One W...

KIMBERLY LANG
NATALIE ANDERSON
HEIDI RICE

Published in Great Britain 2015
by Mills & Boon, an imprint of Harlequin (UK) Limited,
Eton House, 18-24 Paradise Road, Richmond, Surrey, TW9 1SR

ONE WILD NIGHT © 2015 Harlequin Books S.A.

Magnate's Mistress...Accidentally Pregnant!, Hot Boss, Boardroom Mistress and *The Good, the Bad and the Wild* were first published in Great Britain by Harlequin (UK) Limited.

Magnate's Mistress...Accidentally Pregnant! © 2009 Kimberly Kerr
Hot Boss, Boardroom Mistress © 2009 Natalie Anderson
The Good, the Bad and the Wild © 2012 Heidi Rice

ISBN: 978-0-263-25208-8
eBook ISBN: 978-1-474-00387-2

05-0415

Harlequin (UK) Limited's policy is to use papers that are natural, renewable and recyclable products and made from wood grown in sustainable forests. The logging and manufacturing processes conform to the legal environmental regulations of the country of origin.

Printed and bound in Spain
by CPI, Barcelona

MAGNATE'S MISTRESS... ACCIDENTALLY PREGNANT!

BY
KIMBERLY LANG

Kimberly Lang hid romance novels behind her text-books in secondary school, and even a Master's programme in English couldn't break her obsession with dashing heroes and happily ever after. A ballet dancer turned English teacher, Kimberly married an electrical engineer and turned her life into an ongoing episode of *When Dilbert Met Frasier.* She and her Darling Geek live in beautiful North Alabama with their one Amazing Child—who, unfortunately, shows an aptitude for sports. Visit Kimberly at www.booksbykimberly.com for the latest news—and don't forget to say hi while you're there!

To my beautiful, clever, and all-around Amazing Child—although it will be many years before you are old enough to read this book (*thirty, at least, if your father has any say in the matter*), let me remind you that tonight, at dinner, you told me you wanted to be a romance writer like me when you grew up because it was 'cool'. You know what? I think you're cool, too, and you can be anything you want to be when you grow up—well, except maybe a flamingo.

CHAPTER ONE

NOTE TO SELF: never prepay your honeymoon.

Ally Smith sat on the beach under a tattered umbrella nursing her watered-down piña colada and wondered why that caveat didn't make it into any of the wedding planning books. *Probably because no one plans a wedding with escape clauses.*

She should write her own book for brides-to-be. She'd definitely include a chapter on cancellation clauses, the folly of prepayments and how to mitigate the financial toll of lost deposits. Oh, and some fun stuff like how to build a nifty bonfire with three hundred monogrammed cocktail napkins.

And a chapter on how to know you're marrying the wrong guy.

She dug her toes into the warm sand and watched the sailboats bobbing on the waves as they made their way into and out of the marina just down the beach. Why hadn't she pushed harder for the trip to Australia where she could at least be snow skiing right now? June in Oz was supposed to be fabulous. Why had she let Gerry talk her into this when they lived just twenty minutes from the Georgia coast—a popular honeymoon destination in and of itself? She could go to the beach anytime she wanted. She didn't have to fly to the Caribbean for sand and surf.

Because I was too happy to finally be engaged.

In the four months since she'd happened home at lunch-time to find Gerry having a nooner with their travel agent—which explained why he'd insisted they use her to begin with, and probably also why Ally was booked into the worst hotel on the island—she'd come to realize some hard truths: she'd picked good looks and charm over substance, and she should have dumped Gerry-the-sorry-bastard four years ago.

Now, two days into her "honeymoon," she was bored out of her mind.

"Is this seat taken, pretty lady?"

The low, gruff voice pulled her out of her reverie. Shading her eyes from the late-afternoon sun, she turned to find the source of the question.

And nearly spit out her drink as she ended up eye level with the smallest swimming trunks ever made, straining over a body they were never designed to grace.

In any decent movie, the voice would have belonged to a handsome tennis pro with a tan and bulging biceps. This was *her* life, though, so while her admirer did sport a tan, his body bulged in all the wrong places—like over the waistband of his Speedo. Ally bit her lip as her eyes moved upward, past the gold chain tangling in his furry chest hair to the three-day salt-and-pepper stubble, the ridiculous iridescent blue wraparound sunglasses and wide-brimmed Panama hat.

She was being hit on by a bad cliché. This horrible vacation experience was now complete. "I'm sorry, what?"

"You look like you could use some company. How about we have a drink and get to know each other?" Without waiting for her response, the man lowered himself into the adjacent lounge chair, took off his sunglasses and stuck out his hand. "Fred Alexander."

With no excuse to deny the tenets of her proper Southern

upbringing, she shook the proffered hand. The palm was damp. He held her hand a bit too long, and she fought the urge to wipe it on her towel once released. "I'm Ally. It's nice to meet you, but—"

"A pretty girl like you shouldn't be sitting out here alone. No telling who might come along to bother you." He winked at her.

Yeah, no telling. There were plenty of people on the beach. Why had Fred picked her to hit on? *Because you are a loser magnet. First Gerry and now this guy.* At least Gerry had been good-looking, a fact he'd never let her forget.

She had to escape. She should have just stayed in Savannah. Oh, but no, she'd been steamed over the loss of so many other down payments that she wasn't going to let a vacation go to waste, too. It had sounded so practical at the time. She knew better now.

"I was just about to go in, actually. I think I'm getting too much sun." She reached for her bag and slid to the edge of her seat, ready to beat a hasty retreat. Fred placed his hand on her wrist and stroked his thumb over the skin. Ally gently moved away from his hand and out of arm's reach as she stood.

"I'd be happy to rub some lotion on you." Fred's eyes roamed slowly down her body and back up to her cleavage, making her skin crawl. With a slow shake of his head, he said, "That's a crime, Ally. A girl with a body like yours should be showing it off in a bikini." She'd never been so glad to be wearing a one-piece in her entire life, and as he licked his lips in appreciation, Ally felt as if she needed a hot shower.

"Thanks, but no. I'm—"

"Dinner, then. I saw you checking in alone yesterday and figured you'd be looking for some company."

Ugh. She took another step back. "Um, well, I..."

"I'm staying here, too. Suite sixteen. It must be fate that we're both here on our own..."

It was in her nature to make people happy, but this crossed the line. There was "nice" and then there was "stupid." She'd made enough stupid decisions—no more.

"Enjoy the beach." She could hear Fred muttering something about her attitude as she left. *Whatever.* What little enjoyment she'd had just relaxing to the sounds of the surf evaporated in the wake of being hit on by some creepy guy old enough to be her father.

Maybe the TV in her room had a movie channel. She could take that shower, order room service for dinner—if they even did room service in this hotel; she hadn't seen a menu when she'd checked in last night—and plan to do some sightseeing on the island tomorrow.

This was the most pathetic vacation ever. Or was she the pathetic one?

The lobby was mostly empty as she waited behind a couple checking in. More honeymooners. The young woman carried a bouquet, and the red-haired man at her side was having a hard time checking in since he couldn't seem to keep his hands off his new bride. They seemed happy, and Ally silently wished them well as they headed for their room.

"I'd like to see about ordering room service to suite twenty-six."

The hotel clerk shook his head. "Sorry. No room service. Just the restaurant."

Lovely. She thought she'd hit her low spot on this vacation with the arrival of Fred, but obviously there was much more awaiting her over the next few days. Like eating every meal alone.

"But I do have a message for you, Mrs. Hogsten."

"Miss Smith," she corrected automatically. Another good reason not to marry Gerry. She'd never liked the sound of his last name.

The clerk's eyebrows shot up in surprise, and he rechecked his computer screen.

Ally sighed. "I know. It says Hogsten, party of two, but it's just me. Miss Smith."

She saw the flash of pity in the man's eyes as the implications of staying alone in a honeymoon suite registered.

No sense trying to explain she wasn't the least bit sorry to still be single. "The message?"

He handed her a folded piece of paper. "Enjoy your evening."

"Thanks." She flipped it open for a quick peek as she walked back to her room. Her mother's number.

Good Lord, what now? She'd hadn't been gone that long, and she'd made sure all of them were squared away before she left.

Kicking the door closed with her foot, she dug in her bag for her cell phone, only to flip it open and remember she didn't have service here.

The minifridge in her room was well stocked after her trip to the local liquor store last night, and the bottle of Chardonnay called her name. She poured a glass and took a drink before dialing the long string of numbers to call home.

"Oh, honey, it's so good to hear from you!"

Her mom sounded as though the phone call was a nice surprise, which meant nothing was seriously wrong on the home front. That didn't mean she was off the hook, though. Ally drained her glass before she spoke. Instead of refilling it, she took the bottle with her over to the bed and sat down. She might need the whole thing. "You asked me to call. Is everything okay?"

"Oh, we're fine. I guess."

Ally waited.

"Well, other than the fact your sister is going to put me in an early grave with her dramatics…"

Oh, goody. Ring the bell for Mom versus Erin, round 427. Did she really need to be discussing this long-distance?

Breathe in. Breathe out. How typical. Could her family not function for at least a few days without her there? She'd like to think that if she'd really been on her honeymoon, no one would expect her to deal with this. Who was she kidding? If her family tree were any nuttier, squirrels would start showing up at Thanksgiving dinner. She loved them, but not a one had an ounce of sense.

Maybe she'd been adopted. Switched at birth. Or had she been intentionally placed in this family simply to keep them all from spiraling out of control with their dramatics? It sucked to be the grown-up all the time.

When her mom finally paused for a breath, Ally started her peacekeeping duties. "Mom, it is *her* wedding—"

"Maybe so, but you'd think she'd understand how important this is."

It was a wedding, not the trials of Hercules, for goodness' sake. But it took another half hour for Ally to convince her mom of that, albeit temporarily. She banged her head against the headboard gently in frustration.

"And, Ally, honey, the state sent a notice about the property taxes."

"I took care of that before I left."

"So what do I do with the notice?"

"Just set it aside, and I'll get it when I come home. I'll double-check with the state to be sure, but I wrote the check along with your other first-of-the-month bills."

"Oh, then that's good."

The small headache her mother always caused after more than twenty minutes throbbed behind her eyes. "Mom, I'm going to go find some dinner now. I'll see you when I get home, and we'll sort everything out then."

"Of course, honey. Have a wonderful time. We'll talk soon."

With the phone safely back in its cradle, Ally leaned back

against the headboard of the king-size bed and hugged the bottle of wine to her chest. *I'm so glad I don't have cell service here.*

Out her bedroom window, she could see the sun setting over the water. Dammit, she was on vacation. Granted, it was the strangest vacation ever, but it was her vacation nonetheless. She was alone in a honeymoon suite, in a place she hadn't wanted to come to, and staying at a low-end hotel because her travel agent was both spiteful and incompetent. And she'd paid top dollar for this disaster. It wasn't fair, and it wasn't right, but there were worse places to be. She should make the most of it.

She'd *earned* a vacation, by God. She'd put up with Gerry for three years longer than she should have in the hopes he'd shape up and be worth the investment of her time and energy. Instead she'd carried him—financially and emotionally—for all that time. Planning and then canceling the wedding had been stressful, and when she added in her family's constant stream of crises, it was no wonder she'd had a headache for as long as she could remember.

She *needed* a vacation. She deserved it. She would take advantage of it.

After one last long drink straight from the bottle, Ally reached for the phone again. By the time the desk clerk answered, she had a whole new perspective.

"This is Ally Smith in suite twenty-six. No, not Mrs. Hogsten. Miss Smith. I'd like your help in finding a restaurant that delivers and a masseuse who can come to my room tonight for an hour-long massage. And I need to know where the closest spa is. I'd like to get a facial and a manicure tomorrow. Oh, and I'd really love some fresh flowers in here."

"She's a real beauty."

Chris Wells nodded, even if he didn't fully agree. She needed quite a bit of work, but she still held great promise.

He'd wanted to have a closer look before he'd know if the problems were just cosmetic or if they ran deeper.

"She's fast, too," the man continued, pride evident in his voice, "but responsive and easy to handle."

"Her reputation certainly precedes her." Chris stepped onto the weathered wooden deck. At just over forty feet, the yacht was compact, yet elegant in design. Sadly, though, she had suffered from too many years of poor maintenance—the cleats were spotted with rust, the leather cover of the tiller was cracked and peeling. Twenty-five years ago, he'd watched his father skipper the *Circe* to her first win, and he'd known then that he'd race one day, too. In a way, he owed much of his career to the boat rocking gently under his feet.

The *Circe* was long retired, her heavy wooden hull no match for the newer, lighter racing yachts made of aluminum or fiberglass. But he wasn't here to buy a new racer—he was here to buy a piece of history and make her into a queen.

His crew had called him crazy when he'd told them he was taking time off to go to Tortola to see *Circe,* but Jack and Derrick would come around eventually. And he wouldn't trust anyone but them to refit her properly.

"Is she seaworthy? Any reason why she wouldn't make it home?"

Ricardo, the boat's current owner, smiled, obviously pleased with Chris's interest. "A few minor things you might want to look at…"

Chris listened to Ricardo's list with half an ear as he fished his cell phone out of his pocket and called home. "Jack. Send Victor and Mickey down here on the next flight. She needs a little work, but I should be ready to start for home by the end of the week."

"So you're going through with it?"

"Definitely." He was handing the check to a bug-eyed Ricardo even as he spoke.

"Why don't you come on home and let the guys bring her back instead?"

Chris took a deep breath as a feeling of rightness filled him. He was meant to own the *Circe*. "Because she's mine now."

"But we need you here. Paperwork is already piling up on your desk. And, if you're really going to break a record in October, we don't have time for you to putter around the Caribbean."

"I have an assistant to handle the paperwork. Grace can call if she needs anything. October is still a long ways off, and the *Dagny* is ahead of schedule. There's nothing for me to do but admire your handiwork."

Jack sighed and muttered something, but Chris didn't need to hear it. He'd heard it all already. Jack was the world's most compulsive planner—which was great when it came to planning around-the-world trips and designing new boats, but a bit of a pain any other time.

"I'll see you in a few weeks. Have *Dagny*'s sails ready for me when I get home."

"No dawdling in the Bahamas this time, okay?"

Flipping the phone closed, Chris turned back to Ricardo. "I assume you can get me access to the maintenance shed here." He was already making a mental list of what he'd need for the long trip back to Charleston; now he just hoped he could find a good outfitter on the island.

Feeling better than he had in weeks—months, probably—Chris grabbed his duffel bag off the dock and tossed it below. Ricardo was already halfway back to the marina office, presumably to cash the fat check in his hand before Chris changed his mind.

But Chris was already unbuttoning his shirt as he headed

below to change. He was looking forward to getting to know his new addition.

Whistling, he got to work.

A massage, a mud bath and a mani-pedi had worked wonders on Ally's outlook. Tortola was definitely growing on her.

After a fabulous morning of being pampered and polished, she returned to her room feeling so relaxed she wasn't sure how much longer her legs would hold her upright. A short nap and a shower later, her attitude adjustment was almost complete. She just needed to find somewhere to eat—napping through lunch was great for the psyche but left her stomach growling.

The nail tech at the spa had recommended she try the little café next to the marina in order to get a true taste of the local cuisine. It was a short walk, and it gave her the opportunity to appreciate the amazing scenery she'd ignored in her foul mood. Until now.

A smiling teenager led her to a small table overlooking the marina. The same breeze that teased her hair out of its braid also gave her background music as it moved though the rigging of the boats. Sunshine warmed her shoulders, and the fish chowder soothed the grumble in her stomach. By the time she'd finished her second mango daiquiri, she knew she was in paradise.

The bustle of the marina fascinated her. Even though Savannah was close to the coast, she herself wasn't all that familiar with boats. Here, though, sailing was obviously a serious pastime, and the marina buzzed with activity. Curious, and with nothing else on her afternoon agenda, she went to explore.

There were no gates blocking access to the docks like the few she'd seen at home, so she wandered aimlessly. Boats of every shape and size and type bobbed gently in the water, and everyone greeted her with a wave as she passed.

Tranquility. Miss Lizzie. Lagniappe. The fanciful names

painted on the backs of the boats made her smile. *Tailwinds.* *Skylark.* The *Nauti-Girl* made her laugh out loud. *Spirit of the Sea.* The *Lorelei.* The *Circe.*

The *Circe* was smaller than the boats around it, and while the others were tidy and gleaming, the *Circe* looked as though she'd seen better days. Planks from her deck were missing and long scrapings marred her paint. A second look, though, showed the scrapes had uniformity to them and a pile of fresh planks was stacked neatly on the dock.

The *Circe* was getting a face-lift.

"I assure you, it's for her own good."

Ally jumped at the voice and the thump of something landing on the dock behind her. She turned and realized Tortola had spectacular scenery indeed.

Holy moly. He couldn't be real. No mortal man had a chest like that. She blinked, but the image didn't change. Muscles rippled under bronze skin as he off-loaded the supplies in his arms. His pecs bunched, then flexed as he moved, and Ally felt a bit dizzy. Struggling to regain her equilibrium, she forced her eyes upward to the man's face.

But it didn't help to steady her. Sunglasses hid his eyes but not the adorable crinkles that formed as he smiled at her. He wiped his hands over the battered khaki cutoffs hanging low on his hips, then slid the sunglasses up and off his face. Eyes the color of the water surrounding them grabbed her, and she found it hard to breathe.

Real or not, she knew he'd be starring in her late-night X-rated fantasies for years to come.

"Her previous owners neglected her a bit, but she's going to be beautiful once I'm done with her."

The slight drawl made her think of home, and something about the pride and determination in his tone tugged at her. "I'm sure she appreciates it."

"I certainly hope so." He reached to her right to grab the faded T-shirt hanging on the piling, bringing that bronze skin so close she could smell the sunshine and the musk of clean, male sweat. As he pulled it over his head, she stamped down her disappointment at the loss of the lovely view of his pecs. "I'm Chris Wells."

"Ally." She shook the hand he offered. It was warm and strong and slightly calloused, indicating he worked with his hands. The thought of those hands on her... She snapped back to the conversation. "I'm sure she's enchanting."

Chris cocked his head, sending a lock of blond-streaked hair over his forehead before he pushed it back. Those highlights were real—he obviously spent a lot of time in the sun.

Ally cleared her throat. "Circe. The enchantress queen from the *Odyssey*."

"Yes, I know. I'm just surprised you do. Not too many people know who she is." He crossed his arms across that unbelievable chest and leaned against the piling.

"I guess I'm a bit of a mythology geek."

Chris's eyes traveled appreciatively down her body, leaving her skin tingling in their wake. "I definitely wouldn't consider you a geek."

The heat of a blush replaced the tingles, and her brain turned mushy. "She so rarely gets the credit she deserves."

"She turned Odysseus's crew into pigs."

Was that a challenge? "Some might say it wasn't exactly a stretch."

"Ouch," Chris said.

"But she also gave Odysseus the information he needed to find his way home and avoid the Sirens. Odysseus owes Circe one." *Why am I babbling on about this?* She needed to quit while she was ahead. *Find another topic of conversation before he decides you really are a geek.*

But Chris egged her on with another of those smiles. "But they were lovers. *That's* what Circe wanted from him."

Ally laughed and took the opening. Maybe he didn't think she was babbling. "True, but I think that worked out better for Odysseus than for Circe."

"Excuse me?"

She looked at him levelly. "Odysseus and Circe have a fling. After which, Circe gives him much-needed information, and he's gone without a backward glance, leaving her pregnant with triplets. Not so great an ending for Circe." She shook her head sadly.

"What, no romantic sympathies for his desire to get home to Penelope?" Chris teased.

This was fun. She leaned against the opposite piling and mirrored his crossed arms. "Oh, now *Penelope* has my sympathy. Odysseus, the original golden boy of 'all style, no substance,' goes out adventuring, leaving her at home to weave and take care of the kid. She remains faithful while *he* starts the tradition of a girl in every port. Odysseus was a player."

Chris laughed out loud. "You don't sound like you like Odysseus much."

"I won't deny there's something attractive about him, but smart women don't fall for that—at least not more than once."

A blond eyebrow arched upward. "You sound bitter."

She shrugged. "Let's just say I know better. If you ask me, Odysseus got much better than he deserved."

"That's a different take on a classic."

In her primmest voice, she said, "Homer was a man. I don't think he sees it quite the same way a woman would."

"You have a point, Ally."

"Maybe." When he didn't respond, she was disappointed. Were they done now? Should she move on? She didn't want to, but Chris did have a major project underway. He hadn't moved from his lazy pose against the piling, but maybe he was just too polite. She'd wrap it up and let him get back to work. "But you're doing a good thing, bringing *Circe* back to her former glory. I'm sure she'll be lovely."

"She will be. Right now she's just a money pit. I can see now why Odysseus left her. Too needy." He punctuated the statement with a wink.

Feeling better than she had in months, Ally let a giggle escape. "You're terrible."

Chris shrugged. "You started it."

"Well, I stand by my earlier statement, regardless. Your *Circe* deserves the face-lift. I'm sure she'll be a beautiful, *enchanting* ship when you're done."

"Yacht."

"Pardon me?"

"She's a yacht. Not a ship."

"Really? There's a difference?"

"Definitely." Chris levered himself back to his feet. "Ships are those big ones that move cargo and such. These," he indicated the boats around them, "are yachts."

Maybe they weren't done just yet. He didn't seem in a hurry to run her off and get back to work. A little spurt of excitement warmed her blood. This trip was getting better by the second...

"Ally! Ally-girl, I thought that was you."

The voice hit her between the shoulder blades and crawled down her back. *I spoke too soon.* She knew that creepy, gravelly voice. She turned, and, sure enough, Fred was lumbering down the dock toward her like a duck to a June bug. *Why me? Why? I find a hunky guy to talk to and the slimy one has to come and ruin it.* It wasn't fair.

She saw Chris's eyebrows go up in question as Fred lumbered to a stop beside her. "Ally," he puffed, "I saw you headed this way. If you're interested in boats, darlin', I'd be happy to oblige."

At least he's wearing more than he was yesterday. The polo shirt and shorts *were* an improvement, but that didn't mitigate the fact he was *here* ruining her day again.

Fred looked Chris up and down, then glanced dismissively at the *Circe*. "How about that dinner now? We can let this swabbie get back to work."

Chris stiffened a bit at the insult, but he didn't take the bait. *Just when I thought it couldn't get any worse.* Swabbie? How arrogant could one guy be? And how was she going to gracefully extricate herself this time? Short of jumping off the dock and swimming to shore, she was trapped.

She felt, more than saw, Fred reach for her elbow to lead her away. Desperate, she turned to Chris and mouthed, *Help*.

The corner of Chris's mouth twitched. Dammit, this wasn't funny. She didn't want to be outright rude to Fred, but this needed to be nipped in the bud.

Fine. Rudeness begat rudeness, and this jerk started it. Her conscience could be salved by that, at least, as she took a deep breath and opened her mouth to be intentionally rude for the first time in her life. "Look—"

"Ally," Chris interrupted smoothly, "I know you're upset I've been spending so much time on the boat, but you don't need to get even by flirting with another man."

She let out her breath in a rush at the save, but then gasped as Chris looked at Fred and shrugged. "You know how women are about these things. They get so jealous over the 'other woman.'"

Her mouth was open to argue with such a sexist statement when she realized Fred was nodding in agreement. She closed it with a snap and accepted the hand Chris held out to her. One quick tug, and she was against his chest with his arms wrapped around her.

And everything else ceased to exist.

The men were talking, but Ally couldn't hear the exchange. The heat from Chris's body and the solid wall of muscle surrounding her had her blood pounding in her ears. Closing her eyes, she inhaled, and the summertime smell of him filled her senses. Every nerve ending sprang to life, and she fought against the urge to rub sensually against him but lost. Her breathing turned shallow and her inner thighs clenched. But when Chris dropped a warm kiss on her bare shoulder, lightning raced through her, causing her to arch into him in response.

His arms tightened around her, and she melted into the pressure...

"Ally?"

The whispered question sent chills over her skin as his breath caressed her ear. Her eyelids felt heavy as she attempted to open them.

"He's gone. You're safe now."

The words hit her like cold water. Reality snapped back into focus, and... Oh, *no*. She felt the hot flush of embarrassment sweep up her chest and neck.

She'd been writhing against him like a stripper against a pole, and her humiliation was now absolute.

This vacation sucked.

CHAPTER TWO

ALLY WAS A WONDERFUL ARMFUL, but the situation was about to become embarrassing for them both if he didn't release her. The colorful sundress she wore had concealed the lush curves he could now feel as she fitted perfectly into him like a puzzle piece. Curly dark tendrils of hair that smelled like sunshine and citrus caught the breeze and tickled over his skin. When she'd sighed and moved against him, he'd been unable to resist tasting her.

Her plea for help might have spurred him to reach for her, but in reality it had only provided an excuse to act on the need to touch her that he'd felt the moment she'd lifted her chin and started her defense of Circe. A need that had intensified when that Euro-trash wannabe had tried to stake a claim on her.

But now that he was gone, Chris no longer had a reasonable excuse to continue holding her—beyond his own enjoyment, of course. But that enjoyment was beginning to press insistently against her, and in another moment he was going to take advantage of the situation.

As he gave the all clear, Chris felt her stiffen. Ally extricated herself awkwardly, clearing her throat as a red flush colored her chest and neck.

Maybe I'm not the only one who got a thrill from the contact, he thought.

"I, um, ahem, uh—" Ally paused, closed her eyes and took a deep breath. "Thank you for the save. Fred must not have gotten the hint yesterday that I wasn't interested. Maybe now he'll find someone else to stalk."

"My pleasure." *Definitely.* He'd never been one for saving the damsel in distress before, but if this was what it was like, he'd reconsider playing Lancelot.

Ally attempted to smooth the loose hair back from her face, then smiled uncomfortably. But she wasn't beating a fast path off the dock, which was good since he was already hoping he'd have an excuse to touch her again soon.

"Would you like to come aboard? See the *Circe* up close?"

He was treated to a brilliant smile that lit up her deep brown eyes. "I'd like that a lot. I've never been on a boat before. A yacht, I mean."

"You can call her a boat, just not a ship."

"Good, because yacht sounds a bit pretentious." Her cheeky smile was contagious, and he knew he was grinning like an idiot as he stepped onto the deck and held out a hand to help her board.

"I can't believe you've never been on a boat before."

"Never. Well, unless you want to count a canoe at camp one summer."

He'd spent his entire life on, in or around boats. Sailboats, speedboats, rowboats, tugboats—if it went on the water, he'd built it, raced it or at least crewed it. He'd never met anyone who hadn't even seen one up close before.

Ally seemed to be taking the inspection seriously, as she asked questions about the sails and the cleats and how it all worked. As she trailed a hand along the tiller, his blood stirred, wanting that hand to caress him instead.

He cleared his throat. "She was designed to race, so she's lean. No frills to weigh her down."

"Is that what you're going to do? Fix her up and race her?"

"No, I can't race her. Her hull is too heavy to compete with what's out there now."

Ally looked at him. "But you do race, right? Or you're wanting to?"

Was she serious? A look at Ally's heart-shaped face told him she was. She honestly had no idea. How long had it been since he'd had a conversation with someone who didn't know who he was? Wells Racing and the OWD Shipyard really had consumed his life—to the extent that it had probably been at least five years since he'd met anyone who wasn't as obsessed as he was. Maybe more like ten. And while part of him wanted to impress Ally with his list of credentials, he held it at bay. It was nice to be incognito for once.

"I race…among other things." It wasn't a lie. Pops still kept his command in the offices of the OWD Shipyard—in name at least—but Chris found more and more of the day-to-day business crossing his desk these days. He juggled a lot, but Wells Racing was still his main focus.

Ally grinned at him. "But do you ever win?"

He laughed before he caught himself. "Occasionally."

"Is it dangerous?" She didn't meet his eyes as she asked that, but the too-casual way she poked at the deck line belied her interest.

"Not really. You *can* get hurt, don't underestimate that, but it's pretty hard to kill yourself."

Her shoulders dropped in relief. "That's good. My brother races dirt bikes for fun. It's pretty easy to kill yourself doing that." Ally poked her head into the hatch. "Not a lot down there."

"Like I said, she's built for racing. Bare necessities only."

He liked watching her explore the *Circe*. As the breeze molded her dress to her curves, he realized he liked watching her, period. The erection he'd only recently got back under control stirred to life again.

Ally sat on the edge of the cockpit and ran her hands over the smooth planks of the deck. "This is neat. Thank you for showing me."

Unable to resist, he sat next to her. Possibly a little closer than was called for, but Ally didn't move away. "Neat?"

"Yes, neat. I like to learn new things." She looked sideways at him and shrugged. "In fact, I've decided that this vacation is going to be all about new things. I came by myself, which was definitely a first. I've—"

"You came on a Caribbean vacation by yourself?" Even though she'd been wandering the dock alone, he assumed she had friends or family somewhere on the island.

"It's a long story, but, yes."

He started to ask another question but she cut him off.

"Seriously, it's a long, *boring* story. But I'm here now, and I'm making the most of it. I've tried new foods, let the spa spread mud all over me, and now I've been on a boat for the first time. I'd say I'm off to a good start."

He was still reeling at the mental image of Ally nude while mud was painted sensuously across her breasts. He cleared his throat. "You're quite the adventurer."

She beamed, her brown eyes lighting up. "I wouldn't go that far. But I am taking baby steps." Ally closed her eyes and leaned back to enjoy the sun. It was an artlessly erotic pose— back arched, breasts thrust temptingly toward him, the gentle curve of her neck exposed. "This is wonderful. The wind and the water are very relaxing."

He was anything but relaxed. "Would you like to go out?" he blurted.

Ally sat up and opened her eyes, the shock readily apparent. "I'm sorry, what?"

Well, that hadn't been his smoothest move. He cleared his throat. "Sailing. Would you like to go out sailing tomorrow?"

"Oh, I don't know…"

"Come on. It'll be fun."

"I've never—"

"I thought you were being adventurous on your vacation."

Ally shifted uncomfortably. "There's adventurous and then there's the fact that I'm not a very good swimmer."

"The chances of you going overboard are pretty slim unless you jump."

Ally looked over the mess he'd made of the *Circe,* a wary look in her eye. "But—"

He followed her gaze and laughed. "Not on the *Circe.* She's not up for company yet. I'll borrow a little cat or something. Start slow."

Confusion furrowed Ally's forehead. "A cat?"

"Catamaran. Like the ones you see on the beach down there."

She looked to where he was pointing and nodded. "It's kinda big, don't you think, for my first time? Maybe something smaller, like those over there?" She pointed to some dinghies tied up at the dock.

"Ah, Ally, you don't want to start too small. You want to get the full experience." He dropped his voice and teased, "Bigger really is better, you know. It's not the same sensation at all."

She caught her lip in her teeth, the picture of indecision. "Um…"

"We'll take it really slow and give you some time to get comfortable. We won't go very far until you're sure you're ready. Just nice and easy." He stroked her arm and gooseflesh rose under his fingers. "We won't go too fast, I promise—

unless you decide you want to, of course. And I think you will once you get into it. Otherwise, you can relax and let me do all the work while you just enjoy yourself."

Ally's eyes were wide and dark as she exhaled gently. "Are we still talking about sailing?"

Who cares about sailing? He stopped and gave himself a strong mental shake. "Of course. Well? Are you game?" He could see the indecision in her eyes. She wanted to go, but something was holding her back. "Are you afraid? Of the water?"

She hesitated as she looked away. "No. Not afraid, just not any good—I mean, I'm not a good swimmer."

"Do you trust me?"

One eyebrow went up. "I've known you for less than an hour. No, I don't trust you."

Ally was a breath of fresh air—and honest to a fault. "I'm hurt," he teased.

Looking sideways at him, she amended her statement. "But I don't *dis*trust you, either."

That easy smile was really starting to work on him. "It's a start."

"And you did save me from Fred."

"Very true. Surely that merits something."

"If you were a Boy Scout, maybe a badge of some sort." She bit her lip again, sending a jolt through him. "But I don't think you're a Boy Scout."

"You do know how to wound a man. I may not be a Boy Scout, but I am a good sailor. You needn't have any worries about surviving the experience. I'll bet you'll even enjoy it, despite your reservations."

She didn't pick up the gauntlet, but she was coming around. "How about the medium-size one? I can work my way up from there."

"How about dinner instead? If you still want to start small

after that, then I'll get the dinghy. But I think you'll come to see the benefits of not setting your sights too low."

Confusion crinkled her forehead, and it took all he had not to reach for her and drag her below, but there was nothing below but a couple of narrow bunks, completely useless for what he had in mind. "Dinner?" she asked.

He feigned shock. "Of course. You don't expect me to go sailing with a woman I barely know, do you?"

Ally laughed and nudged him with an elbow. "I don't know what to expect from you."

"Just a good time, that much I can assure you." *For us both.*

"Then it's a deal." Ally stuck out her hand, but instead of shaking it, he squeezed it gently.

Slightly flustered, she stood and brushed at her dress with her free hand. "Should I, um, go change?"

"You look amazing." She blushed at the simple compliment, and something primal and protective stirred in his stomach. It was an odd feeling. "I, on the other hand, need to shower. You can't be seen in public with an unwashed swabbie."

Ally squeezed his hand back as she apologized. "Fred's a jerk. That comment was uncalled for."

"I've been called worse by better."

"But still…"

She seemed so earnest in her apology and need to console. "Forget it, Ally. You're not responsible for the actions of others."

A shrug was her only response.

"Where are you staying? I'll come get you around seven."

"The Cordova Inn. How about I meet you in the lobby?"

He nodded, and steadied her as she stepped onto the dock. The *Circe* bobbed as she did, and the boat felt a bit empty once she'd left. He was admiring the gentle sway of her hips when she turned and gave a small wave. Another moment and she was around the building and out of sight.

Well, this was an expected turn of events. He'd come to Tortola to get the *Circe* and found the delicious Ally, as well. His father had called the *Circe* a lucky boat, and now he had proof. Not that he was ever one to question his luck—he'd learned early on to take advantage of whatever winds came his way.

He went below to get his shaving kit and wished the repairs were further along. Or that he'd at least gotten a proper bed installed. He didn't mind crashing on the narrow bunks, but the *Circe*'s cabin was low on creature comforts and not exactly conducive to pastimes other than racing.

That would change, just not soon enough.

Of course, the arrival of Mickey and Victor tomorrow would also put a damper on any on-board activities with Ally. Which reminded him—he still had supplies to stow and he needed to call home.

He'd call and check in with Grace, just to be sure there wasn't anything too pressing, then he'd call Pops and mollify him over the extended absence.

Thanks to the *Circe,* the company, the *Dagny,* and his grandfather were all far away and would remain so for the next few weeks. He stretched, and his fingertips grazed the *Circe*'s bulkheads. He was a free man. *Somewhat free,* he amended as his phone alerted him to an incoming text message.

It could wait a while though. Ally was far more interesting than another discussion of the *Dagny*'s sails or OWD business.

He grabbed his shaving kit and a clean shirt and headed to the marina to shower.

Ally held her composure until she was sure Chris was no longer in sight, then she sagged against the wall of one of the marina buildings. Her legs felt shaky as she let out her breath in a long, unbelieving sigh.

Had that really happened? Had she really just met a real-life

Adonis and agreed to…to… She shook herself. *Technically,* she had only agreed to dinner and a sail, but deep down she was pretty sure she'd agreed to something far more. Chris's interest went beyond taking her sailing. She wasn't *that* naive.

She was, however, completely out of her league. Men like Chris just didn't appear in her world every day. Men like Chris were the stuff of fantasies. Or movies. They certainly didn't appear out of nowhere like a dream come true and take an interest in mousy little accountants.

"God, I love this island."

She wrapped her arms around her stomach and enjoyed the thrill. She had an urge to find that fiancé-banging stupid travel agent and give her a big kiss. Checking her watch, she was amazed to realize dinner wasn't that far off. She only had a little over an hour to wait, but at the same time, that hour seemed like an eternity. Not that she was interested in food. That feeling in her stomach definitely wasn't hunger pangs.

Taking a deep breath, she pushed off the wall and found that her legs still weren't completely stable. Which was appropriate, since she wasn't sure she was mentally stable at the moment, either. These things just didn't happen to her. But it had, and she was willing—make that more than willing—to grab this moment and run with it.

She covered the short distance between the marina and the inn in record time and hurried to her room. The light on her phone blinked, indicating she had a message waiting at the front desk, but she ignored it. She wasn't the least bit interested in her fruity family or whatever crisis they'd concocted for themselves today.

Her wardrobe was limited, as she'd never considered *this* possibility while packing, and she grimaced at the selection. All of it plain, boring, unexciting—rather like her at times. She wished she had time to go shopping, to find something better, but the clock was ticking. When she got home, she'd do some serious shopping to remedy the sad state of her wardrobe. She did find another sundress that was dressier than the one she had on and wasn't shaped like a potato sack. It would have to do.

She showered again and took extra time getting ready, wanting to look as good as possible, but her hair wasn't cooperating. Sighing, she settled for another braid, tucking in the frizzing strands as best she could. At one minute after seven, she took a deep breath and headed for the lobby, half expecting Chris not to show up.

But he *did,* looking like something out of a magazine in loose linen slacks and button-down shirt with his blond-streaked hair brushed back from his face. That fluttery feeling in her stomach bloomed back to life, followed rapidly by the urge to suggest a quiet dinner in her room.

Chris leaned in to kiss her gently on the cheek, an innocent enough greeting under any other circumstances, but in this case, one that melted her insides and made her knees wobble.

"You look fantastic."

"Thanks. So do you." Those blue eyes were going to be the end of her. Seriously. She could stare into them for hours, but when he smiled and they lit…

"Mrs. Hogsten!" The desk clerk approaching her was a wet blanket on her rapidly heating thoughts. She sighed in disgust. Whatever happened to impersonal hotels where none of the employees knew or even cared who you were? She'd *love* that about now.

"Not Hogsten. Smith. Or even Ally is fine."

"Of course, my apologies." At least the pitying look was gone. Instead the desk clerk looked amused as he saw Chris standing so closely beside her. "We have a message for you."

"Thanks." She took the piece of paper and glanced at it

quickly as the clerk left. "Call home." Not tonight, she thought, as she stuffed it into her purse. Turning to the far more interesting Chris, she smiled. "Let's go."

"Is everything okay?" The concern she saw in his eyes was kind, but she wanted that other light back. The light that said he was interested in *her,* not what was on a piece of paper in her purse. The one that made her insides turn over and her skin tingle.

"Just my family checking in."

That other look came back into his eyes, and the butterflies in her stomach fluttered to life. "Good." Chris took her hand and led her toward the door. "It's a beautiful evening and the restaurant's not far. Mind if we walk?"

At the moment she'd gladly walk to hell and back if he'd keep looking at her like she was dessert. *Pull yourself together before you jump on him. At least try to act casual about this.*

The evening *was* beautiful and warm, and Ally inhaled the hibiscus-scented air deeply as they walked. This was the stuff books were written about, walking at night on a tropical island hand in hand with a gorgeous man who—

"There seems to be some confusion about your name at the hotel."

I will not let reality spoil this moment. "Yeah. Well, it's kind of a—"

"Long story?" Chris finished for her, flashing a smile that made her gooey inside.

"Exactly. And boring to boot. How about you tell me where we're headed instead?"

"Have you ever had pepper-pot soup?"

She stomped down the urge to skip. "Nope, but it sounds great. Remember, I'm all about new experiences this week. I'm game for pretty much anything."

Chris stopped walking and pulled her into the shadow of

a huge mango tree. Warm hands settled on her shoulders, and Ally forgot to breathe. "Glad to hear it. In fact…"

It was all the warning she got before his mouth touched hers.

His lips were warm and soft and gentle, but she could feel the restraint, the tension in his hands as they moved up to cup her face and his thumbs stroked over her cheekbones. Rising up on tiptoe, she wrapped her arms around him as his tongue touched hers.

And everything changed.

This. This was the kind of kiss myths were built around. Heat and hunger radiated from Chris's body, warming her blood and making it sing through her veins in answer to the need he stirred in her.

She'd never been kissed like this before, and her world shrank until all that existed was Chris and the feel of him against her and the taste of him on her lips.

A brief jolt of anger moved through her at the thought of all the kisses she'd wasted on Gerry. His lazy, perfunctory, be-happy-you're-getting-anything kisses had never moved her like this.

Like this, she thought, and banished Gerry from her mind as Chris's fingers massaged her scalp, and her knees turned to water. Chris caught her weight as she wobbled, fitting her tightly against him, and what little sanity she had left fled at the sensation: scorching kisses along the tender skin of her neck; the play of muscles under her fingers and the thump of his heart against the chest pressed tightly to hers. The bark of the mango tree bit into her back, but she didn't care.

"Ally," Chris whispered, the sound slowly filtering through the erotic haze around her, and she shivered at hearing her name on his lips.

She opened her eyes to find him staring intently at her, his fingers still tangled in her hair and his thumbs gently stroking her temples. But there was nothing gentle in the way he looked at her, and the fire burning in those blue eyes sent a shiver deep into her stomach.

Chris shuddered, his breath coming in quick pants like her own. She was glad to see she hadn't been the only one to be shaken by the power of that kiss. She didn't have much experience to draw on, but she knew the feeling was mutual. Tightening her fingers on the fabric of his shirt, she pulled him closer, wanting more.

"This isn't exactly the right place."

Belatedly, she realized he was right. While not crowded by any stretch of the imagination, there *were* other people on the street, and several of them were watching the display with interest. She should be mortified, slinking away in embarrassment, but surprisingly she didn't care in the least.

"And, if you plan on actually having dinner tonight, we should probably stop." His fingers slid out of her hair, and she could feel the braid hanging drunkenly to one side as he toyed with the loose strands. A rueful smile played on his lips.

Dinner? She didn't give a tinker's damn about dinner. The only thing she was hungry for was the man plastered against her like some kind of fantasy in the flesh.

Chris sighed and shifted his weight and Ally tightened her grip to keep him from moving away. For a brief moment indecision nibbled at her. She should let him go. She should go on to dinner. She should act nonchalantly about what just happened. A lifetime's experience of responsibility and rationality told her to backtrack to the getting-to-know-you steps they'd leapfrogged over with that kiss.

I don't want to.

The realization shook her to the soles of her plain brown sandals. The sandals were the tipping point. They were practical, boring and suddenly symbolic of her entire existence.

She didn't even have sexy, pretty shoes in her life, much less men like Chris.

Chris.

He hadn't moved since she'd tightened her hold on him, but she wasn't sure how long she'd stood there dithering with herself. When she looked up to meet his eyes, she saw the heat and the question there, and her decision became crystal clear.

"I'm not in the least bit hungry, but if you are, I do know a place that delivers to my hotel."

CHAPTER THREE

ALLY SHOULD COME with a warning label attached. Her words came out of nowhere—okay, not exactly nowhere but close enough—to slam into him with a desire that was almost painful. Underneath that artless, wholesome sensuality and cheeky grin was a woman very dangerous to his sanity.

He hadn't meant for the kiss to get out of hand. He just hadn't been able to go another moment without tasting her. The sweetness had been expected, but it was the fire that had caused him to lose control of the situation.

Hell, he'd lost what was left of his mind. Ally deserved better than a mauling against a mango tree in full view of a dozen witnesses. She tensed and he dragged his attention back to her face, only to immediately wish he hadn't. Her eyes were dark and hungry, her lips swollen and moist from his kiss. Public or not, up against a mango tree or not, he didn't care.

He just needed her hands on him again.

"Food can wait."

Her breath caught and she reached for his hand as she turned.

Thank God they hadn't made it very far. Retracing their steps took only a minute, but it seemed like an eternity. Ally's hands shook as she tried to unlock the door, fumbling the keys.

He took a deep breath to calm himself and took over the

task, silently agreeing with Ally's muttered "Thank goodness" as they were able to close the door behind them.

One lamp glowed beside the very inviting bed, its sheets already turned down by the hotel staff. The window stood open, allowing the quiet evening sounds of the island to drift in.

Ally seemed slightly uncomfortable once they were alone, her movements stiff as she dropped her bag in a chair and reached up to feel the lopsided braid and try to tuck the haphazard strands back in.

Her hands fell to her sides as he reached for the band securing what was left and freed the curls to riot around her tense shoulders.

"You should wear your hair down more often, Ally." He threaded his hands back through the silkiness, and her shoulders relaxed as his fingers found her scalp.

Eyes closed, Ally's head lolled back, exposing the lovely line of her throat, and his lips took the invitation. She hummed in pleasure, and the vibration moved through his body as he pulled her close once again.

The contact brought her to life once again, the tension leaving her body as she moved against him. He took a moment to just enjoy the sensation, patient this time to savor it as he knew he'd be able to feel all of her in just a few more minutes.

But Ally's hands locked around his shoulders as she moved into him, pressing her lips to his in needy hunger, and all of his good intentions to go slow went up in the flames she fanned in his blood.

Ally felt like she was on fire. She needed to touch him. Needed to prove to herself he was real. Needed to feel him against her, in her. And she wanted all of it *now*.

The buttons on Chris's shirt gave way easily, and the chest she'd admired earlier in the day was hers to explore. Her fingers traced the ridges of muscle, and when she retraced her path with her tongue, Chris sucked in his breath in pleasure as his hands tightened in her hair.

A boldness she didn't know she possessed surfaced and she reached for the waistband of his pants. Chris's stomach contracted at her touch, giving her room to release the button and slide the zipper over the bulge, causing her thighs to clench in anticipation.

"My turn." Chris stopped her hands and lifted them over her head before he grabbed the cotton sundress and tugged it off in one smooth movement.

For one brief moment, she felt exposed and uncomfortable, but that feeling was soon chased away as Chris tumbled her to the bed. An acre of bronze skin loomed before the hot weight of him covered her and blocked out any thoughts beyond the screaming need his hands were creating as they moved over her skin.

One toe-curling kiss melded into the next as Chris's tongue flicked against hers like a promise. But when his mouth moved lower, trailing moist heat along the swell of her breasts, she nearly arched off the bed in response. The loss of her bra vaguely registered, followed by the whispery slide of her panties down her thighs.

The featherlight kisses across her stomach were driving her mad. She reached for him, but his fingers locked around her wrist and pulled it over her head. Her other wrist soon followed, and Chris wrapped her fingers around the iron rails of the headboard.

His chest pressed against hers, the crisp hairs tickling sensitive skin, as she savored the feel of him against her from breasts to toes. Blue eyes locked into hers as he held her wrists in place.

"I told you I'd do all the work. That all you had to do was lie back and enjoy."

"I thought we were talking about sailing." Lord, was that whispery voice hers?

Even in the shadows of the room, she saw his grin. "No, you didn't." Then his head dropped to capture her nipple between his lips.

Yesss, she thought, and then she wasn't able to think anymore.

"This is amazing. Really wonderful." After an hour of worrying she'd fall off the boat—yacht, catamaran, whatever it was called—she was finally growing used to the feeling and began to understand the attraction sailing held.

"Then could you quit white-knuckling the edge of the tramp? You're doing serious damage to my ego."

"Your ego is in no danger at all." Sure enough, though, she was still gripping the edge of the trampoline suspended between the two hulls as though her life depended on it. With a great show, she let go of the edge and stretched her arms out to catch the wind.

"That's better." He leaned over to give her a quick kiss.

Ah, yes, sailing was becoming more attractive by the minute. Or at least sailing with Chris was. Completely in his element, he controlled the boat with ease as the wind ruffled his hair.

She had vague memories of Chris kissing her goodbye in the small hours of the morning, saying he had some things to do before they set sail. She'd half expected never to see him again and had gone back to sleep with a touch of regret. Not about sleeping with him—oh, no, *that* topped her list of best decisions ever made—but that she didn't have the guts to ask him to stay.

So when he'd shown up around ten that morning with a heart-stopping smile and a picnic basket, Ally had had to fight the urge to pull him straight back into bed and spend the rest of her trip there.

But this was good, too. She had a great view of his gift-from-the-gods body as he pulled on ropes and adjusted sails. Blue shorts rode low on his hips, and now that she no longer needed a death grip on the trampoline, she itched to touch him again.

She still couldn't believe she'd actually…well, not to put too fine a point on it, that she'd had the most amazing sex of her life with this man. He was too good to be true. But, oh, Lord, the things he'd done to her. She hadn't *known,* never even dreamed of the possibilities. Even now, her nipples tightened with need, and a fire burned low in her belly.

The little Beach-Cat, as Chris had called it, had one major flaw: zero privacy. The open design of the boat meant anyone could see what they were doing. Not that there were many folks in sight…

She resigned herself to just putting her hand on his leg instead and looked forward to getting back to shore as soon as possible.

"Are we headed someplace specific?"

Chris adjusted the sails again and the little boat leaped forward as it caught the wind. "There's a little cove just around the point of the island I thought we could explore. I understand it's pretty secluded."

Her stomach flipped over at the thought. Maybe Chris's thoughts were headed in the same direction as hers.

"But we have a little while before we get there. Why don't you tell me that long story of how you came to be on Tortola alone."

Ugh. Her blissful fantasy was torpedoed by the thought of home. "In a nutshell, I was supposed to come with someone, but that was canceled months ago. The trip was prepaid, and I didn't want it to go to waste, even if none of my friends could come with me."

"Let me guess. That 'someone' is an ex."

Gerry's blond good looks and petulant pout flashed into her mind. Why had she been willing to settle for someone so shallow? "Very much an ex. Thank goodness."

"Agreed. His loss is my gain."

Looking for a way to change the subject before Gerry could spoil her good mood, she went back to sailing. "Does the *Circe* go this fast?"

"We're not going all that fast. Three or four knots, maybe. You could probably get out and run faster than this. And the *Circe* will go a lot faster than four knots."

Pride filled his voice every time he mentioned the *Circe*. "That ship—"

"Yacht."

"Sorry, that 'yacht' means a lot to you, doesn't she?"

"I've been wanting to buy her for a long time, so yeah, I'm pretty pleased she's now mine. But, as you saw, she needs a lot of work. A couple of my friends came by today to work on her, in fact."

A tiny twinge of guilt nagged at her that he'd ditched his repairs of the *Circe* for her. At the same time, she was very glad he had. She stretched out on the trampoline, belatedly realizing she must be getting used to sailing to want to get comfortable. Or maybe it was just the matter-of-fact way Chris handled the cat that put her at ease. The man was born to be on the water, which led her to wonder what he did when he wasn't.

"Where's home for you?"

Chris ran a hand down her side and over the curve of her hip, where his thumb slid under the string of her bikini bottom. "I guess you could now say it's wherever the *Circe* is."

"Really?" She hadn't thought about that possibility. She'd just assumed...well, she wasn't sure what she'd assumed. "But you are American. In fact, with that accent I'd say you grew up somewhere on the southern East Coast."

"South Carolina."

"I'm a Georgia girl myself."

"Let me guess. Savannah."

"You're good."

"At many things." He wagged his eyebrows suggestively at her, and the hand at her hip moved promisingly.

"Oh, I fully agree with that." And she smoothed her hand across his thigh and felt the muscle jump. Chris wanted her. She reveled in the feeling; just a couple of days ago, she had believed she was a boring, plain-Jane loser magnet, but here she was. It couldn't be real: Ally Smith, Femme Fatale. Oh, her ego *definitely* needed this.

Another circle of his thumb reminded her that her ego wasn't the only needy part of her. She couldn't see his eyes behind his sunglasses, but she could *feel* them roam over her body. Even with the heat of the sun on her, she shivered.

A sail flapped and Chris cursed, reaching for the rope and quickly running it through a cleat. Ally was almost glad for the distraction; Chris's undivided attention was a heady thing. She leaned back and closed her eyes, letting the movement of the water lull her as Chris made easy conversation.

But she could still feel his eyes on her.

A bump pulled her out of her languor, and she opened her eyes just in time to see Chris jump off the boat. She sat up quickly. "What the—ouch!"

"I told you to watch out for the boom."

Turning to find his voice, she realized the bump she'd felt had been the cat's hulls reaching the shore. Chris gave a mighty pull, and the boat slid partially out of the water onto the sand.

"Are you okay?" Chris splashed in the shallow water to her side of the boat, his brow wrinkled in concern.

"I'm fine."

"Then come on." He held out a hand and pulled her into the surf with him.

The water was cool, a nice contrast to her sun-toasted skin, and clear enough to see her feet on the bottom. Chris moved into deeper water, pulling her gently along with him. She lifted her feet and held on to his arm, allowing herself to float slightly. The shoreline was empty, and no other boats had moored in the little cove. They were very much alone, an advantage Chris seemed keen to act upon as he pulled her legs around his waist. Strong hands dug into her hips as Chris's mouth found that magic spot on her neck.

"You've been driving me crazy," he growled. "That bikini wouldn't adequately cover a Barbie doll. I nearly ran us aground on the sandbar." His teeth found the string holding her top up, and untied the bow with a simple tug. The grip on her hips loosened, forcing her to grab his shoulders for support as he made quick work of the second string around her back. A second later, her pink top was floating toward shore.

"Um, Chris…"

"There's no one here but us. No one to see you except me. And I want to see all of you."

His lips captured hers for another mind-blowing kiss, but she felt him unhook her legs and quickly slide the bikini bottom off. Chris's trunks bobbed to the surface as he hooked her legs around him again, but this time, no fabric separated them. She moaned at the sensation and he echoed the sound as she moved against him, wanting to feel more.

Although the bathing suit hadn't covered much, being naked in the water was still a shock. She hadn't been skinny-dipping since…well, *ever*. It was decadent and natural and intensely erotic.

Her breasts felt overly sensitized as the water lapped over them, and the position she was in offered him easy access.

One arm held her firmly around her waist as his hand captured her breast, caressing it as his thumb grazed across her nipple.

"Ever made love in the ocean, Ally?"

"N-no," she managed to wheeze.

One eyebrow arched up, and the gentle caress became more insistent. "Then I'm glad you're open to new adventures this week."

She hissed as his tongue swirled around her nipple before he pulled it into the heat of his mouth. Oh, *yes*. New adventures. Sign her up for more, as long as Chris would be her trail guide.

While the nips of his teeth drove her insane, one hand snaked between her legs to find her core. She shuddered as he teased her, his fingers urging her to the edge. How could his skin feel so hot in the cool water? A finger slid inside her, and she rocked her hips into his hand, seeking more. Chris returned the pressure, the heel of his hand hard against her as he urged her on with hot words whispered into her ear.

All she could do was hold on, her fingers digging into his shoulders as she climaxed.

Still thrumming with aftershocks, she opened her eyes to meet Chris's deep blue stare. The intensity there rocked her, causing a rush she couldn't identify, but she couldn't look away.

She kissed him instead, holding his head and pressing her lips to his in an urgent need to share the feeling. Chris's hand moved, withdrawing from her and she ached at the loss.

But it was blessedly short-lived, as Chris cupped his hands under her thighs, lifted her, and slipped easily inside. Gasping, she tightened her legs, squeezing herself against him until their bodies met. Shudders gave way to full-out tremors as he filled her.

Her senses seemed to sharpen, bringing everything into focus—the gentle lapping of the water against their skin, the waves landing on the beach behind her, the warm rays of the sun on her back and shoulders, the throb of Chris inside her, the rapid pounding of her heart, the sounds of their ragged breathing.

Then Chris started to move, holding and guiding her, and her focus narrowed. Nothing existed except this man and the pleasure rapidly peaking inside her. She trusted him to take her all the way, to hold her, please her and not let her drown, so she let herself go, chanting his name in rhythm to his thrusts. As she shattered, she felt Chris pull her close. A moment later, he held her hips tightly against him as powerful shudders moved under her fingers.

"Still feeling adventurous, Ally?"

With a huge effort, she was able to lift her head from his shoulder and open her eyes. One corner of his amazingly kissable mouth curved up in a challenge.

"Definitely."

"Then let's head to shore. I have a surprise for you..."

She felt drunk, more so than the bottle of wine she'd shared with Chris in the cove hours ago could be responsible for. No, she was definitely drunk on sex and sun and the sea—and, of course the man responsible for the best day of her entire life.

Chris helped her off the boat, his hands holding her waist longer than necessary, but she was having trouble keeping her hands off him, as well. The sun had been setting by the time they left their little cove, and a full moon now rode high in the sky, giving her just enough light to see the adorable crinkles around his eyes as he smiled at her.

He brushed his lips gently across hers before pushing the hair back from her face. "I really hate to leave you here, but I need to get the cat back, and there're some things on the *Circe* I really need to check on..."

"It's okay. Go. I'm completely exhausted. I desperately need a shower and some sleep. Lots and lots of sleep. You've worn me out." She rose up on tiptoe for one last kiss. She meant it to be quick, but Chris held her head in his hands and deepened it into a libido-rocking kiss that was both gentle and powerful at the same time. Little flames of desire began to lick at her, and she wondered if she'd ever get enough of him.

"Tomorrow," Chris whispered as he broke the kiss. "Be ready by ten."

"Be ready for what?" Not that it mattered as long as he would kiss her like that.

"It's a surprise. Bring a hat so your nose doesn't get any pinker."

She crinkled her nose experimentally and, sure enough, felt the tightness indicating she'd burned it.

"You're adorable when you do that." Chris pointed her in the direction of her hotel and patted her butt lightly. "Go. Sleep. I'll see you in the morning."

Trekking up the beach to the hotel was difficult on such wobbly legs, but somehow she made it. A deep sigh at the perfection of the day escaped, followed quickly by a yawn. She glanced back at the beach, and saw the sails of the boat in the moonlight as Chris took it back to the marina. *The best day ever.* And if Chris's promises could be believed, she'd have another—possibly even better, though she couldn't imagine how—tomorrow.

She couldn't wait. She wrapped her arms around her waist and curled into the T-shirt she wore—Chris's shirt. Alone now, she lifted the shirt to her nose and inhaled the scent of him.

Oh, get ahold of yourself. With a shake of her head, she went inside.

Few people were still in the lobby, and she realized that it was later than she had thought. She dug through her bag as she walked, searching for her key.

"Miss Smith! Miss Smith!"

Glad she was no longer Mrs. Hogsten to these people, she turned to see the desk clerk closing in on her fast. Pink message slips fluttered in his hand. "We've been looking for you all day," he said as he thrust the stack at her.

She started to roll her eyes, but caught the anxious look on the clerk's face. All the languor vanished as adrenaline rushed through her veins. "What? What's happened?"

"There's been an accident, Miss Smith. It's very important you call home immediately."

He was early, he knew that, but Ally didn't seem like the kind of woman who would mind. She was just lucky Victor and Mickey had greeted him with a litany of problems with the *Circe*'s repairs and a Must Call message from his grandfather when he'd returned to the marina last night, because he'd been sorely tempted to turn right back around and join her for that shower. And, of course, sleep would have been out of the question after that.

Instead he'd spent the evening sorting out the *Circe*'s issues and placating his grandfather. But things were back on track and Ally was now foremost in his thoughts.

Sweet, delicious, tempting Ally.

A few phone calls and he'd borrowed the *Siren,* a sixty-foot cruiser with every amenity—most importantly, a plush captain's cabin. The mental picture of Ally stretched across those sheets was enough to quicken his step. *Siren* was stocked with food and wine and ready to sail. They'd moor off Virgin Gorda tonight, maybe go snorkeling in Devil's Bay tomorrow. He knew of a great secluded trail up from the beach...

His attraction to Ally was a bit of a mystery, but that combination of sweetness and sensuality was both intoxicating and refreshing, and had lifted a weight off his shoulders he hadn't realized he'd been carrying. Victor and Mickey had

teased him about his uncharacteristically good mood, something they said they hadn't seen since the America's Cup win
three years ago.

In response, he'd left them to replace decking and caulk
seams today.

The lobby of the Cordova Inn was deserted, and in the light
of day, he noticed how shabby the hotel really was. Ally
needed to fire her travel agent for booking her into a place like
this. Ally's room wasn't far off the lobby—another thing her
travel agent should have handled better—and he could see the
door standing open.

Good. She's ready to go.

"Pack a toothbrush and a change of clothes, because we
won't be back…" Ally's room was empty, the bed stripped of
its sheets. A maid came out of the bathroom carrying an arm-
load of towels and started in shock at seeing him there.

"Where's the woman who was in this room?"

"I don't know, sir. I just know to clean the room for the
next—"

Chris didn't wait to hear the rest. In a few quick strides, he
was back at the front desk, asking the clerk the same question.

"Miss Smith checked out."

"Yes, I can see that," he gritted out. "Where did she go?"

"Home, sir."

"Why?" He really didn't want to play Twenty Questions
with the clerk, but the young man wasn't being very forthcoming with answers.

"There was an accident. Her brother, I think the message
said. We helped her arrange emergency flights, and I put her
in a taxi to the airport myself this morning at six." He seemed
pleased with himself. Apparently Ally could bring out the
Lancelot in every man.

"Has her flight left yet?"

"Yes, sir. The first flight to San Juan left at seven-thirty."

He cursed, and the clerk's eyes widened.

"However, if you are Mr. Wells, Miss Smith left a message for you." At Chris's nod, he passed over a folded piece of hotel letterhead.

Chris—

I'm so sorry to leave in such a rush, but there's been an emergency and my family needs me. I wish I could say goodbye in person, but the taxi is waiting and my flight leaves in an hour. Thank you for a wonderful day yesterday—it was possibly the best day of my life. Meeting you was the high point of this trip, and I really wish I could stay longer. Take care. I hope you and the *Circe* have wonderful adventures together. Love, Ally.

That was it? No phone number? No e-mail address? Not even a "look me up if you ever come to Savannah"? All that was missing was "Have a nice life."

His good mood evaporated. Ally had left without even saying goodbye.

CHAPTER FOUR

WELL, THAT WAS UNPLEASANT. Not the best way to start a Monday, either. Ally leaned on the sink and took a deep breath. Then she grabbed the toothbrush she'd learned to bring to work with her and brushed her teeth. Wiping the moisture from the corners of her eyes, she was glad she'd switched to waterproof mascara last week.

"Look, Kiddo, I'll make you a deal. You let me keep my breakfast and I'll give you a new car when you turn sixteen, okay?" Another wave of nausea had her leaning against the bathroom door taking shallow breaths until it passed. "No deal, huh? Your loss."

Turning off the light, she opened the door to the office she shared with her friend and business partner. Molly stood waiting with a peppermint and a bottle of water.

"Seriously, now. How much longer is this going to go on?"

Ally took both offerings gratefully. The peppermint helped settle her stomach these days. "According to all the books, about six more weeks if I'm really lucky." She sank into her desk chair and rested her head on her hands.

"You're kidding me, right? Six more weeks of listening to you yak up your toenails every morning?" Molly's pixie face wrinkled in an amusing mixture of concern and disgust.

Ally sipped at her water cautiously, but the nausea had gone as quickly as it had come. "So sorry to inconvenience you, Molls."

"It's not that. I'm just worried."

Ally sighed. Snapping at Molly made her feel as if she'd kicked a puppy. "I know, and I'm sorry to be so witchy this morning. Dr. Barton says this is normal. Unpleasant, but still well within the range."

It was Molly's turn to sigh. "'Unpleasant' is an understatement."

"You're not wrong about that." Six weeks to go? Between the sickness in the mornings and the unbelievable fatigue that set in around three o'clock, this first trimester wasn't going well at all.

"Can I get you anything? Crackers? A soda?"

"Just help me find the Miller paperwork. I swear, this baby has stolen all my brain cells."

Molly casually tapped a folder sitting just left of Ally's elbow. "By the way, I talked to the landlord. He said we can have that storeroom for just a little more each month. I thought you could move your desk back there along with the baby's stuff, and we'll put a conference table out here to meet with clients."

Tears gathered in Ally's eyes. After the initial shock of Ally's announcement had passed, Molly had gone into "prep mode," never once questioning her decision to keep the baby, focusing instead on how they'd work out the logistics. Ally sniffed and reached for a tissue. Seemed she could check "overly emotional" on her list of symptoms, as well.

Thank goodness for Molly. She'd be a wreck without her. Her mom had flipped at the news, seemingly shocked that anyone accidentally ended up pregnant in this day and age. Ally had had to bite her tongue not to bring up her brother's pregnant girlfriend, Diane—no one seemed overly surprised about *that* baby. Molly had been the voice of reason then, too.

Her family was just too used to Ally being the sensible, smart, reliable one, she'd argued. In a rare moment of snark—showing how truly angry Molly was with the lot of them—she'd postulated that the real reason the family was upset over the news was that Ally's attention would be focused somewhere else in the future. God forbid her family might actually have to take care of their own problems and not be able to run to her to sort them out.

Molly frowned. "You're leaking again."

Ally fanned her face. "No, I'm not. Just something in my eye."

"Hey, I'd cry, too, if I went on my honeymoon alone and still managed to wind up pregnant." Molly tossed the comment over her shoulder as she returned to her own desk.

"Yes, yes, I'm aware of the irony." Right after she'd recovered from the shock of seeing a positive result on the pregnancy test and had realized she'd somehow ended up in the two-percent failure rate of the Pill, *that* irony had hit her right between the eyes.

It would almost be funny if it were someone else.

Molly's keyboard clicked as she went back to work, and Ally tried to focus on the books from Miller's Printing Company. She had to get their payroll data entered and their checks printed before the need for her afternoon nap hit, but she was having trouble concentrating.

From the moment her plane had taken off from San Juan, she'd tried to put Chris out of her mind. She knew she needed to forget him, to just let him and their hours together fade into a dim memory. But it hadn't worked. She'd felt like a different version of herself, as though she'd been on the verge of *something* only to have been jerked back by her family responsibilities.

She'd caught a cab directly from the airport to the hospital, expecting to find her brother barely clinging to life. Instead,

Steven was slightly battered from flipping his dirt bike, but awake, lucid and not near death at all—a situation she'd been tempted to remedy when he'd shown no remorse at all for ruining her vacation. After all, as her mother had added, Steven needed someone to deal with the hospital billing department and transfer money from his small trust to pay bills with.

The bitterness of missing out on more delightful days with Chris because of her family...well, she'd almost been over it by the time she'd missed her period, but any hope of forgetting about him had vanished at that point.

She was carrying his baby—a permanent reminder of those two wonderful days. How long would it take for her not to remember him every time she looked at their child? *Her* child, she corrected. This baby was hers alone.

Chris climbed the stairs to his office on OWD's second floor two at a time. His mornings had taken on a pattern these days—an hour at the gym, a few hours on the *Circe*'s renovations, lunch, then into the office. Today, though, he came straight from the yard, bypassed his assistant's desk without stopping for messages and went straight for his computer.

The damage to the *Circe*'s keel was greater than expected, and he'd contacted a friend for suggestions when he and Jack had clashed over the best course of action. He'd snapped a few quick photos with his phone, but couldn't get them to send properly for some reason.

He dug the USB cable out of its drawer and waited for the files to download onto his computer. A few clicks later, and the photos and measurements were off to Pete. Aesthetically, *Circe*'s rehab was going well, but structurally they kept finding new issues to deal with. He'd barely gotten her home—the constant problems had stretched his trip to almost four weeks, much to Victor's and Mickey's amusement and Pops's dismay.

Hopefully, this problem with the keel would be the last.

With the photos sent, Chris closed his e-mail account. The window open on his screen, though, showed another file had been in the download. *That's odd.*

He clicked it open, and Ally filled his screen. Something heavy landed in his stomach at the sight of that cheeky smile. He'd forgotten he'd taken it. They'd been almost ready to sail back when his phone had fallen out of his kit bag. She'd caught it before it went overboard and handed it to him, saying something about…what was it? Boys and their toys, he remembered. In response, he'd snapped a quick photo of her. She'd protested, grabbed the phone away, and distracted him with a kiss.

It had been another hour before they'd set off.

Ally.

He didn't need to look behind him at the bulletin board on the wall to know that Ally's note with her name and phone number scribbled on the back was still there. A hundred bucks slipped to the desk clerk had gotten her contact info from the computer, but after the initial shock and anger at her abrupt departure had abated—and the struggle to get the *Circe* home in one piece had helped distract him nicely—he'd never followed up on his knee-jerk reaction to want to find her.

He'd put her from his mind, if not his dreams, and gone back to his life, even if the blithe way she'd dismissed him had left a bitter taste in his mouth.

Mickey had taken his life in his hands once to tease him about it—shortly after he'd returned to the *Circe* instead of sailing off with Ally on the *Siren*—telling him it was a fair turnaround considering his own love-'em-and-leave-'em past. That was the closest he'd ever come to hitting a crewmate.

He wasn't sure why he'd even kept her note and number, much less pinned it on the board with the photos of him and his crew in various races over the years.

"Chris?" Marge, Pops's secretary, stuck her head around his office door. "I brought you a sandwich."

After thirty years with the company, Marge was more family than employee, and she'd mothered Chris shamelessly since day one. She was well past retirement age, but had said the place would fall apart without her and claimed they'd have to carry her out of there in a box. He and Pops certainly weren't arguing with her or forcing her out of the door.

Crossing to Chris's desk, she laid the sandwich on the blotter and ruffled his hair. "Jack said you two had a disagreement about the *Circe*."

The sandwich smelled delicious, and his stomach growled at the reminder he'd skipped lunch when the keel had distracted him. "Jack always comes running to you, the tattletale. She's not his boat."

"And I'm sure you're right about the keel. Just don't forget to eat. Who's she?" Marge was peering at the picture of Ally, still open on his desktop.

"Just someone I met on Tortola." He closed the picture.

"And you took her sailing? You never take anyone sailing. She must've been some girl." With a confidence not every employee would have, Marge clicked the photo open again and studied it carefully. "She's pretty, but not what I'd call your usual type."

He closed it again and unwrapped the sandwich. His favorite. Marge was too good to him. "Well, Ally was an aberration."

One of Marge's penciled eyebrows went up. "Ally is it? Ally of the mystery phone number, perhaps?"

He nearly choked on the large bite of roast beef but managed to swallow it painfully instead. "Is there anything you don't know?"

"It's right *there*." Marge pointed. "It's not like I had to go looking or anything. Eat."

Dutifully, he took another bite.

"That's a Savannah area code. Have you called her?"

Oh, good Lord. "No. And I doubt I will. Too much going on."

"Piffle." Marge waved the excuse away. "You just don't want to. I hope the poor girl isn't pining away waiting for your call."

"I doubt it." *She would have had to have left a phone number.*

With a shrug, Marge walked back to the door. "That's a pity. Oh, and your grandfather wants an update on *Dagny* when you have a minute."

No, Pops wanted to try to talk him out of it again. Finding fault with the *Dagny*'s progress was only his newest tactic.

Once Marge left, Chris ate and debated with himself as he stared at the icon on the desktop that would open Ally's picture if he clicked on it again.

What the hell. He probably should have called her already, just to be sure that her brother was okay. It would have been the right thing to do, after all.

He closed his office door, then dialed.

"AMI Accounting Services. This is Molly."

A business? Did he even have the right number? "I'm looking for Ally Smith."

"She's, um, away from her desk at the moment. Can I take a message?"

This was actually good. He'd salve his conscience *and* avoid further meddling from Marge by putting the ball in Ally's court. He'd called. Done his part. "Sure. This is Chris—"

"The contractor?" Molly interrupted, but didn't give him a chance to answer. "*Great.* Ally said you'd be calling. Actually, I can give you the information since she's busy."

"I'll just—" he started again, only to be interrupted with another torrent of words.

"We just need an estimate right now, but we don't need to start work right away. We've got until March to get it ready, after all." Molly laughed, but then hurried on before he could say anything. "We need to finish out the storeroom into an office for Ally—did she mention the lighting? She'll need to be able to darken the back half of the room where the crib will go. She doesn't think it will be a problem, but I think we should go ahead and have the electrics for that done while y'all are finishing out the walls. Don't you agree?"

One word out of the flood stopped him cold. "Excuse me, did you say crib?"

"Oh, it won't be a huge crib—I don't want you to think the space is *that* big." There was that laugh again, but he was still stuck on *crib*. "It's really just a cubbyhole for Ally and the baby."

Ally and the baby. And Molly said they had until March. A quick count backward meant that if Ally was pregnant, she'd conceived the baby in June. They were on Tortola in June. She'd told him she'd broken up with her ex months before, which meant she'd gotten pregnant on Tortola.

Adrenaline surged through his system.

"What time do you close today?"

"Oh, we'll be here until at least five-thirty or so. Can you come this afternoon?"

Without a doubt. "And your address?"

"Four seventeen West Jefferson, suite C. We'll—"

Chris hung up.

Ally was pregnant. There was a strong possibility the baby was his. Not only had she fled Tortola without saying goodbye, she hadn't bothered to try to find him and let him know she was carrying his child? Maybe she'd tried to, but...no, he wasn't that hard to find. Chris Wells might be a common enough name, but between knowing he was from Charleston and the sailing, she'd have found him quickly enough with one search on Google.

She had no intention of telling him. Unexpected anger coiled in his chest.

Keys. Phone. That was all he needed. He opened his office door to find Marge and his assistant in the outer office.

Without slowing his pace, he talked as he passed them. "Good. You're both here. That saves me time. Marge, tell Pops I'll talk to him about the *Dagny* tomorrow. Grace, I'm gone for the rest of the day."

Marge recovered first. "Where are you going?" she called after him.

"Savannah, damn it."

Okay, this was getting ridiculous. Morning sickness was for mornings. If she was going to start losing both her breakfast *and* her lunch every day, she and the baby were going to starve to death long before they made it out of this phase.

She brushed her teeth for the third time that day and went back to her desk where the rest of her lunch awaited her. One look at the guacamole on her taco salad caused her stomach to heave in protest.

"What now?" Molly asked around a mouthful of burrito.

"Can you get that off my desk? Just get it away from me, please. The guacamole is—ugh."

Molly, bless her heart, moved quickly, closing the box and carrying it outside without question. Once the offensive condiment was out of sight, her stomach felt much better.

Molly brought her the peppermints once she returned. "That's so sad. You love guacamole and it's so good for you."

"But the baby doesn't love it, obviously, and I'm willing to give in on this."

"Since you're the color of guacamole right now, that's probably a wise choice. Tortilla chip?"

That seemed safe enough. It was the craving for something salty and spicy that had led her to suggest they order Mexican for lunch in the first place. She would just omit the guacamole for the foreseeable future.

"By the way, one of the Kriss brothers called while you were indisposed."

The peppermint actually tasted quite nice with the salsa. "Really? That was fast. Their office manager said they were out of town until tomorrow."

Molly shrugged. "I think they're going to come by this afternoon and give us the estimate." Her brow wrinkled. "He was kinda rude on the phone, though. Are you sure this is the company you want to go with?"

"Michael Kriss did that work for my mom last year. She raves about him."

"Your mom raves about a lot of things."

"Yes, but when it comes to updating or decorating the Dingbat Cave, she is remarkably focused."

"Then I'll withhold judgment until we meet them and get the estimate."

Ally nibbled on another chip. "Speaking of judgment, Erin kicked me out of the wedding last night."

"She didn't! *Why?*"

"Because I'll be seven months pregnant and she doesn't want my big belly drawing attention away from her on her 'special day.'"

The picture of outrage, Molly nearly sputtered. "That's insane. What did your mother say?"

"Oh, she's on board, but it all kind of got lost in the melee after Steven made *his* big announcement."

"Do I even want to know?"

It was a good thing Molly understood her family. "My brother is now a Scientologist."

Molly spat her water across the desk. "Just like that? He woke up one morning and decided he was converting?"

"Pretty much. My grandmother swears she's seconds from a heart attack at the news, Mom is convinced she'll never make it into the Junior League now, and Erin claims Steven is just seeking attention since he's recovered from the accident." Leaning back in her chair, Ally propped her feet on her desk and crunched another chip.

"And your dad?"

"Dad went fishing, so he hasn't weighed in yet."

"Erin just wants all the attention on her and the wedding."

"You got it."

"I'm so glad you passed the edict they were no longer allowed to call here unless someone was bleeding."

"Me, too. I finally took the phone off the hook last night and went to sleep around eight. I was just too exhausted to deal with any of them."

"Good for you. Can I slap Erin next time I see her?"

Bless Molly and her loyalty. "At least I don't have to wear that ugly green dress now."

"Small favors." Molly trailed off into her usual mutterings about Ally's clan, but was thankfully distracted by the phone before she worked up too big a head of steam on Ally's behalf. Once Molly got wound up it was hard to calm her back down.

Ally entered the last few numbers into the computer file, waited for the screen to update, then hit Print. Payroll for other companies was AMI's bread and butter, and she normally found the process boring. Today, though, the monotony of folding and stuffing checks was just what her mind needed. Between her own problems, her family, and the brain-numbness the baby caused, the simple, repetitive action felt soothing.

Two hours later she had all the checks for all four of their biggest clients ready. She took a few minutes to log on to her mother's bank account and pay the bills before she logged on to her e-mail account. Four e-mails from her sister. Ugh. She did not want to deal with that right now.

She eyeballed the stack of checks. Molly normally took care of delivery, but the prospect of getting out of the office for a little while was tempting. Two businesses were within walking distance, and a walk in the August sunshine would be good for the baby. And she could stop for a smoothie on the way back.

The sunshine helped clear the cobwebs from her head and being out in the neighborhood improved her mood. She loved the entire City Market district with its variety of restaurants, interesting stores and true community feel. The rent on the office was high, but worth every penny. Ally dropped off both sets of checks, then dawdled in Franklin Square for a little while to enjoy the afternoon. Next year she could bring the baby here when they needed a break from the office.

She shouldn't delay getting back any longer. After a quick stop at the vegan deli for a banana smoothie for herself and a mango one for Molly, she rounded the last corner.

A very sleek red sports car like the kind James Bond would probably drive was parked in front of their building. As she approached, the driver's side door opened and a tall blond man got out. There was something vaguely familiar about the man...

Recognition hit a split second before he turned around. Her pulse jumped briefly in excitement before reality hit and her heart dropped like a stone into her stomach.

Casually, as though he had every reason in the world to be right outside her office, Chris leaned against the car and crossed his arms across his chest, eerily reminiscent of that first day on the dock weeks ago. Only last time he'd seemed relaxed, open and approachable. Today he looked like he'd been carved from stone, and his jaw was tight. In a tone that could easily cut glass he simply said, "How are you, Ally?"

CHAPTER FIVE

HOLY HELL. Ally tightened her numb fingers around the cup she held as her heart jumped back into her chest and pounded erratically. She leaned against a mailbox for a moment as she tried to gather herself. *Breathe. Be calm.*

"This is certainly a surprise." Pleased her voice didn't shake too much, Ally punctuated it with a small smile.

Chris didn't return it. "Seems we're both having surprising days, then."

She didn't know what to make of that statement. In fact, she didn't know what to make of *anything*—not why he was here, not what she should say in response. "I thought you were still on Tortola with the *Circe.* What brings you to Savannah?"

His voice was clipped, succinct, the lazy drawl disappearing. "I brought the *Circe* home to Charleston. I came to Savannah to find you."

She'd dreamed once that Chris had come to her, and he'd said almost those exact same words. But the reality version wasn't at all like the dream. No, in her dream, Chris had smiled as he said the words, causing those adorable crinkles around his blue, blue eyes. Those eyes were cold now, and one eyebrow arched up in a mocking challenge. What *kind* of challenge, she wasn't sure.

She nearly blurted out, "Why?" but caught the question in time. From the look on his face, she didn't think she'd like the answer. Instead she went to her next pressing question. "How'd you find me?"

"You mean since you didn't leave a number on your brief goodbye note?" he mocked. "Seriously, Ally, in this day and age it's not all that difficult to find someone when you want to."

Something nasty lurked behind his words, sending a cold shiver through her insides. Her hand went protectively to her stomach, but she caught herself at the last second.

The instinctive movement didn't pass unnoticed, though, and she winced as Chris's eyes narrowed. "My question is, why didn't you find me?"

There's no way he could know. Bluff your way out of this and leave gracefully. "I enjoyed our time together—honestly, I did—but it was over and done with. I had no idea you'd leave Tortola. Or that you'd be so close to Savannah." That was the truth. *Why* did he have to be from Charleston, for goodness' sake? Why couldn't he be from Florida or someplace far, *far* from here? "It seemed best just to let it go."

Chris levered himself off the car and took a step toward her, his voice dropping dangerously. "That's not what I'm talking about, and you damn well know it. It would have taken you approximately five minutes to find me if you'd tried. And you should have tried as soon as you found out."

He knew. Oh, God, he knew. How? Paniclike flutters in her chest made it hard to breathe. No, there was no way he could know. "When I found out what?"

"Don't play dumb, Ally. It doesn't suit you. You're pregnant. About six weeks if I understand correctly. And six weeks ago you were with me."

There was the nausea again. She swayed on her feet as it washed over her. Chris grabbed her elbow. "Are you all right?"

She took a deep breath—inhaling the scent of him and letting it coil through her—and blew it out slowly, trying to will the nausea away. Game over, time to just face it. "How did you find out?"

He tilted his head in the direction of the office. "Your business partner—Molly, right?—she told me today when I called."

She needed to sit down, but there was nothing on the sidewalk to use as a seat. This was too much to process at once. The happy thought of Chris calling her *before* he knew about the baby was quickly stomped down by the need to wring Molly's neck. She took deep breaths to calm herself. It didn't work.

"I take it from your reaction that it is my baby."

All she could do was nod. The swimming feeling in her head was too much for anything else.

"And you had no intention of telling me?" Each word was clipped and sharp. This wasn't the Chris who'd taken her sailing and made her laugh. And made her cry out with his touch. This Chris was livid. Cold.

"I just—"

"There's no 'just,' Ally. Yes or no."

"No! I mean yes. I mean—" Over Chris's shoulder, she could see that Sarah, the owner of the bookshop across the street, watching her carefully, a worried crease on her forehead. A quick glance around showed Sarah wasn't the only one paying attention. No one was headed in this direction—*yet*—but they had an audience. At least her office didn't have street-front windows, or else Molly would be out here wanting to know what was going on. This public display had to stop.

She lowered her voice. "Look, I can't talk about this. Not now. And certainly not *here*."

The muscle in his jaw twitched. Chris looked around, noted the interest they'd garnered and nodded sharply. "Agreed."

Relief swept through her. She set the smoothies on the

mailbox and rummaged though her bag for a pen and piece of paper. "I'll call yo—"

"Where do you live?"

Her head jerked up so quickly a neck muscle spasmed. "What?"

"We need to talk. Privately. Your place seems like the obvious choice."

She'd hoped for a reprieve. A chance to plan strategy. A chance to at least get her heartbeat under control. "But…"

"Right here, right now, or your place. Take your pick."

How dare he sweep in here and start ordering her about? She didn't have to "take her pick" about anything. She didn't need this kind of upset. She should just walk away. But guilt nagged at her. To be fair, he did have cause to be angry.

As she argued with herself, the tension in Chris's jaw seemed to increase. She wasn't going to get out of this, so she needed to pull herself together and deal with it as gracefully as possible. Better to get it over with now.

Yeah, keep telling yourself that.

"My apartment is about ten minutes from here. I'll need to get my stuff and tell Molly I'm leaving for the day. I'll be a couple of minutes."

Another nod, this one so small it was barely perceptible. The man was so tense, the cords in his neck were visible.

She managed to open the office door calmly enough and made it inside. Once out of Chris's eyesight, though, her knees began to wobble again as the magnitude of the situation hit her.

Zombielike, Ally placed the mango smoothie on Molly's desk before collapsing in the adjacent chair.

Molly brightened as she reached for her drink. "Thanks. Yum." She took a sip before looking closely at Ally, and the corners of her mouth turned down in concern. "Are you okay? You look pale. Are you going to barf again?"

Possibly. "I'm fine." The emotional toil of the last ten minutes—not to mention the thought of what was still to come—washed over her and she rubbed her eyes tiredly.

Molly took her answer at face value. "Some guy came in looking for you about twenty minutes ago."

A hysterical giggle tried to escape. "Oh, he found me."

"He was *all* shades of cute. Who is he? Is he single?"

Fatigue—probably not all due to the baby this time—washed over her, and she rested her head in her hands. "Molls, *please* tell me what possessed you to tell a stranger over the phone that I was pregnant."

Indignant, Molly nearly choked on her smoothie. "I did no such thing."

"Really? Chris says he called here today and you told him I was pregnant."

"Chris? Who's Chr— Oh." Molly's lips puckered. "Someone did call, and when he said Chris, I thought it was the Kriss Brothers. I mentioned why we were fixing up that room. Are you telling me he was… That the guy who came in here… That he's—" Ally watched as all the pieces fell into place for Molly. "Oh, Ally, I'm *so* sorry. No wonder you look so pale."

There was that hysterical laughter again. Ally went to her desk and turned off her computer. "I'm taking the rest of the afternoon off. I'll see you tomorrow."

"Of course. Go home and lie down. We'll sort this all out tomorrow. I have to say, though—hummina, hummina. No wonder you…"

"Molly…" she warned.

"Okay, okay. What did he say?"

"Let's just say he's a bit angry I didn't find him when I found out."

"I told you that you should. He has a right to know."

"I know." Overwhelmed again, she swung her chair around

and sat. "But being pregnant was complicated enough, I didn't need anything else. I thought he lived on his boat in the Caribbean, for goodness' sake. How was I to know he really lived in Charleston and wasn't just 'free spirit sailor boy'? Like I needed *another*..."

"Another Gerry?"

"Exactly. I have enough folks—not to mention the baby—relying on me as it is. I just got one unemployed pretty boy off my hands, I didn't want to get another one to support. For all I knew, Chris Wells was just another Gerry waiting to happen."

"Wait a minute." Molly's eyes widened. "Chris Wells? And he's from Charleston? He's *the* Chris Wells?"

"Maybe. Why? Who's *the* Chris Wells?"

"I thought he looked familiar. Good Lord... Ally, I know you didn't want to contact him, but are you really telling me you didn't at least look the man up on Google out of curiosity?" Molly was already at her computer, fingers flying across the keyboard.

"I didn't want to know. It was just easier if I didn't. Look, he's waiting for me, and he's not in the most patient of moods right now."

"He can wait one more minute. Come here." Molly swiveled her computer screen around as Ally sat in the chair across from her. "You need to see this."

Chris on a sailboat, grinning at the camera. Her heart did a quick double beat as that was the Chris she remembered—not the very angry man waiting for her outside. "And?"

Molly sighed deeply. "Listen carefully. Ever heard of the OWD Shipyard outside Charleston? The *W* stands for Wells. OWD is the primary sponsor of Wells Racing, and the owner's grandson, *Chris*, captains their boats. Team Wells has won every major race in the last five years—including the America's Cup. They're considered unbeatable. My God, Ally, you certainly know how to pick them. Chris Wells is the Tiger Woods of sailing."

Slowly, Molly's words started to sink in, and the information on the screen in front of her corroborated her story. "How do you know this?"

Molly waved a hand dismissively. "Back when I was dating Ray, he was really into ships and racing. It was all he talked about."

"Yachts." She couldn't believe what she was seeing. Chris was a celebrity. And the heir to the OWD Shipyard to boot.

Molly looked at her blankly.

"Those are yachts, not ships." He'd lied to her. Said he raced some and occasionally won. Yeah, right. He was the freakin' god of the sailing world and he'd led her to believe… Well, he hadn't really led her anywhere, but he certainly hadn't been totally honest, either. Chris wasn't the only one angry now.

Not caring much anymore that Chris was waiting for her, she continued to click through the links, and each Web page brought a new emotion. She welcomed them. By the time she heard the chimes over the door, announcing that he'd gotten impatient and had come to get her, she no longer felt quite so shaky or defensive.

"Are you ready yet, Ally?" Anger still radiated from him, but she no longer cared how mad he was.

Molly, bless her heart, tried to defuse the situation. Extending her hand to Chris, she introduced herself. "We didn't meet properly earlier. I'm Molly, Ally's business partner."

Chris nodded, but his eyes never left Ally. He seemed to be trying to stare her into the ground, but she felt steady and refused to give him the satisfaction of cowering this time.

Grabbing her things, she stood. Time to get this over with. "Yes, I am. You drive. I'll see you tomorrow, Molls."

* * *

Chris watched as Ally led the way to his car and climbed in without waiting for him to assist. Something had changed in the last few minutes, and he now felt anger radiating from her.

Other than the terse directions she provided, she sat in silence as they drove. What did she have to be so irritated about? He was the wronged party here. When he'd seen her come around the corner, his body had leaped to life, his blood heating and his hands itching to touch her again. But the look on her face when she'd recognized him had killed that feeling as it answered almost every question he'd asked himself on the drive down from Charleston. She was pregnant. The baby was his. And she hadn't planned on ever telling him.

When he'd realized it was all true, the anger had boiled over and he'd blasted her with it. He hadn't handled the situation as well as he'd planned, and now guilt nibbled at the edge of his ire.

The only important answer he didn't have yet was *why,* but he planned to rectify that soon enough. With Ally practically vibrating with hostility as she sat next to him, though, he doubted he'd get a satisfactory answer at the moment.

In an attempt to both appease his guilt and ease the tension between them, he backtracked to less volatile territory—at least while they were in a small, enclosed space. "How are you feeling?"

Ally's eyebrows went up and she seemed poised to attack. Instead she closed her eyes and took a deep breath. "The mornings are pretty rough, and I'm tired a lot."

"And that's normal?"

She nodded. "Unfortunately." Her lips twitched in amusement, and, for a brief moment, he flashed back to Tortola, back to when her inability to hide her reactions had charmed him.

But the moment passed quickly, and her amusement faded as rapidly as it had come. "Turn left. That's me on the corner."

The two-story Victorian sat gracefully among its historic neighbors, beautiful and well cared for despite its age. He'd been so occupied on the short drive, he hadn't noticed she was directing him to the heart of Savannah's historic district. "*This* is your place?"

Ally didn't break stride as she climbed the steps to the spacious verandah and slid her key into the lock. "The first floor is. I may not be the heir to a shipyard or have zillion-dollar endorsement agreements, but I do all right."

So she did know who he was. She may not have known when they met, but at some point she'd done her homework. Which meant she could have contacted him if she'd wanted to. His ire flared up again.

Ally's sandals slapped against hardwood floors, and the sound echoed off the high ceilings as she moved around the room before settling on an overstuffed red sofa. The apartment suited her—or at least the little he knew about her—old-fashioned around the edges but still modern. The absurdity of the situation hit him at that moment. A woman he barely knew was carrying his child.

"You wanted to talk. Let's talk."

The challenge was there; he no longer had the element of surprise on his side, and Ally must feel as though she had the home court advantage now. "How long have you known?"

"That I was pregnant? About three weeks."

"And in all that time, it never occurred to you that you should tell *me?*" Agitated, he paced in front of the sofa she sat on, hoping the extra expense of energy would keep him from lashing out again as his temper built.

"To what end? As far as I knew, you lived on a boat somewhere in the Caribbean and hooked up with a different girl every night of the week."

"And you assumed the swabbie wasn't worth telling? He was good enough to sleep with on vacation, but not good enough to help you raise a child?"

"Be reasonable, Chris. It's not a matter of 'good enough.' I was just trying to be rational about this."

"When you found out differently, you didn't call me because…"

"I only found out about the great Chris Wells twenty minutes ago, so it didn't affect my assessment of the situation."

"You expect me to believe that when you found out you were pregnant, you never once tried to find out more about me?"

For the first time in this ridiculous conversation, Ally's temper seemed to flare. "To be brutally honest, I had enough on my plate to figure out. I wasn't all that worried about *you*."

"Oh, no. I can't see why the *father* of the baby would have any impact whatsoever on your plans."

As fast as it had come, the heat fled from her voice and her tone became conciliatory. "Don't take it personally. I loved every minute we spent together, but it was just a summer fling. It was over, as far as everything was concerned."

He gestured at her stomach. "I beg to differ."

Ally sighed and rubbed her face. "Look. My hormones are a mess right now, I cry at the drop of a hat, I'm so exhausted I can barely keep my eyes open, and I haven't been able to eat all day. I can't deal with this level of hostility, and I don't see much sense in continuing to shout at each other. Let's just cut to the chase, okay?"

Personally, he felt there was a lot of ground still to cover, but only a true jerk would continue to upset a pregnant woman. It wasn't good for the baby.

His baby.

While anger had been driving him since Molly unwittingly dropped the news, the magnitude of the situation finally slammed into him. He was going to be a father. Hard on the heels of *that* realization was the even more shocking understanding that he wanted this baby.

Now he needed to sit down. He chose a chair across from Ally and nodded for her to continue.

Ally took a deep breath before she spoke. "I didn't try to find you because I didn't think it would matter. You didn't strike me as the kind of guy who was looking to be tied down, so telling you about the baby—even if I'd been able to locate you—didn't seem like a winning situation." He started to interrupt, but she hurried ahead. "*Obviously,* I was mistaken with that assumption, and for that I apologize. I didn't set out to get pregnant, but I know I want her. Or him. You don't have to worry, though. I have a good job, plenty of friends and family, and I can handle this. I don't expect anything from you."

Wringing Ally's neck sounded very tempting at the moment. "What if I expect something? This is my child, too, remember."

Genuine shock at his statement sent Ally's eyebrows upward. Had she never once considered that possibility while she was "handling" things?

"Well, um, I'm sure we can work something out. Visitation arrangements or…"

"That's not good enough."

"Then what *do* you want?" There was a beat of silence before Ally laughed. "It's not like we can get married or anything."

Actually, that was a possibility he hadn't considered yet. He hadn't had three weeks to make decisions. Hell, he'd barely had three *hours*. "Why not?"

"Be serious."

"Maybe I am."

"I'm not looking to get married at the moment." A shadow crossed her face but disappeared a second later.

"Neither was I, now that you mention it, but the circumstances have changed."

That seemed to spark something, and her calm facade dropped. She stood and paced, and her hands moved agitatedly as she talked. "But the century hasn't. We don't have to get married because I'm pregnant. There are other—"

"I'm not going to be delegated to the occasional weekend." He'd had enough of that with his own parents in the early days after their divorce. Until his mother had decided not to bother anymore, at least.

"Then what do you want?"

Before he even realized what he was doing, he was on his feet and his hands were gripping her arms. "To be a part of my child's life. To be his father!"

Ally shook off his grip. "I'm offering you that. We'll just have to figure something out that works for both of us. Charleston is only a couple of hours away…"

As unbelievable as it sounded, Ally seemed to think he was really going to settle for whatever little plan she had turning in her head. Not likely. "Damn it, Ally—"

She spun on him in a fury. "Don't even look at me like that. How dare you come storming down here and start making demands? This is *my* baby, and *I'll* be the one making the decisions."

He moved toward her, and she took a step backward. "*Your* baby? Hel-lo, you didn't get pregnant by yourself. That baby is just as much mine as it is yours."

She lifted her chin and tossed down the gauntlet. "Maybe not. Maybe I lied and it's not yours after all."

So much for cutting to the chase and discussing this like adults. "Don't try me, Ally. You won't like the results."

Brown eyes narrowed and a flush rose on her chest. "Is that some kind of threat?"

"I don't make threats. Just promises."

The flush continued to rise up her neck, and Ally's lips compressed into a thin line. "Get out," she snapped. "Now."

He stood his ground. "This conversation is not over—"

"Oh, yes, it is. Leave." Stalking across the room, she picked up the phone. "Leave or I'll call the police."

"Now who's making threats?"

"You're not the only one who doesn't make empty threats. Get out of my house."

He'd never had anyone try his temper the way Ally did, and he was moments from saying or doing something he might regret later. Maybe it was best he leave before then. As he opened the door, he warned her one last time. "This doesn't end here. This is far from over."

"Oh, no. It's over. I assure you of that. Goodbye, Chris." She slammed the door behind him and he heard the lock click into place.

She thought it was that easy? That it was over just because she said so? She might have gotten away with it on Tortola, but the circumstances had changed dramatically.

He had his phone out of his pocket and his assistant on the line before he even had the car started.

Ally was in for a rude awakening.

Ally's anger carried her as far as the kitchen for a glass of water before it deflated in a rush that had her knees buckling. Ice rattled in the glass as she filled it from the tap with a shaky hand. Easing onto a bar stool gratefully, she sipped carefully and cursed Chris for making her lose her temper.

She *never* lost her temper. She was the calm one while everyone else spun out of control. Molly had always praised her flair for diplomacy, a skill she'd honed over years of dealing with her family and their constant dramatics. Why had it failed her now? Instead of calmly—rationally—coming to a workable agreement and smoothing ruffled feathers, she'd managed to make the situation worse. Where was her famed calm and diplomacy today? It had to be the hormones. This pregnancy was really messing with her head.

But now that she could see something other than a red haze… Ugh. She may not know Chris very well, but she had a sinking feeling she'd made a huge tactical mistake in firing up his anger.

Her five minutes with Google earlier today had told her a lot about the great Chris Wells. A true golden boy, he came from old Charleston money and had the whole sailing world worshipping at his feet. Maybe she should have given in to her curiosity sooner; then she wouldn't have been at such a disadvantage today.

"You sure know how to pick them," Molly had said it with a kind of begrudging awe, but Ally knew that wasn't the case at all. Molly saw his good looks, his charm and his money, and therefore branded him a good catch. Ally, though, knew better. Looks, charm and money didn't equal squat in her book. Gerry had looks and charm to spare, yet he'd been an emotional black hole. She'd invested far too much in his dreams, only to get nothing in return except four years of doing his laundry. Golden boys had a tendency to expect the world to revolve around them, and she had learned her lesson the hard way. Hell, her own brother was a shining example—handsome and full of charm, he'd been dazzling girls since junior high. But he was self-centered and expected everyone to dance to his tune just for the privilege of basking in the reflected glow. His girlfriend, Diane, would have been history by now if she hadn't turned up pregnant, and even impending fatherhood hadn't tamed Steven.

If she'd found all this out about Chris and hadn't been carrying his child, she probably wouldn't have contacted him. Once bitten, twice shy. Between her brother and Gerry, she had enough experience to know that Chris would be a very bad idea.

And now she had someone else to think about, someone she *had* to put first. How long would Chris want to play Daddy before he got bored and went back to his far-more-exciting world? No way she'd put her son or daughter through that.

Most likely Chris was just reacting out of shock, anger and guilt. It would pass now that he knew she didn't expect anything from him, and his sense of responsibility would fade. She just needed to wait it out. After all, even as mad as he was at the moment, what could he do?

Glad she hadn't completely lost her ability to be rational, she sent a quick text message to Molly to let her know everything was okay and that she was now going to take a much-needed nap. The usual afternoon fatigue was even worse in the aftermath of such emotional upheaval.

She pulled the shades to darken the bedroom and didn't bother to do any more than kick off her shoes before stretching out across the comforter. As she closed her eyes, the image of Chris climbing out of that car—that one second when she'd recognized him, before he had turned around and she'd seen the anger on his face—was waiting for her. And now that she was alone and sleep was crowding in from all sides, she couldn't ignore the fact her heart had skipped a beat in excitement, and for a fraction of a second her whole body had screamed to life.

If only things were different….

Don't go there. Ally rolled over and punched the pillow into shape. This was not the time to play If Only. She knew better than that. Things were what they were, and the sooner she got that through her head the better.

But it didn't stop her mind from toying with the might-have-beens until sleep dragged her under a few minutes later.

CHAPTER SIX

THE WORST PART of Chris's job had to be the paperwork. He had no patience for the pages of numbers and reports that cluttered his desk on a daily basis. He'd rather be down in the yard doing something—*any*thing, even welding, which he hated—rather than be stuck inside buried under a pile of paperwork. But, as Pops reminded him daily, OWD was still a family business, and as the only direct family Pops had left, Chris had to do his part.

That was soon to change, though. Chris being the only Wells left in line, that is. The news of Ally's pregnancy had thrilled the old man and put a new spring in his step. A great-grandchild—security for keeping OWD in the family—had shifted Pops's focus. He'd been a little disappointed Chris hadn't chosen to go about procreating in the old-fashioned way and that more children wouldn't be forthcoming anytime soon, of course, but he'd been more than just a little pleased, anyway. In the past few years, Pops's encouragement to get married had crossed the line into harping, so Chris knew Pops would see this as hope Chris did intend to settle down and have many more children—if not with Ally, then with someone else.

But it had shifted—at least temporarily—focus off the *Dagny* and the solo attempt.

He understood all too well where Pops's concerns stemmed from, but sailing had come a long way in the last twenty years, and his father's boat, the *Fleece,* had lacked many of the technological and safety features currently being installed on the *Dagny.* Yes, any attempt to sail solo around the world was dangerous, but the chances of him ending up like his father were considerably less.

Nope, no matter what Pops's hopes and plans were, he'd still be making his announcement at the club's annual gala on September tenth. That would be just enough time to get a buzz going before he set sail in October, but not so long that it lost its newsworthiness before it happened.

In the meanwhile, though, he still had to go over the shareholders' reports. Resigned, but determined to get it done in the least amount of time possible, he dug into the stack of papers. Engrossed and concentrating, he didn't know Marge had even entered his office until the large manila envelope landed on his desk.

"The courier from Dennison and Bradley dropped this by for you. Can I ask why that shark has been circling the office recently?"

Marge always referred to his grandfather's attorney as "that shark." Where the animosity came from, Chris didn't know. Marge seemed to like everyone else in the world, but she always absented herself whenever Dennison came around and spoke disparagingly of him afterward.

"He's taking care of a few things for me." Opening the envelope, his copies of the papers served to Ally this morning slid out in a satisfying bulk of legalese.

"That's what worries me." Marge's brows drew together in a concerned frown. Marge, too, had received the news of the baby with a mixture of joy and shock, and had tossed in an "Aren't you glad you called her?" as well. But in the three days since he'd returned from Savannah and shared the news, Marge had hovered about, watching with great interest and asking vague, random questions about his plans. As she closed the office door and settled in the chair across from his desk, he assumed he was about to find out why.

Marge squared her shoulders and took a deep breath. "Your grandfather is going to either kill me or fire me but, either way, I'm not just going to stand by quietly again."

He knew his grandfather would do no such thing, and he knew Marge knew it, as well. "Again?"

"It wasn't my place to get involved before. I was still new here and figured there was a lot more going on than I knew about. But after seeing how it's turned out…" Marge stopped and shook her head. "Porter talks to me, and he's simply bubbling over with the idea of a great-grandchild. And if he's called in that shark Dennison, he's falling back on the same dirty tricks he and your father—God rest his soul—used years ago on your poor mother."

"My poor mother?" It was all he could do not to laugh at the turn of phrase. "My mother got exactly what she wanted in the divorce—freedom."

"And I'm telling you that wasn't what Elise wanted at all. You were too young to understand at the time, but I'd hoped that over the years you would learn the truth. Maybe if Paul had lived, you would have found out, but after he died, Porter closed ranks around you even tighter than before. He's basically a good man, so I always assumed his behavior was fueled by Paul's anger and then later his own grief over Paul's death. But now, I'm not so sure."

He'd never heard Marge speak a single ill word about Pops, so the clipped words and barely concealed distaste in her voice came as a surprise. Her hesitancy to just spit out whatever was bothering her was also odd. Marge had practically raised him, and she'd never once held back. Obviously, whatever she was stewing about was important.

Marge wasn't making a lot of sense, but she had his attention nonetheless. "Start at the beginning."

"Your parents started off with a bang—all fireworks and excitement. Elise was sweet and shy and very sheltered, and she never stood a chance against Paul's looks and charm and money—something I'm sure you're familiar with, seeing as you're him made over." Marge's stony facade cracked a little as she smiled at him with pride.

"But that's neither here nor there." She waved away the comment. "Unlike you, Paul never could be convinced to take an interest in the business, and Porter indulged his obsession with racing. Paul was always gone—another race, another title, other women—and your mother simply couldn't continue to put up with it. All she wanted was a simple, amicable divorce."

"Which my father gave her."

Marge's brows went up at the interruption. "At first, yes. Then a couple of years later she met that nice man and wanted to marry him. It wasn't a problem until she told your father she'd be moving to California after the wedding and they'd need to work out a new custody agreement. I think that was the day your grandfather finally went gray-headed from the news. Your mother left here in tears. I'll never forget it. Next thing I knew, that shark Dennison was in the mix and he buried your mother in restraining orders, custody papers and competency hearings. Money buys a lot of legal experts, and Elise wasn't able to fight back."

A vague memory stirred of his mother on the phone, holding papers in her hand and crying. He glanced at the stack of papers Dennison had drawn up, and guilt nibbled at him.

"I think you're beginning to get my point. They just wore

her down until she couldn't fight them anymore. Then, to compound the issue, they let you think she'd willingly walked out of your life."

No wonder Marge had been the one to comfort him after his mother had left. She'd known the reason why. He felt the slow burn of anger in his stomach, but there was nowhere to direct it. His father was dead. His mother was dead. Marge had done the best she could in the situation. And Pops…well, it was tough to stir up too much anger towards a seventy-year-old man who was all the family he really had left.

"All I'm saying, Chris, is that if those papers are what I think they are—and the look on your face tells me they are—then *don't.* Don't do to Ally and your child what was done to you. You can work this out. She doesn't deserve it and your child deserves to have its mother."

Marge sat back in the chair and folded her hands in her lap—the signal that she'd said her piece and was done. Now he was faced with a dilemma. He'd let his temper carry him to this point—Ally had been served with these same papers first thing this morning. At least he had Marge's information before he had to talk to Ally about them and made the situation worse. In fact, he was surprised he hadn't had an angry phone call already. It was a lot to think about, and he needed to plan his next move carefully.

The intercom on his desk buzzed, and Grace cut in. "Mr. Chris, there's a— Hey! Wait!" At the same moment, his office door burst open and Ally stood there, chest heaving and curls rioting around her head. She held a familiar manila envelope in one white-knuckled hand.

"You bastard! How dare you. You—" Anger choked off her words.

Grace was right behind her. "I'm sorry. I tried to stop her."

Three women looked at him. Grace in apology, Marge in question and Ally... Well, he was just lucky looks couldn't kill.

So much for time to think and plan.

It was a good thing she didn't own a gun. It had taken a little while to figure out the legalese, but once the meaning of those papers had sunk in, fury consumed her. Even the unflappable Molly had been taken aback at the extent of the lawsuits.

That fury had only grown during the drive to Charleston, and she'd broken every speed limit in two states in her rush to confront Chris. Now that she was here, she was itching to do him physical harm, especially since he had the gall to look surprised to see her.

She couldn't form words. Every phrase she'd practiced on the drive was trapped behind the anger choking her.

While the blond-haired assistant sputtered behind her, a matronly woman rose from the chair in front of Chris's desk. As she turned, Ally saw both concern and, oddly, affection in her eyes.

"You must be Ally. You're even lovelier in person." The woman's kind smile and gentle pat to Ally's arm as she passed seemed surreal. "Let's go, Grace."

The older woman ushered the younger one out and closed the door behind her, leaving Ally alone with Chris, who looked remarkably calm and unperturbed for someone who'd just served enough legal papers on her to put that lawyer's child through college with the expense.

"Would you like to sit?" Chris came around from behind his desk and gestured toward the chair the woman had just vacated.

Had she crossed into the freaking *Twilight Zone?* "I don't know if I should. You'd probably use my decision to sit against me later."

She couldn't tell if the slight inclination of Chris's head

was meant to be mocking or conciliatory as he perched on the edge of the desk. *The jerk.*

"I expected I'd hear from you today. I kind of assumed you'd call, though."

Molly had suggested the same thing, claiming distance would make it easier to deal with Chris and his outrageous demands. She'd been too mad to listen. "You questioned my competency, my fitness to be a parent. You're demanding my medical records and serving me with an order to keep me from traveling outside Georgia or South Carolina, and you wonder why I came to confront you in person? Maybe we should be questioning *your* mental stability."

"Actually, my attorney did all of that. I just told him I wanted my child and that you were unwilling to come to an agreement."

How dare he try to blame *her* for this? "So you decided to serve all this—" she tossed the envelope onto the desk "—on me? It won't work. I'm not going to let you take custody of this baby. I'll fight you."

"But you won't win."

A red haze clouded her vision, and she curled her hands into fists, her nails digging into her palms. "This is the twenty-first century. I have rights, and no judge in the universe would rule in your favor. I'm not incompetent." She lifted her chin in defiance. That much she was sure of. She was the poster child of competency.

"Maybe not, but it'll still cost you buckets of money to prove it."

All the air left her lungs at his matter-of-fact pronouncement, but Chris just shrugged. "I hate to be the one to break this to you, but it doesn't really matter if I can do half of what's in that envelope. My lawyers will serve you with motion after motion, and you'll be forced to respond to each one."

The possibility of a long, legal battle sobered her. It wouldn't matter if she was in the right; the repercussions would be horrific—not only on her, but on her family, on Molly, on the baby. *Especially* on the baby.

"Zillion-dollar endorsement deals will buy a lot of legal expertise, Ally."

Dear God, he was right. She didn't have the money to fight. She'd be bankrupt just responding to a *fraction* of the motions in that envelope. And if she couldn't fight him, would he win simply by default? Her stomach dropped. She'd made a horrific mistake in angering him, and she'd walked straight into this mess with her pride and anger. But what could she do now?

Chris seemed to realize when that last thought crystallized for her. He indicated for her to sit again, and took the other chair. "Maybe now you'll be more open to negotiation."

Negotiation? Just the two of them? She looked carefully for the trap, but Chris's face was the picture of friendliness and conciliation. Oh, she'd love to kill him. "You mean to tell me... You did this to... This was all just scare tactics?" Hesitant relief now mingled with her earlier anger, and the emotional toll left her drained as her head spun. As much as she'd like to turn on her heel and march out of there, she needed to sit.

"No, not just scare tactics. If we can't come to a workable solution, I will do whatever it takes. Hopefully, it won't come to that."

She tried to sort her scrambled thoughts, but those blue eyes locked on hers didn't help the process. She'd spent the past three days trying to figure out what to do, and she wasn't any closer to a solution than she was when Chris had stormed off her front porch. Trying to balance what was right for the baby with what would be good for them both in the long run... Chris's arrival had thrown all of her carefully made plans into the wind.

Then those papers had arrived and she hadn't been able to think at all. Chris's sudden willingness to be reasonable just brought back all of her earlier problems—this time coupled with the suspicion she wasn't going to like these negotiations.

Anger had kept her not-just-in-the-morning sickness at bay so far today, but as it ebbed, nausea swept back in. She fumbled in her purse for the bag of saltine crackers stashed there. She nibbled slowly on one, grateful for the stalling tactic, as Chris frowned. Then he left, returning a minute later with a paper cup.

"Ginger ale. It should help."

She nodded her thanks and sipped carefully. A few deep breaths later, her stomach settled some and the queasiness waned.

"I'm guessing discussing this over lunch is out of the question?"

Looking up, she saw a hint of laughter in those blue eyes, and the corner of his mouth twitched. He found her nausea amusing, did he? Next time, she'd just let fly on his shoes. See how funny he thought *that* was. "I'll stick with the crackers."

Of course, sitting in Chris's office with those horrible papers still on his desk waiting for him to tell her what he wanted from her wasn't helping her stomach much, either. Chris certainly had the upper hand in this "negotiation," and she knew it. *You have no one to blame but yourself,* her conscience nagged. *You fired the opening shot.* She needed to forget about her stomach and focus on keeping Chris reasonable—

"How's your brother?"

The change in topic jarred her, and she looked at him blankly.

"Your brother got hurt. That's why you left Tortola so suddenly, right?"

How'd he know that? "He's fine now. He flipped a dirt bike in a race and it landed on him. He was banged up a bit, but

Mom just did her usual freak-out and I had to come sort everything…" *Don't give him more ammunition to use against you later.* Her batty family was a liability now. Great. She tried to shrug off the statement. "You know how moms are."

Chris didn't answer. Instead, he leaned back in the chair and crossed his legs at the ankles, looking far more relaxed than was at all fair, considering the emotional mess *she* was at the moment. "And you're in business with your best friend. That's interesting. You're a bookkeeper, correct?"

These questions she could answer properly. Nothing about AMI could possibly be used against her later. "Bookkeeping and general accounting, payroll, taxes—we do it all. My degrees are in accounting and finance, and Molly is also a CPA." She couldn't keep the pride out of her voice. "We've been in business for six years now and we operate totally in the black. Our clientele continues to grow, and we've won several small business awards…" At Chris's amused smile, she stopped. "What's so funny?"

"This isn't an interview. You don't need to read me your résumé."

Confusion reigned. "Then why did you ask?"

Chris sighed. "I'm trying to get to know you a bit better. We're about to have a baby together, and we hardly know each other." His eyebrow quirked up suggestively. "We didn't spend much time talking before."

In a flash, the memories of how they did spend their time hit her, and the muscles in her thighs tightened as the images caused a physical response. She hadn't allowed her thoughts to go there since Chris had shown up so unexpectedly and turned her life upside down. But now they were alone, he was within arm's reach, and he was smiling at her knowingly.

Argh. She tamped the memories down and focused on the moment. Chris wanted to play get-to-know-you games, but she wanted to get this over with so she could figure out what her next move should be. The suspense was killing her.

Just don't antagonize him again. Be calm. Be diplomatic. "Can we get back to the matter at hand? I apologize for the other day, and obviously you do have a right to be a part of your baby's life. I want to work this out amicably, but you have to tell me specifically what you're after." Proud of herself, she sat back in the chair.

Chris steepled his fingers and looked thoughtful. "You're sure you don't want to get married?"

Oh, God. "Positive," she managed to choke out.

"It's a simple, obvious solution."

"And one that's guaranteed to put us right back in this situation in a few years—only then, we'd be fighting out the divorce as well as custody arrangements." She wasn't ready to think about marriage to anyone—not now. She'd already had one narrow escape—a lucky one—but it had taken its toll. Plus, she wouldn't be able to resist his golden-boy looks and charm forever, and then she'd be in real trouble when it all went to hell. "Like you just said, we barely know each other. Great sex is hardly a foundation for a good marriage." *Did I actually just bring up sex again? Damn.*

Chris leaned forward in his chair, and now only inches separated them. Her pulse kicked up a notch and her skin grew warm. "Great sex? Try amazing, Ally." One finger trailed down her arm, causing the hairs to rise. "And there are worse places to start. At least we know we're compatible in that aspect."

Compatible didn't even begin to describe it. Her entire body was screaming for him now. She swallowed hard. "Chris, stop." To her utter amazement and relief, he did, leaning back to put space between them. She took big gulping breaths of air to clear her mind, but his scent still hung in the air between them, and inhaling only made the sex-charged cloud worse.

Stay angry. Don't let hormones confuse this issue.

But maybe she wasn't the only one having a hard time pulling it together. Chris dragged a hand through his hair and shook his head as if to clear it. Then, blowing out his breath in a loud rush, he stood and extended a hand to her. "Come on. I'll take you down to see the work on the *Circe*."

Now what? She needed a map to keep up with him. "Why? We still need to ta—"

"We're not going to find any solutions today, Ally, because we're on opposite sides of the table. You've agreed that we barely know each other, so it seems the next logical step would be for us to get to know each other. We have some time before any decisions have to be set in stone, and it will make the whole process easier if we're friends. So I'm going to take you to the yard and show you how the *Circe* is coming along."

Chris stood there with his hand out to her, but she hesitated. After the roller-coaster ride she'd been on this morning, she didn't trust herself to see clearly. She didn't understand the mercurial changes of Chris's attitudes, and she had a hard time keeping up. She wanted to believe he was sincere, but from the corner of her eye, she could still see the hateful envelopes on his desk. Of course, her traitorous body was on board for "friendliness" and anything else that might come from it, and her hormonally confused brain kept going back to that If Only game where everything had turned out differently. The tiny part of her mind that was still able to think rationally tried hard to tamp down the other emotions and feelings confusing her. It was enough to give her a pounding headache as she tried to figure out what to do.

Then Chris smiled at her, and the crinkles nearly did her in. He had a point—regardless of how they worked out the details, they were going to be attached to each other for the rest of their lives through this child.

Six weeks ago, she'd made a decision that had changed her life forever by sleeping with him. Now she had to decide how she wanted to go forward, and animosity wouldn't be a good choice—for her or the baby. "You want this baby, don't you?"

"Very much."

Options. Decisions. She had to choose quickly. She was caught between Scylla and Charybdis, and ironically, the *Circe* was offering her a possible safe navigation through with minimal losses. She was slowly gaining a new—albeit grudging—respect for Odysseus.

But that didn't mean she was going to just roll over. "Are you willing to phone your lawyer right now and call him off?"

"Yes. I'm willing to be reasonable as long as you are."

"Do that first," she said, putting her hand in his as she let him help her to her feet. "*Then* you can show me the *Circe*."

"You've done an amazing job. She looks much better than she did." Ally ran her hand over the new seats in the *Circe*'s cockpit. "And the cabin is going to be positively decadent—I guess her racing days really are over."

The cavernous OWD workshop was usually alive with people and noise, but with most of the men gone to lunch at the moment, it echoed instead. Glad for the lack of an audience, Chris watched Ally carefully as she explored the dry-docked *Circe*. While she seemed to accept his offer of a truce, she was still wary.

Ally's arrival, so hard on the heels of Marge's revelations, had thrown him. But he was used to thinking fast on his feet, making the most of whatever opportunity came his way, and he was secretly quite pleased with how quickly he'd managed to adapt the situation to suit him.

Dennison hadn't been pleased to get the phone call and had tried to convince him to reconsider, but Chris was now hopeful he and Ally could work this out. Therefore, he concentrated on repairing what little relationship he had with Ally.

As she sat back in the cockpit and gave the tiller an experimental push, Chris assessed his options. While he'd originally floated the idea of marriage halfheartedly, it had oddly taken on new appeal. Marriage had never been on his radar before, and it would certainly solve a lot of problems. Ally was smart and beautiful, and she was already carrying their child. They got along well enough—especially in bed. Successful marriages had been built on a lot less.

The thought of Ally in bed led to the thought of Ally in the ocean, Ally on the beach, Ally on the trampoline of the catamaran…his entire body grew hard at the memories. Oh, yes, they were certainly more than compatible there.

"What's that one called?"

Ally's question brought him back to the matter at hand. He looked where she pointed at the yacht dwarfing the *Circe*. "That's the *Dagny*. It means 'new day.'"

"And it's a racing yacht? It's awfully big."

"Ninety-six feet, but designed to go long distances very quickly with only a one-man crew. I'd offer to take you aboard, but Jack is a little possessive of the *Dagny* at the moment."

"Jack?"

"A cousin who designs all of Team Wells's racers. The *Dagny* is his latest pride and joy."

"And how far is a 'long distance'? I mean, I would have considered Tortola to Charleston a pretty long distance but the *Circe* made it, and she's tiny in comparison."

He laughed. "I said the *Dagny* would cover long distances *quickly*. The *Circe* might make it around the world, but not in any reasonable amount of time."

Ally looked at him strangely. "That's what you're planning to do? Sail the *Dagny* around the world? Alone?"

"And break the record at the same time."

"Wow." She sat quietly, her brow furrowed as she thought. "How long does that take?"

"If I'm going to break the record, less than sixty days."

The furrows got deeper. "Oh."

"Ally? Is everything okay?"

The frown lines disappeared as she brightened and plastered a smile across her face that didn't quite reach her eyes. "I'm just trying to reconcile this Chris with the one I met on Tortola."

"Same guy." He grinned at her.

"Not exactly."

"But close enough."

"Maybe."

She fell silent, tracing the pattern on the seat cushions with a finger, and he wondered what she was thinking about. In the silence, Ally's stomach growled. Loudly.

She blushed, placing a hand over her stomach. "Excuse me. I haven't eaten much today—between the morning sickness and, well, everything else that happened."

He stood. "Then I get the chance to feed you, after all. Let's go."

Ally hesitated. "Um, I should probably head home…."

He'd almost forgotten Ally's overly cautious nature, but even coupled with what she euphemistically called "everything else," he didn't realize he'd have to coerce her just to get her to have a meal with him. Of course, she was probably still a bit distrustful of his motives, but they had to get past that if they were going to work anything out. And if he'd learned anything as the captain of Team Wells, it was how to build a crew. Food helped.

"I never did get to take you out for a meal before, so I think I'm due. You need to eat, the baby needs to eat, and I haven't had lunch, either."

Her brow started to furrow again, but she seemed to catch it in time and shrugged instead. "You're right. Food would be good. Just not Mexican."

He jumped to the ground as Ally carefully descended the ladder propped against the *Circe*'s hull. Reaching up, he grasped her waist to guide her down the rungs and felt a tremor run through her. Like an electrical current, it vibrated through his fingers and shot through his veins, and he was loath to let her go when her feet finally touched ground.

Ally didn't turn around, and his fingers tightened on her as the heat of her skin seeped through the thin cotton of her dress. He remembered the feeling. Obviously so did she.

With her back to him, those wild curls tickled his face, the fresh citrus smell of her filling his nose and warming his blood. Experimentally, he moved his thumbs in small circles and another shiver shook her. Only inches separated them. If she'd just lean back a little...

Voices filled the room, chasing the silence away as the men returned from lunch, and Ally stepped away.

As she faced him, he noted the flags of color on her cheeks and the way her teeth worried her lower lip. Ally might be angry with him or wary of him or any other number of things, but she wasn't immune to him.

Satisfied with that knowledge for the moment, he allowed her the space she seemed to need to get herself back under control.

"I think— I mean we... Um, I, uh, guess..." She blew out a deep breath and brushed her hair away from her face. "Let's just go, okay?"

She turned on her heel and took two steps in the direction of the door before she stopped. The *Dagny* was right in front of her, and she looked at it carefully, her eyes tracing over the rigging before returning to the three hulls of the trimaran. Her mouth twisted briefly and she nodded, almost imperceptibly, before she set her shoulders and turned back to him.

Her smile—a real one, this time—snared him. "Are you coming? I'm hungry."

CHAPTER SEVEN

"AND AFTER THAT, everything went fine. We had a nice lunch, and I came home." She'd been too tired to do much more than send a quick text to Molly last night, so Ally brought her up to speed on the revelations of yesterday while they tackled the much overdue and mindless chore of filing.

"You certainly seem in better spirits this morning."

"My breakfast stayed down, so that was a nice way to start the day."

"That's not what I mean."

"I know." Ally grinned. "But it's still good news, right?"

"You just seem to be in a really good mood for someone who still has the threat of a massive, ugly legal battle looming over her."

"You don't get it, do you?"

"Obviously not."

"Dagny."

"It's a boat. It's what the man does for a living. I don't see the connection."

"Okay, pay attention. Chris got all upset over the news of the baby, then I escalate that by handling the situation badly, too. Like any man, he had to fight back."

"And he used the big guns."

"The biggest. *But* right now, this is still fresh news for Chris. That will fade. At this very moment, even with impending fatherhood on the horizon, he's still planning on going off on this around-the-world race thing. We talked about it a lot yesterday, and he's bordering on obsessed with it. That, and rehabbing the *Circe*. After that, there'll be another race and another boat vying for his attention. He'll lose interest in me and the baby soon enough—between the distance and everything he has to do for this race, we're not going to be high on his radar—and by the time the baby gets here, Chris will have figured out that he doesn't want to be tied down with a child." Ally closed the file drawer with a satisfying bang. "He'll have moved on. Maybe we'll work out some kind of settlement to salve his conscience or some visitation plans or something, but I guarantee he'll tire of this baby stuff soon enough."

"You sound pretty sure of that."

"Molls, racing is everything to him. He only works in the shipyard to make his grandfather happy. Wandering feet and an adventurous soul don't exactly equal Father of the Year. Look at my brother. Diane's been slow coming around to this simple fact, but even she's starting to realize that Steven will never marry her and settle down." Hungry again, she dug in her desk drawer and found an apple. Biting into it, she savored the taste and the lack of roiling nausea. "Nope, all I have to do is just bide my time and ride this out and Kiddo and I will be fine."

Molly's shoulders relaxed. "I'm glad to hear that. Oh, and by the way, the Kriss brothers are coming by Monday to work up an estimate on your new office."

"Excellent." And she meant it. After the upheaval of this week, she was finally feeling as if she had things back under control. TGIF indeed. She had about a thousand things she needed to do today. She'd been next to worthless most of the week, and poor Molls hadn't been able to pick up all of the slack, but her to-do list was manageable, if long, and without continual distractions she'd be able to get caught up and still enjoy the weekend.

But she found it hard to concentrate. The radio played softly, Molly's keyboard clicked away in the background, and the phones were silent, yet she couldn't seem to make the columns of numbers on her screen add up properly. After two hours of working on the same account, she'd made little headway, and she closed the file in disgust. She did mundane things instead—balanced her brother's checkbook, renewed her father's fishing license—but those simple chores didn't require much of her attention.

Her e-mail inbox was empty—since Erin had kicked her out of the wedding, she was no longer forced to referee the ongoing battles between her mom and her sister over caterers and flowers—and the lack of family drama felt odd. Maybe that was why she was unable to focus; she wasn't used to working *without* constant interruptions.

She'd certainly have plenty of interruptions once Kiddo arrived. The thought made her smile. She should enjoy the peace while it lasted—Erin couldn't stay mad at her forever, Steven would do something else stupid soon enough, and she'd be back in the mix. Plus, with two new babies in the family…

She shook her head to clear it and reopened the file from earlier. *Focus.* It took her another hour to find the mistake, and she was relieved to see it was the client's error, not one caused by her inattention.

When the phone rang, she jumped on the distraction eagerly.

"Hi, Ally." Her heartbeat accelerated at the sound of that now-familiar baritone, before she reminded herself she didn't need to panic. She only needed to humor him.

She tried for an upbeat, noncommittal tone. "Hi, Chris. What's up?"

"I'm done for the day and should be headed that way in another hour or so. Can you be ready by six?"

"Six?" She nearly choked on the word. "Ready for what?"

"Dinner."

"You want to go to dinner?" Her voice sounded strangled and Molly looked over, eyebrows raised in question.

Chris chuckled, and the sound did strange things to her already confused insides. "I'd heard forgetfulness was a side effect of pregnancy, but really, Ally. I told you I'd call and we'd go to dinner."

"I didn't know you meant tonight." *Every other male on the planet waits at least a week before they call—if they call at all.*

"Do you have other plans or something?"

Lie. Tell him you're busy. "Um, well…"

"Good. I'll pick you up at your place at six. Bye, Ally."

She was still sputtering her refusal when the line went dead. She placed the phone in its cradle and buried her head in her hands.

"What was that about?"

Ally didn't bother to look up. "He's taking me to dinner tonight."

She heard something that sounded suspiciously like a snort from Molly. "So much for staying below the radar."

"Molls…" Lifting her head, she saw a smirk playing at the corners of Molly's mouth. "This is not good."

This is not good was rapidly becoming her mantra. She left work a little early and took a nap, waking up still groggy an hour later. Cold water splashed on her face helped wake her up a bit, but the fatigue still grabbed at the edges of her mind.

Molly's lecture about the importance of appearing keen on Chris's ideas—for the time being, at least—echoed in her head as she pulled on a simple skirt and a sleeveless silk shirt. After clipping her unruly hair at the nape of her neck, she tried to add some color to her pale face. Deciding it wasn't going to get much better, she took one last critical look in the mirror before turning off the bathroom light.

She still had a few minutes before Chris was due to arrive, so she booted up her laptop and took it to the couch. She typed Chris's name into the search engine, but hesitated over the enter key.

Part of her still didn't want to know. She'd convinced herself weeks ago that the less she knew about Chris the better off she'd be. But that had backfired in her face. Molly had been more than willing to play research assistant, but Ally had held her off, still undecided about how much she did want to know. Even last night, after she'd returned from Charleston, she'd purposefully left the computer turned off, willing to just ride this out. But now, with Chris headed to her door, seemingly serious about this get-to-know-you game, she had no choice but to learn everything she could about him.

Taking a deep breath she hit Enter, and seconds later Google returned its list.

The impressiveness of Chris's accomplishments floored her. From his earliest races when he was still in his teens to his most recent win, Chris had racked up an impressive résumé around the world. It didn't seem to matter where or what kind of boat he raced, he rarely lost, and never finished lower than third place. It seemed Wells Racing had several teams, and while Chris captained their most successful one, he also oversaw the entire racing operation.

OWD Shipyard built a variety of yachts—not just the ones Chris sailed—and their designs were popular all over the world. From what she could find, Chris had his hands in that aspect of the business, as well.

Oh, and here was a mention of Chris meeting with the OWD stockholders in his grandfather's place. And look, he ran summer camps for inner-city kids to learn sailing, and donated huge chunks of cash to environmental causes.

Good God, when did the man sleep? How on earth had he found the time to go to Tortola and sail the *Circe* home? Of all the men in the world she could have hooked up with, how had she, of all people, found the one who just happened to be the world's only zillionaire businessman/champion racer/philanthropist paragon? It boggled the mind.

Remembering their discussion yesterday, she added "world solo record" to her search terms to narrow the results. Google returned very few this time. While several sites speculated Chris would one day attempt to do it—and most likely break the record in the process—none seemed to know that plans were in the works to do just that.

The last link on the page had a very odd headline, and Ally clicked through. The Charleston *Gazette* must have put all of their archives online because the date on the article was close to twenty years ago. She scanned the first few lines quickly and almost closed the window before the impact of the words sunk in. Carefully, she started over again.

After an intensive nine-day search, rescuers have located the boat of missing sailor Paul Wells floating abandoned ten miles off the coast of Darwin, Australia. Based on the heavy damage to the hull, rescuers believe Wells, who was attempting to break the solo circum-navigation world record, perished in recent storms in the Timor Sea. Wells was a native of Charleston and is survived by his father, Porter Wells, and his eleven-year-old son, Chris.

A rock landed in her stomach. Chris wanted to attempt the same stunt that had killed his father? Was the man insane?

Wait, hadn't Chris told her before that sailboat racing wasn't all that dangerous? "It's hard to kill yourself," he'd said. She changed her search terms to give her more information about solo circumnavigation, and from the results it seemed it wasn't all that hard to die after all.

Great. The father of her child had a death wish. Maybe that's why he was so keen on claiming this baby—he'd have a piece of immortality in case his boat sank in the middle of the Pacific Ocean.

That thought made her a little sick.

The doorbell rang and she quickly shut down the laptop before she went to answer it. Taking a deep breath to prepare herself, she opened the door to Chris.

Who looked so good the air in her lungs came out in a painful rush.

With the sun behind him, he seemed surrounded in a golden glow. A black T-shirt hugged those strong shoulders and skimmed over the planes of his chest before disappearing into the waistband of low-slung faded jeans. He grinned, and her heart melted a little as her senses sprang to life. *This* was the Chris she'd flipped for, and her body definitely remembered him. He leaned in to give her an innocent peck on the cheek in greeting, but even that brief touch of his mouth burned her.

"Come on in." Ally stepped back to allow him to pass as she tried to compose herself. How different this time was from Monday when he'd been here, so angry the air around him had nearly burned from the heat. Today he seemed comfortable, almost relaxed.

Well, at least one of them should be, and it wasn't shaping up to be her. With a sigh, she closed the door behind him.

"You look great, Ally. Are you hungry?"

"Starved." Amazingly enough, she was, but she would've lied if necessary. Her living room usually seemed open and spacious, but Chris seemed to fill it completely, making her overly aware of him and creating an uncomfortable feeling of intimacy.

"Then let's go." Chris reached for her hand, and the touch of his hand sent a shiver through her. Yesterday she'd chalked up her immediate physical reaction to his touch as a simple aberration—something to do with all of those pregnancy hormones sweeping through her—but the repeat of the sensation today underscored her need to keep him at arm's length.

Literally.

But he made that extremely difficult to accomplish. He kept *touching* her—to help her out of the car, to guide her as they walked, to tuck a wayward strand of hair behind her ear—and her nerves were a complete jangle by the time they reached the restaurant on the riverfront.

Chris made small talk, and although her mind kept wandering to deeper places, she managed to keep up her end of the conversation. At the restaurant Chris sat opposite her, and finally she had enough distance to begin to incrementally relax.

A drink would have helped, but when Chris waved away the wine list, she remembered it would be a long while before alcohol touched her lips again. She'd have to find her courage outside of a bottle.

"I brought you a present." Chris slid a small black box across the table.

Jewelry. Jewelry came in boxes like that. "That's really not necessary." She scooted the box back to his side of the table.

"Yes, it is. It's what men do when they're trying to impress a lady."

She thought about Gerry and muttered, "Not the men that I know."

"Then you know a sorry class of men. No wonder you dumped your ex."

She looked up sharply to see if he was teasing. The look on his face didn't help her any there. "The fact he was sleeping with someone else had a lot to do with it."

Chris nodded sagely. "Then he wasn't only sorry, he was stupid, as well. I don't know what you ever saw in him."

That comment brought a laugh and suddenly the wariness lifted. "Me, neither."

He pushed the box back to her. "Then open your present."

Sliding off the red and white ribbon, Ally pulled the lid off carefully. Inside, nestled against black velvet, she found a circular gold disk attached to a delicate chain. Holding the disk to the light, she could see the design: two lions rampant, flanking a pillar.

"It's beautiful." From the twitch of his lips, she realized she was missing something. "Okay then, tell me what it means."

"I thought you said you were a mythology geek. It's the symbol of Rhea."

Rhea, mother of the Titans, the goddess of female fertility and motherhood. Rather appropriate, considering. "Of course. Those are the lions that pull her chariot." She ran her thumb over the design. "I've never seen anything like it before. It's lovely. Thank you."

Before she realized it, Chris was behind her, seemingly uncaring of the curious stares of the other patrons as he took the necklace from her fingers and placed it around her neck. The disk settled perfectly in the hollow between her breasts. His fingers brushed lightly against her nape as he fastened the clasp. The touch was gone as quickly as it had come, and Chris returned to his seat.

His eyes moved over her like a caress. "It suits you."

The words and appreciative stare caused her face to heat,

and she was very thankful for the dim lighting in the restaurant and the well-timed arrival of their server with their food.

As they ate, the conversation moved easily through current events, how she was feeling, and the book she was reading before Chris casually mentioned something about the *Dagny* that gave her the opening she needed.

She tried to keep her tone light. "It's a really ambitious goal, but isn't sailing around the world by yourself a bit dangerous?"

Chris set his drink down slowly and looked at her strangely. A moment later he nodded in understanding. "You've been doing some research. It was an accident. It's not likely to happen again."

"But that doesn't change the fact…" She trailed off, unable to finish the sentence.

"That my father died doing the same thing?" he provided for her.

"Exactly." She pushed her plate away, suddenly not hungry any longer.

"Things have changed a lot in the last twenty years, Ally. We've come long way. GPS systems, automatic emergency beacons, satellite communication, improved ship design—it's very unlikely anything catastrophic will happen."

He sounded so calm and sure about it. She wanted to smack some sense into him. "But from what I've read, there's at least a thousand easy ways to die out there."

"Concerned, Ally? I'm flattered. Just yesterday you would've been pleased to hear of my possible imminent demise."

"That's not funny." *Maybe a little bit true, but still not funny.*

Chris shrugged. "Don't worry, though. Should I be lost at sea or eaten by sharks, you and the baby will still be well taken care of."

For the first time that day, nausea rolled through her stomach. It must have shown on her face, because Chris leaned forward to take her hand, concern pulling down the corners of his mouth. "Hey, I'm just kidding about the eaten-by-sharks bit. I didn't mean to upset you."

"I don't see how you can treat this so lightly."

"I'm not. Trust me when I tell you the *Dagny* is the safest, most well-built ship on the planet, and I don't plan to take unnecessary risks." His thumb brushed over her knuckles, soothing her. "I need to do this—not only for me, but for my dad and the company, too. But you don't need to worry about it. I fully intend to make it home in one piece."

I'm sure your father had the same intention. She didn't say the thought aloud. After all, she really didn't have any business getting involved in his plans. She shouldn't have brought it up in the first place.

The light brush of his thumb increased in pressure until he was practically massaging her fingers. The mood was getting too tense and his touch too familiar. To break it, she mimicked his earlier tone. "Then I'll just cross my fingers you *don't* end up as shark bait."

"I appreciate that," he said wryly.

At that tentative understanding, Chris signaled for the check. As he paid, Ally nibbled on her thumbnail and wondered why she cared so much all of a sudden.

Ally had to be the most incomprehensible woman he'd ever met. It could be downright frustrating at times to try to figure her out. The upside, of course, was that she was utterly fascinating. Her moods changed rapidly and without warning, like a squall rising from nowhere, but that unpredictability was part of her allure.

And that allure was becoming increasingly impossible to resist.

He wanted her. Intensely. It didn't seem to matter whether

she was spitting fire in his direction or trying to freeze him out, his body burned for her. From the moment he'd met her on Tortola, she'd been a craving he couldn't seem to satisfy.

Wanting her had gotten him into this situation, and eventually—in spite of her objections—he and Ally would have to come to a workable solution, even if right now they were in complete disagreement as to what that solution would entail. The idea of marriage had grown on him, but Ally still seemed dead set against that. He'd have to convince her differently. Sex might work in his favor there—after all, he knew she wanted him, too, and it might be just the right angle to work. Logic argued he should take this slow, win her over the old-fashioned way, but logic wasn't controlling him at the moment.

He wanted her. Pure and simple.

Now, preferably.

Ally kept a careful distance as she walked beside him to the parking lot. If she only knew what was running through his mind…

She seemed lost in thought on the short drive back to her place, occasionally biting a fingernail as she stared out of the window at the darkness. He was still easing the car into a space in front of her house when she had her seat belt unbuckled and her hand on the door.

"Thank you for dinner. And the lovely necklace. I'll see you—"

Nice try. "I'll walk you up."

Ally seemed poised to argue, but she did wait for him to come around and assist her from the car. At the front door, she put her key in the lock and tried again.

"Good night."

"Aren't you going to invite me in?"

"I don't think that's a good idea, Chris. Let's just take this one step at a time. No need to rush things."

He stepped closer, close enough to feel the heat radiating off her and see her eyes darken. "Who's rushing?"

Ally stepped back a pace, the door blocking a further retreat. "I'm not stupid, Chris."

Her hair had escaped its clip again, and he caught the lock that trailed over her shoulder, winding it around his finger. "I never claimed you were."

Ally stammered as her breathing picked up pace. "We... we...we can't just pick back up where we left off. Everything is diff-different now." Even as she spoke, her hand slid gently over his forearm, belying her words. "There're so many complications..."

"It's not that complicated at all." He shivered as her hand worked its way over his chest, coming to rest over his pounding heart. He traced a finger along the stubborn curve of her jaw, and she lifted her chin, putting her mouth only inches from his. "This is pretty simple."

Ally lifted her eyes from his mouth and met his gaze. The hunger there rocked him. A second later she rose on tiptoe, and the hand on his chest slid to his nape. "I'm probably going to regret this."

Her lips landing on his blocked his response, and as she fitted her body against him his argument died in the flames that stroked him.

This he remembered all too well. The inferno Ally stoked in him. The feel of her mouth moving hotly under his. The taste of her as his tongue swept inside her mouth to explore. The little moan that vibrated through her as his hands slid over her back and pulled her tightly against him.

The sound of a car passing penetrated the sensual haze Ally wove around him, bringing his attention back to the fact that they were on her porch, providing a show for the neighborhood. He reached behind her, found the key still hanging in the lock and pushed the door open. Ally stumbled backward, pulling him over the threshold, and he was able to kick the door closed with a foot.

In the half-light and privacy of her living room, Ally's kiss deepened, turning carnal with need. Her hands tugged at his shirt, pulling it free from his jeans and over his head, and her hands slid over his skin, causing his muscles to contract at her touch. He worked the buttons of her shirt quickly, and it slithered to the floor.

Ally broke the kiss and stepped back. Even in the dim light, he could see the flush on her chest and the rise and fall of her breasts with each shallow breath. With a long look that scorched him, she reached for his hand and led him down the hall.

CHAPTER EIGHT

YOU'RE CRAZY. SEND HIM HOME. Don't do this. Her conscience hammered the words at her as she led Chris the short distance down the hallway. Her whole body was alive, though, for the first time since she'd left Tortola, and the electric hum thrumming through her easily outweighed any arguments her brain might want to put forth.

Chris had a pull on her she didn't quite understand, but now wasn't the time to try to work it out. The light in his eyes and the promise in his kiss were irresistible, and she really didn't care about tomorrow's complications tonight.

It wasn't as if she could end up pregnant or anything.

Chris traced a finger gently down the line of her spine as she walked, and goose bumps rose on her skin. His hand splayed across her back. Two more steps and they were in her room, the bed beckoning.

He caught her shoulders and pulled her against him. The skin of her back met the hard planes of his chest as he nipped the sensitive skin of her neck. Warm hands smoothed around her waist to massage circles on her stomach before moving up to allow his thumbs to graze tantalizingly over the flesh spilling over the cups of her bra.

Her breasts were more sensitive these days, and the exquisite sensation had her grasping at his thighs for support. Her fingers dug into the denim as he increased the pressure and circled a finger around the hard point of her nipple. Her head fell back against his shoulder, allowing him greater access, and the heat of his breath tickled her ear.

She moaned as he slid her straps off her shoulders, and her breasts were released into his hands. Chris murmured in appreciation as he teased her aching nipples, causing her to writhe against him.

One hand on her stomach held her in place as he moved his hips against her, his erection pressing insistently against the curve of her bottom. The other hand inched her cotton skirt upward to the tops of her thighs, and she hissed as Chris's fingers slipped beneath the lace edge of her panties and found her.

She exploded almost immediately at his touch, bucking hard against his hand as the orgasm moved endlessly through her. Chris whispered words of erotic encouragement in her ear, fanning the flames, until she sagged against him, her trembling legs no longer able to support her weight.

He turned her then, his mouth moving over hers hungrily, stealing her breath, as he made quick work of her remaining clothes. Ally cursed her numb fingers as she fumbled with his straining zipper, the need to touch him overwhelming. When it finally released, she hooked her hands in his waistband, drawing his clothes downward as she sank to her knees.

Chris's hands threaded through her hair, massaging her scalp as she took him into her mouth. She heard his sharp hiss of pleasure as she ran her tongue over his hard length, and his fingers tightened.

In two quick moves, Ally found herself between the soft bed and Chris's hard body, and every erotic dream she'd had in the past six weeks came true as he slid into her and sighed her name.

The husky sound of her name on his lips caused her to open her eyes. While the shadows of the room cast hollows around his features, she could see the intensity in his eyes as he moved against her, pushing her to another release.

Her fingers dug into his shoulders as she held on, greedy for what he could give her, and when the tremors began, he redoubled his efforts, holding her hips firmly and picking up the pace. She arched as the pleasure turned too intense, only vaguely aware that the sounds she heard came from her as she went over the edge. From a distance, she heard Chris groan as he gathered her close and stiffened, and time seemed to freeze as he held her while the aftershocks moved through them.

Chris's breathing was harsh in her ears and his heart thumped heavily against her chest. Ally chased after her scattered thoughts, refusing to listen to the small voice in her head saying, *This is where you belong.*

She'd given in to the sensual pull of Chris, knowing full well it would only complicate their situation further. The intimacy of Chris, in her bed holding her while her heartbeat slowed to normal, unnerved her, but even as she worried, her fingers toyed with the fine hairs at his nape, loving the feel of him against her again.

After one last deep, shuddering sigh, Chris rolled to his back, pulling her with him to pillow her head on his chest. His fingers combed through her tangled curls as she listened to the even thump of his heart.

The silence wasn't quite a comfortable one, and the longer it stretched out, the more tense Ally became, the wonderful afterglow evaporating as quickly as the moisture on her skin.

Fatigue was catching up with her, fuzzing her brain as she tried to think. Was he planning to stay the night? He certainly didn't seem in any rush to move. Should she let him stay or usher him to the door? If she let him stay, it would only make things much more difficult later.

Yeah, because I don't want to get too used to having him around.

"Chris," she whispered, only to be interrupted by her own jaw-cracking yawn.

Chris's hand circled on her back until she completed the yawn and tried again. "Shh. Just sleep now. We'll talk later."

We should talk now, she told herself, even as her brain latched onto the idea of sleep and the weight pulled on her. But the soothing caress of Chris's hands was too much to resist, and she started to slip away. *But this is really nice, too,* her body told her, already relaxing against him.

Just don't get used to it, she reminded herself.

Ally's breathing deepened, evening out as she slept, each exhale sliding across his bare chest like a caress. She talked in her sleep, mumbles he couldn't understand. He tried to pick up a word here and there, but nothing she said made sense.

It would be too easy if, like in a movie, she'd tell me everything I needed to know while she was asleep. Insight into her thought process would help. A lot.

He knew Ally was humoring him, to a certain extent, simply because of the leverage his legal team gave him. He could tell by the wary look she couldn't quite hide completely. But her response to him tonight hadn't just been an attempt to play along. Passion had brought down that wall, revealing the Ally he remembered, and at least while she slept, she couldn't argue with him.

Ally turned over and snuggled her back up against his side. Pushing up onto his elbow, he curved around her, spooning her to his chest. She sighed deeply in response.

Chris smoothed a hand down her arm and over her stomach, stopping at the flat plane beneath her navel.

Their child was right under his hand.

Something primal swept through him—a feeling of possessiveness, a need to protect. Slowly, an inkling of what had driven his father to battle his mother so ferociously dawned on him. It didn't make what he had done right—far from it—but Chris was starting to understand the sentiment.

He didn't want to fight Ally. To drag her and their child through the courts until one or all of them were destroyed by the process.

Ally mumbled in her sleep, and it brought a smile to his face. He was making the right decision; he knew that for certain now.

He closed his eyes, his hand still in place, rising and falling slightly with Ally's breath. As he drifted toward sleep, he realized that, unlike for his father, that primal feeling extended to his child's mother, too.

Ally woke to the smell of bacon. It didn't make sense to her groggy brain. Her mom knew better than to drop by early in the morning or without warning, so it must be the neighbors upstairs. Why did they have to be so loud on a Saturday morning…

She rolled over, intending to put a pillow over her head and go back to sleep, but the mess of covers on the other side of the bed reminded her she hadn't slept alone last night.

That memory caused her to sit up as the details fought for notice: a pair of men's shoes on the floor by the door; her bra hanging drunkenly off the back of a chair; the noise and aroma coming from her kitchen…

Chris was still here. And he was now cooking breakfast.

She nibbled her thumbnail, unsure how she felt about that. One thing was for sure—she wasn't going to take the risk of facing him naked with bedhead. She padded quickly to the bathroom, grabbed a robe and did her best to make herself presentable. She came out, still knotting the robe, just as Chris stuck his head around the corner.

"I thought I heard you." His shirt was a bit wrinkled from a night on the floor, and a dark shadow traced his jaw, but he still looked too good for her equilibrium to handle. Especially when he grinned like that. "Are you hungry?"

After so many weeks of morning sickness, the absence of nausea felt strange. Maybe she was finally getting past it. Thank goodness. She nodded and let Chris lead her into the sunshine-lit kitchen.

She loved her kitchen. She loved to cook. But never in the three years she'd lived here had anyone cooked for her, so the neatly set table for two caught her off guard. It was a very simple breakfast, just bacon, toast and fruit with a cup of tea steaming invitingly on the side.

A lump rose in her throat. Chris had made her breakfast.

She tried to clear the lump. "It smells wonderful. Thank you."

Chris just grinned at her again as he moved through her kitchen with ease, bringing milk and jam to the table. "I tried to keep it simple, as I wasn't sure how the whole morning-sickness thing was going."

"I think I'm getting over it. I'm certainly starving today."

"Then eat." He slid several strips of bacon onto her plate before sitting back to sip his coffee. The bacon was extra crispy without being burnt—just the way she liked it.

"You're a good cook."

Chris accepted the compliment with a nod of his head. Ally didn't know what to say next. On the rare mornings Gerry had gotten up anywhere close to breakfast time, he'd read the paper while eating, claiming mornings were too early for civilized conversation. Since he'd moved out, she'd taken up the newspaper habit herself for lack of anyone to talk to. What did people talk about at breakfast?

Chris picked up the conversational ball, but as he asked, "When's your next doctor's appointment?" she wished for a different topic.

"End of this month. They'll do the first ultrasound then."

"I'll be there. Just e-mail me the time and place."

"You don't have to—"

"But I *want* to, Ally."

She nodded as she buttered her toast. "So when are you heading back to Charleston?"

One eyebrow went up. "Eager to get rid of me?"

Not at all. Where had that come from? Even with the slight awkwardness she felt, she kind of liked having him here, doing something simple and homey like eating breakfast. *Don't get used to it,* she reminded herself. "You're welcome to stay, but surely you have other things to do."

"I do have to leave in a little bit. I have a club meeting this afternoon." Much to her surprise, it wasn't relief she felt at his words. If she was going to be honest with herself, she'd have to call that sinking feeling disappointment.

Chris leaned forward, his eyes lighting up. "There's a race next Saturday—a short one just for fun and bragging rights. Would you like to come?"

Ally chewed her bite of bacon slowly, stalling for time. Chris was trying to include her in his life, and she got the feeling that inviting her to a race was a milestone of sorts. Maybe he really did want this to work out between them. Her chest expanded at the thought, and that raised an even bigger question.

Did *she?*

She could be her normal, cautious, rational self, or she could be the adventurous Ally she'd discovered on Tortola. Normal Ally said to keep her distance and stay safe; adventurous Ally wanted to take the chance, enjoy whatever came her way for as long as she could.

Good Lord, she was becoming as crazy as her family.

Chris reached over casually to refill her mug, and the simple gesture warmed her, making her feel she was making the right decision. "I'd love to see you race."

His grin confirmed it.

Her phone rang, disturbing the coziness of the moment. Chris handed her the cordless handset from the counter, and she glanced at the caller ID. She set the phone down and picked up her tea instead. At Chris's questioning look, she shrugged. "It's my mom. I knew the silence was too good to last. Let the machine get it."

A chuckle was his only response, but it was soon drowned out by her mom's voice.

"Ally, honey, where are you? You haven't called in days. You can't still be upset at Erin. I know she hurt your feelings, but it is her wedding, you know."

Ally rolled her eyes.

"Just be thankful your sister is nothing like mine. Now, lunch has been pushed back to one-thirty tomorrow, and I need you to stop by the store and get the wine. With everything going on today, I just don't have the time. I swear, your grandmother is going to put me in an early grave…"

Ally walked across the room and turned the volume down on the machine. Chris did not need to hear her mother carrying on about the crisis of the day. "That could take a while. I'll listen to the rest later."

"I take it Erin is your sister, but why would you be upset with her?"

Ally tried to think of a tactful way to put it, but came up empty-handed. "She kicked me out of her wedding."

"Why?"

"Because I'll be seven months pregnant at the time."

Chris frowned. "I know this is your family we're talking about, but isn't that…"

"Selfish? Self-centered? Slightly sanctimonious?"

Chris leaned back in his chair and spread his hands. "Well, I wasn't going to say it."

"Erin's turned into a Bridezilla over this wedding. I'm kinda glad to have an excuse to be out of the fray."

"And you're expected to have lunch with her tomorrow?"

Ally returned to her chair and poked at her fruit. "The Sunday family lunch. Isn't it a time-honored tradition for every family?" She sighed.

"You don't sound too keen on that tradition."

"As I'm sure you've gathered by now, my family is a little bit nutty. They're not happy unless they're driving me insane." Ally wanted to take the words back the moment they left her mouth. She'd gotten so cozy with Chris this morning, she'd forgotten her need to keep her crazy family under wraps.

"I understand the feeling."

That got her attention. "Seriously?"

"I can't sympathize completely because I don't have siblings, but I do have several cousins. And Pops can be over-the-top sometimes." The corner of his mouth curved upward. "Families drive everyone insane. It's just part of the package."

"Well, my family has a jumbo-size package of crazy going on. It's almost like they try to outdo each other."

"Is your mom a good cook?"

Ally nearly choked. "Are you angling for an invite to lunch?"

"I should probably meet them at some point—we are about to be related, after all. Plus, you shouldn't have to bring the wine since you can't drink it."

Related. Chris said it so offhandedly, like it was a foregone conclusion. Technically he was right, but it still sounded like something else entirely. But showing up to a family event with Chris… "I don't know."

Chris looked at her oddly. "I take it you haven't discussed me with them yet."

"Not exactly. I mean, they know I'm pregnant, but I made it clear the topic of the father was off-limits."

"That was before. Now that you know I'm going to be around, they should probably get used to the idea." At her skeptical look, he added, "What, you don't think they'll like me?"

"Oh, they'll like you." *And then I'll never hear the end of it if this doesn't work out.* On the other hand, she'd never hear the end of it, anyway. She'd held her family at bay for the time being, but eventually… Of course, once Chris met the Bat Crew, he'd probably beat feet back to Charleston, solving a number of her problems right there.

She just wasn't sure if that's what she really wanted anymore.

"Then it's a date." Chris drained the last of his coffee, and Ally watched in amazement as he grabbed empty plates off the table and efficiently put everything in the dishwasher. She didn't know people with a Y chromosome could load a dishwasher.

She stood to help, only to be waved away with an "I've got it." The surprises just kept coming from Chris. Domesticity was not something she expected from a golden boy like him.

Chris closed the dishwasher with a snap and came to kneel next to her. "As much as I hate it, I have to go. I'm going to be late as it is." He kissed her gently on the forehead. "I'll see you tomorrow."

Ally followed him to the door. "That's an awful lot of driving for one weekend. You don't have to come tomorrow. It's okay."

He was threading his belt through the loops of his jeans and didn't look up. "The driving is a pain, but it's not an issue anymore."

"Oh." Had he changed his mind in the last two seconds?

"Victor had the tail rotor taken apart this week, but he promised to have the helicopter back in working order sometime today."

Her mouth dropped open. "Helicopter? You own a helicopter?"

Chris smirked, then hooked a finger under her chin, closing her mouth and turning it up to his at the same time. "Not personally, but the company does. It saves a lot of time." He brushed his lips across hers. "Bye."

Ally closed the door and leaned against it. She could hear the powerful motor of his car roar to life, then fade into the distance as he drove away.

Like she didn't have enough to process. He owned a freaking helicopter, as well. And he'd be flying down tomorrow just to have lunch with her family. Suddenly, the hundred miles between Savannah and Charleston didn't seem like such a stumbling block.

Just when she'd begun to think she had her feet under her and a plan in place, Chris had pulled the rug out. Bit by bit, he was slowly chipping away at her entire wall of defense.

How this vapid family produced someone like Ally baffled him.

She'd picked him up at the helipad, then spent the entire drive to her mother's house "preparing" him, saying her family was a bit crazy but generally harmless. He hadn't said anything in response to her anecdotes, because everyone thought their families were a bit insane or embarrassing.

Instead, he'd been introduced to the most selfish, narcissistic, self-centered people on earth. They were quick to put two and two together and realize he was the father of Ally's child, but that hadn't stopped the snide remarks made to Ally about her unwed, pregnant state. Yet no one seemed to make the same comments to Steven or his obviously pregnant girlfriend, Diane.

Ally favored her mother, Hannah, who didn't look old enough to have three adult children, but the similarities ended there.

Hannah vapidly bounced from topic to topic, complaining about everything from wedding plans to the way Ally wore her hair. Erin, whom he mentally dubbed "princess," treated Ally to condescension while simultaneously expecting Ally to manage everything. Ally's brother was a real piece of work, a man-child who was obviously used to the women of his family waiting on him hand and foot. It extended to his girlfriend, as well, who even in an advanced state of pregnancy perched on the edge of her chair waiting to care for his next need. Through it all, Ally's father wore the look of a man who'd learned it was easier not to interfere while his family swirled around him.

The entire lot disgusted him. Was Ally sure she wasn't adopted?

After half an hour, he'd been hard-pressed not to drag Ally out of that toxic atmosphere, but she'd given him a pleading look and a whispered "It's okay. They'll get it out of their system soon."

No wonder Ally approached the world with such caution. Her entire family had the emotional maturity of fifteen-year-olds, and no matter what happened, it was Ally's job to fix it or else take the blame and to soothe ruffled feathers. When her brother handed Ally a checkbook for her to balance, it was almost the last straw. Couldn't these people handle anything without Ally?

An hour later it hadn't gotten any better, and Chris's appetite and patience were long gone. When his phone rang, he went onto the porch to take the call and stayed out there to cool off before facing her family again.

"They're usually much better behaved in front of company." Ally spoke from behind him. "I'm sorry."

Her heart-shaped face was earnest and concerned, and all the light had gone out of her eyes.

He bit back the disparaging remarks. This was Ally's family, after all, and she obviously cared for them. He wouldn't score any points with Ally by insulting her family—however well-deserved and correct the observations were. "They're certainly…" He searched for an adjective.

"Crazy?" Ally provided. "I told you that," she added with a sigh.

It wasn't the word he would have chosen, but it would do. "They're nothing like you, that's for sure." He touched a finger to her chin.

"Somebody has to be the grown-up. Can you imagine how they'd function if I weren't around?" The corner of her mouth tipped up like she thought it was amusing.

"They're adults," he said, although it was a loose interpretation of the word. "They can take care of themselves."

"You'd think." Ally seemed to ponder that statement as she leaned against the porch railing. "It's just easier to humor them than it is to deal with the fallout."

"Let me guess. The reason you left Tortola so unexpectedly wasn't simply because Steven had been in an accident, but because someone had to come deal with the grown-up stuff."

Ally inclined her head slightly. "Of course I was worried about Steven, but, yeah, they needed me to deal with the hospital and the insurance companies and such. They don't deal well with actual emergencies."

He tried to keep his voice light. "What are they going to do when you're busy with the baby and not able to drop everything when they call?"

She paused, seeming to think about something, so he let the silence stretch out. "Molly asked me the same thing."

"Maybe it's worth thinking about."

Ally kicked off the railing and started to pace. "Sometimes I get really fed up with them. They're flighty, they can't hold down jobs or be responsible about *anything*. They loved my ex, and looking back, I can totally see why. He was just like them. Happy to just sit back and let me take care of everything."

Bitterness tinged her voice, and she seemed to be talking to herself now. "Calling me home from my vacation was par for the course. And at the time, I actually thought they'd done me a favor."

"A favor?"

"After I got over the anger at having my vacation interrupted, I realized that given a few more days, I probably would have latched onto you. Tried to bring you home with me."

Understanding dawned. "And I'd be just someone else for you to take care of. A beach bum with no job."

She nodded. "No offense intended. I still toyed with the idea of trying to find you for a little while, but then I turned up pregnant."

"And you figured the baby would be enough responsibility."

"God, yes. I just didn't have any more to give."

"So doing it alone was your solution?"

"It was easier than trying to figure out how *you'd* fit into the picture." She snorted. "Of course, that's before you showed up and proved you didn't need me to take care of you, too."

"That's because I'm an actual adult—not like them." He jerked his head in the direction of the house. She winced, then nodded in agreement. "I don't need a keeper."

"I know that now. I misjudged you, and I'm sorry."

He stepped forward and smoothed his hands over her crossed arms. She'd provided him with an opening. "I'd like to help take care of you, you know. You and the baby."

Ally's eyes met his, and he could see the confusion there. She really had been flying blind through this. And while the front porch of her parents' house wasn't exactly a good place to be having this conversation, he forged ahead.

"We kind of went about this all backward and out of order, but that doesn't mean we can't make it work."

Ally inhaled sharply. "You're talking about getting married, aren't you?"

He took a deep breath and asked for patience. "Yes, Ally, I'm talking about getting married. But not immediately."

Her shoulders dropped and she sighed audibly in relief. That irked him a little. "But this game we're playing—dancing around like there's a better solution—is crazier than your family." His voice turned husky. "There's a lot to build on." This time when she inhaled, he watched her eyes darken and knew she was also thinking about the night before last. His body hardened in response.

"Chris, I—"

"Shh." He pressed a finger over her lips. "You brought me home to meet your family. You're carrying my baby. We get along fine—when we're not antagonizing each other, that is." Her mouth twisted into a small smile. "I think that's a good start."

From inside he heard the noise level increase, then the sound of Erin's voice. "Ally! We need you in here!"

Ally's eyes flicked in the direction of the door. He moved closer, until he could feel the warmth that always radiated off her body.

"Forget them for a minute. Hell, forget them altogether. Think about yourself. About the baby." He pressed a kiss against her lips. "About us."

"Al-ly!" Erin's voice took on an impatient whine.

Ally seemed lost in thought for a moment. When her eyes met his again, the spark was back. Her lips curved into a conspiratorial smile. "Can you get me out of here?"

Relief—followed quickly by desire—flowed through him. "My pleasure."

"Get the car. I'll grab my purse." Ally raised up on tiptoe to kiss him—a lighthearted, happy kiss like he hadn't felt since Tortola. She was out of his arms and in the house in a flash.

Whatever she told her family, they weren't happy to hear it, and she burst back through the screen door to a litany of loud complaints. She grabbed his hand and pulled him down the steps and to the car.

He opened the door and she slid in, giving the open-mouthed assembled crowd on the porch a wave as he started the engine.

As the wind picked up speed through her open window, Ally's hair came loose, flowing around her face as she leaned against the seat back with a happy smile and closed her eyes.

"Where to?"

"My place."

He floored the pedal.

CHAPTER NINE

LIFE WAS JUST TOO GOOD to be true. Ally wanted to pinch herself, but she'd be black-and-blue by now if she acted on the impulse every time she thought about it.

After their escape from her mom's house on Sunday afternoon, she'd spent an unbelievable afternoon in Chris's arms, taking him back to catch his ride long after sundown. Victor, Chris's crewmate and pilot, had worn a knowing grin as Chris had given her a goodbye kiss that thrilled her to her toenails, reigniting a spark that should have been sated by then. If Victor hadn't been waiting, she'd have dragged Chris back to the car for a quickie in the backseat.

The look on Chris's face said he wouldn't have objected.

Molly had taken one look at the dopey grin on *her* face Monday morning, and not a lot of work had been accomplished as she'd insisted on a play-by-play recount of the weekend. When Ally got to the part about Chris and her family, Molly had merely snorted and said, "I like him more and more."

Her family, on the other hand, wasn't speaking to her—other than one message from her mother on the answering machine, chiding her for her behavior. The four days of silence had been…well, not quite bliss, but a least a welcome break from the norm.

The scent of stargazer lilies filled the air in her and Molly's office, and Ally knew she still wore the same dopey smile for the fifth day in a row. It was hard not to; Chris had only managed one quick trip down to see her on Wednesday night for pizza, but he called and sent e-mails—not so many or so often that she felt smothered, but enough to make her feel, well, *special.* The flowers arriving this morning just intensified that feeling.

She still worried a bit that she wasn't making the smartest of decisions right now—that the hormones shaking up her normal equilibrium and the heady rush of Chris's attentions were affecting her judgment—but she wanted to believe she was. Even Molly encouraged it and joked about expanding the business to an office in Charleston.

That was a little further ahead than Ally liked to plan at the moment. Being caught between a dreamlike possibility and a contingency plan wasn't good for her higher brain functions, but she was hopeful—even if she didn't say it out loud too often.

"Why don't you just go ahead and call it quits for the day. Head on up to Charleston and get the weekend started early." Molly grinned. "You're not doing me much good here, you know. All that smiling and sighing is getting on my nerves."

"Can't. Chris has meetings tonight with sponsors and he has to be at the yacht club early in the morning to prep for the race. I'd just be in the way."

"I doubt that."

"Anyway, there's work to be done here." She scooted her chair up to the desk, determined to actually work now. "I'll try to keep the mooning to a minimum."

"Yes, please do try." Molly shot her a mocking smile before turning her attention back to her own keyboard.

The concentration lasted for only a few minutes before her cell phone rang. Chris's ringtone—he'd downloaded it himself on Wednesday night while they'd eaten pizza on the floor of her living room. She glanced up at Molly as she answered and saw her eyes roll.

"Hey."

"Hey, yourself. Any chance you can sneak out early today and come on up?"

"Molly just asked me the same thing. I thought you were busy tonight."

"Technically, I am. But I'll make time for you."

A warm glow settled in her stomach, followed quickly by that need to pinch herself again. Molly waved for her attention from her desk, and when Ally made eye contact, Molly mouthed the word, "*Go.*"

"I guess I can get away."

"I'll send Victor down to get you. What time?"

The thought of flying in that tiny helicopter made her feel queasy—as if the morning sickness was coming back. "I'll just drive, if that's okay."

Chris made an exasperated sound.

"One step at a time. We're not all daredevils like you."

"It'd be easier my way, though. Faster, too. Plus, you don't know where you're going."

"I'll get a map."

Thankfully, Chris didn't push and instead agreed to e-mail directions to her. She told him she'd call when she was on the road, hung up and started shutting down her computer.

"I'll make this up to you, Molls," she promised as she headed toward the door, mentally reviewing her packing list as she walked.

"Like you'll ever have the time." Molly waved goodbye. "Drive carefully and I'll see you Monday."

Molly's parting words bothered her as she threw her clothes and toiletries in a bag, but she couldn't put her finger on why.

She finally shrugged it off as yet another side effect of pregnancy brain—right up there with her new case of forgetfulness—and simply enjoyed the drive up to Charleston, singing along with the radio.

It wasn't until late that night, as Chris curled around her in bed, his hand absently stroking across her stomach as he dozed, that she realized what Molly's words meant.

No matter what happened with Chris, things would never go back to "normal."

The man was an absolute god. Neptune, Poseidon and Chris Wells. *Mercy.*

Ally's eye hurt from peering through the telescope for so long, but she couldn't pull away from the sight of Chris, two miles out at sea and rounding the second buoy.

She'd known the water was his element, but a simple day sail on a borrowed catamaran hadn't prepared her for *this*. Watching Chris skipper his seven-man crew…damn.

Although the water was choppy, sending up spray as the boats moved through the waves, Chris stood sure-footed at the helm, moving in perfect harmony with the boat—as though it was an extension of his body instead of an inanimate object. The wind whipped through his hair and fluttered the sails. When he shouted an order across the decks, men scrambled. Then Chris was working the winch, drawing her attention to the movement of back and arm muscles outlined under the shirt the wind nicely plastered to his skin. Her mouth went dry.

"Taylor's hoisted a flag." The words came from beside her, and Ally snapped her attention to the man who'd been her tutor for the day. Carl Michman held the impressive title of vice-commodore of the racing association, but as far as Ally could tell, his main job today seemed to be to keep an eye on her and explain what was going on.

She hadn't heard Chris get up this morning, but she did have fuzzy memories of him kissing her goodbye as he went early to prepare for the race. He'd left keys to his apartment and car on the table for her, along with a note giving her directions to the club and the instruction to find Carl when she arrived.

Ally's heart thudded in her chest. "What does that mean? Has something gone wrong?" Her confidence in Chris's assurances that sailing was perfectly safe had been shot down after only a few hours listening to the stories being passed around the observation deck. Near drownings from falling overboard, horrific head injuries from being hit by the boom—the people surrounding her had plenty of war stories that had her hair standing on end long before the gunshot started the race.

One boat had already dropped out when a crew member got caught in a rope and dislocated his shoulder. Hell, even her new friend, Carl, a spry man in his late sixties who embodied every stereotypical image she had of an old sailor, had his own stories to tell—including one where something called a jammer had left him with only nine fingers.

These people obviously had no sense of self-preservation.

Carl chuckled and patted her arm kindly. "It's just a protest flag. It got tight around that buoy there, so I'd bet it's a right-of-way argument."

"Oh." Carl had tried to explain the rules, but she still didn't understand much of what was going on. And to be honest, she wasn't that interested in the race itself—watching Chris in action was enough to hold her full attention, and she focused the telescope back on her only object of interest at the moment.

The boat was easy to find, thanks to the colorful spinnaker with the Wells Racing logo. From there, she could focus on the cockpit.

Although Chris said the race was only for fun, he was obviously intent on winning. Even through the scope, she could tell he was loving every minute of it. Forget golden boy; Chris was a golden *god* out there. It was what he was born to do.

Would the baby take after him? Was the love of water and wind genetic? The multigenerational makeup of the members of the yacht club seemed to imply it was. At what age would Chris expect to have their son or daughter—there *were* mixed gender crews out there, after all—on the water, risking loss of fingers and brain damage? The thought made her a bit sick.

She gasped as Chris artfully ducked the powerful swing of the boom and the boat shot forward as the wind filled the sails, increasing the distance between Chris and the other boats as they raced hell-for-leather to the last buoy. But there was no way the other boats would catch up. The familiar ear-to-ear grin spread across Chris's face as he savored the moment.

"And that pretty much seals it." Carl rubbed his hands together.

Ally heard movement behind her and she turned to see a mass exodus off the platform.

It took a while for the boats to make it in, and she hung back from the crowd, unsure what she should do and not wanting to be in the way as they helped tie up boats. Sure-footed, Chris jumped to the dock, and the throng converged on him with much backslapping and high-fiving. It didn't take long, though, for Chris to make his way through the crowd and catch her up in an embrace that lifted her off her feet. Then, in front of everyone, he kissed her.

She could almost taste the adrenaline and endorphins pumping through his blood, and the powerful arms that held her radiated energy and excitement from the thrill of the race. The rush made her light-headed. Only when her toes touched the dock again, bringing her back to reality, did the catcalls and wolf whistles intrude. She felt her face flush, but Chris was unrepentant at the public display.

Chris kept hold of her hand as the crowd swept inside, but as the glow of his kiss faded, the hollow feeling inside her chest grew, getting worse with each round of drinks as the party stretched into the evening.

Ally sat on a picnic table on the verandah of the clubhouse, just outside the sphere of activity. She didn't want to intrude on something she obviously wasn't a part of, but she didn't want anyone to think she was being antisocial, either. It was just easier to watch the waves and think.

Easier didn't mean less painful, though. She had a lot to think about, and none of it felt good.

Chris was different today—not the Chris she was used to, the one who made her insides do all kinds of funny things when he smiled at her; the Chris she'd met on Tortola; the Chris who downloaded silly ringtones onto her cell phone; the Chris that had almost made her believe they'd be able to pull this strange relationship off.

Here, he was "the Chris Wells," and she was seeing a part of his life she hadn't been able to imagine before.

She couldn't compete with this. Racing wasn't just part of Chris's life—it *was* his life, a major piece of who he was, and she'd never stand a chance at equaling it. And since it wasn't in her blood, she'd never fully be a part of it, either.

Until today "Chris Wells" had been an abstract idea; she'd kind of seen racing as simply Chris's job, much like bookkeeping was hers. Something easily compartmentalized—a nine-to-five job that was put aside at the end of the day.

But it wasn't, and the knowledge was forming a painful lump in her chest. Her job wasn't a lifestyle—a dangerous lifestyle at that. She thought of the hollow look in Diane's eyes as she'd sat beside Steven's hospital bed, bandages swathed around his head and arms, and realized that Steven's daredevil hobby took an emotional toll on her. Could *she* handle that?

"Are you okay?" Chris's voice shook her out of her mental wanderings, and she found him staring at her with concern.

She forced a smile. "Just a little tired. Long day." It wasn't a complete lie. It had been a long day, and she was worn-out.

Belatedly she realized the sun had fully set. How long had she been sitting here lost in thought? The breeze off the water kicked up, and she rubbed her arms to ward off the chill bumps.

Chris shrugged out of his team jacket and wrapped it around her shoulders, cocooning her in warmth and the smell of him. "Then let's head out. I just need to say goodbye to a couple of people first."

"You don't need to leave because of me. I'm fine."

He shook his head. "I just forgot you get worn-out easily right now. I'll be right back, and we'll go."

And so it begins, she thought as he disappeared inside. Chris would eventually come to resent her and the baby for infringing on this part of his life. The pain in her chest intensified. She should have thought this through more carefully, *before* she'd jumped in with both feet.

She was still making excuses as Chris opened the car door for her. "Seriously. We don't have to leave."

"You're practically swaying with fatigue. Let's get you home."

His casual mention of "home" rattled her and warmed her at the same time. "Then just drop me off at ho—your place, and you come back here. Enjoy your party."

He chuckled as he shifted gears. "It's not really *a* party, Ally, much less *my* party. Just people hanging out."

"That would be a party," she grumbled.

"We probably should have left hours ago. You must be bored to tears by all that talk of boats."

"Actually, it was pretty eye-opening." *Understatement of the year.* "And if you want to go back, I'll be fine."

"And miss the possibility you might get a second wind later?" He cocked his head and winked at her. "Not likely."

She opened her mouth to argue, but Chris cut her off. "Ally, it's no big deal. I see these people all the time." He laced his fingers through hers and squeezed. "I'd rather be with you."

The knot in her chest finally loosened as warmth spread through her at his words. Maybe she was worrying for nothing.

"Anyway, you'll see them all again in a couple of weeks."

"What?"

"The end-of-the-summer gala." He stretched out *gala,* giving it a formal sound. "Now, *that* is an actual party. Did the baby borrow your brain again?" he laughed. "You said you would come."

"Oh, yeah." She'd marked it on her calendar in pencil, not sure she'd still be around by then. "Sure. Black tie. I remember." He'd said he wanted her to be there when he made his big announcement about the *Dagny* and the solo attempt. *That* whole idea still put a knot in her stomach when she thought about it. When had her thinking changed from "Oh, goody, he'll forget about us because of the race," to "Oh, no, what if he kills himself?" It made her head hurt.

Ally closed her eyes and dozed, the hum of the motor and the background music from the radio lulling her as Chris stroked his fingers over her knuckles. Next thing she knew, the bright lights of the parking deck under Chris's building were blinding her as she tried to pry her eyelids open. Chris guided her to the elevator, and when the mirrored doors closed, she cringed at the sight.

A day in the wind hadn't done her hair any favors. Her braid hung drunkenly to one side, while the curls that escaped frizzed randomly around her face. Her cheeks were pink from either the wind or the sun, only emphasizing the dark circles under her eyes. The fluorescent lights weren't helping any, either.

Chris just laughed as she tried to smooth the loose hairs back from her face. *Easy for him.* Being outdoors all day was a good look for him. His tanned skin glowed—even under the harsh lighting—and the blond streaks in his windblown hair looked artfully arranged.

Hell, who was she kidding? *Everything* was a good look for him. The man looked godlike even while he slept. It was enough to give a girl a complex.

"Go to bed before you fall over," Chris said as he opened the door to the loft and dropped his keys on the table.

She wanted to argue, but the exhaustion dogging her heels kept her from even making a token protest. Ally slipped out of her shoes and headed toward the bedroom, turning back questioningly when he didn't move to follow her.

"But if you wake up feeling better, let me know." The suggestive grin sent a bolt of desire through her—a surprise since she felt half-dead. She nearly retraced her steps.

Chris shook his head. "Sleep, Ally."

She did. But when Chris slid carefully under the covers later, the movement woke her up. Still groggy, she turned into his arms anyway.

Her blood sang as his hands moved over her. As always, she couldn't think straight when Chris kissed her, but in her slightly fuzzy state, she didn't mind. And with her brain not working overtime, the realization that she was in love with this man slipped into her consciousness.

Adrenaline slammed into her veins, heightening the already exquisite sensation of Chris's mouth on her skin. Blue eyes locked with hers as he slid inside her, nearly pushing her over the edge with one thrust.

For her, at least, this was making love—not just sex anymore. The connection of her emotions to the act caused a strange ache in her chest and at the same time brought a pleasure to her body that had her seeing stars. She shouted Chris's name as her orgasm rocked her.

Chris held her in the aftershocks, his fingers brushing the hair out of her eyes until she could see the small smirk of male satisfaction he wore. The strange ache increased as he kissed her gently, and Ally finally put her finger on why.

He now had the power to break her heart.

CHAPTER TEN

"SHE LOOKS GOOD, son." Pops backed up his assessment of the *Circe* with a low whistle. "I'll admit I had my doubts when she limped into port."

"I didn't." He never would have brought the *Circe* home if he had, but the results of her rehab *were* even better than Chris had hoped. Jack had outfitted her with the most cutting-edge advancements in sail design and navigational equipment, but he'd managed to integrate it without detracting from her original style. The *Circe* was sleek and beautiful, and he had no doubts she'd be fast in the water. Right now she was still in dry dock, but she'd be where she belonged by the end of the week and he'd find out for sure.

But her interior was the true marvel. Turning a racer into a luxury cruiser provided a challenge, but the results were better than expected. The galley was tiny but had all the necessary comforts. Most importantly, though, the *Circe* now had a small, private cabin tucked neatly under the bow, fitted with a custom-designed, very decadent bed. Ally would look spectacular tangled in those sheets.

Pops opened the door to the head and laughed. "Interesting choice."

Chris merely shrugged. Yes, the design had taken up space

most people would have reserved for a larger main salon area, but he wasn't planning on much shipboard entertaining. Using the space to install a proper shower just big enough for two suited his purposes much better.

"Makes me wish I was twenty years younger." Pops sat on the portside couch and extended his arms along the back. "Quite the bachelor pad."

Only Pops could still use the phrase "bachelor pad" in this century without any trace of irony. "I think you could still find use for one—age notwithstanding. You're pretty spry for an old guy." He sat on the opposite couch and stretched out his legs while Pops chuckled. But amusement aside, the comment gave him the opening he needed.

"But I prefer to think of the *Circe* as a private retreat. I don't need a bachelor pad anymore."

White eyebrows went up. "Really? You're planning to marry Ally after all?"

"Just as soon as I can talk her into it. She's a little gun-shy when it comes to weddings."

"Then, congratulations. And let me say how glad I am to hear it. All these young people today having babies out of wedlock…" He shook his head sadly. "In my day, if you got a girl in the family way, you took responsibility and married her. It's the right thing to do." A pause, then he added, "It's how I got your grandmother to marry me."

That got Chris's attention. "Really?" In the few memories he had of his grandmother, she seemed so proper and circumspect. He never would have dreamed Gram would have needed a shotgun wedding. He chuckled. "I guess it runs in the family, then."

"Back then, it was worse on the girl. More of a stigma—not at all like now. But if you ask me, you make a baby, you get married. Kids deserve to have both a mother and a father around."

"I think my mother would be shocked to hear you say that." Pops pulled back like he'd been hit, and Chris regretted not easing into the subject differently. The opening had been there, and he'd taken it without thinking.

"Your mother is a different situation entirely."

"Not really. From what I understand, when I set Dennison on Ally a couple of weeks ago—" had it really been less than two weeks? "—all he had to do was copy over the paperwork from twenty-five years ago. That was just a replay."

"We did what we had to do to protect you."

"From what? My own mother?"

Pops leaned forward, his face pulling downward into a frown. "I don't know what you think you know, but I assure you that removing you from your mother's custody was the best—the *only*—choice at the time. That man she wanted to marry…"

Talking about this was only poking at scars that were long healed—uncomfortable and nonproductive. He never should have brought it up. But he had. "Well, she's not around to refute your claims, is she?"

"You don't understand." Pops tried to wave the discussion away.

"You can't justify what you did. And you nearly let me do the exact same thing." He snorted. "Hell, you practically *encouraged* it."

"I don't need to justify it. One day, when your own child is here, you'll understand what the prospect of losing that child will drive you to do. Am I proud of what we did to Elise? No." Pops shook his head ruefully. "Would I do it again? In a heartbeat, if it meant the difference between keeping my grandchild close or losing him."

The thought of not being a part of his child's life was a physical pain. He knew how the idea felt now; it would only be a thousand times worse once the child was here, a part of his life. But, still... "There had to have been other choices."

"Your mother wanted Paul to sign away his parental rights so her new husband could adopt you. Wanted to move you to the West Coast while you were still young enough to forget everything here. There was no way in hell I was going to allow that to happen."

"So, you deprived me of a mother instead. Let me think she'd walked out on her own. And I never bothered to follow up once I got old enough to do so. I guess that's my loss, and I'll just have to deal with it."

"Have you ever considered that *she* could have tried to get in touch with *you?* Your father was awarded custody, but your mother had visitation rights. She just chose not to exercise them."

That was news. And it put a different perspective on things. "Marge said—"

Pops nodded in understanding. "So *Marge* is who got you all riled up. Figures. Marge was still new then. Her take would be skewed by the fact she wasn't privy to all the facts. Like she is now, it seems," he grumbled.

Chris understood that grumble all too well.

"The fight didn't turn ugly until the end. There was no middle ground as far as your mother was concerned. Your Ally seems more reasonable."

"Only because Dennison hit her with the full package straight out of the gate. She didn't have a choice."

"So why are you complaining? It's all working out quite well, I'd say."

Only Pops would see it that way—without noticing the absurdity of the situation. Arguing with Pops had the same effect as railing at a storm, only with less satisfying results. Maybe stubbornness was a prerogative of old age. The choice was with him, though, whether to let this go or continue to carry the grudge.

If he was going to move forward with Ally, he'd have to let the past go. But just in case… "Let me be very clear *now*, though—Ally and the baby are my business, not yours. I'm taking care of it, and no matter what might happen, you aren't to try that trick again."

Pops's eyebrows rose, and Chris could see the wheels turning in his head. He knew the old man too well: Pops was trying to decide if that was a threat or a challenge. Chris raised one of his own eyebrows in return, and Pops laughed.

"You're a Wells, through and through, that's for sure." Sobering, he added, "I just hope that when you kill yourself on the *Dagny,* you'll rest easy knowing your child is being raised by strangers."

He'd won the round, even if Pops refused to admit it. "Ally hardly counts as a stranger, and again, I have no intention of killing myself. You're just shopping for another reason for me to call the whole thing off."

"You're damn right I am. I'd pull your sponsorship if I thought it would help."

"I'd only find another sponsor."

"And I know that, which is why I haven't." Pops took a deep breath, and as he released it, he suddenly looked every one of his seventy years. "Your father was uncontrollable. A risk taker. He thrived on the adrenaline. And you're like him in a lot of ways. But unlike Paul, you have a good head on your shoulders, so think about this. You have a child on the way. A woman you want to marry. A whole future ahead of you. Why would you want to risk all of that, risk destroying the people you care about most, just for *another* title? You have plenty of those. You're glorymongering *and* making the same mistake Paul did—putting his own dreams ahead of the well-being of others. If it was just me and the business, that would be one thing, but now you have a whole new set of responsibilities that you're not even considering."

It was the longest, most impassioned speech he'd heard Pops give on the subject. In the past, Pops had just called it a "damn fool stunt" and left it at that, his own bad memories clouding the issue.

"Pops, this is much more than just 'glorymongering.' Do you know how many people are depending on me for this? What it would mean for the business? You've seen the economy—you *know* the importance of diversifying so that if the bottom falls out again, OWD will stay afloat. Jack's designs for the *Dagny* will bring us a ton of new business. Every piece of equipment on the *Dagny* will be in high demand after this—*those* businesses need this to happen. Our stockholders need this to happen. There's a lot more going on here than just my quest for another title."

"Don't deny this is personal, son."

Chris pushed to his feet, nearly banging his head against the top of the cabin. "Of course it's personal. But it's business, too."

Pops shook his head. "It doesn't mean I have to like it."

"You'll like it when I break the record, I promise you that much." His attempt at humor didn't erase the worry lines on Pops's face. "I'll make you a deal. One attempt, then back to normal. Even if I don't break the record, I won't try it a second time."

Pops's mouth twitched into a small smile. "Normal for you is on the edge anyway, you know."

He returned the smile. "True. But the solo is still over a month away, and since I don't have anything edgier on the cards than taking the *Circe* out, you can scale back on the worry."

"Good. You do know every one of these gray hairs is your fault."

Pops had finally relaxed some. Good. "But they look good on you. Very distinguished."

"I'll remind you of that when your son—"

"Or daughter."

"God help you if you have a daughter." He gestured at the interior of the *Circe*. "Of course, if Ally's impressed with this, you may end up with more than one."

That was a sobering thought. He hadn't thought about more children.

Pops didn't seem to notice. "When will she be in the water?"

"Later this week. If all goes well, I'll be able to take Ally out for a sail this we—"

They heard the shouts first, Pops's head snapping up. Chris bolted to the stairs, Pops close on his heels. A second later a crash shook the *Circe,* causing Pops to stumble slightly on the stairs. Chris reached to steady him, holding his arm as his head cleared the cabin opening.

Smoke rolled in through one of the open bay doors. Men rushed in that direction carrying fire extinguishers. Chris swore loudly, and he heard an identical curse from his grandfather.

"Go. Find out what's going on. I'll call 9-1-1."

Leaving his grandfather in the *Circe*'s cockpit, Chris bypassed the ladder, jumping to the ground and running to the accident.

"Problem at shipyard. Must cancel tonight. Will call tomorrow. Sorry."

Ally read the short message for the fortieth time, hoping more words might have appeared since the last time she'd checked. None had. Her heart sank as she flipped her cell phone closed and leaned back against the headboard.

She'd been disappointed, yes, when the message had arrived yesterday afternoon, but as today wore on with no call or additional messages from Chris, the vultures of doubt had begun circling. At sundown, they'd perched on her shoulders, the disappointment and doom palpable.

It's exactly what you expected.

Yes, but being right didn't make her feel any better.

Maybe it's not what you think. Things do come up, you know.

Another truism, but also unhelpful. That only made her feel worse, because it meant she was mooning so much over Chris that she was unable to handle the simple fact that he might have more important things on his plate than her.

When had she regressed back to her teen years? Adults didn't act like this. An adult would remember her earlier decision to take one step at a time. Adults didn't pout or stare at the phone willing it to ring.

Obviously, she wasn't an adult where Chris was concerned.

She grimaced at the phone and tossed it to the foot of the bed in childlike disgust.

It rang immediately and she scrambled to find it in the folds of the duvet, cursing herself the entire time.

"Allison Renee, enough is enough."

Ugh. She should have checked the number. "Hi, Mom." Leaning against the headboard again, she closed her eyes and fought back the disappointment.

"I've stayed out of this spat between you and your sister—"

No you haven't.

"But whatever is going on with you has gone on long enough."

"Mom, I'm pregnant. If Erin is too immature or selfish to appreciate that it isn't always about her, there's nothing I can do about it."

"You could try to be more understanding of the stress she's under."

"It's a wedding, for God's sake. Sorry, but I can't stir up a lot of sympathy for her stress levels."

"Allison…"

Maybe it was the disappointment of Chris canceling dinner, maybe it was the extra hormonal edge from the baby, maybe it was the memory of the look on Chris's face when her family had acted so abysmally, but this time, her mother's patented warning whine grated across her the wrong way. Instead of feeling guilty or just relenting because it was easier, she felt angry at her mother—and her family in general.

Her family wasn't crazy. Or eccentric. Or even flighty. They were just selfish and immature. Why hadn't she realized this earlier? And why had she let it get this bad?

"Mom, here's the thing. Erin is *your* daughter. I've gone above and beyond sisterly duty, and I'm tired of it. She's a spoiled brat and I'm tired of mollycoddling her. You want to do it? Fine. But I'm over it."

"Ally—"

She cut her mom off. She was just getting warmed up now, and everything she'd been holding back just seemed to flow out of her. "And Steven is just as bad. If he can convince everyone else to cater to him, that's great. But I'm out of that, too. He's a big boy. He can handle his own life.

"Not a one of you has asked me how *I'm* doing. How *I'm* feeling. How *I'm* handling things. It's like y'all don't even care."

"That's not true at all."

"Mom, stop. I love you and Daddy both, but somehow we all got flipped around and I turned into the grown-up. I'm about to have a family of my own, and that's where my attention needs to be. I can't parent the whole clan. I shouldn't have to, and I certainly don't want to."

With the words out there, Ally felt better than she had in months—*years,* possibly.

"What has brought this on, Ally? Why are you acting like this?" Her mother's voice broke.

What did I expect? Sympathy? Understanding? An apology? She'd brought a lot of this on herself—she knew that—but it also meant it was her prerogative to change the game. "Mom, this is way overdue. I'm sorry your feelings are hurt, but things have to change. When y'all are ready to act like a family—a family that I'm a part of, not in charge of—then we'll talk again."

Her mother sputtered, and Ally had a suspicion she'd made her mother cry. Her outburst didn't feel so great *now.* But she couldn't back down; this was long overdue. "I'm sorry, Mom. I do love you, though. Call me back after you've had a chance to think about everything I've said."

This time she placed the phone on her nightstand. Just in case.

She slid down under the covers and hugged her pillow to her chest. One good thing about being pregnant was the fact she could always nap. It was a good way to pass the time. But her dreams were scattered and wild. She was alone on a boat in the ocean with wind and rain pelting her. She could see the shore, but couldn't figure out how to set the sails properly, and the boat just rocked helplessly on the waves, being pulled farther out with the current. She could see people on the shore, but no one heard her calls for help, and they went on with their business, unaware or uncaring she was out there.

She woke when she heard her phone beep, indicating a new message.

She pried her eyes open, but the room was now totally dark—her nap had lasted a good three hours and the display on her bedside clock now read eleven-fifteen. She couldn't shake the lingering unease from her dream, and she fumbled for the phone.

Her heart jumped when she saw the message was from Chris: "Didn't want to wake you. Will call soon. Sleep well."

He hadn't forgotten her after all. That put a smile on her face, and she rolled over and went back to sleep.

* * *

Chris let the wind catch the *Circe*'s sails as he cleared the entrance to the bay and headed into open water. He was right—she handled like a dream. He had about three hours to put the *Circe* through her paces before he had to be back. He had plenty of time to make his lunch meeting and then meet Victor for his ride to Savannah for Ally's doctor's appointment.

After the mess of this week, just thinking of seeing Ally was a balm to his brain. Although the explosion was a stupid, careless accident—and the workers responsible for creating it had been disciplined appropriately—no one had been seriously hurt and the clean-up, while slow, was progressing. That hadn't kept everyone from OSHA to the union reps from crawling all over his shipyard and creating a nightmare, though.

Even worse, the ensuing mess had kept him close to home all week, cooped up in his office from dawn till dusk. He hadn't been anywhere—much less Savannah—for days.

The sea air worked wonders, clearing the debris from his mind, and he turned the *Circe* away from the wind. Maybe he could get Marge to stock her with provisions while he was gone this afternoon. He'd be able to bring Ally straight back to the dock tonight and they could anchor for the night a couple of miles up the coast. He was eager to christen the *Circe* properly.

They could head out by six, maybe seven, depending on how long it took at the doctor's office. Granted, he didn't have a clue how long that would take—he didn't frequent obstetricians' offices as a rule—but they'd have something to celebrate tonight. He'd like to have that celebration on the *Circe,* even if they stayed tied up at the dock. It seemed fitting somehow.

He thought about the ring, locked up in the safe at the office. He'd save *that* for tomorrow, giving them a different reason to celebrate. He wanted Ally to marry him—soon. Enough dancing around the subject. Enough splitting his time between two cities and going home to an empty apartment every night. He wanted Ally here, and the only way to work that would be to get her to marry him sooner instead of later.

The wind was slightly erratic, but the strong breeze soon caused the boat to heel. He let the sheet out, letting the sail go wide, and the boat leveled off.

He hoped Ally would choose a small ceremony—something they could pull together before he left on the *Dagny*—but he'd settle for her moving into his place. If she wanted a big wedding—one to rival her sister's—then she'd have two months to plan it. That, plus supervising any work she wanted done converting the spare bedroom into a nursery, should keep her occupied for fifty-some-odd days.

Maybe it wasn't ideal timing, what with the solo coming up, but they'd make do. Nothing in their relationship had been normal to date, so why start now? He smiled at the thought.

Now to convince Ally of his plan.

After weeks of fighting with seemingly everyone—from Ally and Pops to his lawyers and now the union—and having both his professional and personal life turned upside down, the contentment he felt now seemed odd and out of place. He inhaled deeply, sure life would be on an even keel from here.

The snap of the mainsail caught his attention, and his head jerked up in time to see the sail sag. A second later the wind was in his face, changing direction completely and filling the mainsail from the other side. Cursing his inattention, he turned, only to see the boom swing violently toward him.

Everything went black.

CHAPTER ELEVEN

ALLY SAT IN HER CAR in front of Dr. Barton's office staring at the ultrasound image the tech had given her. To her, the baby looked a bit like an alien peanut, but the tech had assured her everything was perfect and as it should be. She'd heard the baby's heartbeat; she had a DVD of the session tucked in her purse, showing the baby doing slow somersaults. It had been the most amazing, awe-inspiring thing she'd ever seen, and it brought tears to her eyes.

And Chris had missed the whole damn thing, the jerk. That brought tears to her eyes as well, and she swiped at them angrily.

"I want to be there," he'd said, and she'd believed him. When he hadn't shown up at her office to pick her up at the agreed-upon time, she'd started calling his cell. Nothing but voice mail. She'd waited as long as possible, finally heading to the doctor's on her own so as not to miss the appointment. She left messages, including the address of the office, telling him to meet her there if he was running late. She'd held out hope until the tech had dimmed the lights to start the procedure, but the disappointment had tainted the excitement of seeing their baby for the first time.

Their baby. Ha. So much for that.

"Sorry, Kiddo," she told her stomach. "Sorry if I got your

hopes up. I was pretty hopeful there, too." She put the car into gear. "It won't happen again."

The bitter taste stayed in her mouth as she called Chris every name in the book on the way back to her house. She saved a couple of choice insults for herself—naive, foolish, harebrained, besotted, blind, lovesick…she had plenty to choose from.

Somehow she wasn't surprised to find Molly waiting on her porch when she got home. Molly had been livid when Chris didn't show, and she'd even offered to go in his place. At the time, Ally had still been holding out hope he was just late and would still show, so she'd gone alone.

Molly's pixie features twisted when Ally got out of the car alone. She even looked down the street as if to see if Chris was following in his own car. Ally shook her head.

"The bastard."

While the show of support warmed her, it also caused tears to gather again. "We knew it was coming, right? Better sooner than later."

"He's still a bastard."

Ally unlocked the door and Molly followed her in, still muttering epithets. "So we're back to plan A. It's a good plan. A sound plan." Her voice broke a little and she swallowed hard. "You want to see the video of the ultrasound? Kiddo looks like a little alien peanut."

"Later. Right now I want you to call Chris's office and find out where the hell he is."

"Molls…"

"Here," Molly handed her a piece of paper. "He may not be answering his cell, but someone at the shipyard will answer the phone and they'll know how to find him."

Ally eyeballed the note, recognized the number of the shipyard and looked at Molly suspiciously. "Did you…?"

"No. I didn't call. I wanted to, but I decided to give him the benefit of the doubt. Which he obviously doesn't deserve. The rat."

She stalled. "Molls, it's not—"

"Fine, I'll go start the popcorn and warm up the DVD player. You call and find out. It's one phone call. Then you'll know."

"Fine." Ally sank onto the sofa and dialed. The phone rang and rang—more times than most offices would allow—before a woman answered breathlessly.

"Um, hi. This is Ally Smith and I'm trying to find Chris—"

"Oh my God." She heard a scraping sound like the woman was covering the phone with her hand, then she heard a muffled, "It's Ally. She's looking for Chris."

What in the world was going on there? Another muffled scrape as the phone was handed to someone else, and another woman came on the line, the voice cautious and placating. "Ally? This is Marge Lindley. We met when you came to the office."

Okay. "Hi, Marge. I'm looking for Chris. He was—"

"Honey, I'm so sorry we didn't call you sooner."

Something in Marge's voice set off alarm bells in her head. Ally took a deep breath.

"Chris took the new boat out this morning, and… Well, he said he was only going to be gone for a couple of hours, so we didn't know until he didn't meet Victor as planned…"

Her lungs froze, and the alarm bells rang louder.

"We've called out the Coast Guard, and Victor's still out looking for him in the helicopter—"

The subject the woman was dancing around finally crystallized. They didn't know where Chris was either. If Victor was out looking for him…and, oh, God, the Coast Guard?

This was bad.

Chills ran over her skin, and her stomach fisted painfully.

Marge was still talking, but it barely registered as background noise.

"Ally? Ally?"

It was hard to breathe around the knot in her chest. "I'm here."

"They're pinging his GPS. They have coordinates for the boat. They'll find him."

Pinging his GPS only meant they'd find the *boat*. If Chris wasn't answering hails or his phone… She felt lightheaded and dizzy.

Molly pushed open the kitchen door. "Popcorn and orange jui— What's wrong?"

"Chris." It was all she could manage. Oh, God.

"You. Head between your knees before you pass out." Molly took the phone from her hand and put pressure on her shoulder blades, forcing her head down. Ally could hear Molly take over the conversation, asking questions while rubbing comforting circles over her shoulders.

She'd been cursing him, and all the time he'd been… The horror stories she'd heard just last weekend provided more than enough fodder for her imagination.

She tried to breathe slowly. Deeply. Tried to remember that Chris was half water god and therefore whatever was going on didn't necessarily mean the worst. Tried to calm herself because worry and panic weren't good for the baby.

"Are you okay?"

Ally sat up slowly as Molly placed the phone on the side table. She hadn't heard the end of the conversation. "What did Marge say?"

"The harbormaster saw him leave the docks a little after seven. From what I understand, that's not unusual—him going out by himself early in the morning. His assistant knew he had a lunch meeting, so they assumed he'd gone straight from the dock to the meeting." Molly moved purposefully around the house as she talked, taking the food back to the kitchen, bringing Ally a pair of jeans and indicating she should put them on. "His lunch date just assumed something had come up, so he didn't bother calling the office when he didn't show. When he didn't show up at the helipad to come here, Victor sounded the alarm."

Molly handed Ally her purse, folded a sweater over her arm and picked up two paperback books from the shelf. "Let's go."

When Molly was in full Managing Mode, it wasn't wise to argue. Anyway, Ally wasn't in much of a state to argue. Between her overactive imagination, anger at herself for not realizing something might have gone wrong and anger at Chris for putting himself in this situation to begin with…well, there wasn't much room for higher cognitive functions. "Where are we going?"

"Charleston. Victor can't come get you, because he's assisting with the search, but I know you'll want to be there when they find him. I'm driving."

Chris looked terrible. Well, as terrible as it was possible for a man like him to look. He was pale beneath a bad sunburn, caused by lying unconscious in the cockpit of the *Circe* for several hours, and a huge white bandage swathed his head. According to his grandfather, a white-haired man everyone called Pops, Chris had a nice-size gash under there.

But he would recover. Ally sat in semidarkness, the late-afternoon sun still peeking through the hospital window shades next to his hospital bed while Chris slept. Although he'd been unconscious when the Coast Guard boarded the boat, they'd been able to wake him and do tests that showed the injury, while scary, wasn't going to cause long-term problems. Other than the laceration and the concussion, he'd suffered dehydration from the blood loss and being in the sun, but the IV drip in his arm would fix that up, as well.

Marge had called her cell to let her know Chris had been found and was en route to the hospital, but by the time she'd arrived, he was already stable, sedated and in his hospital room to rest. Ally had agreed to stay while the others went home to rest, promising to call with an update as soon as she could. Molly had gone back to Savannah, and with Chris asleep, Ally had plenty of time to think.

He'd been gone for over eight hours before anyone even knew he was missing. Stupid men and their testosterone-driven need to do crazy, stupid, reckless things. Although she'd only known he was missing for an hour or so, she'd aged ten years in the interim. Chris's grandfather looked as if he'd been pulled through the wringer, poor man.

She couldn't handle this kind of stress. What was more important, she didn't want to. She wanted a nice, normal life. To think, a couple of months ago she had been bemoaning her boring, uneventful existence, and had jumped on the chance to shake things up when Chris had arrived like a gift from the gods.

She'd shaken things up, all right. Let's see, she was now pregnant and in love with someone who seemed to eat adrenaline and risk for breakfast every morning. Boring and uneventful had never sounded so good.

"Ally?" Chris's voice was raspy, and her head snapped up.

She moved to the side of the bed and carefully touched his arm above the IV tube. His blue eyes stood out sharply under the white bandage. "You're awake. How do you feel?"

"My head hurts like hell."

"No doubt. You took a good crack there."

Chris's warm hand caught hers. "Good thing I'm hard-headed." A small smile crossed his face, then faded. "Sorry I missed the doctor's appointment. How'd it go?"

Although she knew it was far too early, she could swear

she felt the baby flip over. "Kiddo's fine. Perfectly healthy. I've got pictures to show you."

"Good." His eyes slid closed. "Wish I'd been there, though."

Yeah, me, too. "I'll let you rest."

"No, I'm okay. The lights just make the headache worse." His fingers stroked over her knuckles. "I'd planned to take you sailing tonight. Guess we'll have to reschedule."

"Pops said the *Circe* didn't suffer any damage, so they towed her back in and put her in her berth—whatever that is."

That brought another small smile. "So you met Pops."

"Yeah. Sweet man. By the way, I didn't know your middle name was 'The Damn Fool Idiot.'"

Chris chuckled, then grimaced as he put a hand up to his head. "I shouldn't laugh. It makes my head hurt."

"I think a better idea would be to not get in the way of the boom if you don't want your head to hurt." She hooked a foot around the chair leg and pulled it closer so she could sit. "Or at the very least, maybe you should tell people what time to expect you back."

"Duly noted."

Ally sighed and leaned her head against the bed rail. "You certainly had everyone worried."

The hand holding hers squeezed slightly. "Sorry about that." His words slowed as his body gave in to the need to rest. "Remind me to have Jack check the GPS systems on the *Dagny*…" The sentence trailed off as his breathing deepened and evened out in sleep.

But Ally's head jerked up at his words. The *Dagny?* The solo attempt? The man was lying in a hospital bed from his most recent solo sail and he was thinking about the next one? One that was far more dangerous than just being a couple of miles off the coast? Did he have no sense of self-preservation? If *this* could happen on a simple day sail, the possibilities of what might happen in the middle of the freaking ocean... Oh, dear God. She wanted to pull her hair out.

She untwined her fingers and eased her hand from under his. The man was insane. Twisted. Cracked. Not firing on all cylinders. That boom must have hit him pretty damn hard to knock *all* the sense out of his head.

Anger flared. She'd been so caught up in everything else, she'd lost sight of the one thing she'd known from the very beginning: Chris was a golden boy, expecting the world to dance to his tune, regardless of the costs to others. Just like Gerry. Just like her brother. Hell, just like her whole damn family—selfish and self-serving to the core. Chris needed the thrill, needed the adrenaline rush, the glory, and the adulation like he needed air to breathe. Let someone else pick up the pieces.

God, she had to be some kind of masochist—how else could she explain her compulsion to love people like that?

After he raced the *Dagny,* then what? What would be the next rush he'd chase? Obviously she and the baby wouldn't be able to compete with that need for very long. They'd never be enough. A bitter laugh escaped. Last week she'd convinced herself it was silly to be jealous of a boat, of a hobby—hell, of a lifestyle—but now she realized it wasn't jealousy talking. It had been the rational part of her brain trying to get through the rainbow-hued gauze her hormones had wrapped around her mind and body.

But now she was thinking clearly. Finally.

If only she'd realized this before she'd fallen in love with him. Before she spent the last few weeks tying herself in knots over him. Before she'd taken years off her life worrying about him.

At least she wouldn't be sitting home biting her nails and pacing the floor while he took off on the *Dagny* or whatever other harebrained scheme he came up with to court death.

What about the baby?

Well, plan A had been shot down, and now plan B was in pieces at her feet. She'd move on to plan C. That's what lawyers were for, after all. She'd just hope Chris could be reasonable and wouldn't let his lawyers bury her the way he'd threatened before.

Chris shifted, drawing her attention back to him. Her heart cracked and tears sprang to her eyes. Getting over him would be tough—especially since he'd always be a part of her life, however tangentially. But she had to do what was best for her and for the baby, and keeping herself as distant as possible seemed the wisest course.

Even if it did hurt like hell.

She slipped into the hallway, closing the door silently behind her so as not to wake him. She was dialing Marge's number when one of Chris's crewmates came down the hall. Jack, maybe? Derrick? She'd met so many people so quickly.

"How is he?"

"Sleeping," she answered. "He woke up for a few minutes and was lucid, so concussionwise, I think he's okay."

The man nodded. "Do you need anything?"

"Actually, something important has come up and I need to get back to Savannah. Chris is resting comfortably, but could you stay with him until Pops or Marge comes back?"

"Sure."

"Thanks." She tiptoed back into Chris's room and grabbed her belongings. Leaning over to kiss his sunburned cheek, she whispered, "Thank you for the fun times. I'm sorry, though."

Tears burned in her eyes, drawing strange looks from Chris's friend as she hurried past him. She was in the hospital parking lot before she realized she didn't have a ride home. Molly had figured she'd want to stay the night, and Ally hated to call and make her drive the round trip for the second time in one day.

Victor. Victor could have her home in no time, and he'd volunteered his services anytime she needed him. Her mouth twisted. She doubted Victor or Chris extended the offer for a situation like *this*. But she didn't have a lot of other options, plus Molly would only have to drive to the helipad.

She couldn't do that. Instead, she went to the reception desk and asked for a phone book. In no time, she had a rental car lined up and a taxi on its way to get her.

See, she reminded herself. *There's always a plan C.*

This time when he opened his eyes, the room was dark, the only light coming from somewhere to his left. The pain in his head was receding a bit, but his skin felt tight and dry. What time was it? How long had he been sleeping?

It must have been a while, since he remembered nurses waking him up several times to ask him silly questions about his phone number and the president of the U.S. The grogginess he remembered from earlier had passed, though, and he was clearheaded now.

Chris turned and saw Jack dozing in a chair next to the bed, a book resting on his chest. "Hey."

Jack started, then rubbed his eyes. "You're awake."

"Where'd Ally go?"

Closing the book, Jack shook his head. "Good to see you, too. You look like hell."

"I've been worse."

Jack shrugged. "True. But to answer your question, Ally went back to Savannah. She said something came up."

Ally had left? "Did she say what?"

"Nope. Just that it was something important she had to take care of."

Something to take care of. Probably her family. Not a one of them could get dressed without Ally's assistance. She'd probably be glad to move to Charleston—at least they wouldn't expect her to drop everything every time someone broke a nail. Hell, no wonder she'd said she'd like to have a pet but that she didn't have time to take care of it; it was probably a nice way of saying she didn't *need* something else to take care of.

Still, it stung a bit to think she'd left him in the hospital and gone rushing home to deal with the crisis of the day.

Jack looked at him closely. "I'm sure she'll call."

"I'm sure she will. It's just irritating that her family has her on call twenty-four/seven."

"You're not in any danger of dying. Maybe she has bigger fish to fry," Jack teased.

"If I'm not dying, when can I get out of here?" He pushed the button to raise the head of his bed into an upright position.

"It's five in the morning, so not for a while. Might as well get comfortable. But the nurses said that if everything checked out, you could go home later today."

Good. He had things to do.

Jack shook his head. "Don't get any ideas. You'll be home-bound for the next couple of days at least."

Ugh. But if Ally would come and stay with him…

Jack knew him too well. "*And* on restricted activity. Nothing, um, strenuous."

"You're such a killjoy."

"Hey, I talked Pops out of hiring a home nurse to look after you."

"I'm much obliged." He reached up and felt the bandage around his head. "So how bad was it?"

"A concussion from the boom. There's one hell of a goose egg on the left side of your head. You've got ten stitches above your right temple from where you fell after you were knocked out. It looks like you landed on a cleat and sliced yourself open. Some blood loss, mild dehydration, sunburn. Just enough to mess you up, but you'll survive."

"And the *Circe?*"

"Other than blood in the cockpit and a dent in the boom, she's fine. Pops had her towed back to the docks."

"That's what Ally said." Except then she'd left while he was asleep. What *was* this penchant she had for leaving without saying goodbye properly?

Jack settled back in his chair and stretched his legs out in front of him. "Do you need anything? Water? Painkillers? I can get the nurse for you."

"How about my phone? I could check my e-mail." Call Ally and find out what's going on. No, it's five in the morning.

He shook his head. "Pops would kill me. You're supposed to be resting."

"I'm plenty rested. I feel fine." In fact, he was already itching to get out of bed and move around, and he *would* have, if not for the IV tube tethering him. He drummed his fingers on his thighs, impatient to get out of the small, depressing room. A muffled noise caught his attention, and he looked over to see Jack smothering a laugh.

"What?"

"You."

Jack was the closest thing to a brother he had, so he wouldn't strangle him. *This* time. "So I'm ready to leave. You would be, too. Why are you here, anyway?"

"Keeping an eye on you. Making sure you stay in that bed. Pops told me to sit on you if I had to." His lips twitched. "I'm still holding out hope you'll push me to it."

"Try it and you'll be the next patient," he threatened. His head did still hurt, even though he wasn't all that tired anymore. "Fine. I'll stay put like a good boy. Unless you have a book there for me, though, you'll have to entertain me. What did I miss yesterday?"

"Not a lot. The *Dagny* passed inspection and rumors are

buzzing about her. Pops got the union folks calmed down, and the repairs to the building are almost done. Pretty boring day—until you went missing, of course. That added some excitement."

"Glad I could help." He snorted, then regretted the action as his head throbbed. "I can't believe you had to call out the Coast Guard, though. I'll never live that down."

Jack howled with laughter. "*I* can't believe you got hit with the boom. Maybe we should send you back to sailing school."

"Very funny. The thing jibed out of nowhere. I was a bit distracted, that's all." *Yeah, thinking about Ally.* That was a newbie mistake, daydreaming like that. One he would not make again. Jack's grin didn't fade. "Keep laughing, and the next time you fall overboard, I won't come back for you."

Schooling his features, Jack cleared his throat. "Still…"

"How's Pops?"

"Claiming you're going to be the death of him." Jack grinned again. "But he's found an ally and kindred spirit with Ally. They both think you're too reckless for their sanity."

Chris rolled his eyes. "Ally thinks going swimming less than thirty minutes after eating is too reckless."

"Oh, good. She and Pops can tag team you."

"Don't think I haven't realized that. You're going to have your hands full with the two of them while I'm gone. They'll just feed off each other."

"Maybe I'll go with you…"

They were both laughing when the nurse poked her head around the door. "Well, you seem to be doing much better. I thought I'd pull your IV." She nodded her head toward the light growing stronger outside the window. "We'll get you lined up for some tests, and maybe you can go home this morning."

"That sounds like a plan."

CHAPTER TWELVE

By Sunday afternoon Chris was bored out of his mind. He'd been released yesterday with strict instructions to rest and take it easy, and only by promising to actually do so had he avoided Pops sending a babysitter to his loft to look after him. But being locked in was wearing on him. His head was still tender, and the stitches looked ghastly, but the confinement was driving him crazy.

It was a beautiful day. The sun was shining, no clouds in the sky, and a good breeze moved through his open windows. He could easily think of twenty places he would rather be instead of here, watching TV.

Of course, the fact that he was supposed to be out on the *Circe* with Ally grated across his nerves. Where *was* she, anyway? During the one quick, unsatisfying conversation yesterday, when she called to check on him, her voice had sounded wrong. Flat, like someone had taken all the air out of her. She'd skated over the subject of her family, leaving him to wonder what they had her in the middle of now and if that was the cause of her deflation. Something wasn't right in Ally's world, and whatever it was, she wasn't sharing details.

She'd called earlier this morning—still not sounding quite like herself—saying she'd be up to visit later in the afternoon.

He'd offered to send Victor to pick her up, but she'd declined, saying she'd rather drive.

Lord, everything was chafing at him today—even Ally's dislike of the helicopter. Hell, even going to the office was starting to sound like a good idea. At least it beat staring at the same four walls.

He checked the clock. Surely Ally would be here soon, and that would calm his restlessness and need to get out of here. If he had to be trapped indoors, Ally was the one person he'd choose to be with.

Plus, he was feeling a *lot* better.

Where the hell was she? He grabbed his phone, only to hear a knock at the door. Finally. It had to be Ally—otherwise the doorman would have called up.

He crossed the room in three quick strides, his body already awakening at the thought of her. "You have a key, you know," he said as he opened the door, but the sight of Ally's drawn, pinched face stopped him. "Are you all right?"

Her forced smile didn't fool him. "I should be asking you that question. How do you feel?" Ally sounded even more distant, if it were possible, than she had on the phone.

"I'm fine," he answered carefully as Ally stepped forward, and he closed the door behind her. She carried a tote bag—not really large enough to be an overnight bag, but big—clutched tightly to her side.

"You look much better."

Her stilted words had him moving cautiously as he leaned down and kissed her cheek. Whatever was going on with her, well, it wasn't good, that was for sure. She moved stiffly, like she might break, and she seemed to be holding herself together by sheer force of will.

"Chris, I—"

"Why don't you sit," he said at the same time.

Ally nodded and moved to the couch and perched on the edge, placing the large bag in her lap. He sat next to her as she took a deep breath.

"We need to talk. Well, *I* need to tell you something, and I'm not sure how." She sounded cautious, hesitant. Something was wrong.

"Okay." He watched her face closely, saw her mouth twist, and a chill ran through him. "Is it the baby? Is something wrong?"

"No, no." She shook her head, and a curl slipped out of the ponytail. "The baby's fine. In fact, I brought a copy of the ultrasound for you." She patted the bag halfheartedly.

There was more than just an ultrasound in that bag—he'd bet the *Dagny* on it. "Then what?"

Ally chewed on her bottom lip and stared at the coffee table as if it was the most unusual thing she'd ever seen. He realized she hadn't made eye contact with him since she'd walked in the door. Finally she took another deep breath, rubbed her hands across her face and exhaled noisily. "Okay. I'm just gonna say this, so…"

He waited for her to continue.

"I can't do this anymore." Ally's shoulders dropped as she said it, and her eyes finally met his. They were as distant as her voice had been.

She wasn't making a lot of sense. "Do what, exactly?"

"This." She waved her hand between them. "You and me and the whole thing. I just can't do it."

The punch in his gut barely registered as Ally hurried ahead.

"I've had some time to think recently, and you and me— we're just not going to work. We're too different and I can't handle the stress and the worry and…"

He reached out to touch her hand. "Ally, I'm sorry about Friday—I know it worried you—but it was just an accident."

"I understand that. But I can't handle waiting for the next accident. Waiting to hear if you…" She cleared her throat. "Waiting. Look, you love it—sailing, racing, all of it. I understand that, I really do, but *I don't.* And I can't deal with it. I can't compete with it, and I can't handle it, so I'm getting out while I can."

"Did Pops get to you? If this is about the *Dagny*—"

"Pops didn't have to get to me. I got here all by myself." She sighed. "It's all of it, Chris. You and I are too different to get along."

"I thought we were doing pretty well."

Ally got up to pace, giving him a sense of déjà vu. "Yeah, the fireworks, and the chemistry, and the excitement—that's all really great. *Now.* But long-term? No. I want my life to have a lot less drama in it. We're from different worlds—you love the limelight and the thrill, and I'm just an everyday accountant. I can't keep up with you.

"And more importantly, I have to think about the baby. What's best for her."

"And having her parents together isn't good for her?" He saw her wince as he raised his voice, and he tried to tamp down his temper. "Ally, you're not making sense."

"If you're off racing or whatever, then her parents aren't actually together. And I can't be a good parent if I'm always worried about you."

Astonished and not quite getting it, he nearly sputtered before he pulled it back together. "You don't want me to race?"

"I would never ask you to do that. It's too much a part of you. To ask you to give that up would be asking you not to be *you* anymore and…" She sighed again. "I don't expect you to change who you are. But I can't change who *I* am, either. And that's why this won't work with us."

Ally was taking Friday's scare a bit far. "Take a deep breath and calm down for a minute."

She spun on him, her eyes blazing. It was a nice change from the emptiness. "Don't patronize me. I'm an adult, and I've made my decision. We want different things, and we can't provide them for each other. What kind of *true* relationship could we ever have? You want *this*—" she looked pointedly at his injuries "—and I want…" She stopped, shrugged and picked up the bag she'd let slide to the floor.

Angry, he grabbed her upper arm. "What do you want, Ally? Tell me."

She simply stared at his hand until he released her. He felt like a jerk, reacting like that, but, damn, *where* had all this come from?

Ally pulled a large manila envelope out of the bag and handed it to him.

He knew without opening it he wouldn't like the contents.

Ally took a deep breath to stabilize herself. This was even harder than she'd thought it would be, and the whole conversation was like digging her heart out with a rusty fork. And Chris wasn't making it any easier.

Why'd he have to look at her like that? And why did her libido jump up and dance every time he did? The man was recuperating from an injury, for God's sake, why couldn't he at least look a little less…a little less…well, a little less godlike. He looked remarkably hale and healthy, aside from the stitches over his ear, which made her feel slightly less like a true witch for breaking up with him just forty-eight hours after he got hurt. His sunburn wasn't even peeling—it had darkened into a tan that stood out sharply against his white T-shirt.

This hadn't gone according to the careful plan she'd spent hours thinking about and rehearsing repeatedly in the car on the drive up. She'd let him get to her, and she'd nearly lost what little control she had over herself more than once. She'd come so close to sounding like a complete idiot, too. If she hadn't caught herself, she would have said, "I want someone who loves me more than a boat."

God, it sounded juvenile. She was still jealous of a damn boat. And in reality, it *wasn't* the boat—she just knew she couldn't settle for second or third place in Chris's life. Couldn't be the cheerleader and housemom for his frat-rat, golden-boy lifestyle. She loved him for what he was, but at the same time, she couldn't handle it. She just couldn't put it into words properly.

Saying those things to Chris had been the hardest thing she'd ever done. Handing him the envelope he was now staring at like it was a snake was the second hardest.

He looked at her questioningly and weighed the envelope in his hands. "What's this, Ally?"

"I talked to my lawyer on Friday night." Granted Uncle Joe was her father's oldest friend, but he'd been willing enough to meet with her on Saturday and draw up the documents Chris now held. Of course, if Chris chose to fight her, she'd be doing Uncle Joe's bookkeeping for the rest of her natural life to pay him back the legal fees. "I'm hoping we've moved past the anger and the threats and can discuss this like adults. It's a fair agreement—very liberal visitation, no child support—"

"No child support? Are you sure, Ally?" he mocked.

"I don't need your money to feed and clothe my child."

"*Our* child," he corrected, and she didn't like the snarl in his voice.

"As I said, I don't need money for day-to-day maintenance. There's a clause, though, about extras like braces and dance lessons and college. If you have a problem with any of it, my attorney will be able to work with you to come to an agreement."

"Dammit, Ally." He tossed the envelope onto the coffee table where it landed with a thunk. When he turned to look at her, her breath caught. Was that hurt in his eyes? She gave herself a strong mental shake. No, probably just anger that she'd thrown a kink in his plans.

"We gave it a try, Chris. It didn't work."

"I'd hardly call a couple of weeks a good try," he scoffed.

"It was enough." *Enough to let me fall in love with you. Enough to give you the power to hurt me.* "Take a couple of days to look over the papers. I'm sure you'll see I'm being very reasonable, and I'm only asking the same from you."

God, why did this hurt so much? It was all she could do to keep the tears at bay. She needed to leave. Now. Get distance between them again so she could see straight. So she could let her heart start to heal.

Digging through the bag again, she took out the rest of the contents. A copy of the ultrasound. A T-shirt he'd left at her house. The keys to his loft. The small box containing the necklace. Everything she could find that would remind her of him—save one. Her permanent reminder. The only one she could keep. But with her luck the baby would look exactly like him and break her heart all over again every single day.

Chris didn't say anything, but the muscle in his jaw twitched. She couldn't tell what he was thinking, but she knew if she stayed much longer she'd be lost.

And she couldn't risk that again.

"Bye, Chris." She forced a smile. "I'm glad we had the chance to get to know each other. It'll make things with Kiddo easier." The lie tasted sour in her mouth. Although his silence unnerved her, at the same time it was probably a good thing.

Then he turned those blue eyes on her and her heart seemed to shatter. They were cold.

Barely holding herself together, she turned on her heel and

forced herself to walk calmly toward the door. Only once it closed behind her did she give into the tears, and by the time she reached her car, her shoulders were shaking with sobs.

The hollow place in her chest ached, and she took a deep breath, cursing every decision she'd ever made when it came to Chris—all the way back to agreeing to go sailing with him on Tortola in the first damn place. If only she'd known that one decision would come to this painful moment.

But now. *Now* she was thinking straight. Making good decisions. She welcomed back the predicable, rational, reliable Ally she'd lost track of when Hurricane Chris had blown through her life.

Too bad she didn't like that Ally anymore.

The chime of the doorbell woke her up. Seeing Chris had drained her emotionally, and the round-trip drive hadn't helped her physically, either. While she'd managed to get the tears under control, the giant gaping wound in her heart hadn't eased any with the drive home, and she'd gone directly to bed, needing the relief from reality only sleep could provide.

But the room was dark now, and she rolled over to check the clock. Nine-thirty. A little late for visitors, but when she heard the key in the lock she realized this was no average visitor.

Great. Exactly what she didn't need today.

She barely had her feet out from under the covers when she heard her mother's voice.

"Ally, honey, where are you?"

"In here, Mom."

"Why are you in bed so early? Are you feeling all right?"

The simple question brought tears to her eyes, making her glad the room was dark and her mother couldn't see. She wasn't all right. She'd probably never be all right again. "I'm tired. You had three kids. Surely you remember how it was."

Her mother laughed. "That I do."

Waiting for the other shoe to drop always tried her patience, but considering their last conversation, Ally wasn't sure how long she could wait for her mother to dance around the subject. "What brings you by, Mom?"

"I wanted to check on you." She crossed the room and turned on the bedside lamp before sitting on the edge of the bed.

Ally squinted against the light as she pushed herself to a sitting position. "I'm fine. My doctor's appointment went great, and Dr. Barton says the baby is one hundred percent perfect."

Her mom frowned. "I'm glad to hear it, but I'm here to check on *my* baby, not yours. Are you ready to talk to me again?"

Warily she searched her mother's face, but the brown eyes held only concern. "I don't know, Mom. Did you think about what I said?"

"Of course I did. I just wish you'd said something earlier." She sighed and pushed Ally's hair back from her face, tucking it behind her ears. "I always said you were my little adult. You came out of the womb running the world, so sure of the right thing to do all the time. You never seemed to need me as much as the others." A weak smile crossed her face. "You're my strong one, the one I don't have to worry about all the time. I guess I just got lazy because I knew you'd be there to take it all in hand." Warm hands cupped her cheeks, bringing tears to Ally's eyes. "I am sorry about that, sweetie."

Ally nodded, words trapped behind the lump in her throat. She swiped at the tears on her cheeks.

"I can't promise I'll be able to change overnight, but I will try." With a sigh, her mom wiped at the tears, as well. "And I'll let you handle Erin any way you want to—or not at all. That's completely up to you. If it makes you feel any better, I'll confess Erin is driving me insane, as well. Honestly, you'd think she was the first person to ever get married."

As her mother rolled her eyes, Ally was able to laugh. "Without me to complain at, Erin must be all over you."

"And then some." They shared a moment in silence. "So, are we okay now? I've missed you."

"I've missed you, too, Mom." Though she should feel better now, she felt worse. Without the anger at her family helping to distract her, the pain washed over her in waves. Fresh tears welled in her eyes and rolled down her cheeks.

"Oh, honey, what now?" Her mother wrapped her in a tight hug, and Ally's fragile hold on her control snapped. Sobs shook her as her mom stroked her back and whispered nonsense words of comfort.

Just giving in to the tears helped. It didn't help the hollow feeling in her stomach or the ache that had set up camp in her chest, but she did feel a bit more in control as the sobs abated.

"If we're okay, and the baby's okay, then this must have something to do with Chris."

Ally straightened and nodded.

"Whatever it is, you know I'm there for you. Whatever you need."

So glad her mother was finally being a *mom,* Ally laid her head in her mother's lap and let the whole story flow.

"You're working poor Grace to death. I sent her home early." Marge brought in a stack of papers and dropped them on his desk. "Those are the financials on the Newport yard. Your grandfather has already had a look and made his recommendations."

"Good." Unfortunately, without Grace here he couldn't get much more done about *that* today. When Marge settled into the chair across from his desk, he realized *he* might not get much more done today, either. She had that look on her face.

Oh, he really didn't need this today. He hadn't slept properly in days—not since Ally had ripped his guts out with her exit from his life—and he was already on edge. Burying himself in paperwork helped precious little, but at least it gave him something he could control, something he could make work.

"You know," she started conversationally, but he wasn't fooled a bit. Marge had something on her mind. "Grace isn't the only one who needs a break. You've been cooped up in here for days, and we're all tired of looking at you. Newport will still be there tomorrow...and Friday. It will even still be there on Monday. Take the *Circe* out or something."

He rubbed a hand tiredly across his face. "I appreciate the sentiment, Marge, but if we want to expand to Newport, we need to get moving before I leave in October." *And it helps pass the time.* "I've got the gala in two days, paperwork from the accident in the yard, and you've just sent my assistant home when I need her. I can't just slip out right now. Anyway, I have a meeting this afternoon—as I'm sure you well know."

"Oh, yes, Grace did mention that." Her nose wrinkled in distaste. "That shark's partner. The little barracuda. Smaller fish to fry this time?"

"Let's just say Dennison is a little overenthusiastic about what I need. The barracuda will do just fine." At Marge's raised eyebrows, he added, "Just a personal matter. Nothing to concern yourself over."

Marge turned a remarkable shade of red. "I've known you practically your entire life and you tell me not to concern myself? That's rich. This meeting is about Ally and the baby."

"Yes, it is."

She waited, but when he didn't offer any additional information, Marge huffed. "That's all you have to say? What is that barracuda up to?"

"Ally and I are in the middle of a custody dispute. Lawyers are the usual accessories."

"I thought you and Ally had come to an agreement already."

He shrugged.

"You're not planning to…to…" Marge went and closed the office door then returned to her seat. "Chris…" she started with a warning tone.

"Don't start. I won't be dragging out the cannons again. I'm not my father. I don't plan to fight dirty."

"Porter said you were getting married."

"That was once the plan, but not anymore. Now we're back to lawyers."

Marge studied his face carefully, then nodded. "I see. She turned you down, did she?"

He tossed his pen down in disgust. "You know, I bet other executives don't have their employees meddling in their personal lives all the time."

"I wouldn't know," Marge answered cheekily, making him want to take a hard look at her pension benefits. "Can't say I blame her, though."

"Gee, thanks for the show of love."

"Oh, I do love you, honey. Any woman would. I just wouldn't want to marry you." She shook her head, but her lips twitched.

Fine, he'd bite. "Do I want to know why?"

Serious now, Marge leaned forward in her chair. "I've known you since you were a child, and I know you're a good man, but you have to try to see this from Ally's point of view."

"Ally thinks what I do is dangerous."

"And you can't claim it's not."

"Well, no. But it's not like I'm parachuting into war zones or something."

"Granted, that would be worrisome, but it's a totally different situation, as it would be for a good cause. You've grown up in a world full of men—I think you're missing a very important point about women."

"Then please enlighten me." It was the only way to get her out of his office so he could get back to work. Talking about

Ally wasn't going to help his mood any, either. It only made him recognize how much he missed her.

"I'd bet your boat that Ally's not like the women you're used to. That's why she's gotten under your skin. At the same time, you want her to be like those other women—impressed by who you are and what you do. Ally's not, is she?"

"Ally doesn't know a buoy from a bowline."

"Exactly. I got to spend some time with her at the hospital while you were off getting that thick skull of yours X-rayed, and let me tell you, she was trying to understand and accept your life, your people, and even your boat. Did you do the same for her?"

"Excuse me?"

"Ally was trying to meet you halfway—more than half-way if you ask me. You just weren't holding up your end of the bargain. I'm not surprised she wouldn't marry you. She wants more."

Marge's matter-of-fact tone rankled him in a way she'd never done before. She was stepping way outside of the line, but she had too many years invested in his company and his family for him to call her on it. "Thanks for your concern, Marge, but I've got this under control. Would you take these files by Billing on your way back to your office?"

Marge stood. "I'll take the files. *And* the hint. Chris, honey, don't expect Ally to settle for second best. She's not that kind of girl and she deserves better. And if you want happiness—for either of you—you wouldn't expect her to. Just think about it."

"Fine. I'll think about it. But right now, I need to think about capital financing and stock options."

Smug now that she'd had her say, Marge left and closed the door behind her. He wondered briefly if she was taking some kind of new medication or something as he tried to focus on the paperwork in front of him.

What "more" could Ally possibly want? He snorted. He'd

hardly asked her to "settle" for anything. She and the baby would have everything they wanted. They could be happy together if Ally wasn't such a worrywart and a control freak.

He shook his head and looked at the financials again. The numbers all looked good—everything seemed to add up properly.

Add up.

Ally was a numbers person; everything had to add up properly for her. She liked things in proper columns and rows and nothing about the two of them lined up neatly anywhere. Well, except maybe their bodies. *That* brought a blood-heating mental image.

What had she said about her family? They needed her. So did he, but in an entirely different way.

That thought brought him up short, and the papers in his hand were forgotten. When exactly had she become a need? He'd wanted her since the moment he'd seen her on the dock inspecting the *Circe*. Her impassioned defense of Circe and disparaging remarks about Odysseus had enchanted him much the way Circe had enraptured Odysseus. But *need?* That was a new feeling.

He didn't like it very much, that was for sure. Marge was right that Ally was under his skin, but until this moment, he hadn't realized how much he wanted her there.

He thought of Ally—wearing that shapeless cotton sundress that hid the luscious curves of her body while her hair escaped the braid and flew randomly around her face in the breeze—as she argued her case against Odysseus in defense of women everywhere.

She'd snared him and he'd never denied it. Unlike Odysseus, though, he had no plans to sail off into the sunset and forget her or their child.

Aren't you? It might look that way.

Was *that* it? Did Ally's objections to him taking the *Dagny* around the world go beyond the possible danger? "It's a whole different world," she'd said. Christ. He was as thickheaded as Marge had said. Ally didn't think she would fit in that world and he'd done nothing to convince her she did. The silly woman thought he'd pull an Odysseus eventually. She'd called Odysseus a player, the original golden boy. No wonder she'd tried to keep herself distant from him.

Tried was the operative word. This whole thing with Ally had spun way off course. She wasn't the only one who'd gotten a hell of a lot more than she'd bargained for that day on the docks. Now he just had to enlighten her.

He opened his drawer and pulled out the manila envelope containing Ally's laughable custody agreement and the necklace she'd returned.

He slid the necklace into his pocket and tossed the papers into the recycling bin.

CHAPTER THIRTEEN

PLAN C WAS A HELL OF A LOT harder than she'd figured—especially when trying to get over Chris had her feeling like a junkie in rehab. Not thinking about Chris was just as hard as thinking about him, and both had her craving him like a drug.

Work didn't help. No matter how deeply she buried herself in paperwork and numbers, the pain in her heart was a constant reminder of what she was trying so hard to forget. She caught up on the backlog at work. She'd cleaned and organized every closet in her house. She began to regret the truce she'd called with her family—at least fighting with them would give her something to do with the long hours. Plus, they were actually taking her new rules of running their own lives seriously, so she didn't have *their* day-to-day business to occupy her. Briefly she even considered making up with Erin—surely her sister could supply her with enough wedding-related drama to keep her busy.

But the dreams were the worst. She could try to keep Chris at bay during daylight hours, but he seemed to own her subconscious. Heartbreaking, erotic, fanciful—her dreams all had one vivid thing in common: Chris.

With all the work done, she had no reason to stay at the office. Molly was long gone; plans of a hot date with the guy who owned the architecture firm two blocks over had her skipping—literally—out of the door an hour ago.

She opened her e-mail program one last time. The last e-mail from Uncle Joe hadn't helped her mood any: Nothing from him or his lawyer yet. Give it until next week before you worry any more. Easy for him to say. Maybe knowing Chris's signature was on the agreement would help with this whole healing process. Wondering if that horrible lawyer of his was going to make her life hell could be partly to blame for the continuing hollowness in her stomach.

No e-mail from Uncle Joe or anyone else, but a reminder did open up in her window: Get a manicure on the way home.

Well, no need for a manicure now. She'd made that reminder when she was still going to Chris's yacht club thing tomorrow night. Now that she wasn't going, her unpolished, slightly gnawed nails weren't an issue. She'd even given Molly back the lovely red dress she'd borrowed for the event. Instead, she'd spend tomorrow night safely ensconced under the duvet, trying very hard not to think about the announcement Chris was going to make with the official unveiling of the *Dagny*. That thought still made her ill. It was probably a very good thing she wasn't going to be there. There was no way she'd be able to smile and react appropriately while Chris made his announcement.

What did constitute appropriate in a situation like that? Not that it mattered. It wasn't her business anymore. God, this whole situation made her head pound, and she wished alcohol wasn't bad for the baby. She could use a strong drink about now.

She missed Chris. Part of her was willing to do whatever it took, put up with whatever she had to, just to have him for however long she could. Rational Ally was up against a formidable foe when it came to her emotions.

With a sigh, she deleted the reminder for the manicure, wishing she could manipulate her feelings as easily.

Habit took over after that—shutting off her computer, adjusting the office thermostat, turning off the lights, locking the door. She was on the bus before she knew it, and the familiar sights of her neighborhood were almost a shock since she had no recollection of the ride home.

"Have a good weekend," the bus driver said as she got off at her stop.

Yeah, right, she thought, but she managed a polite response.

Fall hadn't arrived on the Georgia coast yet, but it was cooler as she walked down the tree-lined street, letting her mind wander.

The red car in front of her house didn't register at first, but when it did, her heart jumped to her throat and she stopped dead on the sidewalk.

She had to be hallucinating. Or it was a different car that just looked like Chris's. She closed her eyes, cleared the image from her mind, then peeked.

Nope. South Carolina plates. Yacht club sticker in the back window. Her knees nearly buckled. *Oh, God.*

This is why Uncle Joe hadn't heard anything. What part of "contact my attorney" didn't Chris understand?

She approached the car carefully, but the front seat was empty. Taking a deep breath, she turned up the walk to her house.

Sure enough, there—perched on her porch rail and looking too good to be real—was Chris.

Breathe, Ally. She repeated that to herself as she climbed the stairs. Chris sat easily, his back against one of the support posts and his arms crossed casually over his chest. With sunglasses hiding his eyes, she couldn't tell his mood, so she aimed to keep this meeting light.

And hopefully quick. Painless would be too much to ask for.

"Be careful up there. You'd hate to fall and bash your head twice in one week."

Chris pushed his sunglasses up onto his head and grinned at her as he levered himself off the railing. "Well, I certainly don't want to worry you." He sounded cheerful, amused even, and the crinkles around his eyes clawed at her heart, distracting her as she tried to figure out what he was here for.

She scanned the furniture on the porch, looking for evil manila envelopes with lawyers' return addresses, but found none. Chris leaned against the railing, putting his hands in his back pockets and causing the muscles under his formfitting T-shirt to bulge against the fabric. Her mouth went dry and her thighs clenched.

Forget breathing, try focusing. "Okay, I give. Why are you here?"

His eyebrows went up, and she realized how sharp her tone was. "I was hoping we could talk. Should we go in?"

No! Her living room was too small and he filled it far too easily. She needed to breathe, to be clearheaded if they were going to talk. "I think we should talk out here."

She moved to the porch swing and sat, sending it swaying slightly. The movement sent a strong enough signal that she didn't want him joining her there, so he shrugged and lowered himself into the wicker rocker to her right.

"If you wanted to talk about the custody agreement, you should really call my—"

Chris shook his head, causing a lock of hair to slide out from under the sunglasses and fall across his forehead. Her fingers itched to smooth it back, so she twined them together in her lap.

"I don't want to talk about the custody agreement."

That caught her off guard and her mind spun as it searched for possibilities. "Then what?"

He stretched his legs out in front of him, causing the rocker to tilt forward slightly, and leaving only inches between his denim-clad legs and her bare ones. She quickly tucked her feet under the swing. "I thought we'd talk about mythology."

She certainly hadn't been expecting *that*. "Mythology? Seriously?"

He nodded. O-*kay,* mythology was the topic. Why *this* topic was a different question altogether…

"I've been thinking about what you said about Circe and Odysseus."

Oh, dear. "Look, I was just babbling that day. Trying to make conversation, you know?"

"I thought you made some good points. About Odysseus at least. I'd never thought about it from Circe's point of view before."

She fumbled for sensible words. This was surreal, but she'd play along. Maybe she'd figure out where he was going soon. "Well, it was Odysseus's story. He gets the hero treatment."

"I watched the video of the ultrasound. It doesn't look like you're carrying triplets."

Okay. New topic. "I should certainly hope not."

"So unless you have some secret power to turn men into swine I should know about, I think it's safe to say you aren't Circe."

"Um…" The nurse at the hospital had sworn he didn't have brain damage, but now she wasn't so sure.

"And since I don't plan to pull an Odysseus and leave you and the baby behind, can we move past that?"

Mythology riddles were *not* what she needed right now. "Chris, I don't know what you're talking about. I just—"

"I love you, Ally."

Everything froze. Her heart seemed to skip a couple of beats while the happy bubble in her chest inflated at his words. The need to savor that thought—*Chris loved her*—nagged at her, as did the need to throw herself into his arms…

No. She closed her eyes, blocking out the intense blue stare and his beautiful face. It was a wonderful thing, but it changed nothing. *Remember that.* "This won't work."

She opened her eyes in time to see one blond eyebrow arch up. "That's your response when a man tells you he loves you? You sure know how to deflate the moment, don't you?"

"Don't think I don't, um, appreciate the sentiment—I do, really. But love and good sex are two different things—"

Chris smirked. "But they go together quite nicely." She opened her mouth to say more, but Chris continued, seriously this time. "I know you've been burned, but it wasn't by me. You can't judge me based on your ex or anyone else."

That ticked her off. "I'm judging you based on *you* and our history. It's all the information I need to make a decision."

"But, my little number cruncher, did you factor in the fact that you love me and that I love you?"

Ally felt her chin drop and she closed her mouth with a snap. How to answer *that?*

Chris exhaled loudly, an exasperated look on his face, then moved to the swing next to her. "You're not going to help me out here at all, obviously. Fine."

He looked so exasperated, it would almost be funny if the topic weren't so serious.

"I love you. I want to marry you. I want this baby and hope-fully more someday. I'm even willing to put up with your family—or run interference for you, whichever you prefer."

The words washed over her, bringing tears to her eyes. God, she wanted to believe him, and from the look in his eyes, she knew he meant what he said. At least he did right now. While it was perfect in so many ways, it also meant nothing at all.

She didn't know what to say, and Chris frowned at her silence. "Maybe this will help convince you." He pulled a folded sheet of paper out of his back pocket and handed it to her.

The film of tears in her eyes made the print blurry, and it took a minute for her to realize she was holding a press release. "Wells Racing Announces Record-breaking Around-the-world Solo Attempt." There was that knot in her stomach again.

"We'll make the official announcement tomorrow night, but that's the press release faxed to all the major papers and sailing press this afternoon."

"That's...that's...that's great, Chris. I wish you nothing but luck."

"How about you read it first?"

What, so the knife in her heart could slice even deeper? But Chris leaned back, setting the swing gently moving again, and didn't say anything more. She blinked against the moisture in her eyes and skimmed the short paragraphs. *Sponsored by OWD Shipyard, world-class racing teams,* blah, blah, blah, *the newly designed* Dagny, *skippered by the internationally known John Forsythe...fifty-nine-day record to beat.*

Wait. Who? She skimmed back. John Forsythe? She looked at Chris questioningly.

"You didn't get to meet John—he wasn't at the last race since he was in Scotland at the International Sailing Federation meeting. Excellent sailor. He's been itching to attempt the record for a couple of years now."

Confusion reigned. "But I thought *you* wanted to break the record."

Chris captured her hand and threaded his fingers through hers. "I do. But not as much as I want you."

Said simply like that, Ally knew he meant it, and her heart expanded until she felt her chest would burst. *He did love her.* Loved her enough to give up the chance to...

"Chris, I can't ask you to do this."

"You didn't. I've never had to take anyone else into consideration before, and it didn't occur to me to try to see it your way. I'm used to being in charge—I forgot we'd have to be a team."

"You'd give up racing for me?" Chris needed racing like he needed air; it wasn't something she could get her head around easily.

Chris's mouth twitched. "I didn't say *that*. This race, definitely. Future races? Well...let's just say it's open to negotiation."

He squeezed her hand gently as he spoke, and this time she squeezed back. She was too happy to say anything at the moment. She just wanted to savor the feeling.

"Ally?"

"I love you."

Happiness lit his eyes, and they glowed a deep Caribbean blue. Tugging her hand, he pulled her into his lap for a kiss that seared through her, healing old wounds as it did. Ally's arms twined around his neck, her hands burying into his hair, holding him close. She never wanted this moment to end, but Chris was shifting awkwardly under her.

She pulled back, breaking the kiss. "Don't tell me I'm too heavy already."

"Hardly," Chris mumbled, capturing her lips again. One arm hooked under her bottom, lifting her slightly as he shifted, then settled her comfortably back on his lap. "I thought you might like this back."

Her necklace dangled from his fingers, the medallion catching the sunlight and sending rainbows over her skin. She felt the smile split her face as he hooked the necklace around her neck.

Chris toyed with the medallion as it nestled between her breasts, and the air around them became charged. Her skin started to tingle and an ache built between her legs. She traced a hand over the expanse of his chest and sighed. "Let's go inside."

Skilled fingers tickled over her collarbone, sending lovely

shivers over her skin. With a small smile, Chris helped her off his lap and to her feet. He stood and kissed her gently on the forehead. Suddenly, everything seemed to click into place. She could do this. Loving Chris might be easier than she thought.

"I'll race you," he challenged.

Well, at least it wouldn't be boring.

HOT BOSS, BOARDROOM MISTRESS

BY
NATALIE ANDERSON

Possibly the only librarian who got told off herself for talking too much, **Natalie Anderson** decided writing books might be more fun than shelving them—and, boy, is it that! Especially writing romance—it's the realisation of a lifetime dream kick-started by many an afternoon spent devouring Grandma's Mills & Boon® novels…

She lives in New Zealand, with her husband and four gorgeous-but-exhausting children. Swing by her website any time—she'd love to hear from you: www.natalie-anderson.com.

I still can't believe I've been fortunate enough to have one story published, let alone getting to this— my tenth title. But my real luck was when a certain editor pulled my manuscript out of the pile and saw something she could develop.

So, to the hugely supportive Sally: for all your help and effort, I cannot thank you enough.

CHAPTER ONE

AMANDA snatched a second to glance up, checking the manufacturer's plate detailing the date and location of construction, on the upper inside of the door frame. Yes, it was real, it had been built in a proper factory and fingers crossed it wouldn't fall out of the sky with her in it. Only once she'd scanned it did she step over and onto the plane. She'd never board without seeing that little rectangle of metal with its punched-in lettering first.

Ritual reassurance achieved, her gaze dropped again, right to the floor, thus avoiding the censorious glares of the air stewards as they grimly gestured to her seat. She knew they were cross, had heard the huffing and puffing from the internal phone system. Taking two steps down the narrow aisle she could feel the equally burning glares of the passengers—having held them up for a full five minutes. Not that long in the grand scheme of things, but seemingly an eternity for plane passengers. She could hear their murmurs of grumbling discontent.

Too bad. She tilted her chin and tried harder to ignore them. This had been an emergency—too many people were counting on her. Thank heavens for her old university buddy Kathryn who'd got her onto the flight last minute and managed to get the ground staff to hold the plane for her as she'd sprinted down the corridor. One second later and that door would have been shut. And if she hadn't got this, the last flight out today, she might not have made it back to Auckland tomorrow in time for the meeting. The risk of fog in the early morning was too great. So she'd made the hour drive from Ashburton to Christchurch in record-breaking time—just keeping within the legal speed limits—and then Kathryn had worked her magic.

Without so much as a glance at the person occupying the window seat next to her aisle one, she pushed her laptop bag into the stowage compartment in front of her feet. She'd get it out again as soon as they had levelled out and get to work. The flight was only a little over an hour but every minute counted. This pitch had to be perfect—the company needed the business to stay afloat and she needed to keep her job. Money mattered—and yes, it was a life and death thing.

She snapped together her safety belt; the plane was already taxiing down the runway and the stewards were quickly covering the mandatory safety basics. She could just about recite the phrases with them—having made this trip too many times in the last two months. It was only then that she noticed that she was seated in the small business class section. She hadn't travelled in this exclusive section of a plane in years.

Bless Kathryn.

But as the plane paused at the head of the runway the old anxiety sharpened. She put her head back, closed her eyes and mentally ran through all the probabilities—facts and figures and how it was planes actually stayed up in the air...

It didn't work. The cold sweaty feeling spread.

She'd think about the pitch—that would take her mind off it.

Impossible.

She'd think about Grandfather.

Equally impossible.

Her heart was beating high in her throat—clogging, choking. And she was sweating more than when she'd been challenging the record for fastest airport dash ever. The last thing she could do now was have a panic attack and cause more disruption to the others on the plane. But her heart pounded harder, louder.

Just think about breathing.

Her lungs jerked, resisting as she took a breath. The engines roared. Her blood competed, trying to beat a louder noise in her ears. She curled her fingers around the edge of the arm rest, clinging on tight. Squeezing her eyes tighter, she concentrated on flexing her muscles. Never mind that she was supposed to start at her toes and tense then *relax* them, it was all she could do to focus, to stay aware. Now was not the time to faint. Or scream. Or worse.

Breathing. In and out—was how you did it.

'Of course, someone inconsiderate and selfish enough to hold up a plane? It could only be you, Amanda.'

She opened her eyes and turned her head. That voice had cut through the din like a diamond on glass—silencing everything.

Eyes darker than the dead of night stared back at her, framed by thick black lashes. The bridge of his nose had a slight bump from an ancient break, his cheekbones were high, his forehead broad. His lips were full, but there was no hint of a smile. Not for her.

It was a face she knew better than her own, yet she hadn't seen it in years.

'Hello, Jared.'

She hardly heard the bellow of the engine as the plane

kicked off from the ground. Head pressed back against the seat, she couldn't look away from the cool derision in his face.

'It must be at least ten years,' he drawled. 'I'd have thought things might have changed but I guess not.'

It was nine years. Nine years, seven months.

'Some things change, some things don't.' She flicked a glance over his clothes. Jeans. Jared always wore jeans—in school, out of it, when working the ride-on mower, when stacking boxes of files, when cleaning cars…

Under the blazing summer sun and on the coldest winter morning, Jared wore jeans. Maybe he knew how fit he looked in them?

But as she looked at the dark stitching she saw the jeans were different now. His jeans today were designer—not old and faded with dust on the thigh, holes in the knees and fraying ends. She looked up at the black wool jersey—fine merino.

Yes, some things changed.

The plane soared higher and she barely noticed.

Jared James—of all people. The trickle of cold sweat slid down her spine while her heart thudded even more uncomfortably. Well, today had been awful—why should she have thought its last few hours would improve any? She leaned around, looking longingly down the aisle at the rest of the plane. Hoping to spot a spare seat, but all she could see were shoulders and bits of leg protruding all along the edges.

'You'd go to cattle class just to avoid me?' he murmured. 'How touching.'

She twisted further, trying to scan the window seats as well as the aisles. Surely there must be another seat. She couldn't be held responsible for her actions if she had to stay near him. Not tonight.

'You're still only thinking of yourself?' His brows lifted.

'Look how busy that woman is.' He pointed at the steward, efficiently pulling out the trolley to serve refreshments. 'Are you really going to bother her more?'

Amanda felt both embarrassment and rage burn through her like twin rockets heading to Pluto. The twisting mass of resentment Jared inspired in her had been on the back-burner for nine years, seven months and now it blasted off with enough power to make that longest journey.

Some things could never be forgotten.

He was wrong—things could and did change. Like her cringe-tastic crush. Two years in the brewing, it had taken only one night for him to destroy it.

Because of him she'd been forced to leave the town she'd spent all her life in. Because of him her relationship with her grandfather had been damaged. Because of him she'd had to live out her last years at school in loneliness and isolation.

And ever since there was never a time when she returned home without thinking of him—seeing his shadow on the land, hearing his heavy-booted tread along the path. Always she had the momentary wondering of where he'd gone, what he'd done—before quickly stamping out the errant thoughts. She didn't want to know; she didn't want to think of him.

Because she had cared. No matter what he thought she really had cared. And he'd left a wrinkle on her heart that she couldn't iron out no matter how hard she tried—no matter how much she told herself she was over him. Such a mistake—a young girl seeing a hero where there was only a heartless youth. His action had resulted in a punishment far more severe than her silliness had warranted.

Why had she been so foolish to have believed herself to be in love with him?

Then she turned back to face him and saw exactly why. No inexperienced sixteen-year-old could possibly resist those darkly handsome looks. His Latin colouring—the olive complexion and almost-black, dangerously gleaming eyes, the thick dark hair that had always had that slightly rough, tousled look. Mystery, rebellion, a hint of scarring—he was too intriguing, too much of an enigma for her not to be curious. Add to that the toned physique honed by hours of hard, heavy work. And then there was the attitude. No man had attitude like Jared James.

She hadn't been immune—no female in town had. But she had been the most foolish.

'Amanda Demanda.' His laugh rasped across her like a sand-roughened desert wind.

The old name still had the power to hurt. She'd known about it. Had heard it muttered behind hands when she'd walked past. But no one ever said it to her face, only Jared. And now he'd managed to do it more than once.

His eyes taunted her, mouth teased her. But there was no warm humour. Amanda's chin lifted. There was only one way to handle this. Icy politeness. Manners maketh the woman, right? And manners weren't something Jared tended to bother with—at least not with her. Not that she could really blame him. There'd been a time there when she'd been rottenly ill-mannered towards him—rudely insisting he carry out her orders around the property. It had been an immature girl's method of getting his attention and it hadn't succeeded. At least, not in the way she'd desired. So then she'd tried something far more stupid. Having heard the way the girls talked about him, looked at him—the rumours that he was a dangerous, demanding kind of lover, and one they all wanted. She'd naively thought that if she offered him everything she'd get the kind of attention she craved from him.

So stupid. His reaction had cost her the last of her girlhood and she could never forget or forgive that.

Well, she didn't want his attention now. Now she'd give him nothing but 'nice'—converse a little, do some 'pleasant' catching-up, and then excuse herself into her work. As much as she'd like nothing more than to blast him and then flounce off, she'd made enough of a scene on this flight already; besides, there wasn't another seat available.

She dropped her gaze for a millisecond as she inhaled some calm and then turned fractionally further towards him with the biggest smile she could manage. OK, so it was tiny, but it was there. 'So, Jared, how have you been?'

His eyes narrowed. 'Busy.'

Naturally. Jared had always been busy. Every spare moment outside school he'd been working—making the money that his father had been too drunk to be able to. 'Visiting old friends?'

Incredibly his face closed up even more. 'This was a transit stop for me. It should have just been ten minutes to load the passengers from Christchurch. But it was fifteen because of you. I'm flying up from Queenstown.'

She ignored the dig. 'Been skiing?'

'Snowboarding.'

'How nice.' But Jared in jeans with snow-dusted hair wasn't an image she wanted to envisage. He'd be so cool on the mountain. He was too damn cool, too good-looking and sitting too close. And with a skittering pulse she knew that a twenty-five-year-old woman might not be any more immune to his looks than a sixteen-year-old had been.

She tried to inhale deeply, trying to suppress that scary realisation and bring her anger back to the boil. That was enough polite chat for her to get away with. The plane had levelled—she'd barely noticed the ascent after all, what with the shock of finding her first crush seated beside her. And he'd crushed her all right. All her secret dreams and fantasies. He'd exposed her and changed the course of her life. Not that she'd ever let him know it. Masking her breathlessness, she reached forward and lifted up her laptop bag. Time to retreat behind a screen and extreme concentration, although admittedly that kind of concentration was going to be tricky. Her mind whirled as fragments of memories she'd tried to bury deep long ago started floating up to the forefront of her brain and her blood pounded harder than it had been just prior to take-off.

The humiliation felt as raw, real and recent as ever. She wanted to shrivel up and be washed away like a slug down a drain. Instead she calmly lifted the lid of her laptop, determined to maintain poise and dignity. She wasn't sixteen any more.

She politely accepted the coffee from the air steward, sat back as the woman passed another to Jared.

'What about you, Amanda—you been busy?' he asked after taking a sip from the steaming cup.

Oh, so he'd mastered some rudimentary conversational skills, then, had he? And only just remembered?

'Very.' She, on the other hand, was over it.

There was a sound that might have been a snort or a laugh. She had to look at him—just to make sure he wasn't choking to death or something. She encountered an expression of disbelief so dry she could have been transported to the Sahara.

'Sweetheart, you don't know the meaning of the word.' He spoke casually, sat casually but those eyes of his were still sharp and dark and digging right through her.

'Jared,' she said softly but firmly. 'You don't know me any more.'

He had no idea of how her life had played out. Maybe back then she'd been the spoilt, wilful, foolish girl he so clearly thought she still was. But she'd grown up—finally taken on responsibility.

'I know enough.' His piercing look roved right over her.

He couldn't see much, she reasoned as her temperature began to rise. Not beneath her brown wool coat. Several years old, it was classic enough to still wear and it hid the skirt and shirt that had been the height of fashion several seasons ago.

But despite the thick wool of the coat and the opaque stockings covering her legs, she felt as if Jared's gaze were stripping her close to naked. It was the sexual, animal element of him—she'd recognised it all those years ago as the woman in her had become awakened. But she'd had no idea of the power of it. And while she'd had no hope of resisting it, she'd had no hope of coping with it either.

Yet even now, as she observed the thick lashes almost resting on his cheek as he looked down her arm, her blood raced and she was so tempted to beat that spark into a flame—just to see what would happen. Because the one wild taste she had got back then had become the measure for all.

And then she remembered the aftermath.

Jared James was bad—bad-mannered, bad-tempered, badly behaved and bad for her.

He picked up her hand. Immediately she tried to pull it away but his grip became lethal and she stopped trying to resist. His hold instantly softened but he didn't let go, instead pulling so her wrist crossed the arm rest and he could study her fingers more closely.

Her erratic breathing stopped altogether. Her skin sizzled where it was in contact with his.

'I don't believe these pretty hands have ever known

hard work.' He turned her hand over and the index finger of his free hand made circles in the centre of her palm.

It tickled and she wanted to pull it away but at the same time…at the same time…the rest of her started to—

Want.

More circles teased.

Her fingers quivered in his as she shuddered in a wisp of air.

A smile softened his mouth. The kind of smile that he'd never turned on her before—one that both tempted and made her nervous. It deepened, becoming the kind of smile that would have a woman on a bed and spread in seconds.

Oh, no. She couldn't let him do this—she couldn't fall again just like that…

'Hands like these are all about pleasure.' He walked two fingers even more lightly across her palm and then lifted his head to catch her wide-eyed, mesmerised gaze on the full. 'Aren't they, Amanda?'

CHAPTER TWO

AMANDA curled her fingers into a fist and jerked it free of Jared's, burning with embarrassment. And what made it worse was her suspicion that he knew that embarrassment wasn't all she was burning with. All grown-up maturity and attempts at politeness escaped her. She glared at him. Breathing again. Hating the effect he had on her—the effect he'd *always* had—smile or not.

But he, the swine, was laughing. Those dark, bottomless, devilish eyes were creased at the corners. She daren't look at his mouth. She daren't…but her eyes slid and then she did. Oh, it was that smile again, only now it was tainted with a touch of sarcasm.

This was just too humiliating. To bump into the man who had been the cause of so much heartache and discover he still could make the world tilt with just a look?

'Will you excuse me, Jared? I have some work to get on with.' Cool practicality could be her only defence. She'd deal with her hormones later.

'Really, Amanda?'

'Actually yes. Contrary to what you may think, I'm not independently wealthy and do actually have to earn money to be able to eat.'

'But not at this hour surely?'

She glanced at her watch. A little after nine and it meant that there was still about an hour of this hellish flight to go. She stared at the laptop screen, wishing she could disappear into it like in some weird sci-fi movie.

'You know you were always beautiful, Amanda, but you're even more beautiful now.' He sounded coolly detached, as if he were discussing the weather.

'Do you think?' She almost managed a disinterested inflexion but choked on the last word and then was unable to stop herself looking at him again.

He took the opportunity to give her another searing once-over.

'Very much. A little pale, perhaps a bit thin, it's hard to see under that coat, but your cheekbones are a little gaunt. Been burning the candle?'

Not in the way he meant. While there had been many sleepless nights, not one of them had been spent partying or clubbing or indulging in wild, hedonistic sex. His gaze lifted as that last option popped into her head, and his knowing smile came slow.

'As I said, I've been busy.' She turned back to the screen, back to work, back to oblivion—*please*.

He sat angled side on, obviously watching her, waiting. In the end she couldn't resist. What he'd said…had he really thought she was beautiful back then? If that was the case, then why had he done it?

She gave up the mental gymnastics and looked at him, decided to brazen it out. 'You had your chance.'

'Meaning I won't get another?' His eyes were all daring now.

She looked straight into them, cool as she could. 'No.'

His smile curved into a gentle crescent—like a stretch

of sand along a beautiful beach that tempted you to race across it and dive in. 'Your mouth says one thing, your body another.'

'Oh, please.' Sarcasm flooded from her that time. 'You think that line's going to get you anything but a knock-back?'

'Too close to the truth?'

'Too much male chauvinist.'

'Tell me no and I'll listen. Whether you mean it or not.' He leaned closer to her, holding her gaze with his as he spoke soft and slow. 'I've never needed to pressure a woman. Usually they come on to me.'

A second passed before Amanda blinked. Finally absorbing what he'd said…what he'd meant…what he was reminding her of…

'I was young.' She couldn't cover the wobble in her voice.

'You're not so young now.'

For a long second she fought the urge to tip her coffee over him. Instead she lifted the cup with trembling fingers, clamped them round the plastic.

'Ask me again,' he murmured. 'The answer might be different this time.'

She forced herself to take a deep sip instead, not caring how scorching the wretched stuff still was—it was nothing on the way her insides were boiling already.

'It wouldn't take much to get me to say yes.'

She nearly spat the coffee out all over him. 'Dream on, Don Juan.'

He laughed then. A deep chuckle that was so rude, so outrageous and so damn genuine. 'Is that it?' He shook his head, looking both sorrowful and scornful. 'So *refined*, Amanda. What happened to that wilful, take-what-she-wants girl?'

And then she got it. He was teasing her—just winding

her up. He didn't mean a word of it and had played her for the fool she was. The more polite she'd got, the more impolite he'd got, until she snapped and he laughed. And he'd known exactly the angle to take…her attraction to him.

Humiliation times fifty.

Did he do this to every woman? She was certain he could be charming if he wanted—but women would fall at his feet even if he wasn't. Just as she had. Yet here he was flying back from a holiday solo—clearly there was no wife. Was there really no lover?

But, of course, she gave herself a mental slap, there'd be more than *one* lover.

'Have you been to Ashburton recently?' If he was determined to talk, she'd control the topic and from now on it would be safe.

'Not for nine years, seven months.'

Satisfaction flashed through her like wildfire. So he knew exactly how long it had been. He'd left town the week of her birthday. She hadn't seen him again since that night.

'Why not?' She genuinely wanted to know.

He turned, seeming to study the safety-belt sign in front of them, and when he turned back his eyes were bland. 'No reason to.'

No person. No family. No love.

She'd longed to give him love. She and the rest of the female population. Angry Jared James, whose mother had left him and whose father had boozed so much he was barely cognisant and certainly not 'there' for his son. Alone and isolated and gorgeous.

'Not even curiosity?'

'What could there possibly be to be curious about?' His answer was curt.

'Quite.' Determined not to feel wounded at the question,

she focused on feeling pleased because his lack of interest meant it more than likely that he wouldn't know about her grandfather. Not many people did, but in a small town it was hard to keep secrets—especially when he'd been such a public figure. But he deserved dignity and Amanda was working harder than she'd ever worked in her life to try to ensure that he got it. And for some reason it was important to her that Jared not think badly of Grandfather—he could think what he liked about her, but not the old man.

She turned back to her screen. Read the same sentence five times over before getting the gist of it and trying to move on to the next. But it was hopeless. She might as well tinker with colours and formatting.

The pitch was at ten a.m. tomorrow and it was vital they win it. The consultancy had been hit hard by changes in the economic climate and was teetering on the brink of closure. But if they could secure this contract it could be enough to see them through and they could build on it. It seemed to be her luck that when she'd finally landed a well paid job in the big city, it was far from certain. And she needed certainty—her grandfather was counting on her.

But now, with her concentration shot, she knew she was in for a long night of uncomfortable memories mixed with nerves and adrenalin. She might as well pop the migraine pills already. Except she couldn't possibly be woozy tomorrow.

Rats. Why did Jared James have to be on this flight *tonight*?

Jared sat back as not so deep inside him irritation duelled with amusement. Eventually amusement got the upper hand. It took a while though and its dominance was precarious. She'd looked so cucumber fresh when she'd appeared—despite the thick wool coat. Only the hint of a flush had touched those pale cheeks when she'd walked on board, blanking the passengers. Not even a small smile of apology or embarrassment sent in their direction. Nothing.

Amanda Winchester. Owned the world and acted like it. She was everything he wasn't, and all those years ago she'd had everything he hadn't. Money, leisure and freedom, whereas he'd had nothing, worked 24/7 and been imprisoned by the broken background from hell.

He'd changed though. Moved up in the world. Indeed here he was sitting in *her* class—he'd earned the right. But a sudden flash of discomfort made him stretch and shift in his seat. Despite being able to pay the fare a zillion times over, seeing her brought that old feeling back: the desperation to control, to escape, to succeed, and to *have*—not just material things. And with it came the bitterness that he'd felt towards her—back then she'd symbolised all he'd lacked and been everything he'd wanted.

He stared at her, unable to look away. She hadn't changed. Still spoilt. Still selfish. Oh, sure, now she had the ice-princess thing going on the surface. All polite poise and butter-wouldn't-melt-ish. But the fact was he knew what she was really like and her behaviour proved it. What Amanda wanted, Amanda got—even if it meant two hundred people got held up because of her.

An over-indulged minx and damn if she didn't still stir his blood—more so now, incredibly enough. He'd never forgotten the sight of her in that get-up…her pale skin had seemed luminous next to the black silk. Where on earth had she got it from? Mail order?

Nine years, seven months rolled away just like that and he was hit hard in the groin by a need that had never been indulged—and the accompanying frustration because she'd been forbidden. He gritted his teeth at the memory and then forced relaxation as he tried to think—reminding himself it was a long time ago and he was no longer the less-than-nothing youth he'd been back then.

In fact, he mused as he sucked in a breath, it might be all right to want her now. One night with Amanda Winchester wasn't necessarily taboo—not any more. Not now they were both out of that town and all grown up. That thought doused the discomfort and roused the hunter in him.

So as she oh-so-determinedly ignored him he cast his eyes over her screen. Not caring about how rude he was—in fact he was doing it deliberately, wanting to annoy her into betraying herself again. She was a spoilt, demanding brat all the way. She'd tried testing her new-grown claws on him all those years ago, but he bet she'd be one hell of a vixen now. And yes, if she asked again, his answer would be very different. The wilful, wanting teen would translate into a wild, wanting woman. Hadn't he just caught a glimpse of it in her eyes? Hadn't he been unable to resist touching her—just a little, to see if that spark would flare? And it had. How would she burn if he touched her where he really wanted to?

He blinked to refocus his eyes from the internal fantasy that was going to get him very uncomfortable if he didn't shut it down. Too long since he'd had a lay—that was the problem. As he shifted in his seat again he saw what it was she was working on.

Hell, no way!

He took a moment to regulate his reaction and then asked, 'So what do you do to earn money to eat, Amanda?'

'I'm in advertising.'

He smothered another snort. Of course she was. She could sell ice to an Inuit, had that knack of getting people to say yes. But not him. Not unless he controlled the situation.

'Which agency?' He figured it'd be one of the top two.

'Synergy.'

He clamped his jaw to stop it falling open. It was the wild card he'd selected. By far the smallest of the three agencies he'd shortlisted for the pitch, and, from what he'd heard on the grapevine, the one most in need of securing the contract tomorrow.

He was glad he'd found out. Forewarned meant fore-armed and now he had the time to plan his strategy. No way could he work with her, but at least he was spared the shock of having her walk into his office tomorrow.

He took a sidelong glance at her coolly remote expression. He was not gentleman enough to give her warning. But then, he'd never pretended to be a gentleman. In fact, he spent the rest of the flight trying to suppress the most ungentlemanly thoughts.

As the plane descended he watched the way she was gripping the arm rest between them and figured it wasn't worth fighting her for it. 'Don't you like flying, Amanda?'

'Not much.' Her lips barely moved as she answered.

'Don't like being out of control, huh?' The almost ad-mission of a weakness amused him.

'I have a strong self-preservation instinct.'

He chuckled. A strong selfish instinct, more like. Not to mention lazy. He would never forget the tone she'd used to order him around on her grandfather's farm and the way she'd sat at a distance with such indolence and watched him carry out her wishes.

Finally they landed and the second the seat-belt sign was switched off she was standing, bags in hand—arrogantly asserting her priority status without even being conscious of it. Her sense of entitlement was so ingrained. Jared counted to ten as he waited behind her while the stewards opened the doors. Her high heeled boots gave her an extra inch, meaning the top of her head made it to his mouth. He breathed in, caught the gentle scent of her shampoo, and his flare of anger became a flare of something else.

The first thing he'd do would be to free her hair from those clips—see if it was as long and golden as it had been back then. She'd always worn it loose—he'd seen it, like a flag heralding her arrival, and he'd known not to look. She'd been out of bounds but she'd pushed it. She wasn't out of bounds now.

He shortened his stride to stay alongside her as they walked along the corridors. She pushed buttons on her mobile and so did he. He had five messages. All of them could wait. It seemed she had none—or at least none urgent enough to warrant immediate attention. They got to the ground floor and the signs pointing to the luggage carousels. He, like she, ignored them and headed straight for the exit.

'Don't you have baggage to collect? Not your snow-board?' she asked.

'I like to travel light.' Habit from the old days, he figured. When he'd finally got out of Ashburton he'd taken almost nothing with him. Nothing but a bunch of memories—and most of them were bad. It wasn't that he didn't have the material possessions now—if anything he'd have to admit he had too many. So he kept his snowboarding gear and a complete wardrobe at his holiday home in Queenstown.

It was an odd relief to see that she was disconcerted by his presence—to know that he affected her too, just as she did him. Not that he'd let her know it.

Oh, yes, despite her polite façade it was as obvious as anything that she wanted him to go. Just to be perverse, he stayed close. She was slowing now as they reached the exit.

But there was no one to meet her. No boyfriend waiting at the gate to pull her close and kiss her like crazy.

He shouldn't care, but he was pleased about that too. No rings on her fingers, no calls on her mobile. They went through the automatic doors together. He expected to see her dive straight into the nearest taxi but instead she paused.

'Lovely to see you again, Jared.'

Lovely? Oh, sure, like she really thought that. Why couldn't she be honest about it?

'It was interesting seeing you too, Amanda,' he said casually. 'Who knows? Maybe we'll see each other again soon.'

She gave a plastic smile, turned and walked. Fast.

He watched her for a moment, appreciating the neat ankles and slim calves as her legs clipped along. He wished he could see more of her. She'd had long, slim legs as a girl—damn the wool coat. He forced his head to turn away, figuring she must have her car parked in the long-stay area.

He headed to the short-stay building and got into his car. It felt good to be back and now he had some fun to look forward to. He was going to enjoy seeing her perform tomorrow. Pulling out of the building, he looped round and caught sight of her—waiting for the bus service? No way. He'd pulled over before it hit that it could be a bad idea— not tonight. Maybe after tomorrow.

But the words popped out regardless. 'Can I give you a lift somewhere?' What the hell was she doing at a bus stop anyway?

Her gaze was cool as ever. Those blue eyes lancing through him like beams of dry ice—burning cold. 'Thank you very much, Jared, but I'm OK.'

He stared hard at her. Under the light from the street-lamp above the shadows under her eyes seemed more pronounced. So did the shadows in them. She looked slim. She looked pale. She looked tired. And suddenly he wondered whether she really *was* OK.

'It's winter and it's dark.' Wasn't that good enough reason to say yes?

She glanced down the street as if praying the bus would suddenly come into view. Her reluctance made his irritation resurge. So it was him that wasn't good enough.

'Who am I?' he growled. 'The big bad wolf?'

'Of course.' Her chin tilted. 'You know you are, Jared.'

CHAPTER THREE

WOLF or not, Amanda should have taken up Jared's offer of a ride. She'd seen him slide into the sleek black sedan that had been parked in a priority space and knew it would be the ultimate in comfort on wheels. Not some low-to-the-ground flashy sports car—that would be too small for legs the length of Jared's. He was a big, strong man and he had the equivalent in a motoring machine. But she'd refused— cutting off her nose to spite her face, as it turned out. The bus had been late and had then broken down on the side of the motorway, delaying her even further. It had been almost midnight before she'd got back to her room and, as she'd predicted, sleep had been elusive, brief and peppered with memories and dreams she wished she could forget.

She jabbed the button to summon the elevator. She wasn't late. Having woken before sunrise and knowing there was nil possibility of more sleep, she'd got up and ready hours ago. Even now she had no need to race up the stairs, for she was still over an hour early. But she wasn't the first in the office. Bronwyn was already there, carefully studying the mock-ups.

'Hey, Bron.' Her manager was lovely and talented and Amanda wanted to help keep her small company afloat.

There were four of them and Amanda was the most junior, but she'd been the one to come up with the concept that they'd run with for this pitch and Bronwyn had insisted she lead the presentation. Amanda figured her boss was too fair for her own good.

'Are you sure you want me to be the one to do this?' she asked.

'Of course—it's your idea, your freshness, your conciseness, and you have a fantastic presentation style. I wish I could bottle it and sell it. I'd be a squillionaire overnight.' Bronwyn looked at her. 'Are you feeling nervous?'

'A little.' More like a lot. There was too much resting on it and they all knew it.

'I'll be there. Just give me the look and I can help you out.'

'I'll be OK.' Amanda put her bag down. While it was wonderful to have been given the opportunity to really prove herself, she needed to do more than that. She needed to win. Grandfather was depending on her. She'd put all her hope on the new medication—but it cost the earth.

At nine-thirty she and Bronwyn got into the taxi. Sean and Danielle stood and waved them off as a gesture of solidarity. Amanda checked her reflection in the car window. But in the two minutes that had elapsed since she'd exited the bathroom her tight, precise French plait was still tight and precise. Not a hair out of place, no lipstick on the teeth, no creases in her skirt. She was—outwardly—as ready as she could be.

Fresh was a medium-sized local beverage company that specialised in fresh-made juices and smoothies. Headed by the gregarious iconic Kiwi actor Barry Stuart, it already had high brand recognition and good market share. But now the brief had changed—Barry wanted his face off the product. They wanted a new campaign that would get results, and an ad agency that would drop everything and come running. Demands would be high, but the results would be worth it—generating enough business to keep the company afloat.

It was a fifteen-minute drive to the factory on the edge of the CBD. They waited in the spacious foyer for several minutes. Amanda avoided her nerves by studying the paintings showcased on the bright white walls—a small but solid selection of emerging New Zealand talent. Someone had a good eye.

The funkily clad receptionist took a call in quiet tones and then came over to them.

'If you'll follow me.' She guided them to the lift and pressed the button for the third floor. Once there she led them to a large meeting room with wide windows looking across the city.

'If you'd like to set up in here. Barry and the CEO will be in shortly.'

Amanda glanced at Bronwyn—she'd thought Barry *was* the CEO. Bronwyn shrugged and got the mock-ups from the portfolio she was carrying. Amanda pulled her laptop from her bag, scoping for power sockets.

'Hello!' The loud tone heralded the unmistakable arrival of Barry. The smile that he pulled from everyone flashed onto Amanda's face. He had the kind of presence that made everyone relax even when you'd never met him. So familiar—like the friendly uncle who spent his Sundays turning the sausages at the family barbecues. Then she saw who had come into the room behind him and her heart arrested.

Jared? What was *he* doing here? She looked behind him to see if someone else was coming in. But with a glint in his eye he closed the door.

There was a painful thumping in her chest as her heart remembered to work and made up for the gap by going triple-time.

She'd never known what it was Jared had done after leaving town. It wasn't as if she could ask Grandfather. She'd have been mad to mention his name to him—not after what had happened. She swallowed back the memories. *Not now.*

But she suddenly knew he must have done OK because he was standing here with Barry as if he owned the place.

Oh, no. No, no, no.

Maybe he was the financial guy? *Please?*

She couldn't help staring. Couldn't stop either. He looked incredible. The Jared she'd known nine years ago would never have worn a suit. Certainly not one made to measure. For one thing he wouldn't have had the money, for another he wouldn't have cared to. But today he looked as if he were born in it—so neatly and naturally it skimmed his broad frame. It was dark, the shirt navy, the tie dark too.

And those eyes—they drew you into their darkness. Like velvety night in the most remote countryside, they held the promise of a million stars once you got to the heart of it.

Bronwyn was talking, introducing herself and Amanda to Barry and Jared. But Amanda was standing still and silent like a French mime artist with stage fright.

Barry was laughing as he made the return introductions. 'I'm just the front man. Truth is I sold out the controlling share of the company a couple of years ago but my boss likes to keep private. It's Jared here. You should be talking your talk to him.'

So it was the worst. Jared was the CEO—the person she had to win over today.

As if that would ever happen.

Jared spoke, inclining his head towards Bronwyn but keeping his eyes on Amanda. 'I'm sorry for the confusion.' The look in his eyes said he wasn't sorry at all. The look in his eyes grew in sharp amusement.

'But it shouldn't make much difference.' He kept talking. 'Fresh is a privately held company and I'd prefer it that you don't disseminate the management information. At this stage Barry is still very much the face of the company—until you guys do your stuff, of course.'

He smiled suddenly. That killer charm of a smile again. It was all too rare but when it flashed it had any female in the immediate vicinity weak at the knees and needy in the womb.

Amanda, still recovering from her exposure to it last night, felt a double impact.

Last night. Her brain clicked on—whirring while she read the continued amusement in his expression—and the implication became obvious. Her blood beat faster. He was not *surprised* to see her here. He had an expectant air— he'd *known* she was going to be at this meeting.

Her anger built as images from the flight flashed—she'd been working on the presentation, or at least trying to, for half the time in the air. He'd been right beside her; he'd have seen her screen easily. In fact, she knew he had. And she'd even told him for whom she worked.

But he had said nothing. Given no clue that they were destined to meet again today. It had to have been deliberate. A red mist of rage swirled before her eyes as she remembered his parting words about maybe meeting each other again 'soon'. *Totally* deliberate.

The swine. The arrogant, calculating swine.

'I want to retire,' Barry was saying in his jokey manner. 'He keeps working me too hard.'

Amanda didn't smile back. Too angry, she turned. This just couldn't be happening. She needed to win this pitch, Synergy needed the account, and she needed the money for Grandfather. She pressed her lips together, refusing to unleash the venom she ached to vent.

The men got seated on the other side of the table and Bronwyn sat too, leaving Amanda to launch into the presentation.

She switched on the screen. But it stayed blank. She switched it off and then on again. Still blank.

'Mandy?' Amanda hoped that the sharp hint of panic in Bronwyn's voice was audible only to her.

'One moment please,' she said. This was so not what they needed right now.

The power cord led right past the chair where Jared now sat. As she bent to check the plug was pushed right into the socket he murmured, 'Mandy? You're never a Mandy.'

She straightened and met his eyes for one furious moment. He was laughing—*laughing*. She knew her face was flushed, could feel it growing all the more so as she absorbed the full extent of this living nightmare. Was this just some trivial joke for him? From the expression in his eyes he wasn't expecting anything much at any rate. He was out to enjoy himself, not take her seriously.

For a moment hopelessness swept over and almost sank her. Had this blown all chances of them actually winning the contract?

Heck no, she couldn't allow that to happen. Her fighting spirit kicked in. Their pitch was a good idea, it was her first chance to prove herself and more than anything she needed the money. And now she had quadruple the incentive. She was going to ace this presentation and really show him exactly what *she* was made of.

She made herself smile at him—as if there were nothing wrong—and then stepped back to her computer. She saw the question in Bron's eyes and gave her a smile to reassure her—hoping she'd read her strange new skin tone as a sign of nerves, not fury. This time the cords were in right at both ends and light flickered on the screen. All systems go.

She paused, looked at Barry with his broad, unmistakable grin and then she looked at Jared. No grin, but all cynical challenge and underlying amusement. He really didn't think she could do it. She inhaled, mentally tossed the ball high and hit him with her most powerful serve.

Twenty minutes later Jared had his fingers to his tie, discreetly trying to loosen it, wondering why the hell he'd worn it in the first place. Barry had already ribbed him about the suit—his usual work attire was jeans and a shirt. He'd hardly worn a suit since his banking days. The casual vibe of the company was half the reason he'd bought it and he only wore suits on the days when he needed to assert authority. So what was it about today that he felt the need to assert authority?

It was only Amanda—only the half-naked nuisance of a girl he'd walked away from almost a decade ago. Only the one he hadn't been allowed—and stupidly the one he'd wanted most.

He hadn't known what to expect from the pitch. But he certainly hadn't expected to be impressed. And he was impressed. After a few minutes there he'd even stopped thinking about how delectable she looked and focused on what she was saying. What she was saying made sense.

Damn.

He'd never expected Amanda to turn the tables on him. He'd anticipated a flaky presentation. He'd anticipated a move afterwards. Take her out for a drink. Then somehow get to a place where they could light the fireworks between them and let them explode in a one-night extravaganza. Instead he got her cool ice-princess approach—concise delivery, punchy lines, and, once she'd got going, genuine enthusiasm. So bloody polished, so bloody perfect.

She'd always felt out of his league. And somehow she still did. Somehow just seeing her sent him into a sort of time warp where he was a teen again and fighting his way out of his lot in life. He'd been so at the mercy of those around him—dependent on generosity. He couldn't afford to make a wrong move—not then. But damn this feeling— he was the one in control of everything now, wasn't he?

He refused to relinquish that control.

Yet almost helplessly he watched her, able to see so much more of her today than he could last night. And she was incredible. Her hair was still tied up but looked as gold as it had been all those years ago. Her girlish curves had softened into the fuller shape of a woman. Still trim but with full breasts and a slim waist that was accentuated by the neatly tucked-in blouse and skirt. He wasn't listening again—hearing only the racing of the blood in his veins. Heading south.

He looked down at the table forcing himself to concentrate on the words, not on the image of her.

Amanda was winding down her spiel, talking up the bit about the benefits of going with their agency and not one of the others she knew he was seeing later in the day. She was tired. Had been talking non-stop for nearly twenty minutes and she had no idea—none—about how it was going down. There'd been no questions, nothing. Barry had added a couple of smiles and nods while Jared had been the bronze statue across the way. The sense of hopeless-ness was returning—especially as she saw she'd lost his attention and he had a huge frown on.

'Synergy is a New Zealand–owned company—'

'Why is that a positive?' Jared finally interrupted in a rough tone. 'Wouldn't we be better off with an overseas conglomerate that has a vast pool of talent and resources from around the globe?'

'We can offer a unique viewpoint into your local market.'

'How up to the minute are you?' He fired the question.

'As up to the minute as you can get.' She fired right back.

'So you'd say you're "in touch" with the trends, then, are you?'

'Oh, believe me, Mr James,' she descended into sarcas-tic sultriness, 'we're *in touch*.'

There was a silence as Jared met her gaze coolly, triumph suddenly kindling in the dark depths of his eyes. Her heart pounded and her spine prickled as she recognised danger. She broke away, looking down to her notes.

Bronwyn and Barry were both quiet, Amanda snatched a quick glance at both. There was a question in Bronwyn's eyes and a hint of panic—contrasting sharply with the amusement written all over Barry's face. Amanda realised that the line between professional and personal had been crossed—she'd crossed it. The challenge in the air had been thrown up by her.

Jared suddenly smiled as he reached out and needlessly moved a piece of paper on the table. It was the merest flash of teeth, revealing his moment of satisfaction further. He'd needled her deliberately. And she'd risen to the bait all too easily. Again.

Rats.

She flashed a quick, vitriolic look at him. He must have

sensed her attention because his eyelids lifted and his eyes met hers—veiled with apparent blandness, almost boredom.

Jerk.

But those hideous years at Eastern Bay School for Girls saw her regain her precarious control. She spoke quickly, clearly. 'By choosing a New Zealand partner you're helping strengthen your home economy. You're helping to keep good talent onshore, and good businesses working, which is precisely what you like to do, isn't it, Mr James? Isn't that one of the fundamentals of your own company policy? To generate jobs locally?'

She'd done her homework—spent a good twenty minutes talking to one of the delivery drivers who supplied cartons of the juice to the café nearest to her work. He'd been delighted to talk about the company he worked with. In the last couple of years, he'd said, Fresh had expanded its production significantly. And it ran an in-house mentoring scheme and had a high number of employees who'd come from troubled youth intervention programmes— getting kids off the street and into a job. She'd been surprised—not aware that Barry had such a do-good streak.

But now she knew it was Jared at the helm it made more sense—given his own background. Yet the mentoring wasn't something they used in publicity—once the driver had let it slip, he'd then done so much making light of it she knew it was important. So why didn't Jared want it advertised?

She met his hard gaze and refused to look away.

'Why do you want to go away from personality-based advertising?' Bronwyn piped up, clearly aware of the edge between Amanda and Jared.

'He's sick of seeing my face everywhere.' Barry grinned.

'So why not rebrand it with your own name and face?' Bronwyn asked.

Amanda said nothing, just watched Jared's expression close down.

'You could call it JJ's Juice?' Bronwyn laughed.

Barry laughed too.

Jared didn't.

It wasn't long before silence reigned. Out of the corner of her eye she could see Bron blushing—realising she'd made a gaffe. The only one not wincing was Barry.

'You're not necessarily going to head the company long-term,' Amanda said quietly. She didn't know where she got the prescience from but she knew she was right. 'And you don't want it limited or dominated by one personality.'

He met her gaze for a moment longer and then looked away.

'You know him.' Bronwyn stated the obvious the minute the taxi doors were closed.

'Yes.' Amanda sighed, not wanting to meet her boss's eyes, but honesty compelled her to.

'In a way that means we'll get the contract or we won't?'

Amanda paused and then shook her head sadly. 'I don't know.' She pulled the tie from her hair and loosened the plait, its tight do hurting her head. 'Probably the latter. I'm really sorry. I had no idea he was going to be there.'

'Nor did I. Keeps his cards close, doesn't he? Doesn't want to be in the public eye at all. I wonder why?'

Amanda could hazard a guess. Privacy was important to Jared. He'd hated the whole town knowing his business—all the girls feeling as sorry for him as much as they wanted him. He wouldn't want to be showcased as the underprivileged-kid-done-good. He had too much pride for that.

Bronwyn opened her mouth but closed it again. Next

time she opened it she got the question out. 'How well do you know him?'

It was the inevitable question and Amanda knew exactly what it was she was asking. 'Not that well.'

'OK.' Bronwyn smiled. 'So how *do* you know him?'

'We grew up in the same town. But I haven't seen him for years.'

'There's something, though, isn't there, between you?'

You'd have had to be made of stone not to have picked up on the tension between them. Bronwyn wasn't an idiot. And Amanda knew she wasn't going to let her get off this track without offering up some of the detail.

'A kiss.'

'Only one?'

'He stopped it going further.'

One frightening, exhilarating, life-changing kiss. So often she wished it had never happened. Yet other times, usually when she was kissing someone else, she was glad it had. Because it had been the one kiss that had given her a glimpse of what it could really be like. Amanda had gone in for a lot of kissing in her quest to find a man who could better it. She'd yet to succeed.

She'd romanticised it of course. That was the problem. With the passage of time that hazy memory had become something more than it had really been.

Amanda glanced across to see Bronwyn's glance resting on her—amusement mixed with chagrin swirling in her expression. 'Well, it'll be interesting anyway.'

'I'm really sorry, Bronwyn. I'd never have come along today had I known.'

Bronwyn shrugged. 'If your past is going to make as much difference as all that, then maybe we don't want his business. If he's unprofessional enough to allow personal issues into his decision-making processes, then we're better off without him, right?'

'Right.' Amanda wanted to smile but couldn't. No way were they better off without his business. They needed his business no matter what.

'But for what it's worth, I think your presentation was stellar. Whatever history you two do or don't have, it certainly put fuel in your fire. You could have sold me a three-week-old wet newspaper.'

Amanda flushed once more—this time from pleasure rather than mortification. And then the warm feeling subsided. No matter how good she'd been she was sure Jared wouldn't give them the job.

At that moment Jared was staring at the painting hanging in the far corner of his office, for once not getting any sense of calm from the vast landscape it depicted. He tugged off the tie and undid the top button of his shirt.

This was business. He had to make this decision based on what was best for the company. Which was the pitch more likely to work and which was in tune with his vision? And who could he work with closely to get what he wanted?

What he wanted or *who* he wanted?

He frowned and turned away, looking out of the window and down the road where a few minutes ago a taxi had driven off, taking the infuriating Amanda away.

Damn.

Because he'd liked her pitch. He'd liked the idea. And there was a part of him that wanted to give the job to that company because he wanted to see it succeed—not go under, swallowed up by the global advertising giants. He'd stepped in and stopped this juice company from being taken over by a large offshore firm; it was part of what had driven him to work the hours he had and take the risks he had. They'd paid off too, those risks. Now he was contemplating another.

Could he really work with her?

He frowned. Ridiculous. Of course he could. A little lust attack could easily be stamped out. Because no way could he follow through on the idea of a one-night fling with her if they were to be working together. That would be messy and Jared loathed messy. He worked most of the time, he played outdoors some of the time and he scored even less of the time. The three were kept very separate. So what if he wanted her? He'd wanted her before and said no; he could do that again no sweat. Definitely.

The question was, could she work with him? Could she keep *her* professionalism up?

And that, he realised, was what he wanted to know. Could the spoilt princess cope with him giving the orders? His mouth stretched into a smile, slow and wide. How funny for the boot to be on the other foot. Amanda Winchester answering to his call for once.

It shouldn't matter. Jared was not the kind who liked to abuse his power—but in this case, in this unique case, the temptation was irresistible.

CHAPTER FOUR

AMANDA stared, too scared to believe as she, Sean and Danielle listened in on Bronwyn's conversation.

'Yes…yes…certainly…of course.' Bronwyn glanced up and winked, then spun her chair away to look out of the window and control the big grin stretching wide across her face. 'That won't be a problem. Wonderful, Jared.'

Amanda watched as Bronwyn looked at the receiver and then carefully put it down.

'Well?' screeched Sean.

'People—' Bronwyn looked about to burst '—we have ourselves a client.'

'All right!' Sean did a jig. 'Where do I buy? What do I buy? Radio, TV… Are we doing the web too?'

Bronwyn held up her hand and Sean, well trained, fell silent. 'We'll get to that in due course. Our Mr Jared James is one demanding customer and very particular about what he wants. He had a number of requests relating to the pitch, all of which I've agreed to. The first stipulation is that Amanda manages the account—she's responsible for creative content *and* for liaising with the client. Obviously we're here to help you, Amanda. You're not totally alone in this.' Bright-eyed Bronwyn was watching her too closely.

Amanda felt the blood rushing through her body—but none of it was getting to her brain.

'Manage the account?' Deal with Jared? Be responsible for it *all*? But she'd only been in this job a few months—only moved to Auckland when it became clear she needed to earn serious dollars.

'I need you to do this, Amanda. Are you going to be able to?' Bronwyn came round from behind her desk.

'Sure,' Amanda blurted. 'Of course.' She whirled away and went to her own workstation.

Oh, no. Shock and a sudden desperate need for something sweet—an edible distraction—filled her.

They'd got the contract but she was going to have to work with Jared—spend time with Jared. Food—quick!

Because of course this would all be fine if her body didn't go on heat at just the mention of his name. She was melting inside…

Oh, no. She picked up the box of gourmet chocolates and stuffed the first one she grabbed in.

'Hey, Amanda! Hey, stop!' Sean screeched again. 'They're samples for us to build an ad campaign for.'

Amanda, still chewing the first, added a second to the mix. 'Do I look like I care?' She swallowed and immediately stuffed another in. 'I need them *now*.'

'But, Amanda, they cost a *fortune* and—'

'I can buy more,' she snapped as she devoured yet another.

'Well, you could always get your grandfather to buy the company.'

'Jared?' She spun so fast that three of the chocolates flew from the box like renegade bullets.

'I was talking to Bronwyn on my mobile.' Jared casually picked up a chocolate that had landed on Danielle's desk beside him. 'Guess she hadn't had the time to tell you I was here yet.'

'I…' Amanda glanced over his shoulder and saw Bronwyn's face—the anxiety as she mouthed 'sorry'.

'Let's just make it a quick meeting now, shall we? I don't want to take up too much of your valuable time.' He looked at the chocolate in his hand and then sent the box of chocolates an equally ironic glance.

'Um. OK.' Amanda shoved the box behind her and swallowed, certain she was all chocolate teeth.

He stepped closer, still holding the stray truffle. 'Is there somewhere we could go? A meeting room perhaps?'

'Um—' But as she went to answer he put the chocolate in her mouth. Startled, she gaped, chocolate and all.

Laughing, he licked the small bit of melted chocolate from his finger and then shut her mouth with a nudge under her chin. 'I was always good at the clown game at the fair.'

Unable to do anything else in front of their current audience, Amanda chewed—viciously.

'Now I know how to get you to be a little sweeter to me.' The devil glinted in his eyes. 'Lead on, Amanda.'

Ignoring the gaping stares of Danielle and Sean and the sky-high brows of Bronwyn, Amanda stalked round the corner to the small meeting room. She paused outside the door.

His smile was about as trustworthy as a crocodile's. 'After you.'

She walked in, conscious of him shutting the door behind him. Far too conscious of how small the room was, how tall he was, how she still wasn't used to seeing him in a suit—certainly not one as devastating as this. Even more magnificent than the one he had on at the pitch yesterday, this one was black with the thinnest of pinstripes and set off by a deep red tie. She stared at him. Lost, for a long moment, in the sheer infuriating attraction of him.

Then came the pep talk. *Be professional. Ignore the chocolate moment and the way he's looking at you. Just do the job and do it well.*

She took in a deep breath. 'Thank you very much for putting your faith in Synergy. We're looking forward to working on your campaign and making it a successful one.'

'Of course.'

His bored-sounding air unnerved her.

'Are you sure you don't want Bronwyn to join us?' She glanced to the door. 'Not even to take notes?'

'No.' Lazily he walked towards her.

She stepped back.

'Are you afraid of being alone with me?' He kept walking towards her.

In this small meeting room there wasn't anywhere to go. Three more steps in reverse and the backs of her legs were up against something. 'Of course not. I'm not afraid of you.'

He put his hands on her shoulders and pressed down on them. She sat. It was one of the chairs in the row against the wall.

'But I thought I was the big bad wolf.' He sat on the chair next to hers and smiled that smile again.

Crocodile? Snake? Wolf? Whichever, it didn't inspire faith, courage or hope. It inspired…*other* things.

'That was just a joke.' Her voice wavered.

'You know what they say—spark of truth in every one.' He was deliberately baiting her, deliberately sitting too close.

'I can't work with you being like this.' She jumped up.

'Like what?'

'You know what.'

He rose and prowled, positively prowled towards her. 'Technically, you'll be working *for* me.'

Oh, like that helped? She moved to the door but he stopped her with a hand on her arm.

'Come and sit down, Amanda, and stop acting like a spoilt child,' he said softly. 'You need to put aside your personal feelings and get on with the job.'

That got her. Her personal feelings? He was the one hand-feeding her chocolates in front of people and then sitting too close. '*I* have no personal feelings. Not for you.'

'Is that right?' His hand dropped and his face held no memory of a smile. 'Prove it.'

'Pardon?'

He stepped closer. 'Prove there are no personal feelings.'

'H-how—?'

'Kiss me.'

'*What?*'

'You can show me there's no desire.'

'You arrogant—'

'It's that impossible, huh?' His eyes glittered.

She met their intensity with a deep look of her own. The challenge was back and he'd brought it this time. And Amanda couldn't walk away. This wasn't about the contract any more, this was about closing the door on the past. That long-ago night hung between them. It was the first thing she thought of every time she saw him. It was the big old elephant in the room and it needed banishing.

No desire? She wanted to prove it to herself more than anything. Surely that kiss all those years ago hadn't been that spectacular. It had made her sick, hadn't it? But all she knew was that every one since had been lacking in something. Surely now she could shake off the magic memory and move on. He was an over-confident, arrogant jerk.

But there was an insidious warmth unfurling deep inside her belly. A gnawing hunger. Given how her heart raced at the sight of him, how restless her body became in his presence…

She didn't trust herself.

The room was almost humming with the energy emanating from both of them. And yet they stood still—he like the cat waiting to pounce, she like the rabbit in the headlights.

She forced herself to blink.

'All right.' She was a grown woman, in control of her emotions and her destiny, right?

She took the small step to bring her right into his space, tilted her head to be able to see right into his eyes. He was tall, and he wasn't making it any easier for her. Despite her high heels she had to rise right up onto the tips of her toes. This close she could smell him, could see the faint darkening on his jaw, could feel the warmth from his skin.

That feeling deep inside intensified. She tensed every muscle in her body. Keeping her arms close to her sides, her fists clenched, she pressed her firmly closed lips to his for all of a nanosecond.

Faster than the strike of a snake, his hands shot out, grasping her upper arms, keeping her on her tiptoes, her face close to his.

'That wasn't a kiss,' he muttered, mouth barely moving. 'Kiss me properly.'

His head lowered, angled to catch her lips just at the moment she was about to refuse. That was why her lips had parted, wasn't it? To say go to hell.

But as Jared's warm lips sealed to them, her own only softened and parted more. And although his fingers gripped on her arms, his kiss wasn't hard.

Those words were lost. And it wasn't hell she was thinking of any more.

The last time he'd kissed her it had been fierce and ferocious and deliberately punishing. And then it had blown up into an onslaught of raw sensuality—exposing her to a carnal passion that had both overwhelmed and thrilled her.

But now the touch of his lips was light. He brushed his mouth against hers, almost gently teasing, and all she could do was stay right where she was, up on tiptoe, no longer breathing but feeling every tiny movement.

The pressure from his fingers eased; they no longer controlled, but smoothed down her arms instead. He lifted one hand away only to slide it round her waist to the small of her back, pressing her body closer to his. His other hand went lower, running down the length of her arm to encapsulate her fist with his own.

The pressure of his mouth firmed and asked for more. His tongue teased and suddenly she slackened—her lips parted further and immediately he pressed home, intimately stroking the soft inside of her mouth.

Her fingers relaxed, fluttered and his moved, entwining through hers and he lifted her hand, placing it on his shoulder. The fabric was smooth beneath her fingers and she slid her hand higher, searching out the skin at the back of his neck.

She lifted her other hand all by herself. Coasted light fingers over the broad shoulder of his suit jacket and then up, feeling the warmth of him with the sensitive pads of her fingers. She spread her fingers wide and slid them higher into his thick dark hair, holding his head to hers.

His arms tightened, so she was leaning her weight against him and bonelessly she let him. She could feel his hard body down every inch of hers now. Plastered together but it wasn't close enough. Her muscles moved, her body rhythmically surging, seeking to be closer.

She opened further for him, wanting him to invade the rest of her. Her tongue searched out the mystery of him as the kiss went purely carnal and ravenous. He smelt so good and tasted better.

His hand cupped the underside of her breast, his fingers splayed out, spanning her fullness. His thumb stroked, nearer and nearer to the summit and the tight, aching peak. Finally he grazed over it and she groaned, her hips instinctively driving forward faster with the pleasure of it. His other hand spread wide against her bottom, pushing her closer again, and he pressed his thigh between hers. She wasn't wearing stockings, had only thin silk panties on and through the wool of his suit she could feel his thick, hard muscles. She groaned again as the heat of desire washed over her; he stroked her nipple again and rammed his thigh between hers that little bit harder.

He kissed down the side of her neck. She moaned, eager for him to reach her breasts, wanting his mouth on her nipple, wanting him to feast. But he moved so slowly, so deliciously, tormentingly slowly. His hand moved, his thumb stopped that delicious stroking. She pressed harder down on his thigh as he undid the top button on her blouse, and then the next. His mouth caressed the skin he'd exposed. Not much further, another couple of buttons...

'Please...' she panted.

He cupped her breast again, circling around her nipple with his thumb, and then he scraped hard across the tip of it.

She gasped.

'No personal feelings, huh?' He lifted his head, looked at her with a gaze so cool it was like having a bucket of ice water tipped on her.

She jerked her head back, breathing hard as she realised he'd been toying with her. Again.

Anger made her blood run even hotter. Because, damn it, she *wasn't* the only one who'd been getting excited just then.

'Clearly you have them too.' She thrust her hips against his, crudely referring to his hard, thick erection pressing up against her lower belly.

He dropped his hands from her and stepped back so quickly she almost stumbled. 'What red-blooded man wouldn't react when a woman with a body as curvy as yours writhes against him like that?'

Writhes?

Oh, she had, she had. She had an unbearable ache and she'd been moving against him any which way to ease it. Pressing her pelvis against his, riding his thigh over and over and he'd felt so good and she'd felt so hungry…

She put a hand on the back of a chair for support. 'You should be working with Bronwyn on the campaign.'

Storm clouds chased away the last of the glitter in his eyes. 'No, Amanda.'

'But, Jared—'

'This is the thing, the contract is tied to you. Without you I pull the plug and more than likely the agency will go under.'

'What?' Stunned, she couldn't believe her ears.

'It was your idea, wasn't it? The pitch?'

She nodded.

'Then it's your creative talent I want.'

She shook her head—she could work on the ads here at the agency; she didn't need to deal with Jared directly…

'Can you really do it, Amanda?' He spoke harshly. 'Can you put other people first? Or is it still only about what *you* want?'

She opened her mouth but he overrode her.

'Synergy needs this contract to survive, doesn't it? Well, they don't get this contract without you.' His black brows drew together. 'Have you ever really worked hard, Amanda? Because you're about to be worked really, really hard.'

'You think I've never worked hard?' What the hell did he know of her?

'I don't think you've ever had to. I think you use whatever means you have to hand to avoid it.'

'Wow.' Her eyes opened wide. 'What an opinion you have of me.'

'It's not your fault. You were spoilt. You had a grandfather who indulged your every whim. You've never learnt the meaning of the word no.'

'Is that what you think?' My God, he had no idea—hadn't he been the one to teach her? And as a result—being sent away to that awful school… She'd changed—no longer was she the little madam who'd deliberately left her boots caked in mud for him to clean like some servant boy.

'That's what I know,' Jared said flatly. 'He'd do anything for you, Amanda.'

At that comment she turned away. It was a timely reminder. Grandfather had and would *always* do whatever he could for her—even if it hadn't necessarily been the best thing, he had meant well. He had loved her. And now she had to pay him back. It was her turn. But she defended the way things had been.

'There's nothing wrong with doing things for those you love. For wanting to make their path smoother than the one you had.' Grandfather had only wanted to protect her. In his own way he had been making up for the loss of her parents. The loss she'd been too young to really feel—not overtly anyway. And he didn't want her to have to work as hard as he had. Old-fashioned enough to want her to live 'like a lady'—and have all the suitable accomplishments of a lady. To draw, to dance, to play piano, to speak French—to just about be rendered useless.

'You can't be protected or cosseted for ever. Even real princesses have to work hard at what they do.'

Inside she burned at the injustice. But she refused to rise to his bait. Not again. She shut the lid on the seething emotions inside. Offered the one truth she could manage. 'You have no idea how hard I can work, Jared.'

'No? I guess you can prove it to me.' He smiled—that wolf smile. 'I wonder if you'll do it as well as you proved you had no personal feelings for me.'

She trembled—trapped by circumstance into behaving but unable to stop one last bite. 'You know what, Jared? I admit it. I do have personal feelings for you. I hate you.'

For more reasons than he'd ever know.

His smile broadened. 'I know. It's going to be fun, isn't it?'

That wasn't quite the word she had in mind.

He stepped closer, but she stepped a half-inch back, crossing her arms—an ineffectual barrier but it was all there was.

'And what are we going to do about…about…?'

He raised an ironic brow. 'The way you kiss?'

'The way *we* kiss.' It wasn't as if he hadn't kissed her back—if anything he'd led the dance, his hands had crossed the boundaries, his tongue had teased hers out.

'Nothing.' He shrugged. 'I can control it.'

That got her. As if it weren't anything spectacular? Of course it was. She'd done a lot of kissing and that had been in another class. He thought he'd been testing her? Yeah right. He'd been as breathless as her. As hot as her.

'Oh, really?' she asked, pouring on the sarcasm.

He stood stock-still, meeting her fiery gaze with a banked, black one of his own. 'Sure.'

She deliberately let her eyes trail down his body and back up again. He could control it? She turned and literally flounced out. Determined to prove him wrong on *everything*.

CHAPTER FIVE

THE second Amanda got to her desk she picked up the box of chocolates and put the lot in the bin.

'We're having a planning meeting late this afternoon.'

Damn, he'd followed her through, carrying on the conversation as if that kiss had never happened.

'I'm not free this afternoon.' She didn't turn to face him. 'Tomorrow morning will have to do.'

'I'm not in town tomorrow. It'll have to be tonight.'

'But—'

'This is priority work, Amanda.'

Amanda saw the way Sean was sitting unnaturally still at his desk. The way he was staring at her and then at Jared and then back to her—and down, looking at her mouth and then her blouse.

Hell. The top two buttons were still undone—and Amanda's buttons were never undone. That was the problem with Jared—he made her forget all the important things, such as that now she had to be *nice* to him.

'Where and what time?' she turned and asked him sweetly.

He grinned, knowing how much she was hating having to change her attitude. 'I'll pick you up from here at six.'

'No,' Amanda said hurriedly. She did *not* want to meet

him in the evening. 'I can come to your office at four. Would that suit?'

'I thought you were busy.'

'I can squeeze you in.'

His eyes met hers for a pregnant moment and she felt heat flood into her cheeks—had she really said that? Was he really thinking of what she was suddenly thinking of?

'That would be perfect,' he purred and with a wave to the others was gone as silently as he'd arrived.

Bronwyn looked worried. 'Are you sure you can handle this, Amanda? I mean, things look a little—'

'I know.' Amanda raced into damage-control mode. 'Jared likes to tease. But I can handle him.' She'd learn to handle herself around him. She looked around at the other two and realised just how much they were counting on her. Not to mention Grandfather. She straightened. 'I can handle the account, Bronwyn. I won't let you down.'

No getting close. No proving anything. Not until this job was out of the way and the money was in the bank.

Jared breathed the fresh cold air, opting to go for a walk rather than get in his car and go straight back to his office. What the hell had he been thinking? He hadn't, of course— the minute he'd got her into a room alone he'd been unable to stop pouncing. Hand on heart he hadn't intended to touch her. But hand on heart he couldn't resist. He walked faster as his body threatened to react awkwardly to the memory of that kiss.

She was the hottest woman he'd known. But she was also destined to be his forbidden fruit. He'd set up a business situation; following through on that heated encounter wasn't possible when they were going to be working together. So stupid—he should have stayed away.

Almost ten years ago he could have had her but honour and duty to another had forced him to refuse. Now, it was his own integrity and he would stay in control of it.

But despite that, and despite knowing all about her spoilt streak, he still wanted.

Amanda got to his office two minutes before she said she would. The receptionist told her to go straight up. His office was nice, large, but not ridiculously so, and very informal. She turned her back on the sofa, opted for a chair at the round table in the corner. For the first few moments she felt awkward, but it was as if the morning had never happened. He kept his distance, barely looked at her, as he showed her the previous campaigns and pointed out what he liked and didn't like about them.

She relaxed. Focusing on the work, she started to hit her stride, making notes, making points, asking questions.

'Let's get something to eat.' His suggestion came out of the blue.

She glanced out of the window—when had it got dark? What time was it? After six already? How had that happened?

'Aren't we done for the day?' She had copious pages of notes.

'No,' he answered uncompromisingly. 'I'm away tomorrow and I want you to be able to get on with this asap. I want to meet on Monday and you can show me what you've come up with.'

Monday?

'So let's go to a restaurant and keep going.' He sat back in his chair, looking at her rather than at the papers spread between them.

'But—'

'Think of it as killing two birds with one stone. You need

to work to be able to eat, right? Tonight you can do both. Besides—' he suddenly had that smile on '—a restaurant is nice and bright and public.'

She made herself look away from him, looked around her instead. The office was very quiet and the darkness closing in on them through the window made the scene more intimate. She was drawn back to him again—meeting his eyes...

'OK.' It was a no-brainer.

He drove, his car even more luxurious than she'd imagined it would be when at the airport bus stop on Sunday night, with its spacious seating, the stretch-right-out leg room, gleaming interior and purring power under the bonnet.

Those years ago in Ashburton he'd had no car—had either hitched a ride or worst case, ridden a rusty old mountain bike. Back then Amanda had ridden in her grand-father's Daimler, seated in the back seat like Lady Muck. It was Amanda who had no car now.

'Any preference—Italian? Thai?'

She shook her head, realising she no longer felt that hungry.

He pulled into a park and walked her half a block up the street—giving her a sidelong look. 'They do a really good chocolate fondant here.'

'What makes you think I'd like that?' she asked tartly.

He laughed and reluctantly so did she. OK, maybe she could do with a little sweetening. The warmth of the res-taurant came out of the open door to meet them. The maître d' smiled at Jared and led them straight to a table in a quiet corner.

Amanda narrowed her eyes—had he booked this? When? It was obvious the two men knew each other, and

Jared was clearly used to such quick service. Quite the successful man, wasn't he?

She shouldn't be surprised. He'd worked so hard back then, of course he'd have continued that habit. No doubt he deserved every inch of his obvious success. But somehow it grated. Especially in light of her own failures. While he'd gone up in the world, she'd tumbled down. But she'd never worked like him, never had to—not 'til now. Maybe there was a kind of justice to it? But it wasn't fancy things she wanted—in truth she'd never really wanted them. Right now she'd give up all the riches in the world to have her grandfather healthy again.

She watched Jared sit back in his fine tailored suit, noting the ease with which he spoke to the waiting staff— so at home in a scene of such wealth and sophistication.

He'd be even more irresistible to women now, wouldn't he? What with serious money as well as those superb looks and that sizzling attitude. They'd be falling over themselves to land him. And he'd be happy to make the most of it. Always he'd have the pick of the most beautiful women around.

Amanda glared at the menu card.

'Shall I order the dessert right away?' Jared was grinning at her.

'I think I can hold off.' She winced as she realised this was one of those places that was so expensive it didn't detail the prices. 'What else is good?'

'The veal.' He didn't need to look at the menu to know the dish.

'OK.' She didn't want to take responsibility for deciding how many millions this meal was going to cost.

'I'll have it too.' He added a bottle of wine to the order and a bottle of his own company's juice.

Amanda looked everywhere but at him in the interven-
ing moments. Sure it was bright and public, but they were
in a darker corner near the back and there was something
dangerously intimate about a small table set for two. What
a fool she was for agreeing to this.

Once upon a time they'd been from opposite sides of the
tracks. Now those positions had been reversed. Jared was
the one issuing the orders, Jared was the one in control of
her career—and he was enjoying it, wasn't he?

Payback time. But what she didn't know was why—and
he didn't know the possible ramifications. She wasn't
going to tell him. Wasn't going to play the pity card—he
never had. All she could do was what he had—work hard—
maybe that would make him accept her competence.

'It'll be fine,' Jared assured the waiter when he came
with the wine. 'I'll pour.'

The waiter left immediately and Jared filled her glass.
She lifted it, but paused when she saw him put the bottle
back on the table.

'You're not having any?'

'I don't drink.'

'Is that because of your dad?' she asked straight out.

There was a momentary tightness to his mouth but then
he answered. 'I like to have all my wits about me.' He lifted
his gaze and the irony gleamed at her. 'But you go right
ahead and relax.'

He'd avoided the reference to his father. It had made him
uncomfortable—perhaps even a little angry? But Jared
couldn't constantly dig about her antecedents and not let her
do the same. The fact was they knew a lot about each
other—most of which each preferred the other would forget.

How many of his employees knew he'd gone without
breakfast every day of his teens? That the teacher at school

had given him a bag with an apple and sandwich on the sly and that he'd cleaned her car on weekends as payment? How many knew that James wasn't his surname but his middle name—that he'd rejected his father's name as soon as he could. She knew. And Jared knew she knew. And she was sure he hated it.

Was that the cause of the friction between them? The reminders of what they'd once been? Was his judgment of her grounded in that old imbalance—when she'd had everything and he'd had nothing? She could understand it— because with the turning of the tables, she was coming close to resenting him now.

She looked at the deep red liquid in her glass. 'I'm not having a whole bottle of wine all to myself.'

'No?' Jared's grin became positively evil and he toyed with his cutlery. 'Maybe you'd like something stronger later—brandy perhaps?'

She'd had brandy just once in her life. And she would never, ever have it again. The scent of it turned her stomach. She fiddled with her wine glass. He was deliberately taunting her, reminding her. It wasn't the first time he'd referred to their past encounter and the only way she could think of to stop the unsubtle comments was to take him full on. He thought he was embarrassing her? He was, but she could never be as embarrassed and humiliated as she'd been that night. Did he even know what had happened afterwards?

'It took him a long time to cool down.'

His eyes sharpened. 'Your grandfather?'

She nodded. 'Why did you do it?' Why had he betrayed her so completely?

'You were so young. And you were hell-bent on making the biggest mistake of your life.' His fingers ran over the blade of his knife. 'Did you really think I'd take advantage of you like that?'

He was only a couple of years older than her. It wasn't as if it were a couple of decades. 'I was sixteen.'

'In some countries that would be illegal.'

'And in others we could have been married for two years already.'

He snorted. 'You were too young.'

'It wasn't obvious you were going to be such a puritan.' Had he any idea of the rumours that used to float around about him? About his success and prowess as a lover? Was it any wonder she'd believed that her risqué stunt would be just the thing to turn his head towards her?

'Let you down, didn't I, honey?' He laughed but it wasn't a warm sound. 'Wasn't all the rough rebel you wanted.'

He'd left her in all her glory—a silk and lace negligee on her grandfather's front doorstep. He'd rung the bell so loudly that both Polly the housekeeper and Grandfather had come running. She'd been wickedly angry with him. But not as angry as he'd been with her. Her wrist had been bruised for days from the force with which he'd dragged her out of his car and up to the door. But that wasn't 'til after…he'd taught her the lesson in his own style.

'He did exactly what you suggested.'

'What was that?'

How could he not remember? 'Locked me up 'til I was old enough to know better.'

'Did he?'

'Eastern Bay School for Girls.'

'How awful for you,' he mocked. 'A veritable prison, I imagine.'

'In its own way, absolutely.' Two years in the most hellish boarding school, not even on her home island, and full of the snobbiest, cattiest girls ever to have been born. Add to that a bunch of prison wardens impersonating teachers and the whole place was set for a right old party—*not*.

'And did it work?'

'Save me from myself, you mean?'

His gaze intensified.

She deliberately lowered hers and allowed a smile to touch her lips. Mona Lisa all the way.

The silence was long.

'Why did you do it?' His voice sounded rusty.

Their eyes met full on once more. She looked away first. She picked up the wine and took a small sip. 'I guess I *was* young. At the mercy of hormones or something.'

'And you're still at the mercy of hormones?'

She looked back to him—instantly fell into the velvety darkness.

'You still want me, Amanda.'

She forced herself to reply. 'You're an attractive man.' Only a little bit of a wobble. 'But I'm older now. You don't need to worry. I won't be hunting you down again.'

'I won't find you waiting in my bed for me late one night?'

'My body might still find yours attractive, Jared,' she said, fighting for breath, 'but I wouldn't sleep with you if you were the last man alive.'

'Oh, really?'

She froze at the way he'd so coolly mimicked her words of this morning. Knowing damn well he had as much right to sound sarcastic as she had then. 'You ruined everything.'

'Did I? By not giving the spoilt princess her way? Were you not indulged for a while? I bet it didn't take you that long to wind him round your little finger again.'

She calmed herself with a count to ten. 'Like I said, it

took a long time for him to cool down.' And now he was in trouble. She had to keep that and only that at the fore-front of her brain. She couldn't let this haze of desire cloud her judgment and ruin everything—not again. 'Look, Jared. We're grown-ups now. Let's laugh about it and move on. We have to work together and that's the extent of our relationship. Professional, agreed?'

'If you think you can manage it.'

That was it for her. She'd tried to parry him, she'd tried to be open, she'd tried to reason. No more. She stood.

His hand shot out and gripped her wrist. 'Stay,' he said. 'I'm sorry. I promise I won't refer to it again. We'll leave that night behind.'

She hesitated, thought of Grandfather and Bronwyn and the others. Finally sat.

'Thank you.'

He still held her—his hand completely encircling her wrist, his fingers resting on her pulse point. There was no way he couldn't feel its wild beating. She stared at his bronze skin, but was somehow frozen, unable to pull away.

The waiter appeared with two plates that looked more like art than food—breaking the still moment. And as Jared lifted his hand she pretended she didn't miss the weight of it. She picked up her fork and pushed the food around to mess it up a bit.

'Is it no good?' In what felt like a minute, he'd nearly eaten all his.

'No, it's lovely. I'm not hugely hungry, that's all.'

'I guess my teasing you isn't helping.'

'Not really.'

'How is your grandfather?'

'He's OK,' Amanda answered cautiously. 'Much older of course.'

'But still going strong?' Jared asked. 'He was always a busy man.'

'Yes,' Amanda said. Physically he was OK, his body still pretty healthy for a man in his eightieth year although he'd lost weight recently. But that was all that seemed to be working well—the body. The brain? Not so good. But she wasn't going to share. Grandfather had a right to privacy and she didn't want to open up her heartache to Jared of all people. She turned the conversation on him.

'Why juice? Why this company?'

He grinned. 'I worked there when I first left Ashburton.'

'Really?'

He nodded. 'I got a scholarship to university—double degree in maths and commerce. But I still needed to work.'

Amanda nodded, not surprised at his subject choices. She remembered Grandfather once saying that Jared had the best maths brain he'd ever encountered.

'It was a good job—started early so it fitted in with my studies.' He shrugged. 'And I like juice.'

'So have you been working there all this time?'

'No.' He laughed outright at that. 'After I got the degrees I went overseas. Hong Kong.' He anticipated her question. 'I made money trading foreign exchange.'

Banking—sort of stuff Grandfather had been into. And she knew mega money could be made and lost. She also knew the young guys in the investment firms had some serious party lifestyles too. 'Why did you come back?'

'I hated it.'

That surprised her. 'Why?'

'It was so false. A bunch of suits all gathered round computers watching electronic money grow. I wanted a real job that I could get my hands into. And I hated the lifestyle. But it was a means to an end. I made the money I needed to get the property I wanted and be able to buy the company I wanted.'

'Juice.'

'It's a good little company.' He sounded a tad defensive.

She smiled. It wasn't that little and she sensed Jared had ambitions to take it further—this rebranding was just the beginning. He talked a little more about his time trading. She sensed he was making an effort as much as she. But the cynical gleam was still there. It wouldn't take much to bring the big bad wolf back.

'Are you having the dessert?' he eventually asked.

She shook her head. 'I need to get going.'

'I'll give you a ride.'

'I can get a taxi,' she said coolly.

'I'll give you a ride,' he repeated.

She could feel him bending her to his will, wanted to fight against it but knew he wanted her to just so he could win. She sighed. Hadn't she said they were grown-ups? And purely professionals working together? 'That would be lovely, thank you.'

She didn't speak in the car other than to give directions. He glanced her way more than once. 'Tired?'

'I have a lot to think about.'

She slipped out of the car as soon as he'd pulled over where she told him to. Said she'd have everything prepared for when he got back. Waved goodbye and walked away. Fast.

She did have a lot to think about—a lot of work. But it wasn't ad campaigns or marketing slogans that looped round her brain all through the wee small hours. It was a frame-by-frame replay of that one night. Over and over. When her world had come crashing down.

It had been one of the hottest nights of the summer and she was on holiday. She loved the holidays. It meant Jared was there almost every day—working for her grandfather—as a filing clerk in at the bank, in the office at home, in the fields on the farm. She'd sit at the window and watch.

She knew the deal. She had girlfriends, she lived on a farm for goodness' sake so she knew the facts of life. But the fact was she was turning sweet sixteen and she'd never been kissed. Being Amanda she wanted more than that and there was only one man she wanted it from.

For over two years she'd had a crush on Jared. Tall, enigmatic, sexy-as-hell Jared who never even looked at her. The odd occasion he had it was as if he looked right through her. Well, she'd hatched a plan—one that wouldn't fail.

She'd got the lingerie from the department store while on a trip to the city one day. Had hidden it in her room for her special night. Where had she got the audacity?

Oh, yes, that was right, Grandfather's brandy.

While she'd celebrated her sixteenth birthday with her friends on the nearest Saturday, on the actual night she had her own special present planned. Jared lived in a one-room cottage a couple of kilometres down the road. She put her raincoat on over the top of her negligee and ran. Fast on her feet—she'd been the sprints champion at school. He wasn't home. She'd known he wouldn't be. He'd been working late on something for Bill, Grandfather's best mate.

She remembered hearing his step on the old wooden deck. And the nervous rush of excitement that had flooded her. He'd seen her immediately. Hard not to when she was perched up in the middle of his bed. The door had slammed behind him but the bang was nothing on the bark of his voice.

'What are you doing?'

'It's my birthday.'

'And?' He didn't take a step nearer. 'Exactly what do you think you want from me?'

'I want…' She hadn't imagined it would go like this. What on earth *had* she imagined? Talking hadn't really come into the fantasy.

'You want what?' He sounded icier than she'd ever thought a person could. 'Come on, you're here now. Spit it out.'

'I…' She couldn't do it.

He couldn't even see the funny side. Surely he could have laughed about it. But he was angrier than she'd ever seen a person be.

'I want you to get the *hell* out of my bed.'

Misery and humiliation were boiled up with defiance as she slowly stepped onto the cold wooden floor, trying to keep the slip from riding up her thighs as she moved. The wind was blowing the mercury even higher but she was freezing, wearing nothing but her black lace negligee that barely made it quarter of the way to her knees. He stood and stared, like a block of stone. Finally he moved, only to open the door and wait for her to pass through.

'Forget it.' She masked her mortification with sixteen-year-old attitude.

She brushed past him, head high, but as she stepped out onto the deck his hand shot out and grabbed her wrist.

'Do you even know what it is you're asking for?'

'Yes.' She tossed her head and flung the answer at him. 'But don't worry, I can find myself a real man. One who isn't intimidated by a woman who knows what she wants.'

'A woman? Is that what you are?'

'Obviously one that you can't handle.'

He'd moved then all right. Pulling hard on her wrist so she'd stumbled and fallen against him. His body had been rock and his mouth had come down so hard on hers it had made her eyes water. She'd felt smothered. She'd gasped and struggled and suddenly the quality of the kiss had changed. His arms had still been like bands holding her tight and close but his mouth had moved more gently—just a fraction, just enough. She'd frozen, just feeling and then the warmth had started—trickling, then all of a sudden flooding through her body. She'd softened, pressing herself against him, and somehow his body had grown even harder and he'd hauled hers even closer. His hands had roved then, sweeping down her back, around her waist. And she'd kissed him back, her tongue meeting his and exploring further—tasting him, breathing in the sharp male scent of him, shaking as it had overwhelmed her. She'd been flying, yearning, instinctively moving, aching for something more.

He'd let her go so suddenly—shoved her from him—and she'd swayed on her feet. Her mind whirling, her stomach swirling. And suddenly she'd been so cold and dizzy and terrified. She'd gone to say something, she never knew what because instead she'd turned and heaved out all of Grandfather's reeking brandy all over his deck.

He had sworn long and loud and so furiously. She'd never heard such a crude compilation of taboo words and phrases—never had since.

She could hardly blame him.

He'd handed her a tissue to wipe her mouth and taken her arm again—none too gently. He'd locked her into his ute and gunned his foot to the ground, breaking the speed limit all the five minutes back to her home, leaving her to face the wrath of her understandably irate guardian.

But nothing her grandfather said or did had hurt as much as the way Jared had looked at her—it had felt like a kind of hate and she could never forgive him for it.

CHAPTER SIX

'I'M BACK and want you to spend the morning with me.'

'And I'd do that because…?' Jared was back early. Blast.

'In order for you to design the best ad campaign you need to understand my business from the inside out.'

'I already have all the information I need to be able to produce the best ad campaign for you.' She was hard at work on it now and she needed all day to get it right before their meeting on Monday.

'You don't have hands-on experience.'

'You're promising me hands-on experience?' She couldn't help rising to the innuendo.

There was a micro pause. 'All the hands on you want, sweetheart.'

'Well, thanks all the same, Jared, but I think I have it under control.' She sure hoped she did—herself that was.

'Well, you know I am the client and what the client says goes. I want you to see the factory up and running and so I'll meet you in Reception at nine-thirty.'

He'd hung up before she could get another word in. Hands-on experience? In less than twenty minutes?

She took a deep breath. So far she'd had two days to prepare for this moment. Not just two days but three whole nights as well—but then she'd barely slept a wink of any of them, too busy thinking and then when she had fallen asleep she'd had to make herself wake. Because when she slept, he was with her…and *those* dreams were not allowed. And suddenly two days and three nights didn't feel like nearly enough.

Maybe it was because of the lack of sleep that she felt the need to check her hair was tied neatly and her lips thoroughly coated in pale pink lip gloss.

And surely global warming was to blame for her surge in body temperature when she saw him waiting for her dressed in black jeans and black shirt and intense gaze. For a moment there was the flame in his face too—as he looked over her latest skirt and blouse combo—but it was quickly snuffed.

Professional.

He led her out past Reception and into what looked suspiciously like the tea room.

'OK, so this is a juicer.' He pointed to the bench.

She glanced over to where a bunch of about five young workers were sitting at a table with a pack of cards shared out in hands. Oh, yes, definitely the tea room.

'Yes, I think I've seen one of those before,' she said, turning her attention to the stainless-steel manual press that shone like a mirror. 'Don't tell me you have these poor guys juicing oranges half by half on just one of these?'

There was a collective snigger from the boys behind them.

Jared simply smirked and picked up an orange from the basket on the bench. He halved it swiftly with the sharp knife lying on the wooden board and put one of the halves on the juicer. Then he reached for one of the glasses stacked on the other side of the machine.

She tried really hard not to notice the flexing muscles

in his forearms as he pushed the lever down and the glass filled with the bright liquid.

'Everyone should start the day with a little vitamin C.'

He took out the spent half and put the other piece of orange in. 'Your turn.'

It was a little harder than she expected but at least she didn't splatter juice on her shirt.

He picked up the full glass and held it out to her. Truth be told pure orange was too acidic for her liking. But, with him watching her like that, no way was she declining the challenge.

She took the smallest of sips, aware of his overly intense scrutiny. She licked her lips, the taste making her shiver.

He took the glass off her, shaking his head. 'You don't deserve it.' He drained it and placed it on the bench. 'Come on.'

They walked—but out of the factory rather than through it.

'Why am I here?'

'You're getting to know the client better.'

By walking through his car park? It was a complete sham. She knew it. He knew it.

'Maybe I'll get to better the client?' she said coolly, showing her claws. She couldn't stop the slight flirt—the need to make him strike.

'Is that what you think you can do?' An instant response. With a lower tone, he stepped closer.

Oh, it was too, too easy to go over the mark with him.

She tried to step back. 'Well, aren't you trying to put me off balance?'

He followed—even closer. 'You think?' And what of it? His tone was all insolence.

'Why?'

He turned and pulled her around the corner of the building and right into his arms, his hands around her waist, holding her to him. There was the instant flare but she pushed her hands on his chest, a small barrier blocking her breasts from contact with him—too much, that would be too much.

His gaze had dropped to her mouth; she was trying so hard not to move it, to part or worse still lick her lips—dry and desperate though they felt. He wanted to kiss her, she wanted it too—her attention dropping to his mouth as it curved once more into that wolfish smile that was so tempting.

'Does anything dirty ever come out of your mouth, Amanda?'

'Pardon?'

'Anything dirty. Hot, frisky, carnal, naughty.' The look in his eyes was downright dangerous. 'Do you ask for it how you want it? I'm thinking it must be there. That wilful teenager didn't disappear into thin air at some posh boarding school. She's still there. Still wanton. Still wild as anything.'

She gaped, then tried to hide how his words were affecting her. 'You are so out of line.'

He ignored her words, cocked his head as he studied her expression instead. 'Do you have some great secret life?'

'What do you mean?'

'A lover hidden away somewhere? A series of lovers?'

'*What?*'

''Cos the thing is, you look and act like an ice princess.'

'You mean you think I'm frigid.' It wouldn't be the first time someone had said that—when her kissing quests ended with her rejecting the sample.

He tilted his head side to side, as if he was weighing it up. 'Yeah. OK. Frigid.' His chest moved beneath her fingers as if he was laughing inside. 'That's exactly what you look like. But I know different, don't I? I know exactly how hot for it you really are.'

'Go to hell.'

'You forget, sweetheart, hell was my home.' Through his cotton shirt she could feel his warmth—burning. 'Be careful or I might take you back there with me.'

'Let go of me.' But she was forced to move her arms as he crushed her closer, sliding her hands to push against his biceps—but his muscles were hard and now her breasts were flattened against the equally solid wall of his chest. She daren't breathe.

He just tightened his grip and moved one hand to her waist, then higher, his thumb burrowing between them. 'Ask me nicely.'

That thumb teased her taut nipple.

She shuddered. 'You're an arrogant bully.' But she was breathless.

'Yeah,' he admitted. 'With you I am. Because you're a spoilt princess too used to getting anything she wants.'

'I really don't like you.'

'And I don't much like you either. But the fact is we're meant to end up in bed together.' He growled, pressing her pelvis harder into his to prove the point.

'It's not going to happen.' She didn't know who she was telling—him or her own wayward body.

'Do you honestly think you could refuse?'

'You really are arrogant.'

'But, Amanda—' his eyes locked onto hers '—I have every reason to be.'

She couldn't handle him. Her hand itched with the desire to slap it across his cheek. Never had the thought of physical violence been so tempting. But there was another fantasy even more satisfying—even more shocking. She'd have him beneath her—have him out of control. And she would do everything she'd dreamed of to him—until *he* was the one begging her, until *he* was the one shuddering in desperation for *her* touch.

Bad to the bone was how Jared James made her want to be. But unless he was up front about how much he wanted her, in the same way he was asking her to be, then 'no' was going to be her answer. 'No' *had* to be her answer—she couldn't afford to stuff this up. It took all her concentration to regulate her breathing, to cool her response, desperate to find a way to push him back before she betrayed herself completely and begged for him to touch her more.

'Is this you "controlling it", Jared?' Sounding as frigid as an icicle.

For a second it froze him and she took the chance to push free of his arms.

She tossed her head and met his stormy expression with far more calm than she was feeling. 'Now are you going to show me the factory or not?'

Jared stared into her eyes, watching the clouds thicken in them, feeling her body cool and grow taut even though she now stood the best part of a metre away. The last sliver of his humour vanished and the silence grew.

The weird thing was he'd been so sure he could control it—hadn't he been the one to say no before? Yet now the effort was tearing him apart and she was the one holding fast. It made him all the more determined.

He wanted to hear her say how much she wanted him. He wanted to blast through that icy outer layer and find that passion.

He was a sexual being, well used to being wanted by

women. But he wanted to hear Amanda admit it. Since when was he so needy? He knew already, didn't he? He could see all the signs of arousal in her body. But it wasn't enough.

The hunger infuriated him.

He spent a gruff hour showing her the factory, ignoring the sidelong glances and obvious speculation of his employees—personal tours weren't something he ever did.

Back in Reception she looked no higher than his chin as she spoke. 'Thank you very much—'

'Cut the crap.' He couldn't stand her finishing-school politeness a minute longer—not when he wanted the real, raw response he knew was bubbling beneath her poised exterior. 'I'll see you Monday.'

She worked almost every minute of the weekend, and every second of it she thought of Jared. Could feel his fingers skimming her skin, could catch his scent in the air, could hear his low murmur in her ear—his audacity, his blatant sexual references. They'd end up in bed together, huh?

Hell would freeze over first.

But as much as she wanted it—to have him, to get it over so she could get over it—she couldn't. On Sunday night she spent the early hours tossing and turning before giving up entirely. She was trapped, wanting him beyond desperation but unable to have him—she had to keep control of this job. She had to do a *good* job.

Anxiety stifled her appetite. Nerves made her knees knock. Sexual frustration fogged her rationale. She was held together by the thinnest of threads and it was already fraying in the taxi on the way to meet him.

His suit was the first thing she noticed. The second was his utter lack of smile and that last little thread inside her snapped.

The first thing he criticised was the colour scheme. Then it was the 'f' on the new logo. Then it was something that she didn't even hear.

She tried to nod. Tried to smile. Tried to handle it. Managing the whole thing on her own had been hard enough, but managing her wayward hormones when it came to Jared was just impossible.

'OK, I get it,' she interrupted him mid-critique. 'Nothing about it is right.'

'What?'

'Nothing I do will be right for you.' Standing, she shook her head and shuffled the papers together haphazardly.

'This isn't about you, Amanda. Don't take it personally.'

'It is personal,' she snapped. 'Admit it, Jared. You're determined to think the worst of me. You're just going to rip apart anything I do for you no matter how good it actually is. And you're never going to take me seriously, are you? I'm just one big joke to you. Someone to wind up for your own amusement. You don't even want my work, do you?'

Black eyes stared at her. 'Amanda, this is the first pass at this. We'll take what you've done and refine it.'

But she'd lost it. 'What is this? Some sort of torment? Some warped kind of retribution for my supposed good fortune at birth? Because you once had to clean my boots? Now you're going to make me suffer? Well, I get it, Jared. Nothing I do will ever be good enough for you. *I'll* never be good enough for you. So I quit.'

'*You'll* never be good enough for *me*?' Incredulity flew across his features. 'What the hell kind of rubbish is that?'

'It's true,' she stormed at him, unfettered emotion to the fore. 'You don't want anything I do and you don't want me!'

Shock and then a wild anger crossed his face. An anger

she'd seen once before. In a flash she knew what was coming and adrenalin roared through her blood.

She'd roused the wolf.

Her angry body resisted his for all of two seconds. Then she wriggled her arms up around his neck and kissed him back just as hard. At this kiss, there was no more thought. Only touch and sense and need. Control, now unleashed, had no hope of being recaptured.

Jared ran his hands down her body. Touching her the way he'd been thinking about for too long. And because he'd been thinking about it too long, all hell broke loose when he actually did it—every muscle escaped his brain's command, every cell strained to get closer to her.

She gasped beneath his onslaught, her hands moving as fast and hard on him as his did on her. Pulling closer, yanking at buttons. She was so responsive, with his every touch she trembled. It made him want to touch more and more. But it was no slow exploration. He ran his palms up her thighs, straight under her skirt, gliding over the smooth warm silk of her skin. She adjusted her stance, widening it, and he knew there was no resistance, only equal need surging. He pulled down on the elastic. Once he got her knickers as far as her knees she lifted her feet, wriggling so she stepped out of them. His fingers sought that sweet contact.

Her lips broke from his at just the slightest brush; her moan was his undoing. Looking down at the expression on her face, he could wait no longer. He was so full of energy it was as if she weighed nothing as he scooped her up and took the three strides to the sofa. So easy to lie her down and then be there with her. The relief of feeling her beneath him was equally tormenting because he needed to be closer. Their lips connected, reconnected. Hungrily kissing—deeper, harder, longer. Her arms clung tight around his neck, her hand pulling his head to hers, clutching tufts of his hair. He wriggled a hand between them to pull up her skirt at the front. She was panting between his kisses. He fumbled with his belt, not wanting to lift himself that half-inch away to be able to slide the zip down and yet frantic to get the fabric out of the way. It was only a second but it was too long. He couldn't wait any more. From the sounds of her breathless yeses neither could she. Finally, finally, he snatched a quick breath and with one powerful movement thrust home.

He felt her instant recoil but he was too big, too heavy, and in too deep for her to escape. She was rigid beneath him. Unbearably tight. Every muscle locked hard. And her cry…her cry had not been the sound of pleasure he'd expected.

Shocked, he stared at her. Not wanting to believe her reaction—it had to mean…to mean…oh, hell, no.

'Amanda.' Harsh, guttural—he scarcely recognised his own voice.

Her eyes flashed open. He saw the sheen of liquid magnifying their bright colour—the pain in their depths. She breathed out—a hard burst of air and the rasp as she gasped more air in.

He was as tense as her, braced on his arms, about to lift away from her. But her hands clutched him, her fingers curling hard into his butt, her body not releasing his.

'Make it good,' she whispered on another rush of air. 'Please make it good.'

Frozen, he stared at her, brain working hard to compute this nightmare, his body winding harder. Wanting so badly but devastated at the same time.

It was too late. There was no undoing what he'd just

done. He closed his eyes, grasping hard for control. He had to retrieve this situation—to redeem both himself and her. And the only thing he could think to do was to make it better—to do as she'd asked and make it good.

Every muscle in his body begged for him to move. But he kept as still as still. Carefully he lowered his head, kissed her eyes closed so he couldn't see into her soul and feel the guilt pour in. When he reached her mouth he felt the way she was gingerly keen to kiss him back. He slowed everything. Light, butterfly kisses, starting again, slow and sweet and gentle. Until it was her mouth that parted further, her tongue that sought out his. Gradually he felt her body relax, then he felt it soften and slowly, so slowly absorb his more.

When he felt her hands slide over his back he choked. Kissed her again, more tenderly than he'd ever treated anyone. Only then did he dare move just that little bit. A small rocking movement—a fraction deeper before sliding back. There was no instant tension in her this time and slowly he repeated the action.

Her mouth parted and sought his kiss again—he could feel her hunger building. He slipped his hand beneath her bottom, pulled her closer towards him, lifting her leg over his to widen her position and enable her to move.

'Meet me,' he muttered, moving her hips in time with his, showing her—once, twice, and then she took over, adjusting, rising higher, arching up as she understood and experimented with their sensual dance.

Slow. He kept it slow, drawing out and then pressing close again so she felt every inch as her body accepted and embraced his.

He swept his hand up the side of her torso, brushing aside her blouse and bra so he could return to her breast.

Knowing she was sensitive there, determined to bring pleasure back to her.

Her breathing had stepped up; he kept the rhythm the same but deepened the movement. Kissing her breasts, caressing them with fingers and tongue while matching the deep rhythm of their joining. And then he slipped his hand low, moving to touch her most sensitive spot directly.

Her body was rigid beneath his again but it was different this time. Her breathing was fast and shallow, small moans becoming louder and her fingers curled hard into his shoulders.

'Jared.'

'Yes.' He kept moving, slow, deliberate, intense. Focused entirely on her, keeping the rhythm the same as nearer and nearer she got. So close, so close it needed only one more…

Her eyes screwed shut and she shook and this time when his name left her lips it was in a high cry that slammed satisfaction into him.

His own body burned, blood bubbling, and every muscle screamed with the effort of restraint. Too long. He'd held back too long.

As her cry ended he lost control. Thrusting hard and deep and fierce and fast, gathering her to him, not caring that the buttons on his shirt were digging into his chest or that the cotton was sticking to his back like a second skin. He just had to get closer, closer, closer.

CHAPTER SEVEN

AMANDA lay burrowed deep into the soft leather sofa, crushed by Jared's weight, blown away by what had just happened. So good. So much better than incredibly good. Her body was warm, her cells still singing, and for one blissful moment she felt utterly ecstatic and sublimely relaxed.

But then thought started to return. And all she wanted was a kiss—some sort of seal, an acknowledgement of how intensely together they'd been.

But there was no reassuring touch, no word, definitely no kiss.

Instead she felt his muscles tense and she braced herself for the unknown—*his* reaction. He didn't look at her as he lifted away. Nor did he speak. The silence was louder than the way she'd screamed his name as she'd come.

He turned his back and pulled his trousers up, redid the four or so buttons that had come undone on his shirt. He pulled it away from where it clung to his back. In less than a minute he was back to the businessman. The only giveaway that anything remotely 'unprofessional' had occurred was the way his breathing jerked, the sweat on his brow and the red stains across his cheekbones.

Flushed with the remnants of desire or blazing anger?

Amanda pulled the cups of her bra back over her breasts and clumsily worked a couple of blouse buttons. They'd both been basically fully clothed, and yet had been so intimate—so shockingly, wonderfully intimate.

Finally he looked at her. 'You should have told me.' His eyes burned.

So it was anger.

'There wasn't really time,' she croaked.

'There's always time.'

But he would have stopped. And she hadn't wanted him to stop.

His lips thinned and he turned away again. 'That never should have happened.' He jammed his fists into his pockets. 'How badly did I hurt you?'

She sat up, awkwardly pulled the front of her skirt down and did up the last button on her blouse. She had no idea where her knickers were. Didn't want to know, just felt the imperative need to get out of there as soon as possible because he was so clearly unhappy with her.

'I'm OK.' She almost couldn't believe it had happened. Would have thought it a dream except for the burning between her legs and the residual warmth in her muscles.

'Bullshit. That was unrestrained. Too fast.' He spun to face her. 'It could have been a lot better for you. It should have been.'

'Sleep with a lot of virgins, do you?'

'You're the first. But I know a woman needs to be ready. You weren't ready.'

He swore then. Almost as bad as that night of her birthday.

Sitting on the sofa, she squeezed her eyes shut. Not wanting to cope with the anger she could hear. Past and present merged for a moment, making her feel sick.

'Sorry to sully your ears, sweetheart, but you…you…'

He was pointing at her with his finger like some authoritarian figure from Victorian years. Then she noticed that the finger was shaking slightly.

'Don't think yourself a villain, Jared.' She stood, emboldened by that faint sign of emotion other than anger in him. 'I was willing.' She attempted a laugh. 'I finally got what I wanted.'

'Why are you crying, then, if it was what you wanted?'

'I'm not crying.'

'Then what are these?'

Surprisingly gentle fingers moved fast, wiping under her eyes, then he pressed them to her mouth.

'Taste it,' he insisted. 'Salt, Amanda.'

But not only that. His fingers tasted of *her*. Smelt of *her*. An intimacy she'd never known. Her eyes widened, senses reeling. He snatched his hand away. Swore again. Short and pithy this time.

Another unbidden, unwanted tear rolled down her cheek and turning she swished it away. 'I guess this isn't exactly the aftermath I expected.'

'What the hell did you expect?' He swung her to face him. 'I'm not about to get romantic on you, Amanda.'

'I know that,' she snapped.

'You really are still that spoilt child. You've no clue, have you? You could get pregnant.'

'Actually I'm not that naive, Jared. I'm on the pill. But I guess I might have to worry about other things.'

'No, you don't,' he said, white about the nostrils. 'Incredible as it may seem to you, that's the first time I've ever had unprotected sex. I'm clean. You won't catch anything from me.'

They stared at each other—both lost for any more words. She couldn't believe anything that had happened in the last half-hour. That the conversation had descended like this. There wasn't even the comfort of a post-coital hug. Not even the pretence of friendship to ease the awkwardness.

She walked to the table, started to gather up her papers. Once she'd stuffed them together she turned, caught him looking at her with a face that was now pale.

'We can go over those another time.' He gave her file a quick glance. 'I'll take you home now. You should have the rest of the day off.'

'I'm fine, Jared. I'll go back to the office.'

'You're going to be able to concentrate on work now?' He shook his head. 'You need to go home. You need to…'

Cry some more? His voice had trailed away but she knew he was right. She had no chance of coping with work now. Truthfully she just wanted to click her heels and be home alone and able to bury her head in her pillow for ever and ever and ever.

How could this have gone from something so sublime to so awful?

Instead she glanced at her watch. Good grief. It was only a bit after ten-thirty in the morning. His office door hadn't even been locked. Anyone could have walked in and caught them. She'd just lost her virginity in unplanned, almost un-protected sex first thing in the morning with a man who didn't even like her let alone love her.

But, oh, how she'd wanted it. Hadn't she done it delib-erately? Pushed him?

'Amanda, I'm—'

'Please don't apologise, Jared,' she said, icily polite. 'I asked for it. I wanted it.' What was more she'd enjoyed it—after the initial shock. And she didn't want him ruining it further by making it even more obvious how much he re-gretted it.

He drove on the outside edge of the speed limit. The awkwardness created an impenetrable cone of silence between them.

Stupid, stupid, stupid. Amanda was the one with regrets now.

Not that it had happened—she would never regret that—but she did regret that it could be nothing more and that it would only be that once.

She didn't have to give him any directions; he obviously remembered well from the other night. As they pulled up outside the building she undid her seat belt, eager for a quick escape. But he had the engine off and the key out and was out the door just as fast.

'You don't have to—'

'Don't even go there. I'm seeing you right in.'

'Where does the chivalry come from, Jared?' She didn't want him feeling like he 'had to' just because a situation had flared up between them that had got out of control. He was feeling bad because he'd just slept with her. Taken her precious virginity and not realised until it was too late. Was worried he'd hurt her.

What hurt was knowing that it had been so incredible with him and that it wouldn't be like that with anyone else. She'd tried already—so many times. Kissing every Tom, Dick and Harry and never going a step further because there was nothing in it. Earning herself a reputation as a frigid prick tease. But she'd never come close to feeling a thing with any of them, certainly not the thrilling wildness that she'd just experienced.

What hurt more was the terrifying confirmation that she wasn't over him—and the realisation that she wasn't ever going to be. No one could make her feel the way Jared just had. She wouldn't ever want another.

But he didn't want her.

Who got to have a first time like the one she'd just had? Yes, it had hurt, but then he'd been so careful, building her up again so slowly until she'd forgotten the pain and could only focus on the incredible sensation of having him inside her like that. The way he moved, had taught her to move— so easily, so amazing that she wanted more. Even right now she wanted more. She wanted him to take her in his arms and tell her he'd never experienced anything like that either and then take her straight to bed and do it all over again.

It had been spontaneous quickie sex on the sofa in his office and they hadn't even been naked. What could it be like between them if they had a bed and a whole night ahead of them? And if they weren't arguing?

She longed to find out. But with the man of steel striding beside her she knew she had no hope of it ever happening.

The main door to her building was unlocked. It wasn't supposed to be. Anyone could walk in. She led the way up the stairs to her own room. Not looking to see his reaction as they passed the closed, locked doors of the other residences of the letting house. He said nothing until she'd unlocked her door. She wanted him to go but she didn't have the energy to fight him. Really she just wanted to get into a shower and cry.

'I'll see you right in.'

The mail was on the floor as they walked in. She crouched and picked it up, recognising the logo of the nursing home on the top envelope. The reality of what she'd just done hit her. How could she have forgotten?

Not even the ad agency woes were anything on this.

'I thought you flatted with some friends or something.' Jared's frown had grown exponentially.

'No. I just have a room here.'

'Why?'

Because she couldn't afford anything more. Because she didn't have any friends here other than the ones she'd made at work.

'I like it,' she lied.

He was staring hard at her but she hardly noticed, too busy trying to see through the envelope from the nursing home. Was it a bill? The cost of the new medication for Grandfather was huge but she'd been desperate for him to try it—anything to slow down the deterioration of what had once been such a marvellous mind.

She forced herself to grow some dignity. She had to retrieve this situation.

'I don't regret what just happened, Jared,' she said shakily. 'But I'm sorry things were so out of control. I'm sorry *I* was so out of control.' She made herself look him in the eye. 'I never should have yelled at you. It was extremely unprofessional of me.'

She clutched the envelopes tighter in her hand to stop the rustling sound. 'I hope this won't affect our business relationship.'

For a moment he didn't move, just looked at her hands, looked around her room once more.

'I'll be in touch,' he said at last. Brief. Promising nothing. Then he turned. He couldn't get away fast enough.

Amanda locked the door behind him. Once she'd thought she could never be more humiliated than that night of her sixteenth birthday. Now she knew different. Funny how this time there were no witnesses. Last time she'd had Polly and her grandfather to see how he'd rejected her and then add to it. This time it was just her and Jared. And while she knew he had the power to make her happier than anyone on this earth, he also had the power to make her suffer as no one else could.

* * *

He never should have touched her. Never should have put a finger on her. Hadn't he known the danger?

Hell. He just hadn't realised *quite* the danger. He slammed his car door shut; no way was he going back to work either. He drove and kept driving 'til he was out of the city and heading north towards the beaches as he was forced to revisit everything he knew—or thought he knew—about Amanda Winchester.

He thought of her all those years ago, sitting up in his bed, thinking he'd be thrilled to see her there in a black lace negligee. How many times had he wondered what it might have been like if he'd taken her up on her offer? Never had he imagined it would be like the nuclear bomb that had just exploded in his office.

And, man, the fallout was something else.

He was deeply, bitterly angry. Mostly with himself. He'd been wrong. Jared hated being wrong. Nothing was as it seemed—not concerning Amanda.

He'd thought she'd have done it years ago. Gone and found some other willing stud as she'd threatened. But she hadn't. Why hadn't she? God, she was so gorgeous, surely they'd be beating down her door...

And nor was she living the life of luxury he'd always imagined she would. In reality she was working hard to keep her precarious job, living in a total dive in a crap part of town with a bunch of transients, and then she'd let him take her virginity in a bout of out-of-control, angry sex.

What the hell was going on?

He thought back to that long-ago night once more, tried to focus on her face. He'd been too shocked to see it then, but he knew now how nervous she must have been. Nervous enough to swallow too much of her grandfather's brandy. She'd been foolish—spoilt for sure and impetuous.

Naive. And now, he saw, rather sweet. She must have really wanted him—had she actually had deeper feelings?

No. Not possible. It was physical. It had to have been just physical. It always was, right?

But never to have been with another? He couldn't believe that the young woman who'd so brazenly offered herself to him had never let some other guy come close.

He went hot and cold at the thought of that moment. He'd hurt her and he hated himself for that and he hated her for putting him in that unwitting position. She should have damn well told him. God, how could he have gone from the best experience in his life to the worst and back again in just a few minutes?

Jared lifted his foot from the accelerator, realising he'd just shot way over the speed limit. Bitterness brewed in his blood again. He knew he was attractive to women. Even back when he'd been young and worthless with no family, no money and no obvious prospects, he'd been approached and enticed.

But wasn't it all they wanted from him? It was certainly all he offered. A relationship—commitment—was never something he considered. He didn't have the will or the skill for that.

He'd thought Amanda had been the spoilt young girl going for the boy from the wrong side of the tracks—attracted by the rebel cliché and her hormones had liked the muscles. Lots of women liked them. Even more women liked money. Jared knew this now too. But what did she *really* want? She'd been a virgin, for heaven's sake. She sure as hell better not want a wedding and white picket fences because that wasn't ever going to be his scene.

He'd have to stay away. The situation had totally nose-dived. Messing around with someone so inexperienced wasn't his scene either. Not if there were going to be the kind of expectations that made his blood run cold.

But instead his body burned inside out again as need shot through him and he battled with how realistic that determination was. Because of what he wanted to do to her…what he ached to do…

He pulled his car over to the side of the road and stared at the zero on his speedometer. He had to admit it. The drive to have her overpowered his instinct to reject and run. Staying away was not a viable option.

But he was not going to be caught in her spell a second time. He was not going to spend long lonely nights dreaming of her again. He was not going to lose control.

He turned the car around and headed back to the city. Any idea of keeping things on a purely professional footing was long gone. But whatever happened next between them had to be on his terms.

CHAPTER EIGHT

THE residual ache between Amanda's legs wasn't going away. But it wasn't damage from the initiation she'd had. Oh, no. It was the desire for more. Her appetite had been whetted. She'd tasted. And now she yearned—hunger yawning wide deep within. And all she could think of were ways in which he could fill it. Finally aware of all she'd been missing out on, she was reduced to a sex-starved female fantasising her life away.

She dragged herself to work, dreading facing the others. They'd be wondering what the hell had happened yesterday.

'Are you feeling OK?' Bronwyn was on her the minute she stuck her head in the door. 'Jared phoned yesterday and said you'd come down with a migraine at the meeting.'

Migraine. Was that what you called it? Amanda nodded dully. 'I'm so sorry I—'

'He's coming in at ten. He's changed his mind.'

'He has?' She could scarcely breathe; it was the worst news, then. The agency was losing the business and she'd lose her job. There'd be no money for—

'About having you as the client liaison.'

What? Did he use those words exactly? Amanda felt the colour fire into her face.

Bronwyn looked at her closely. 'He's happy to have your contribution on the ads, but he does want someone more experienced to manage the project.'

'We still have the contract?' Amanda fought back the dizziness, tried to understand. 'I haven't ruined it for you?'

'Quite the contrary—he's expanded the brief. But he wants the benefit of the full team.'

Right. In other words, no more one-on-one time with Amanda.

'For what it's worth I think this is for the best,' Bronwyn said softly. 'It was a lot for someone as inexperienced as you to have to manage.'

Jared was a lot for someone as inexperienced as her to manage. Yes. She knew that. But she was still ticked off.

She left the building at a quarter to ten using coffee as an excuse, not trusting herself to be within a hundred metres of him without screeching at him like a banshee. Half an hour later she slunk back to her desk, hoping he'd have been and gone already.

'Amanda.' Bronwyn appeared. 'Jared has a few questions.'

Her heart sank—no such luck. It had been a remote chance anyway.

She went into the meeting room, casting a glance to the side of him rather than right at him. But her retinas captured his image anyway—another suit—and every fantasy flicked through her head again.

Rats.

She sat and refused to look at him as she answered the couple of questions relating to the logo. Stared at the pages on the table between them as he and Bronwyn wrapped up their chat.

'A lot of great progress has been made.'

Yeah right.

Bronwyn stood and Amanda leapt up too, moving swiftly to the door.

'One moment, Amanda.' It was a command and in front of her boss she couldn't ignore it. She stopped but she stayed standing.

Bronwyn went out anyway. Clearly they'd discussed it—him having a private word with her.

'Are you OK, Amanda?'

'Oh, sure.' She turned to face him. 'You have sex with me and then you pull me from the contract. I'm just fine.' She attempted a laugh. 'And you're the one saying to keep the personal separate from the professional.'

'That's exactly what I'm trying to do,' he said in an annoyingly reasonable tone. 'The agency still has my business, Amanda. But I don't want to hold you to ransom over it. No matter what happens between us, Synergy will be doing that work. But I don't want you doing whatever with me because I'm the one with the power over your job. I want you free of that to make your own decisions.'

Whatever with him? His words slowly sank in. 'Decisions about what?'

He paused. Stood from the table and moved that touch closer. 'Have dinner with me.'

'Is this because you feel guilty?' She wished he wouldn't come closer; it made it difficult to concentrate. But he took another step.

'Do you think I have anything to feel guilty about?'

'No. I think we can share responsibility for what happened.'

'Yeah,' he said softly.

She could feel his attention—despite refusing to meet his eyes. She'd be sunk if she did. 'Don't feel you have to—'

'I don't feel I—' He broke off. 'Just have dinner with me.'

She stared straight ahead at his broad chest and the remnants of her rage disintegrated. She could no more say no to him than she could stop breathing.

Hopeless.

And he knew, didn't he? Because she didn't even have to voice her answer. He just made the plan as he walked out the door. 'I'll pick you up at six.'

He was ten minutes early. Sent a text to let her know and she left her desk immediately.

He pulled away from the kerb as soon as she was in. 'Are you hungry?'

She hadn't felt hungry in days. Not since she'd walked onto that plane and found herself next to him. The gnawing inside had nothing to do with food.

'I'm cooking.'

'Really?' She glanced into the back seat and saw a couple of shopping bags. She smiled but couldn't work up more enthusiasm—too aware of other things. They were going to his place? Why did he want to do this—was it some sort of apology? Some kind of obligation? A belated dinner-date bit seeing how she'd delivered herself as the dessert yesterday?

Or did he want more—as she so desperately wanted more from him—that touch, that fire…

She practised her airplane breathing to try to steady her pulse. Barely ten minutes into the drive he swung into a basement garage. As they got out of the car she saw him cast yet another sidelong glance at her. 'The campaign is going to be great, Amanda. It just needs some fine tuning.'

He thought she was worrying about that?

The apartment complex was small but exclusive. He led her to the elevator and they shot up to the top floor.

'Nice place.' Wooden floors, wide windows, spectacular views. Equally spectacular paintings were highlighted on the walls with specially placed spotlights.

The furniture had sleek, clean lines and looked comfortable. But Amanda couldn't sit, couldn't stand still. She walked, one window to another, from one painting to the next—until she stopped in front of the biggest, hanging above the gas fire.

'This is a beautiful painting.' She studied the stark landscape drawing a kind of comfort from the barren hills.

'You like it?' He looked in from the kitchen to see the one she meant.

'Very much.' She nodded, turning and catching his smile.

'Come into the kitchen,' he said gently.

'Said the spider to the fly,' she muttered. But she followed—unable to refuse that subtle note in his invitation. *Intimacy.*

His head turned sharply and a broad grin stretched his face. 'But who is the spider and who is the fly?'

Oh, like that wasn't obvious? He laughed at her expression, she ignored him and wandered round the kitchen as he unloaded the groceries. He had nice appliances. Great espresso machine. A juicer of course. She paced. Looking, searching for something, anything to distract her from the excitement and adrenalin racing inside.

'Amanda?'

'Hmm?'

He sighed and suddenly swooped, picked her up easily and plonked her to sit on his kitchen bench.

Startled, she looked right into his face for the first time that day—reading the darkness burning in his eyes, seeing the tension in the sharpened angles of his jaw.

Her eyes widened and somehow everything slowed. Inside she shook with each powerful thump of her heart.

He did nothing. He said nothing. But so closely he scrutinised, his eyes reaching deep into hers, seeking something out. She didn't know what he was hunting but she knew she couldn't hide a thing. Because under his burning glare her mouth parted—she could feel the pulse in her lips as her blood sped, and from the depths of her belly came the curling licks of heat and desire.

She wanted him so badly.

His features flared but for a moment she was unsure if the brightening was driven by anger or desire.

His lips barely moved but his low mutter seared her skin. 'I can't resist you.'

Suddenly there was a scuffing sound, one thud, then another—she glanced to the side in time to see his shoes hit the floor by the fridge.

Snapping her gaze back to him, she saw his grin had returned as he undid his tie and tossed it over the far side of the bench. She sat absolutely still as he began to undo the buttons of his shirt, until finally she got her voice to work. 'What are you doing?'

'Taking off my clothes.' He shrugged his shirt off. 'It gets hot in the kitchen, you know.'

Oh, she knew. She released the breath she'd been holding for ever. But the relief was swallowed fast by the excitement as she burned up—fascinated by the body being revealed. His torso was incredible.

'How come you have a tan?' Smooth, lightly bronzed skin stretched over honed muscles.

'Swimming. Surfing.'

'But it's winter.'

'I go overseas.'

He had chocolate-brown nipples that she wanted to lick. Her own nipples were tight and sore. Never in her wildest fantasies had she imagined having him before her like this—she'd known he was strong, but she hadn't guessed he'd have such definition.

'Where do you go?' Any conversation to stop her gawping and drooling.

'Hawaii.'

There was no fat, his body all filled out with muscle and sinew and rippling strength. His hands had undone his belt. In a second he was stepping out of his trousers, sliding socks off at the same time. Then his fingers went to the waistband of his boxers.

'You don't think that could be dangerous in the kitchen?' she croaked, a feeble attempt at a joke.

He just pushed them all the way down. And then he was there, bold, proud and big.

She blinked. Oh. No wonder it had hurt.

'You think this is dangerous?' he asked quietly.

She tried to look away from the beauty of him but she couldn't. And yes, intimidated accurately described her feelings.

His smile softened and he took her face in his hands, lifting it so she looked back into his velvet eyes. 'I won't let it hurt this time.'

This time. Thank goodness there was to be a 'this time'. He kissed her. The kiss she'd been aching for since they'd been together yesterday morning. Gently he took possession of her mouth, then swept into her. And even though she was completely clothed, and he was completely naked, she was the one utterly bared.

His hands slid up into her hair, freeing it from the clip so it tumbled down. She shifted on the bench, sweltering.

His fingers combed the length of her hair and then dropped. Slowly he undid one button of her shirt, and then he kissed the small vee of skin he'd just exposed, then he moved to the next one until finally he pushed the halves apart, slipped his fingers around her back and unclasped her bra, letting the cups fall down. They both looked at her nipples—hard and straining towards him.

'You're beautiful.' He touched her so slowly, spanning his hand below her ribcage and smoothing his way up to the soft globes and their hard buds.

As she sat with the sleeves of her shirt pushed down to her elbows, her bra hanging loose at her waist, her head felt heavy as she watched him tease and taste her. She'd never known it could be possible to be so close to orgasm just by having him caress her breasts like this. She wondered if they'd ever make it to a bed.

'In a minute,' he muttered. She must have asked aloud.

'I think you'll enjoy the method of transportation.' He stood back a fraction and tugged the sleeves of her shirt from her arms, letting it fall to the floor.

He unzipped her skirt and she wriggled so he could pull both it and her knickers off. The bench was cold on her bare bottom. His hands skimmed her sides, gently teasing up and down as he kissed her more, and then they took hold of her waist, pulling her right to the edge of the bench, spread her knees so he could step between them and their chests met. Skin against skin. She shuddered.

As he took her mouth in a deep kiss his fingers delved, gently exploring. He lifted his head and smiled—definitely the wolf. 'Hot and wet.'

She was consumed with heat and want—and then he did give her just a little of what she wanted. Just one finger first, sliding into her silk, before he withdrew and suddenly plunged two while his thumb gently worked that spot just above.

'Oh.' She shuddered as the orgasm crashed over her. 'Oh, no.'

'Enjoy it,' he muttered, nuzzling her breasts. 'We'll make more. We'll make lots more.'

He held her, hands stroking as she recovered and then realised she was still hungry. She looked up at him; the angles of his face seemed to sharpen as he read her expression.

He took her hands in each of his and placed them flat on the bench just behind her so she was leaning slightly back. 'Watch.'

She looked down her length. Saw the broad, blunt head of his erection jutting up towards her. He tilted her back a bit more and pushed her knees wider apart. She was shaking, so exposed, yet so excited.

He held his shaft and rubbed against the heart of her. She gasped. Was it possible to die of excitement? If so such a demise was a serious threat now. So hot.

There was no hiding demurely beneath a sheet with Jared. It was raw, smouldering sensuality and they were facing it full on, fully focused.

Their eyes met. Hers felt huge, as if she'd been drugged.

'Watch,' he commanded again.

Obediently, greedily, her gaze dropped. The head of him was now glossy and slick with her juices. He eased just the tip into her before withdrawing, only to do it again. He was right. It didn't hurt this time; what hurt was not having more of him. Now the hunger roared, the ache desperate.

The air was hot, it was hard to catch and draw into her lungs. Her head felt leaden. She wanted to lie back and be taken, to have him thrust as deep as he could go.

'Jared.' He couldn't miss her need.

'OK?'

'Yes.' Oh, yes.

But he teased her more, entering just a little and then pulling away, then a little more and she grew hotter and wetter, incredibly turned on by the sight as well as the sensation of them joining.

'Please.' A tiny, desperate whisper.

His muscles flexed and inch by slow sweet inch he pulled her from the bench and onto him. Instinctively she curled her arms and legs around him as he took her weight in his hands. She looked right into his eyes as she reached his hilt, unable to speak, drowning in the sensation and in the melting darkness of his eyes.

He lowered his head and kissed her. She could hardly kiss him back for the unstoppable moans of delight sliding from her throat.

And then he walked.

She quivered against him as, supported in his arms, she succumbed completely to sensation. He paused every few paces to emphasise his possession, his hands gently rocking her against him. At one point he stopped, leaning her back against the wall, and thrust harder into her, his actions fuelled by her broken whispers.

Finally they were in his bedroom. Despite him carrying her, him doing all the work, she was breathless, crying as unbearable ecstasy shattered her once more. 'I can't take any any more.'

He lay her down and the full weight of him came onto her. 'But, Amanda, this is just the beginning.'

CHAPTER NINE

SHE should go. But before Amanda had even moved Jared's hand encircled her wrist.

'Stay with me.'

Her heart pounded—stay? 'I'm—'

'Stay the night.'

Oh. Of course—just for now, not for ever. She dropped back to reality.

'Do you have your pill with you?'

She gave him a cold look.

'Family isn't on my agenda, Amanda.' He didn't apologise. 'Never will be.' He rolled half onto her, stopping her sliding along the bed away from him. 'There is no such thing as happy ever after.'

She knew what he was doing. Warning her not to build fantasies he had no desire—or even ability—to fulfil. Laying down the law according to Jared.

'Don't you think?' she asked, wistful—wishing he were wrong. 'I think it's possible. I like to think that my parents would have been happy together had they lived. And Grandfather was devoted to the memory of Grandma.'

'Easy to be devoted when the other person is dead.'

'That's an awful thing to say.'

'Yeah. It is an awful thing to say. But that doesn't stop the fact that it's true. People live together, they get sick of each other. They either decide to put up with each other or they move on.'

'That's not true.' She shook her head. 'Most marriages work because the couples are happy. It's not sufferance. It's friendship. Support. Love.'

'You're such a romantic, Amanda.' The way he said it wasn't a compliment. 'Why on earth did you throw away your precious virginity on a non-believer like me?'

'I didn't view my virginity like that.' She hadn't had much choice. He was the only man to turn her on—unfortunately he was a rogue. 'That was just sex.'

And that was the way she had to view this—and embrace her decision to enjoy it while it lasted. She would make the most of it, because it wasn't going to be for ever. He couldn't be clearer on that.

He looked sardonic. 'Doesn't sex come into your equation for a happy marriage?'

'Of course it's important. But it's not everything. There are other ingredients just as important.'

'Wrong.' He laughed. 'It's the most important bit, honey. If they're not fulfilled they'll eventually go shopping elsewhere.'

'You are the most cynical man there is.'

'Not at all. I'm a realist and you're as naive as the day you turned sixteen. It just goes to prove that I wasn't the man for you then and I'm not the man for you now. I'll never be the man for you.'

She tried to keep her muscles relaxed despite the spreading freeze inside. 'You're the man you want to be.'

He shook his head. 'You're the person your life makes you.'

'No,' she said. 'Not you. If that were the case you should

be down and out in the gutter. You broke the mould. You got out of the cycle. Statistically you should have been thrown out of school and been in and out of jail three times before you were twenty.' She swept her arms round him, stopping him slipping from her. 'Come on, Jared. How many different primary schools did you go to? Five? One a year or more? You had a mother who walked out, a drunk father. What chance were you supposed to have? If you'd let your life "make you" all those bad experiences and knock-backs would have made you like him.'

His face had turned to stone and she could feel his muscles flexing. She carried on regardless.

'But you didn't. You *chose*, Jared. You chose to work as hard as you did. To fight. To make a better life for yourself. You choose not to drink. You choose to work for prosperity. You choose to be the man you are.'

'It's not as simple as that,' he said flatly, hands harder, pressing heavier onto her. 'I had help. I had opportunities along the way. Not everybody gets them like I did. It wasn't all doom and gloom and drama.'

She paused. 'I'm sure it wasn't. I'm sure there were good times.' She hadn't meant to offend him. It was his family after all.

Their eyes met.

Some family. His mother had walked out with another man when he was twelve and his father had moved them to Ashburton—to a cottage where the rent was cheaper and the pub a walk away. The alcohol had finally killed his dad when he was fifteen. She didn't know if he'd suffered physically, but neglect was a form of abuse too. And he'd certainly been neglected.

'I just believe that you can be or do anything you want to, Jared,' she said softly. 'You have that kind of strength.'

He laughed, looked away. 'Yeah, and at night time I put on my superhero cape, fly out the window and save the world.' His grin was boyish and uplifted. Laughter, that kind of laughter, suited him.

'Have you ever heard from her?'

'Who?'

'Your mother.'

The smile vanished from his eyes and she kicked herself for asking that question right then.

'Oh, yeah. Mum eventually tracked me down. It was the one time I got publicity. It was an alumni piece—you know, graduates who've achieved—advertising basically, for the university. I was back on a break from Hong Kong—I'd already made my first million and bought some property here. Mommy Dearest realised her son had done good. She'd left the guy she left my father and me for. Maybe he'd left her, I don't know. Anyway, she tracked me down. Said she'd wanted to keep in touch all those years but that Dad wouldn't let her.'

'Do you think that's true?'

He shrugged. 'I don't know. But I'd have said Dad was too apathetic to stop anyone doing anything that they really wanted to do. She could have gotten in touch.'

Amanda felt for him then.

'She said she wanted to get to know me. To make up for all the time she'd missed out on. But you know what she really wanted?'

Frankly Amanda hated to think.

'What do women always want?'

She shook her head, knowing she wasn't going to like his opinion on this one.

'Money or sex,' he said bitterly. 'And I'm no Oedipus.'

Money or sex. Was that what he thought?

On the face of it all she wanted from him was one of those two things as well. Honestly, she wanted more from him. But he made it too damn difficult to ask. He only offered what he offered and she would take it—instinctively knowing it was that or nothing.

'Is that why you shun publicity now?'

'Yeah. I don't want her coming back into my life. She decided to leave it, she can stay out of it. And I don't want other people coming to me for handouts either.' He closed his eyes. 'I give, Amanda. But I do it my way. That's my right, isn't it?'

'You employ at-risk youth. You give them opportunities.'

He lifted his head from her chest. 'How do you know?'

'I made it my business to get to know the client.'

He lay down again. 'Yeah. Well, you've well and truly done that now, haven't you? But I just want to live in peace. Work hard. Do my thing. End of story.'

Amanda said nothing, just tightened her arms around him.

His hand swept down her thigh. 'Are you going to stay?'

'No. I don't have my pill with me.' Actually it was in her handbag but it was a convenient excuse. Staying overnight would bring additional intimacy that, while she knew she would love it, she didn't think he would. Not yet. Probably not ever. So for her own protection, it was best to leave. Just sex. No expectations. At least that was what she'd aim for.

'I'll give you a key and the security code. You can come after work tomorrow.'

So there would be yet another time. Could she handle this day by day? 'OK, but I'll go again when I want to.' She needed to retain some assertiveness.

'Or maybe it'll be when I want you to.' His eyes glinted.

So he didn't want to cede control either.

'I wonder who will want it first?' she murmured.

'It doesn't matter. It'll end soon enough.'

'So one day I'll wake up and you'll not want me any more? Is that what happens?'

'No. What happens is that one day I'll wake up and you'll not want me any more.'

His mother had done exactly that, Amanda realised. Up and left with another man who had no desire to house some other guy's son.

'Is that what always happens?' She tried to stay casual.

'What do you think?' He asked lightly enough but his eyes were dark.

'I think you engineer it so that happens.'

He'd accomplish it so easily. He didn't need to utter cruel words or behave badly. He'd go into dry wasteland mode and any woman would get frustrated with getting nowhere near the heart of him.

Jared rolled and stretched out in his big empty bed, watched the sky lighten, and felt a kind of relief that she hadn't stayed. It had been a weak moment when he'd asked—since when did he crave a cuddle? He hadn't had an affair for a while, that was all. More often than not he was left unsatisfied—despite the physical release. Sometimes the resulting dissatisfaction outweighed that physical release and he found it wasn't worth it. These days he put his energy into his work, into his sport—with only the occasional spill into sexual conquest.

Amanda might not be experienced but she sure had enthusiasm and a kind of fearlessness that both turned him on and tormented him. She wasn't afraid of her sensuality, wasn't afraid to let go—it was as if she wanted everything he had in that moment. She understood this was only momentary too; he guessed that was why she'd chosen not to stay—because she knew. But right now she was also damn near insatiable. Good thing, because right now so was he.

She was there when he got home that night; pages of mock-ups littered the large rug on the floor of the lounge. She had a glass of wine on the coffee table. She was kneeling over the pages, studying them, barefoot and her hair hung loose.

She turned her head as he opened the door.

'Don't get up,' he said. 'Stay there.'

She looked back at the mock-ups, head angled, hair gleaming in the light as she studied the tiny variants on each. 'What do you think?'

'Incredible.' She had no idea, did she?

Maybe she did because she twisted again and gave him a keen look. He'd already stripped off his shirt and his fingers were hovering above his belt.

A pixie smile appeared and she gave her hips a little wiggle. 'You think?'

His eyes closed for a second at her sweet playfulness. When he opened them again she was crawling a little towards him.

'Come closer and take a good look,' she cooed.

There was a rushing feeling in his chest. 'Amanda—'

'They look really good from down here.' She swivelled and crawled back to the big sheets of paper. Peeked over her shoulder and gave her hips another wriggle at the same time.

She giggled then, a light bubble that contrasted with his low laughter as he sank to the rug, utterly at her mercy.

'Do you know what you're doing, Amanda?'

'Figuring it out as I go.'

'I knew your creative talent was impressive.'

Amanda beat him back to his house again. Cold, she lit the gas fire and flopped into the armchair beside it. Put her feet up on the tile hearth surrounding it to let the flames warm her legs.

The key sounded and she looked up, trying to control the leap in her heart and the fire in her belly. He said nothing, but there was that smile as he walked over and sat on the hearth in front of her. She was falling for that smile—it didn't seem quite so dangerous, more like thrilling. He looked at her bare legs and his brows lifted.

He bent, kissed one knee, then the other, soothing the twin grazes she'd got from the carpet during their wickedly erotic coupling the night before. Watching him tend to each with lips and tongue, she let her legs fall apart, so her inner thighs were open and inviting him in. He took immediate advantage, kissing his way up her smooth, sensitive skin. She groaned, her head falling back on the chair.

'How the hell did you stay a virgin so long?' His words were slurred and she knew he'd discovered the fact she was wearing no panties and that she was already glistening wet for him.

'No one…' She could hardly speak.

'No one what?'

'No one kisses…like you do.'

'You like it when I kiss you?' he muttered, breath hot on her thigh as he hooked her leg over his shoulder. 'Like when I kiss you here?'

'Yes. Oh, yes.'

Amanda stood under the shower for far too long—her body warm and eager and unfulfilled. How could that be? For the first time in her life she could understand addiction. It hadn't even been a week and yet she wanted more, more, more. It was a horrible, desperate hunger. A sanity- and pride-destroying need that would have her accepting anything so long as he'd keep sleeping with her.

Not good. This was why she dragged herself from his warm bed every night, returning home to slide alone between her own freezing sheets. Because he wanted a quick fling and she was falling in love.

But she couldn't stop returning to him in the evening. Taking what he could offer. Surely it was the only way to break the attraction to him—to gorge until she could no more. Yet so far it was having the opposite effect and she was dreaming of drawing closer to him.

For once she was looking forward to flying away.

But late on Friday night she was there again, watching with her mouth watering as Jared stirred the mass of vegetables with a quick action.

He saw her attention and grinned. 'Don't want them to burn or, worse, go soggy?' He lifted the pan off the flame and spooned some on the heated plates where the steaks were resting.

He looked up and caught her out staring again. He smirked. 'Do you want to go sailing this weekend? The forecast isn't too bad.'

Amanda swallowed. The invitation had so casually been tossed out and another weekend—next weekend—she'd have leapt at the chance to spend a day with him. But she couldn't and in her heart she knew it was a good thing. 'Actually I already have plans this weekend.'

'Really?' He paused expectantly.

'Yes.'

'Work?' He can't have heard her note of finality.

'I'm seeing someone.'

'Who?'

It was her turn to pause. She didn't want to tell him

about Grandfather—that would be pulling him into a part of her life that was complicated enough without his presence. 'Um…just a friend.' There was no polite way of not answering. 'Shall I get the cutlery?'

Their eyes met for a moment.

'Sure.'

Dinner was quiet—Jared attacked his steak with vicious slashes of his knife as if he hadn't eaten in a year but Amanda pushed hers around her plate, her mind on the coming weekend. She needed to check in with Grandfather.

She took their plates to the bench and then went to find her phone. Looking at its black screen, she frowned. Stupid. She'd forgotten to charge it.

'Do you mind if I borrow your phone?'

She tried to phone Grandfather every day—so he had some contact with family, but also because his condition bothered her. But she hadn't had the chance earlier and she wanted to remind him she was coming. Something was not right but she couldn't put her finger on what it was. She was bound to be imagining it. Feeling guilty for being away so long and not knowing how quickly he'd deteriorated. Being overly cautious now as a result and probably seeing problems when there weren't any. It was probably just part of his illness.

'Go right ahead.' Jared was cool. 'Use the one in the lounge.'

It was only a brief conversation but at least she got to talk to him. Grandfather sounded confused, as he increasingly did. He still knew her but there was so much else he didn't know. Like the day of the week, his address, his phone number, what it was he'd just been saying. The nurse was keen to take the phone away again. Amanda stalled, wanting some sign that things were OK.

'I'll see you tomorrow, darling.'

She hung up and tapped her fingers on the table, hating that she couldn't go check on him right this instant. Not for the first time she thought maybe she'd have to move. She couldn't be this far away from him. Yet there was the dilemma. Here she could earn the money for his medication—she couldn't get the same kind of salary down there. But she needed to be able to pop in at any time of the day, just to make sure everything was OK—because right now she wasn't sure that it was.

She turned, restless, and was surprised to see Jared leaning in the doorway, grasping a cup of something hot and steaming. 'Coffee?'

She shook her head. 'Actually I'd better get going.'

She couldn't stay here. She'd tell Jared if he asked. And the last thing she wanted to do really was burden him with her family dramas. She could work this out on her own. He was her bedmate, not her best friend. He didn't like women who wanted things from him—not material things, not emotional things. While Amanda wanted physical things from him, that was all she was admitting to. And if she was secretly craving more, that was her problem to solve.

Jared worked to keep his voice even as anger rotted his stomach. 'Sure.'

'I'll get my things and call a cab.'

'I'll give you a ride.'

'Thanks.'

He watched her grab her bag and stand fiddling with the strap of it. She didn't seem to mind that he hadn't even tried to make her change her mind about staying. They hadn't actually had sex yet tonight but there wasn't even a token comment about it.

Who was the *darling*?

He thought about his fine plans for the weekend. He loved getting outdoors and escaping the city. For a second he'd considered taking her to Queenstown except he wasn't sure about letting her invade his retreat. Still, the idea of taking a boat out for the weekend had been very appealing. But she didn't want to spend that kind of time with him—she wanted no more than the few hours in the evening where they pushed each other physically and ate if they were lucky. Tonight she didn't even want that.

She was so preoccupied that she didn't even try to make conversation on the ride to her place. Didn't notice that he didn't either.

Jared fumed. Who was the spider again? 'Cos he was starting to feel like a fly—sucked dry and stuck in her web. He pulled up outside her hideous boarding house.

She'd nearly got out without saying anything but he grabbed her shoulder.

'Look at me.' He wanted all her attention on him.

She did as he asked and as he watched she seemed to come back to the present, her eyes widening as she stared at him.

He kissed her then, a hard, brief kiss that did nothing to soothe the prickles digging under his skin.

'Have a good time.' He pulled the car from the kerb as soon as she got out.

Damn. She was getting to him.

He got back to his apartment and told himself he was glad to have his space back. But where was she going? He prowled through his cavernous-feeling lounge. Glanced at the phone.

Darling. Who was the bastard, then?

He went closer and stared at the machine. Picked up the receiver. Hit redial. Bitterly laughed inside at the simplicity of evil genius.

A woman answered and he listened to her greeting.
'Sorry. Wrong number.'

He put the handset down and groaned aloud at his own stupidity. How could he have thought, even for one second, that she was off to be with another man? This was the woman who'd given her virginity to him only four days ago at the frankly ancient age of twenty-five. He laughed then. God, he was a fool.

He sobered. It was scary that jealousy could turn him into such an idiot. It was terrifying that he'd felt that degree of jealousy.

White Oak Retirement Centre. It had to be Colin Winchester, her grandfather. Why hadn't she just said? Why keep it a secret? The bitter anger bubbled again. Because she didn't want him involved in her life other than as her sex partner. She didn't even want to spend the whole night with him.

Well, that was fine, wasn't it? He didn't want anything more than that either, did he? They were just expunging ghosts and fulfilling teen fantasies. Then they'd move on. Sooner rather than later.

Jared had never had a long-term relationship. Never would. The whole family thing wasn't for him. Security, yes—as in financial—and he'd worked hard to get it.

He stomped into the kitchen. He was glad she was gone for the night. It was good to have his space back as his. He wasn't missing her. Wasn't smelling her scent in every room.

He was a liar.

He saw her in his mind again, couldn't shake her from his head. She'd been so distracted, not even noticing his less than subtle frosty reaction.

Maybe something was wrong? He stopped stomping and replayed those last few words he'd heard her utter on the phone. Listened to the tension that had been so obvious in her tone. It wasn't that she'd been concerned about him overhearing—it wasn't about him at all. All her focus had been on something miles away and she'd been anxious.

His blood chilled. Something really was wrong.

He reached for his phone again. 'Auckland airport, please.'

CHAPTER TEN

AMANDA was on the first flight of the day. Couldn't afford a hire car this weekend so was anxiously hoping the plane would land on time for her to make the bus. She couldn't afford the airfares either but had stuck them on her credit card. Some things were more important than money.

The bus that she'd dashed to catch was slow. Ordinarily the journey was only a little over an hour but it took almost two. She'd booked into the usual motel—not having any old friends in the town to stay with. She'd left Ashburton and not looked back, visited Grandfather only on brief occasions in those university years. Jared was right; she'd been spoilt and selfish.

She walked to the motel and dropped her bag. She'd put the night's bill on the credit card as well—crossing fingers it wouldn't be rejected. Then she walked round to the nursing home. It was early—not yet visiting hours, but tough.

He was sleeping. She crept into the room, frightened at how frail he looked—even more than he had two weeks before. Carefully, so she wouldn't wake him, she sat on the edge of the bed and looked into his sleeping features.

He'd been such a strong man—capable. And she hadn't been easy for him.

She put her hand on his and then caught a glimpse of something dark under the short sleeve of his nightshirt. She lifted the hem a little. There was a big bruise on his upper arm, a few smaller ones above, one old and yellowish but most of them looked fresh.

'We had to hold him down. He got a bit cross,' the nurse said briskly as she walked in and saw Amanda's frown. 'You know how he gets. He bruises very easily.'

He got agitated sometimes. Could get a bit stroppy. But to be held down? Hard enough to get bruises like that? She looked closer, could see individual finger marks. OK, so older people did bruise easily, but still... She stroked her grandfather's hand.

'He'll sleep for a while yet.' There was definitely a defensive note in the woman's voice. 'You might as well go and come back later.'

'I'm happy to sit for a while.' Refusing to add the 'Is that OK?' the over-polite bug in her normally would insist upon.

The nurse paused on her way out. 'He's been more confused recently.'

Amanda nodded. She'd noticed it on the phone.

'Thinks the world's a conspiracy against him.' The nurse smiled the smallest of smiles, but her eyes were keen, as if waiting for Amanda's reaction.

She managed the smallest of smiles back but said nothing.

Towns changed. As the greats grew old they were so easily forgotten. Did that nurse know that it was Grandfather who'd raised the money to rebuild the library? That he'd been a councillor and on the local health board— a small-town dignitary, no less.

At seventy he'd been fearsome. Now at eighty he was fearful. She'd seen him go tense and quiet as the staff went past, seen how thin he was, how he fretted. And Amanda's heart was breaking.

She spent the morning with him, smiling as he woke up. He was pleased to see her. She talked about the rugby with him. Glad it was his team that had won the night before. But then, as he pointed out, they always won—he'd never forget that.

Her tummy was rumbling by the time she left. He'd had lunch and would snooze for the afternoon. She'd go back at dinner time to keep him company and watch the next game of rugby tonight.

She strode through the chemically-smelling corridors and blinked back the tears. She needed to meet with his doctor. But she'd have to be here for a weekday to do that—a five-minute chat over the phone wasn't going to cut it. Things needed to settle down at work before she could ask for time off. But if things were as bad as she feared she knew she was going to have to come back here and look after him.

There weren't any ad agencies in this town. Maybe she could look for a job as a copywriter for the local paper? Or she could work at the supermarket or gas station or anything. Whatever she had to do she'd do. As Jared had said the other night, Grandfather would have done anything for her. Now it was her turn.

The thought of Jared made her heart contract. She'd pushed him from her mind. This weekend wasn't about her or him. She sighed; moving might be good. She'd need a complete change to help expunge him from her soul when their affair was over.

She flicked open her mobile. Searched out the number for Grandfather's old GP. She'd leave a message asking him to call. That would be the start. She could work out more from there.

She stopped just outside the doors. At the bottom of the steps, leaning against the railing, was Jared. The Jared of old in jeans and jersey with unsmiling, penetrating eyes. Despite her distress her heart did a back flip and emotion rushed to the surface. She very nearly cried. She very nearly crumpled, longing for his arms to enfold her.

Instead she repeated her phone number to the answer machine and closed up her phone, not taking her eyes off him the entire time.

She walked down the steps but stopped on the last one. She didn't know what to say.

'You should have told me,' he said, expression unfathomable.

She jerked her head to the side.

His face went even more masklike. 'I know we're just sleeping together, Amanda. But I am interested in what else goes on in your life.'

Was he actually hurt? 'You know what Grandfather's like. Very proud.'

He looked down and pulled away from the railing. 'You had lunch?'

'No.'

'Let's find somewhere and grab a coffee and a sandwich.'

Cafés had changed in the time they'd been away. Gone upmarket with fifty fancy coffee varieties and freshly made gourmet snacks. He chose a little one on the edge of town that had a gallery and sculpture garden to add to the atmosphere as well. Shame it was drizzling or they could have sat outside. As it was he pushed her into a seat at a small table overlooking the garden.

The gas flames of the feature fire warmed her back but still she shivered.

'How is he?'

'Not so good.' She picked up the sachets of assorted sugars from the bowl on the table between them.

'What's happened?'

She sorted the sugars by the colour of their wrapping, unable to look at him as she spoke. 'After school I stayed away. Didn't want to come back here and I was still angry with him for sending me to that school. I went to university in Wellington. Did an arts degree. I didn't want to go out to work so went on and did honours, then a masters. It was a cushy life—Grandfather paid the fees. I figured he owed me some fun. I came back briefly in the holidays. But not nearly as often as I should have.'

She rearranged the sugars into rows according to type. 'I didn't really notice at first. Sometimes when I phoned he seemed confused, but I figured he'd probably just had one too many gins or something.'

'Where was Polly?'

'She died about six years ago. Had a stroke.' And yes, since his housekeeper had died the decline had been even more rapid. Amanda's heart ached. Polly had almost been a mother to her.

'Too young,' Jared murmured.

She'd only been in her mid-sixties. Amanda nodded. 'I didn't realise how vulnerable Grandfather was. He'd always been so much the boss. So strong, the authority figure.' She sighed and swept her hand through the sugars, scattering them wide. 'I came back a couple of Christmases ago and he was stressed. He'd lost a lot of money when all those finance companies went under.' There'd been an economic crunch and many investors had lost out. Her grandfather had lost heavily. At the time Amanda hadn't realised just how heavily. 'But he'd said not to worry. He had fingers in another pie and it would all work out. I thought he was capable. He'd been the big businessman in town. People came to him for advice, you know?'

She looked up and saw Jared nod.

'It was a property development scheme. He'd met the developer. Said he was a gun with fantastic ideas. He bought it all—hook, line and sinker.'

'It fell through?'

She nodded. 'Grandfather pretty much lost everything.'

'The guy was a con?'

'I think so. He got away without paying off his creditors. Last I heard he was involved in a new development on the Gold Coast of Australia.' She rubbed her fingers over her temples. 'Grandfather was agitated. At first I put it down to the stress of the finances. But then it was more. I talked to his GP. Grandfather had never told me but he was already on medication to slow it.'

'Dementia?'

'Something like that.'

'Do you think his ability to make the decision on the property scheme was impaired? Do you think the guy took advantage of that?'

She dropped her hands and looked at Jared hopelessly. 'I could never try to prove it. I'd have to have Grandfather declared unfit or something, wouldn't I? He'd hate that. You *know* what he's like, Jared.' Proud, independent and so sure of what was best for him—Amanda had inherited some of the same failings. She could see that now. 'We sold the big house and managed to get a little unit for him. I came down to see him more.'

'Wasn't there someone else who could help?'

'There's no one around any more. All his old mates have either passed on or gone the same way. Bill's gone to live near his grandchildren in Tauranga. The town has changed. I don't know most of them any more.'

She tried the coffee but it was still too hot. She set the cup down. 'The deterioration sped up even more. He couldn't stay alone. He'd wandered a couple of times and couldn't remember his new address. I worried he'd leave an element on or something.'

'So he moved into the home.'

'It was the nearest one that had a secure unit.'

Jared took a sip of his coffee, apparently not bothered that it was boiling hot. 'What's been going on?'

'I don't know.' She lowered her voice. 'I'm not happy with the place. *He* seems unhappy. But I can't be sure why. I didn't come down for a month when I first got the job in Auckland. That's when I really noticed it.'

'What?'

'He's lost a lot of weight. So I started coming more often. Lately it's been every other weekend. Something's not right.'

'Not right how?' His intensity made her tremble.

She looked around behind her. There were a couple of other customers but they were at tables far away. Music was playing. They wouldn't overhear the wildness of her thoughts. 'He has bruises.'

Jared's eyes were black now. 'And you don't think it was accidental?'

'I don't know.'

'No,' he said low, urgent. 'You do know. Go with your gut. What's it telling you?'

'I think he's been hurt.' It felt so awful to say it aloud. Her eyes filled. She was terrified for him. Too scared to think she might be right.

'Deliberately?'

'I don't know.'

'Are there other things?'

She frowned. A few bruises weren't a lot. It could have been just as the nurse said. 'He's gone so quiet recently. But I don't know, that could be part of his deterioration… I try to phone every day but sometimes they say he's asleep and I know they haven't taken the time to check.' She paused. 'And every time I see him he's thinner. So much thinner than a few months ago…'

'Why don't you move him up nearer you?'

'I can't afford to.'

She'd investigated private care facilities in Auckland but the prices were prohibitive. 'I've been paying extra so he can have medication that isn't government funded. But it's not enough.'

'So what are you planning to do?'

'I'm going to move back here.' She expelled a deep breath. 'That way I can pop in—any time, unexpectedly. Be the annoying relative who's always asking questions.'

He was like stone.

'It's what I have to do, Jared.'

'If you moved him, you wouldn't have to give up your job. You wouldn't have to move.'

'I told you, I can't afford to. And why put him through all that upheaval? He's lived here all his life. This is his home.'

'It sounds like he's not in much of a position to notice that. Get him somewhere with a nice view and a lovely garden to stroll in. And you to visit more often—that's what will make it for him. You'll be the constant for him.'

'How would he cope with the move?'

'He'd cope with professional help and with you being there with him. It's better than leaving him to be abused here.'

She flinched. 'I'm not. That's why I'm coming back.' She dragged in a breath. Tried to minimise her fears. 'I don't know that it's the whole place. It might only be one staff member. It might not even be that. I don't know what else I can do, Jared.'

'Report it.'

'Based on what? A few bruises? Woman's intuition? It would make his position worse, wouldn't it? They'd hate me for it and take it out on him.'

'Whether it's one person or the whole damn lot it's unacceptable. He can't stay there, Amanda. And what about the other residents? Who's there keeping an eye out for them? Don't you owe it to them to make sure the place is being run OK?'

Guilt and impotence and frustration smothered her. 'Damn it, Jared. Don't put it all on me. I can only do so much. He's my responsibility. He's all I can handle.'

'You're the one who said I had the strength to do anything. Why don't you think the same of yourself?'

She shook her head. 'I'm not like you.' She shrugged. 'You were right. I've always been spoilt. Decorative. I studied art history, Jared,' she mocked herself. 'What's the point of that?'

'Maybe we need the beautiful things in life, Amanda. Maybe it helps the human condition.'

Her jaw dropped. 'The *human condition*?'

'I know.' His grin was a little twisted. 'I can't believe I said that either.'

He spent a long time staring into his coffee. She watched him for a while, drinking in the sight of him. But then she let it go, looking out of the window, watching the wet streaking down the panes and forcing in a bite or two of her panini.

He lifted his head. Spoke quietly. 'Let me take care of him.'

'No.' This was exactly what she didn't want. She didn't want to take like that from him. 'No.'

'Why not?'

'It's like why you changed the conditions of the contract with the agency. I want you to be free to make your decisions.' She breathed deep. 'About us.'

'We're over when we're over. And we're not over yet. This will make no difference to that.'

'I can't let you. It would make things too complicated. I don't want what you think all women want.'

Sex or money or both and nothing else.

His mouth tightened. 'This isn't about you, Amanda. In fact this has nothing to do with you. *I* owe him.'

She frowned. 'How do you owe him?'

He looked at the bottom of his coffee, then up at her, steadily holding her gaze. 'He gave me a job when no one else would take me on. No one else would give me a chance. He opened a bank account in my name. It was a savings account—I couldn't withdraw the money even if I wanted to and it meant my father couldn't make me. Colin kept out only enough for me to get basic groceries. He arranged work for me all over the place and saw I was paid in kind by the farmers. Half a beast in the freezer, potatoes, whatever. But no money for Dad to spend on drink. Colin hooked me into a network of support I'd never have been able to break into without his backing. But there were strings. The work was all dependent on my school grades. So long as the grades were good, I got the work. He was a hard man but he was fair and he taught me a lot when I worked directly for him—in the company and on the farm. Thanks to him not only did I survive but I got an education and I grew ambition.'

Amanda's eyes filled. She'd had no idea.

'So now do you understand?' Jared suddenly said roughly. 'I could hardly repay the guy by bedding his precious young granddaughter, could I? No matter how much I wanted to.'

CHAPTER ELEVEN

AMANDA blinked rapidly. 'You *wanted* to?'

'You nearly killed me that night, Amanda.'

Sudden warmth exploded in her chest and she smiled. He'd wanted her.

He frowned. 'I was a kid. A beautiful young woman is in my bed dressed like some wild fantasy. How could I not have wanted you? I wouldn't have been normal if I hadn't.'

Her happiness bubble burst. Oh, so it was just hormones. Any beautiful young woman would have done it for him—it wasn't just because it was her.

'If I can help him now, in any way, then I'm going to,' Jared said. 'And you're not going to stop me. This is between me and him. Not you.'

She sat back in her chair. Coffee cold and forgotten. Stunned by what he'd revealed.

'You really didn't know?' Jared asked softly.

'No, I had no idea the extent of it.' She shook her head. 'I mean, I knew you used to clean Mrs Chalk's car in the weekends and she had a sandwich for lunch for you but—'

'Yeah.' He grinned. 'She was in on it. The old dragon. But I'm grateful to her. She knew I could do it. Knew how badly I wanted to get out of there.'

Amanda felt troubled. 'But if he did so much for you, how come you didn't stay in touch with him?'

Jared fiddled with the spoon. She didn't know the rest of it, then. Colin had come to see him, working at the woolshed, the day after that hell of a night before.

'Thank you for bringing her home. She's young. Head-strong.' The old guy coughed. 'Girls. They get these crushes.'

Jared nodded.

'You're a good bloke, Jared. But you're not the bloke for her.'

And never would be. He didn't say it but he didn't have to.

'You've finished school.' They both knew this. 'Have you heard back about the scholarship yet?'

Jared shook his head. 'Not for another couple of weeks.' He'd applied for a full scholarship to university in Auckland.

'Go anyway, Jared.' To Jared's intense discomfort, Colin held out a cheque. 'You deserve it. You've worked hard for it.'

Jared looked the man right in his eyes. This wasn't about him getting his education and they both knew it. 'I'll go but I'm not taking your money.'

Colin frowned.

'It's time to go anyway.'

Colin waited a moment longer and then put the cheque back in his pocket. 'I'll do your references. Recommendations. Anything.'

Jared shrugged. His work record would speak for itself. When he left this town that was it. He was never coming back.

Colin knew, perhaps, just how close he'd come. He must have seen the way he'd looked at her. Couldn't have failed to notice her swollen mouth. Jared's too had felt puffy. He'd kissed her so hard his teeth had grazed the inside of his lips—heaven knew what he'd done to hers.

'Thank you, Jared,' the older man said softly. 'Good luck.'

He left town the next day.

He worked hard to forget that night. It was easy during the day, when he had work and study to focus on. Harder at night when his mind relaxed as sleep neared. The dreams—oh, the dreams, the way his hand had slid over the delicate shape of her bottom, sliding smoothly over the silk of that killer negligee. And then he'd curved his fingers right around, into the intimate curve of her—unable to stop himself. Discovering her lack of knickers, feeling her fresh, damp desire.

That had been the moment. He'd pushed her from him. Hurled her, really. But it had either been that or take her then and there. He had only been a youth. Control with finesse was something that came with age and experience. Back then it had been all he could do to walk away. Dragging her back to her grandfather, knowing it would kill the thing dead in its tracks.

But it hadn't.

Nine years, seven and a half months later and he still had to work harder than anything to control his body's reaction to her. Even more so now knowing what she was like. The reality so much better than the fantasy. How bloody tempting every inch of her was.

Looking back on it now, he didn't blame Colin. Wouldn't he have done the same? No way would he want his granddaughter hooking up with the son of the town drunk. The local charity case. That fire in Jared had been fuelled even more. To do better. Be better. For the old guy to have second thoughts? Regrets? The 'I'll show you' mentality that many who achieved had been blessed with. Was it a blessing or a curse?

He shouldn't have cared so much what the old guy thought. Had liked to pretend he hadn't. But he had. Pride had made him angry. He wouldn't be paid off. And he'd been so angry with her for wanting only that from him. The irony was that now he suspected she wanted more—and that was impossible.

Jared chose not to tell her any of that old conversation. Not now. Not ever. It was in the past; she might not agree but that was where it would stay. And he still wasn't the man for her.

'I didn't keep in touch because that was what we agreed.' He finally answered her question. 'I wanted to get out of this town and never look back. There was nothing to come back for.'

Her eyes were big and round and hurt danced in the shadows at the back of them.

'It was just one kiss, Amanda,' he said roughly. 'You're supposed to get over your teenage crushes.'

She winced and coloured. Spoke with the finishing-school dignity that both irritated him yet made him respect her at the same time. 'I'm working on it.'

Shame the same couldn't be said about him. One image, one taste had come back to haunt him in the flesh. Now he couldn't seem to rid himself of the obsession.

Amanda carefully placed her knife and fork on her plate. Buying some time to recover from the hurt she'd felt at his comment. Reminding herself that this was just a fling and she'd better keep that fact in mind.

'I'll take care of Colin. Get him out of there,' Jared said. 'But you deal with the rest of it.'

'What if I'm wrong?'

'So what? What's the worst that can happen? Some-one comes in and checks the place out and gives it a glowing report.'

'At the taxpayer's expense?'

He shrugged. 'Taxpayers' money gets wasted on a lot worse things. And what if you're right? What if they're not being treated well?'

She knew he was right to push it. Some of those residents were as vulnerable as small children. Yet she couldn't help but worry. 'Most of the staff in those places work so hard. Most of the time it's the patients who are abusing them.'

'Sometimes,' Jared said. 'And so often those carers are underpaid, short-staffed and over-stressed. Things can and do happen.' Relentless, he gazed at her. 'You know how to write a letter, Amanda. How to make a call.'

Finally she nodded.

'Where are you staying tonight?' He dropped his spoon on the side of his plate with a clatter.

'The Ashcourt Motel.'

'I hadn't booked a place yet. I'll go there.'

'I'm in unit four.' Did he understand that he didn't need to get his own room?

His chair scraped as he roughly pushed it back and stood. 'I'll get working on a solution for Colin.'

'I'll go see how he is.'

He led the way through the tables. The rain still poured relentlessly.

Their progress halted when the door to the café opened and a couple of older women walked in. The first woman pushed back the hood of her coat and saw whose path she was blocking.

'Jared?' She sounded amazed. But more telling was the look on her face. Amanda recognised it—that same mix of embarrassment and hunger that she'd felt when she'd seen him again.

'Linda,' he said flatly.

Amanda suppressed a shiver. Man, he could be an arrogant bastard.

The woman shifted uncomfortably to the side, frowned at Amanda as she walked past. 'You're…'

'Amanda Winchester.' Amanda nodded, one of her polite school smiles coming automatically.

She watched as Linda searched Jared's features once more. Her face was pale now except for two spots of deep red on her upper cheekbones.

Jared appeared not to notice as he walked out the door and casually strode to the car, the rain not seeming to penetrate his hardened exterior.

Amanda ran to the car feeling every cold needle of the downpour as if she were at the mercy of an incompetent acupuncturist.

He had the car idling already and looked impatient as she fumbled with the belt.

'That was Linda Dixon, wasn't it?'

The principal's wife. She'd sometimes helped out in the school office.

He didn't reply. She knew as well as he that it was her. She glanced at him. He had such a 'don't go there' look. He jerked the gears and pulled on the wheel with far more force than necessary.

But Amanda wasn't afraid of his silences. Her curiosity was too great. And her female intuition told her there just had to be history—ugly, messy history—between them. But she'd go casual, relaxed, as if there weren't this churning feeling in her gut. 'Did you know her well?'

He didn't lift his eyes from the road. 'Not that well.'

No? So why was the woman eating him with her eyes? Oh, they were *so* talking history.

Finally he looked at her. His eyes dark, the cynical amusement only fleeting. 'You don't really want to know, do you, Amanda?'

'Oh, no.' She shrugged. She was a woman—*of course she did.*

A sharp bark of laughter. 'You're a crap liar.'

It was her turn to study the road ahead.

'The lovely Linda approached me one day when I was doing some work around their grounds—they were on my longlist of ride-on lawnmower jobs. Mr Dixon was out at some school board meeting. It was a hot day—nor-west wind blowing over the plains sending everyone crazy.' The faintest of smiles touched his mouth. 'You know what she wanted, don't you, Amanda?'

Those needles were being twisted well below the depth of her skin now.

'You know because you asked for the same thing later that very day.' Bitterness rolled out of him.

'My birthday?' She stared. Shock left her mouth hanging. 'Did you—'

'What do you think?' He broke in. 'She was almost old enough to be my mother. What's more she was married. I wasn't going to sleep with her or any of them.'

Them? There were them? Amanda drew breath. Astounded at the revelation. Oh, she'd known there were rumours aplenty about Jared's supposed prowess as a lover, but even so. And he was so angry about it. She inhaled a couple of deep breaths. Tried to lighten it up. 'So did you leave Ashburton a virgin, then?'

He choked, a rough spurt of laughter. 'No. But at least she was my age. Or near to. And she was single.'

The sword of jealousy struck fast and deep, killing the humour she'd been trying to resuscitate. 'Did it last long?'

'It was a casual thing.'

Casual. Like this thing between them.

'What was her name?' Had she known her? Was she pretty? Amanda hated her anyway.

Jared pulled over. Amanda still stared at the road as if the car were moving over it. He reached across and slid his palm down her cheek, turning her face to his. 'You want a spreadsheet detailing every woman I've ever slept with?'

'No.' The thought repelled her. She hated all of them.

'Then let it go. The past is past.'

'Would your spreadsheet run to more than a page?'

'Amanda,' he half laughed.

'It's not fair. You know exactly the detail on mine.'

'It was a lot harder saying no to you than to her.' Softly he brushed back a wisp of her hair.

Well, that sure didn't make her feel any better. The old embarrassment crushed her, doubling in weight. She'd thought she was so special. Had been offering him a precious experience as if she were some princess bestowing a favour on a man she thought worthy.

But in truth she was just one of at least two women throwing themselves at him like cheap tarts. No wonder he'd got so jaded. Part of him must have wanted to laugh but instead he seemed so bitter about it. Why?

'What did she do when you refused her?'

His expression closed over again. 'That's something you really *don't* want to know.'

He looked over her shoulder, nodded to the rest home. 'Now get in there and sort him out. I'll see you at the motel later.'

CHAPTER TWELVE

AMANDA paused at the bottom of the rest-home steps and made herself file away the conversation of the last five minutes in a compartment labelled 'Danger: Do Not Enter'. Grandfather was the priority. Grandfather, whom Jared was going to help. She quickly walked in, far more confident than when she'd arrived first time round this morning. Jared hadn't laughed at her. He'd taken her qualms seriously and invigorated her with the sense that she was right to be concerned and, even more, that she had to do something about it. She'd known that. But it was so nice to have the back-up.

As for what might have been happening to Grandfather? She couldn't think about it. For so long she'd seen him as a pain in the neck, restricting her freedom, limiting her choices—giving her no choices, in fact, not until she was well and truly of age. Underneath she'd known he had her best interests at heart. Thought he was doing what was best for her. That he loved her—as she loved him. But she'd also hated him for it, and rebelled in cowardly fashion, by leaving, barely visiting—only occasionally out of obligation.

She hadn't known the extent to which he'd helped Jared

and there was part of her now that felt jealous. Sure she knew Jared had worked odd jobs—she'd watched him after all—but she'd no idea of the almost paternal care Grandfather had taken over him. He'd kept his business life away from her; it wasn't something she'd 'needed to worry her pretty little head' about—not until he was no longer capable and then it was kind of too late. She wished he'd included her more, taught her more. Maybe she should have asked more, taken a more active interest.

But the hard, determined man had been old school through and through. Women didn't do the finances; that was the man's job. He'd probably spent far more time talking to Jared than he ever had to her. And no wonder Jared felt as if he owed him. He'd made him work for what he got, given him a sense of respect and dignity. She wished he'd done the same for her. She'd been given all the 'things' a girl could want and yet none of the things she'd really needed in life.

Completely spoilt and sheltered right up until that night of her birthday, and then he'd been so angry he'd sent her away to a hell on earth. And she'd been so angry she hadn't come back—not until it was too late.

He was dressed and dozing in his armchair when she got to his room. She shut the door behind her as she went in. Carefully lifted the short sleeve of his tee and got her phone from her bag. Feeling like a spy, she took a couple of pictures of the angry-looking bruise and checked his other arm. There were another couple of bruises. Anger and upset burned in her chest and she didn't leave his side the rest of the afternoon.

The darkness unnerved her as she walked back to the motel. Despite the streetlights the sky was huge and forbidding. She was cold and the heels of her shoes clipped and echoed along the empty street. Her feet moved faster as she saw the lights of the motel. Breathless, she scanned the note taped to her door.

In the next unit...

That was as far as she read because the door next to hers opened. Jared looked at her, took her hand and with a frown pulled her straight into his room.

'How did you get on?' He took both her hands between his and rubbed them.

'OK. How about you?'

'Great.' He smiled and she felt as if the sun had just burst through the storm clouds. 'I found a place for you to look over on Monday. I've made an appointment already but you can take a look at the website now.'

She walked to the table where his laptop was open, the big screen showing bright, high-definition images of a place that looked like a five-star resort.

She skimmed an eye over the features of the exclusive facilities. 'But there must be a waiting list?'

'It's taken care of. You decide if you like it and that's where he'll go.'

So fast. So easy. And while it was wonderful, suddenly she felt so guilty. Why hadn't she been able to do this herself? 'You've been busy.'

'We'll get a specialist to look him over,' he said. 'I've already been on to them about that. There might be other meds they can try and they can assess if there's anything else that we should know about.'

She scrolled through the pages, searching for the finer print. But there was no information on fees. She shook her head. 'This place will cost a fortune.'

'Forget it, Amanda.' Jared put a steaming mug of coffee

on the table in front of her. 'I wouldn't have a fortune if it wasn't for him.'

She sat at the table and went through the website again, torn between being thrilled and feeling so bad. He took the chair next to hers and looked alongside her. This was a huge undertaking, a huge responsibility, and she couldn't really let him do this, could she? But she already knew she had no choice. But it would affect them, it couldn't not. The question was how.

Eventually she turned. 'Jared—'

'Don't worry about it.' He shook his head. 'This makes no difference to us. This is separate from us.'

She understood what he was trying to say. He was under-lining their 'affair' again. And he didn't want her reading more into his actions than he intended. But the questions that had been turning over in her mind all afternoon just begged to be asked. 'How did you know I was here?'

He looked back to the computer.

'Why did you come after me?' she pressed.

'I guess it was my intuition,' he said. 'Something wasn't right.'

'Not right?'

'I was worried about you.'

Adrenalin and forbidden hope surged in her chest at the words. *Worried.* 'Why were you worried?'

'I don't know,' he said sharply. 'You just didn't seem right.'

'How did you find out where I'd gone?'

'Does it matter?'

'Yes.'

'Why?'

Because it was telling her a lot about him—about how he was feeling about her. Surely there must be more to them than sex if he was chasing down half the length of the country to make sure she was OK. Surely that meant he must *care*.

And as the nervous excitement exploded in her chest, sending electrified blood racing through her veins, she realised just how much she wanted him to care.

Try to play it cool, Amanda, she told herself. *Just try.* This was Jared the loner. Jared the sexier-than-anything flirt who had ironclad armour. If she was going to find a chink she had to do it by stealth.

'I have to get back to Auckland first thing.'

She drew breath. He'd realised his mistake, was pushing away and putting up the boundaries again. Well, she wouldn't make the mistake of clinging too tight—not yet. Patience wasn't one of her virtues, but she was thinking she might have to work on it. That and hope.

'Of course.' She nodded. First thing he'd be off to get his distance. But he hadn't been able to answer her questions, couldn't deny what they both knew she was thinking—that there was more going on than either of them was able to admit just yet.

And there was the night between them now—their first whole night together. This night could be on her side.

He was staring at the computer. An avoidance tactic if ever she saw one.

Jared had always made her want to be bold. And now she'd had an extra confidence shot in knowing he'd come after her. She badly wanted to say thank you. But she didn't want him associating this with gratitude. So she kept the words back as she swung her leg over his, straddling his lap, her body blocking the computer screen from him.

He didn't look up to her face, kept his gaze on the same angle—right at her breasts. She took off her top. He still didn't move so she twisted her arms behind her and unhooked her bra. Cupping her breasts in her hands, she pushed them together and lifted them in offerance.

His groan was torn from him. And then he buried his head in her.

'I'm starving.'

Amanda lay back and enjoyed the view as Jared disentangled his limbs from hers, sat up on the bed and stretched.

'Really, really hungry.' He grinned.

'So am I.' Lunch at the café had been hours ago. 'Pizza?'

'Yeah.' He pulled on his jeans and made the call.

The incessant drumming of the rain on the iron roof of the motel precluded further conversation. He stood in the doorway, one arm stretched out, bracing on the frame, looking out into the light, seemingly unfazed by either the damp or the chill—despite wearing nothing but those black jeans. The pizza boy should have been and gone already—but it was Saturday night and with the weather so miserable it probably meant that everyone in town was staying in. And ordering pizza.

Amanda pulled the sheet higher, wondered if she'd ever tire of looking at him—it didn't seem likely, at least not in the next century or ten.

'I used to hate this town.' Jared finally spoke.

'And now?'

'Well, I'll never live here again. But I don't hate it so much.'

'I hate it,' she said.

He turned, brows raised. 'You don't hate anything.'

'Yes, I do.'

He slammed the door shut and walked towards her. 'What else?'

'Not knowing what you're thinking.' She held her breath.

He studied her, head on an angle. 'It's real simple. I can't wait to have the pizza, and I can't wait to have you again.'

'In that order?'

He grinned. 'Yeah.'

She sat up and let the sheet fall to her belly. 'Still in that order?'

His grin widened. 'Yeah.'

She stood right up on the bed, legs apart, running her hands from her breasts downwards as she rocked her hips in a sensuous circle. 'And now?'

There was a knock on the door and she instantly fell on the bed, burrowing back under the covers. His laughter rumbled loud and genuine from some place deep inside. And she couldn't help giggling herself.

Having paid the pizza boy and carried the box in, Jared put it on the table and strode over to the bed where she was still half hiding. 'What are *you* thinking?'

That she loved it when he laughed like that. That she'd never had so much fun. That she could stay holed up in this motel for ever. 'That I hate cold, soggy pizza.'

'That right?'

She nodded, fascinated as he grappled with the fly of his jeans.

'Well, isn't that just tough?' he muttered as he pressed his body close to hers.

True to his word Jared left early. She slid from bed at the same time, quickly showering and dressing, ready to see him off and get to her grandfather.

But as she stood by his rental car the infernal uncertainty smothered her. 'Are you sure?'

He looked annoyed. 'Let's not go round and round on this. It's a done deal.'

But Amanda needed the reassurance; if she was going to go in there and uproot her grandfather, she needed to know there was security in his future. She had to trust Jared. Without doubt she knew she could. His reliability had never been called into question—he'd always turned up when he'd said he would, always worked later, longer, harder than anyone. If he said it, he meant it.

But there was that part of him still so unknown to her— the part he blocked. She wondered if she'd ever get to know him the way she longed to. And she worried that by letting him do this she would in some strange way make their relationship even more remote—even more of an 'arrangement'.

He walked back round the side of the car, all closed man again, but planted a fast, fierce kiss on her mouth. 'Just do it.'

CHAPTER THIRTEEN

Just do it. Amanda repeated the mantra over and over on her walk to the home. A quick check found her grandfather gazing out of the window to the bare wooden fence. Amanda felt guilt stir. He'd have a better view soon. She went to the reception—it being Sunday the manager wasn't there, but the defensive nurse of yesterday was, as was another.

Amanda assumed a bright smile and polite society mode. 'I wanted to talk to you about Colin.' She paused, ensuring she had their attention. 'I'm moving him up to Auckland to be nearer me. I'll be back on Friday to pick him up.'

'Friday?'

'Yes. The wonderful thing is I've gotten him in to see the leading gerontologist up there—he'll have a full medical and go into a new facility.'

'He has the appointment on Friday?'

'Yes.' Amanda beamed. 'I'm so hopeful there may be a different range of drugs that might help him.' And she was certain there was no way that awful bruise would have faded by then—nor would any others, if there were others. They'd be found. And if there was anything else to be found, it would be.

Did defensive nurse look uncomfortable? 'You're supposed to give us notice.' She certainly had an unmistakable sharpness in her voice.

'I'm giving you notice now.' Amanda smiled to ease the edge in her own words. 'But don't worry, his account will be paid for the required length of notice period. But he will be leaving sooner than that. On Friday, in fact.'

Despite the satisfaction, she was shaking as she walked back to Grandfather's room to spend the rest of the day with him. Hopefully her fears were totally wrong, but if they weren't then those carers were on notice and they knew it. She'd follow it up with a letter to the manager and the health board tomorrow. Sitting in the chair next to her grandfather's, she spent half the afternoon composing it. The rest of the time she dwelt on the even bigger conundrum in her life.

How could she reach Jared? While he wanted her it was only on his limited terms—physical and nothing but. And yet there was more, he'd followed her, he'd been worried…but she didn't know how to draw him out and build on it. The darkness in his eyes hid wounds and, while she knew much of what he'd suffered, she didn't know how to breach the walls he'd built. And, without doubt, it was her heart on the line.

Jared moved papers from one pile to another. Just as he'd been doing for three hours now—not counting the ten-minute break for a cold-sandwich dinner. He meant to have the night away from her. Just to underline the point that what he was doing with Colin had nothing to do with her—with 'them'. He winced. Hating the thought of 'them'. But all the same, underneath, the concept was tantalising.

Dangerous.

But there was no future for them. There was never a

future, never a for ever. People came together for a while and then parted. And it was better to part before it got too messy, too painful. And it was better to be the one to initiate the separation.

Because no one was walking out on him again.

But he knew she'd be home. Her flight had been scheduled to land two hours ago and, yes, he'd gone online and checked that it had. On time. Which meant she'd be home—especially as he'd arranged for a car to collect her from the airport. He'd had the call confirming that had gone successfully.

So he knew.

He moved the pile to where it had been on the desk before he'd moved it back. Again. He stood, growling in frustration.

Pointless. Procrastination. Pathetic.

But there'd be no sleep tonight, not if he carried on like this. And so, late as it was, he got into his car.

Sex. It was just sex. That was all she wanted. And him too, right?

Playful. Plentiful. Passionate.

He didn't want more than that. And he knew she didn't. When it came to what she wanted from him, she definitely came down on the sex side of the equation.

She said nothing when she opened her door. Simply stood aside and he walked in. There was nothing to say, was there? There was just this burning attraction, the desire that couldn't be licked. Indeed it only seemed to be growing the more he had of her.

She melted into his arms, pressing her body to his and letting him in where he most wanted to be. The sense of relief was overwhelming. He didn't care about the dingy room and the narrow lumpy bed because when he finally slept, it was a better, deeper sleep than ever.

But consciousness returned ultra early. With it came the awkward silence. He could hear her unspoken questions—the 'what's going on?' that she was so determinedly holding back. Her room was tiny, and they were trying too hard not to fall over each other.

He didn't want to talk about it. Couldn't seem to think straight any more—not when he was with her.

All night together in the motel had been a mistake. Two nights in a row was a huge mistake.

'I'm away for business meetings for a few days,' he fabricated. It was plausible enough. 'Flying out later this morning.' And he would be—to his bolt hole in Queenstown. Some time on the slopes should help clear his head—some time away from *her*.

'I thought you were coming to the agency this afternoon?'

Damn. 'I'm going to have to reschedule. It's a situation that cropped up overnight.' OK, sounding weaker now. He'd turned his PDA off—for all he knew the factory could have gone up in flames and frankly he wouldn't have cared. In those moments in her arms, the rest of the world disappeared. Hell, he needed to get perspective back—like now.

Three hours later he was away from her—in the air with some wintry freedom his destination. But for once the bird's eye view of the Southern Alps didn't thrill him. The snow-laden peaks looked fearsomely clean and cold against the blue sky but he barely noticed them. Tearing his focus off the constant contemplation of Amanda seemed impossible.

The plan for Colin's move was well under way and he was happy with how it was panning out. It would keep Amanda in Auckland and keep the old boy safe. Things could continue as they were for as long as he wanted.

But the discomfort nagged and he mentally put his exit

plans in place. When it was over he could get the bills for Colin processed at work so he wouldn't need to see or know any details at all. There wouldn't have to be any direct contact. She could be cut from his life quite easily.

Good.

He walked into his home, waiting for the relief to hit—that feeling of freedom that came as he breathed the crisp air and saw the huge sky and the magnificent mountain backdrop.

But it didn't come. Instead he wondered what she was doing. Walking around his house, he felt the ache of emptiness. He turned—was that a footstep?

He wished.

He wanted to see her walk into the room. Wanted her to experience the beauty of it with him. He'd stand at the window with her and take her as they watched the sun's rays traverse the snowy ranges…

Oh, for crying out loud! He broke into a run. Ridiculous, mooning around like a teen struck by his first case of calf love. Adolescent hormones run rampant. He grabbed his boots and board and chucked them in the back of the car. Physical activity—adrenalin—for the couple of remaining hours of light he'd work his body into fatigue.

But his brain he couldn't shut down.

Snow, speed, sweat—he went faster, further. But it was as if, the more he tried to escape, the more insistent the thoughts of her became. She was so far in his brain and his body craved hers as if she were a deadly narcotic.

In the end he flew back earlier than he'd planned and drove straight to her place. As he thudded up her stairs his anger grew yet more. He hated the fact that she lived in such a dive but he didn't want her to live with him, damn it. And he didn't want to be missing her when he'd gone to his bolt hole. He didn't want to want her all the time like this.

He banged on the door and called out to let her know it was him.

The expression on her face when she opened it was pure frozen politeness.

'How were your meetings?' she asked. Too polite. Too finishing school. 'Are your clients as good at snowboarding as you?'

So she knew.

The mask fell and fire flashed from her eyes. 'I rang your office to get some info for Grandfather's forms. Your mobile was switched off and your PA said you were out of range for a few days. *"He won't be back from Queenstown 'til Thursday."'* she parroted. 'But it's only Tuesday. What happened Jared?'

'It didn't work out the way I wanted.'

'What didn't? Your precious time out?'

His muscles simmered, ready to flex and fight—but he kept them in check, sensing her body was stretched on an even tighter wire.

'Why lie?'

'I didn't want to offend you,' he trod carefully.

'Why would it offend me? So you wanted some space. You're a free man, Jared.'

True. So why did he feel this guilt, then? 'I did have some meetings.' He fell on the back foot. 'Video conference.'

'Just so long as there is no woman there.'

He froze, the comment knocking the breath from him. How the hell could she think that?

She stood with her legs wide, blocking the doorway, all female aggression. She'd have no hope of stopping him if he really wanted to get into her room, but there was that edge that made him pause. The frisson of danger emanating from her—as if she were perilously close to a precipice and he had no desire to push her from it. Not when he still wanted her so badly.

'There is no woman, is there, Jared?'

'You know there isn't.' Only her. Only the ghost of her following him every bloody where. And the thought of being with another woman made him feel sick—a fact that made his muscles bunch with even more anger.

'Do I?' she countered. 'I only know what little you choose to tell me.'

There was nothing he could say to that.

'And it would seem that even that might not be the truth.' Her chin tilted. 'Exclusivity wasn't something we discussed at the start of this.'

'You don't leave any time or energy for anyone else and you know it.' He leaned closer. 'Let me in.'

'No.' She wouldn't look him in the eye. 'It's not convenient now. I wasn't expecting you back 'til Thursday.' Her voice grew huskier. 'I have other plans.'

So he was being punished. And she was as much of a liar as he was. But he moved forward fast, curling his hand round her neck before she could back away or shut the door on him. The kiss was deep as he let her feel his hunger for her, but it wasn't nearly enough. He lifted his head and simply looked at her, watching for the moment. It happened gratifyingly quickly. She exhaled, leaned that fraction closer, mouth soft and parting, *willing*.

And then he pushed away. Punishing both of them. 'Have fun.'

Amanda cursed as she leaned against the door and jammed her fingers into fists to stop herself running after him like the lovesick fool she was.

Who was she kidding?

That show of bravado and defiance had been nothing but the smoke of an illusionist and it had taken nothing for him to blow it away. She couldn't hold out, couldn't possibly compete with him for control. But why should he be the one to hold all the cards?

On Wednesday there was nothing. No call, no text, no email. She found out that the information the rest home needed had been faxed from his office directly.

On Thursday she caked on the make-up to hide the dark circles under her eyes. Even so Bronwyn frowned at her. 'You look awful.'

'I've not been sleeping well.' At all in fact.

'Go home early.'

She shook her head. Work was a distraction. She needed something to occupy her body and mind for as much time as possible and in chasing that aim stayed chained to her desk well beyond closing. By the time she got home the streetlights were on and the scent of ten different dinners hung in the hallway.

Jared was leaning on the wall next to her door.

Her feet stopped without her instruction.

'I'm back,' he drawled, with eyes dark and fathomless.

She said nothing, couldn't come up with even the smallest barb in defence—there was only the mad acceleration of her heart and the fierce throb as blood poured into her most secret, sensual places. For that moment *nothing* mattered but getting what she needed. He shut the door behind them and she turned to face him.

It was like that first kiss of old—hard and angry and full of passion. Violent need burst through both of them, enhancing their strength and speed. But he broke away, breathing hard. She pulled him back, tender lips begging for more.

'I'm hurting you,' he resisted.

'You're not.' And she took him, mouth bruising, hands moving to get what she wanted. He took a step back but she followed, pushing him right up against the bed and then onto it. Straddling him, she pulled her panties aside and impaled herself in one fast movement.

'Amanda.' He sucked in a shocked breath. 'Are you OK?'

She sighed—a breathy half-laugh of amusement, and sublime sensual fulfilment. 'Never better.'

A gleam grew in the depths of his dark brown eyes. 'This is how you want it?'

'For now.'

He chuckled, a low, sexier-than-hell sound that should have warned her. She felt his muscles ripple and flex. And then, with fearsome self-control, he worked her up to ecstasy, beyond and back again. Until she understood entirely— while she might be on top, he still called all the shots.

Jared could admit it now. The last two days had been hell and merely proved that this thing wasn't over between them. In fact there was more to it that needed addressing. He listened to her breathing slow as he stroked the damp from her cooling skin.

'I'm sorry. I should have been more honest about where and why I was going away.'

There was no audible response, but he felt her body tense just that tiniest bit under his fingers.

'I like the mountains,' he tried to explain. 'They're relaxing.' *Usually.*

'Have you been feeling tense?'

'A bit.' *Massively.* Still was. His body was on constant alert, ready to go into battle—protect and defend mode. It was ridiculous.

He tried to relax again. Made her take it slower this time,

wanting to wring out the last of the sexual tension from her body as well as his own.

It worked only momentarily.

Rampant, unrelenting desire.

Jared cradled her once more as she recovered, her body half on his in the narrow bed of her hideous room. Places like these were rented on a week-by-week basis. Princess Amanda shouldn't be living in such a dump with scary transient neighbours. Even if she did bolt the door. But he had a solution.

His heart thudded in his chest and he swallowed.

'There's a vacant apartment in the building two along from mine,' he said. It was less than a three-minute walk.

'Are you thinking of moving?'

'No.' He cleared his throat. 'But I think you should.'

'I can't afford to move,' she said lazily. 'Things will get better now that I'm not going south all the time and don't have to pay for these extra meds for Grandfather, but it'll take a while for me to save bond and extra rent.'

'Why don't I rent it for you?'

'Pardon?'

'I'll take the lease. You just move in.'

They could be close. Accessible. He could be with her when he needed her, and have his space the rest of the time. He could maintain that distance that was so crucial. But she'd be there for him. He'd know she was there.

His muscles were taut, waiting for her answer. It was the closest he'd ever come to claiming a woman—to offering her a permanent place in his life.

'You're saying you'll set me up in my own apartment?'

'We could be together but…'

'*Not* be together.'

He let her go as she pushed up on his chest. Her tone hadn't exactly been thrilled.

'I thought this was just for a wee while,' she said, looking into his face.

'It's…ah…' He broke from her gaze. 'It's taking longer…'

She nodded slowly. 'And what happens when we do eventually reach our conclusion? Am I out on the street? Given forty-eight hours' notice or what?'

'Amanda—'

'No, I want to know. What is it you're wanting from me in return? Just sex? A specific number of times a week? Do we commit to dinner dates as well or is it just what happens in the apartment? Do we draw up a written contract? Six nights of sex for a bed and a roof. Dinner on a blowjob-by-blowjob basis?'

'Amanda, don't be—'

'No, Jared. Don't *you*,' she said harshly. 'Don't you make it worse.'

'Make what worse? I want you to—'

'I suggest you think about what it is you really want,' she interrupted again. 'And why you want it. Then come back to me. Then we'll talk.'

'You're taking this all wrong.'

'Am I? You want me to be some sort of mistress, Jared? Some kind of exclusive whore?'

'Don't talk like that.'

'Like what? *Honestly?*'

'All I want is to see you set up in a place better than this. This isn't safe.'

'Oh, right.' She stood up from the bed and took the sheet with her. 'So it's all about me. This is for *my* benefit. Well, how generous of you, Jared. First Grandfather and now me. I understand you owe him. How is it you owe me?'

'This isn't about deals or debts.' He sat up, uncaring of his nudity, just frustrated and failing to see her problem.

'No? Then what is it about?'

He fell silent.

'Like I say, Jared. Think about what you want and what you've just done. Is it an offer or an insult?'

'The *offer* is there. It's up to you.'

'I'll think about it.' She took the three paces to get as far from him as possible in the room. 'But right now I want you to leave. This is my little hovel and I need some space. I don't have the luxury lodge in Queenstown to escape to. I want my room to myself.'

He yanked on his jeans. 'You are such a woman.'

'As woman as you can get.'

'You insist on twisting things round.' He jerked his shirt over his head.

'I'm not twisting anything, Jared. I'm calling it as I see it.'

'Well, you see it wrong.' He glared, hands on hips, wanting to shake her. Why the hell couldn't she see how her moving would benefit both of them?

'Get out, Jared.'

He reached into his pocket and retrieved his car key, held it up in front of her. 'I'm leaving this for you. You'll need it tomorrow.'

She wanted to refuse. It was written all over her face and in her rigid stance. She wanted to refuse everything he offered—bar the occasional use of his body.

'I'm leaving it.' He tossed it across the room; it landed on her stripped-back bed. 'Do what you like with it.'

The door slammed behind him and then he heard the bolt shoot home.

CHAPTER FOURTEEN

AMANDA sat on the plane, staring out of the window at the beautiful snow-capped mountains—the spine of the South Island. That was what she needed—a spine. How else was she going to manage Jared?

Every cell felt hurt and it was easier to think worse of him. Whipping up her anger to block the depth of pain pressing into her ribs. How could he? How dared he treat her like that? But she knew the outrage was futile.

He could. He had. He did. And he would some more.

Ride roughshod over her. He did what he wanted, went for what he wanted with no thought of the impact on other people. Well, that wasn't strictly true, she acknowledged; he'd thought she'd be *pleased*—that she'd want to be set up at his beck and call like that. It only highlighted the fact that what they wanted from each other was so drastically different.

But she had such a weakness for him. Saying no for ever seemed impossible. Somehow she had to get away. But that felt impossible too. She still *wanted* him. She longed for him with a fierce need that had never diminished through the course of time—only intensified. But she had to break it, couldn't let her feelings for him control her life like that.

If she moved for him, she'd be on edge all the time expecting the end. And she couldn't make do with second best.

If only he hadn't mentioned it, if they'd continued as they were for a while longer—maybe she could have handled that? She could have kept her hope—deluded herself into thinking more might happen…

But for him to be contemplating some kind of permanent quasi-relationship? That he planned for them to be together but not truly *be* together for however long he liked? That she couldn't stomach.

She pushed her head harder back into the headrest as she admitted she couldn't actually stomach either of those options. She couldn't be his kept woman, but nor could she ever be satisfied with an ongoing fling. She was a fool to even think it.

She wanted more. Truthfully she'd always wanted more. She wanted it all—the commitment, the vows, the kids.

He never would.

She shifted again in her seat, recrossing her legs for the zillionth time.

'Don't be anxious. It'll be fine.' The nurse travelling with her from the new rest home smiled at her over her cup of tea.

'I'm not a very good flier.' Amanda felt compelled to offer an explanation. 'Take-off and landing is the worst but I don't really relax on board at all.'

'Lots of people feel that way.' The nurse nodded.

Truth was she'd been so preoccupied with Jared she'd hardly noticed the plane take off. He seemed to have cured her of that anxiety—by being a far greater source of stress himself.

She'd sat on her bed all night and waited for the dark sky to lighten. Driving in his car—his scent subtly surrounding her…her anger hadn't gone, but was more muted and the pain had pierced as the true meaning of his offer crystallised.

To be some kind of *mistress*? She couldn't imagine a life more lonely than to have only a tenth of the man she wanted everything of. To be compartmentalised in his life so completely. Only to warm his bed on the nights he was cold.

He was ice all through.

She was in love with him. She'd been in love with him for years. But what he was offering wasn't enough—too little, too painful. The fact he'd offered such an arrangement hurt enough already. Yet the proof that he was so emotionless, that he could seriously contemplate such a soulless scheme, didn't destroy her love for him. It made her heart ache for him as well as for herself. He'd been so broken, had so little trust in relationships. She could only hope that there was someone out there who might help him to be whole one day.

But she wasn't that person.

'Your grandfather will settle in quickly. We've got a lot of experience in dealing with patients like him.'

Amanda nodded, blinking to stop the tears from falling, and guilt rolled in like clouds in a sudden squall. She was awful—she should be thinking about her grandfather instead of Jared. Her mission today was far more important. She suppressed the wretchedness with a huge effort, tried to blink the scratchiness from her eyes.

She and the nurse walked from the plane straight to the rental car waiting for them at the airport. It was amazing what money could do. Jared had been right. She'd visited the home and they'd confirmed a place for the next week. It seemed that with the right amount of money anything you wanted could happen.

No wonder he thought he could get her to move too.

It'd be just another transaction to make his life more convenient.

'I'll drive if you like,' the nurse offered. 'You have a rest before seeing your grandfather.'

The woman was worth her weight in gold. And Jared was probably paying her in it. Amanda closed her eyes and let her drive.

Things went smoothly once they arrived. Having the nurse with her meant she had a buffer from the rest-home staff. Colin was dressed and ready. She'd talked to him every night this week, explaining that she was coming to get him so he could live nearer, but not going into too much detail to confuse or stress him. The specialist at the new home had instructed her on how to handle it. She could only be guided by his expertise. Determinedly hiding her own anxiety, she introduced the nurse as her friend who was coming on the trip with them. Her grandfather smiled.

Jared looked at his watch—again. She'd be at the rest home, just as she would have been forty seconds ago when he'd last looked at his watch and thought about where she was, how she was. He seemed to have developed some sort of nervous tic—obsessive watch-checking.

Obsessiveness full stop.

What the hell did the woman want?

He gave up on the report on his desk and went to look out of the window. Still wondering how it was going. Whether she was OK. Whether he should have gone. But he hadn't wanted to go—didn't want to face the old man. Just in case Colin remembered that he hadn't wanted him involved with his granddaughter. He hadn't thought Jared was good enough for her. But things were different now, right? He wasn't the person he'd been back then. He had money now—lots of money. A great job. Respect. Dignity.

That was what the old man had wanted, right?

But Jared couldn't be sure. Or was it something intrinsic, something so much a part of his nature that it couldn't be divorced from him, that the old man had determined wasn't good enough for his precious girl?

Maybe there was something unwanted about him—something his mother hadn't wanted. That nobody wanted.

Linda Dixon had been merciless. When he'd tried to politely refuse her advances she'd simply come on stronger. When he'd been firmer, she'd got nasty. Said she could make life very difficult for him—could cost him his jobs. But it had been the ravings of a bitter, frustrated woman, right?

'You're a stud, Jared. It's all you have to offer a woman, but it's enough to get by. You'll never amount to anything else. You should make the most of your assets now before you fall apart like your father.'

Like your father. He had fought like anything not to be like him. He worked hard, was reliable, efficient, honest.

But even so, was he like him? In the sense that he couldn't commit to a relationship—couldn't give whatever it was that would keep that person with him. Jared knew his father hadn't been interested in either his wife or his son. He'd been selfish—only taking what he wanted—which in the end was simply enough of the stuff in the bottle.

Was Jared as selfish? As susceptible to addiction? Wasn't he addicted now? It was just that his stimulant of choice was Amanda. He wanted her more than he'd ever wanted anything and he craved her in a way that he wasn't sure was at all normal.

But it was just want. His life had not enabled him to love or be loved.

His fingers itched. He could send her a text, see how she was. But he didn't think he'd get a reply—and he'd far rather hear it in her voice, so he could catch the nuances and pick up on any unspoken tension or relief. He ached to know.

Damn. Why hadn't she agreed to move? Didn't she want him any more? But he knew she did; she'd ravished him last night with a hunger that was in no way satisfied, not yet. So why so angry about the apartment idea? It was an arrangement that would give them all the benefits of a relationship and none of the…

What?

He put a hand on the cold pane of glass and asked himself. None of the angst? Concern? *Complications?*

Yet here he was already unable to work, unable to relax, for the worry about how she was getting on today. Wanting to talk to her, to help her, wanting to *be* with her…

The complications were already there.

And he was an idiot.

He pressed both hands on the glass. She was right. His offer had been an insult. He'd pretty much asked her what Linda had asked of him—but without the threat.

He'd treated her as a plaything, not a person.

But he hadn't meant it like that. God knew he hadn't meant it. But his offer had still been based in utter selfishness. He'd wanted her on his terms. Safe, emotionless terms. And in doing so he'd hurt her. Sure she'd been angry, proud, strong. But he'd seen it—the overbright flash in her eyes, the determination to hold herself away from him…

All of a sudden he couldn't breathe.

Why had she been so hurt? Had she actually wanted *more*?

He jerked away from the window. No. He knew what she wanted—she'd implicitly agreed to it, hadn't she? A few weeks of physical fun and that was it…hell, *she* was the one who chose to leave *his* bed every night.

She wanted him as her lover and nothing else. And he had nothing more to give.

But he was in a bind. She was right, he'd needed to think about what he really wanted, then they'd talk. But he couldn't open up to her…

His heart thundered in his chest. *Risk*. The greatest risk of his life—he, who'd played with fortunes for fun back in his banking days, was more terrified now about simply opening his mouth. Because he wasn't sure how he'd cope if he lost her for good.

He formulated a strategy—the heat between them fried his brain—if he was going to be able to express himself then he needed some control. He had to remove sex from the equation—at least until he knew.

He nodded to himself. Right. He wasn't going to be with her again until they had their relationship sorted out.

Relationship.

He breathed out. Whispered the word. Rolled it round in his mouth. A funny little glow burned in his chest. Hell, he was going soft. But he liked the idea of having her around. For as long as she wanted, as much as she wanted. He frowned—there was the rub. She could go at any time. Could he try to keep her happy? Keep her wanting to be with him? He didn't know that he could. He hadn't been able to keep his own mother wanting him—what hope did he have with a woman like Amanda?

The sexual attraction between them was undeniable. But if it burned out, did she feel there was anything else binding them together? He closed his eyes, trying to quell the anxiety.

He had no choice but to ask—find out what she wanted,

and see whether they could keep this thing going. Adrenalin surged through him. His muscles sharpened, he was ready to fight, now knowing what he was fighting for—more time together.

What had been her recipe for a happy marriage? Best friends, support, love. He wasn't capable of the total commitment—but two out of three might do it. Could she accept that?

He had to try. He had to do that for her.

The flight went as well as she could have hoped. Colin was happy to be with her. She'd said she was taking him to stay at a nice new place. Going over the basics she'd been saying on the phone. She helped him into the front seat of Jared's car. The nurse climbed into the back, clearly used to riding in such luxury.

The staff at the new place were welcoming with wide smiles and offered to send along a tray with tea and muffins as soon as they were settled in. She took a breath as she saw the room they'd prepared—stunning, with a magnificent view across the beautiful gardens. He could watch the sport. She could call in any time. There was even a room for her to stay the night should she want to. He'd be safe. Well cared for. And the country's leading specialist in geriatric medicine was at the hospital down the road.

It wasn't 'til after the tea tray arrived that Grandfather started to lose it. Alone with him, she helplessly tried to calm his agitation. But no matter what she said it worsened until he was beside himself—his eyes blank, panicked, a frightened old man, shouting. The nurses came, the doctor, gently calming him, administering a sedative and lifting him onto the bed.

Inside she crumpled—hating the destructive illness.

Wishing there was something more she could do. Wishing to see him happy—desperate to have him back.

The doctor said the stress of the move might make him more confused for a few days but that he'd settle down again. The reassurance didn't help. Doubts about everything brought her own despair to the surface.

The doctor then looked closely at Amanda and told her to go home. Colin would sleep through the night now and she'd be more help to him by appearing early in the morning refreshed and breezy. But she lingered, sorting through his things, setting up the photo frames, the small items of familiarity he'd had at the old home.

It was after eight when she got into the car. There was only one destination. She needed to see him, to feel his touch, to have just that fraction of what she really wanted.

She drove to Jared.

The tears started ten minutes into the journey and were streaming by the time she pulled into the garage beneath his apartment complex. By the time she exited the lift she was barely able to walk.

Tired, hopelessly confused and terrified she was doing the wrong thing in everything. She'd never felt so alone or uncertain in all of her life. Never felt so in need of comfort. She was barely able to gulp back the sobs; her throat, eyes and heart were lumps of burning pain.

She'd give in. She'd take the crumbs. She'd take whatever it was he could offer for as little or as long as he wanted. Because right now she needed him. Needed his arms around her and his strength inside her.

She fumbled with the door key, hardly able to see for the way her tears were rippling her vision. And then it opened from within. Jared's features swam before her.

She was so relieved more tears fell. She hadn't expected

him to be there but he must have been home for a while because he was barefoot and tousled in tee shirt and jeans.

'What happened?' She only half saw it, but she clearly heard his frown—heavier than lead.

She stepped just inside the door and waited as he closed it. As he turned back to her she put her arms around his neck. Not wanting to talk, just wanting to forget and to feel. 'Kiss me.'

'No.' He didn't move.

Her fingers threaded into his hair and she pressed down hard, wanting to bring his head closer to hers.

His hands gripped her wrists, and he removed her arms, pinning them to her sides. 'No, Amanda.'

She didn't understand. Refused to believe.

She leaned forward, sinuously pressing her breasts and pelvis against his body. 'Kiss me, Jared.'

He stepped back, hands sliding up to her upper arms, forcing her to stand alone. 'No.'

No.

She heard him then.

No. No. No.

She was blind to everything but that denial; her tears splashed on her arm—on his hand.

Oh, God, he was rejecting her again right when she needed him most. Right when she was ready to give in and accept anything from him—no matter how little. Now he was taking it all away.

She wrenched away from him. Running.

'Amanda!'

She curled her fingers round the key that she still held—gripping it so tightly her skin was almost pierced by its jagged edge. Not caring that it was his car she was going to escape him with. The lift was still on his floor. She jabbed at the buttons, shutting the door, stopping him from coming in after her.

In the cool gloom of the basement the lights flicked on his car as she pressed the button on the key. She was in and hit the ignition. The engine purred. She jerked the stick into gear. But then she turned on the windscreen wipers instead of the lights.

'Damn!' Bloody European car.

That smallest, silliest of things was the final straw.

She screamed. Gripping the steering wheel as she bent her head over it and howled with the pain and guilt and sheer soul-destroying loneliness. A raw, violent sound that cracked and lurched as she sobbed uncontrollably.

The door opened.

'You're in no condition to drive.' His voice was rough but his hands were gentle as he slid one under her, the other behind her back, and carried her back to the lift.

Her fist clenched on his chest. She could feel his heart pounding. He must have flown down those stairs to have kept pace with that supersonic lift.

'I hate you,' she choked. He'd hurt her and now she had nothing left, not even pride as she broke. The world crumpled and she screwed up her eyes, unable to stop the rivers flowing from them.

'I'm sorry.' He held her close as the lift whizzed up. Walked straight into the apartment—his door still open wide from the crazy sprint they'd both taken. He kicked it and it slammed behind him. Five strides later he was at the sofa and sitting on it; his grip loosened a little then but she didn't have the energy to pull up and away. Every ounce of her had succumbed to grief.

And her thoughts went back to her grandfather. To the terror and despair of those moments before she'd called for the doctor. She cried and cried and cried for the loss of the only parent she'd known, for the heartbreak at seeing him fade. For seeing such a strong, vital man cowed and child-like and so vulnerable. And for her inability to protect him. She'd let him down.

'I should have done more. I should have been there more.' She sobbed, barely coherent.

His lips were on her hair as he answered. 'You did everything you could.'

'It should have been more.' Her voice rose. 'I never should have left.'

'You were young. You had to leave home. He wouldn't have wanted you to stay.'

'I should have gone back more often. I should have seen it sooner.' She was so sorry. So unbearably sorry. 'I wish he'd told me.'

'He's not himself.'

And now she was alone.

Eventually Jared stopped trying to reason with words and just soothed with shushing sounds and gentle strokes down her back. Rocking her and listening and being supportive as best he could. Forcing his own lust down, just cradling her like the sad friend she was. She needed arms and ears more than passionate aerobics. She was in no state for it and he didn't want to confuse things more.

He didn't want to bury her emotion and pain in what was, at present, only a temporary fulfilment. And he wanted to know all her secrets, her fears and sense of loss. And then he wanted to fix it somehow.

His heart filled to bursting as he felt the break in hers. Felt the honesty in her love and sadness for her grandfather. She loved him. And Jared wished he'd had someone to care for him as deeply as that. A family. A real kind of family that was there through thick and thin—those people who made mistakes with each other but who forgave and who still loved regardless.

But he couldn't believe that he could ever make that family with Amanda.

After a long while he moved. She'd cried herself to sleep and his arms were beyond aching and right on into numb. He didn't care. Didn't want to give up the burden of her. He carried her into his bedroom. Laid her down and loosened her clothing, shrugged out of his own. Slipping between the soft sheets, he pulled her towards him, curling around her, listening to her jagged breathing and the occasional hiccup.

Hours later he still couldn't sleep, lay with his head propped on his hand watching her face in the dim room. Her cheeks were pale, a bit blotchy, tear-stained and tired. He bit the inside of his cheek, feeling a strange stinging at the back of his own eyes. He clamped his teeth together then. She made him weak. But somehow she made him strong too. He needed the morning to come. Needed to be able to talk to her when she was calm and rested.

Only problem being that *he* was far from calm, and found any kind of rest impossible.

CHAPTER FIFTEEN

AMANDA woke, her eyes so heavy they wouldn't open properly. They must be totally puffy. Man, she must be a sight. She lay still, trying to ignore the headache, but it thudded anyway.

She was in his bed and he was an arm's length away, sound asleep and, as far as she could tell, naked.

And despite last night's outpouring, her eyes watered again. More for him this time than for her grandfather.

It hurt—she winced and tried to blink them back. Enough already.

He'd refused her last night, when she had wanted him so badly. He'd torn her heart right through and all the pain had tumbled out. But even though it hurt she couldn't blame him. Couldn't hate him how she'd really like to. He could never give her what she wanted. She understood that now. He simply didn't have those feelings in him—not for her. That was why he'd made the offer he had. He hadn't understood her angle—hadn't even thought that she longed for something more. He just wanted her around for fun-filled nights. Not needing or wanting anything else. Happy to pay the money to make it more convenient, surprised that she'd been angry. At least he hadn't worked out why she'd been so angry. At least she thought he hadn't then, he must know now. But she was beyond the humiliation.

It no longer mattered. She knew what she had to do. It would be difficult now that Grandfather had moved here, but distance should be able to be maintained. Jared wasn't about to go visit him. And if she found a new place, got a new job, there would be no reason for their lives ever to intersect again. It would be over.

But there was one last thing she couldn't resist. Was it wrong to take advantage of a man when he was vulnerable—physically at least? She figured he wouldn't really mind. It was merely sex for him and she knew how much he enjoyed it. And she wanted one last memory to take with her.

She justified it for a few moments more—she was giving to him. She wanted to give everything to him. She loved him. She'd always loved him. And this one final time she'd show him exactly how much she loved him. Show it with her body not with the words that she didn't have the courage to say.

Then she'd leave. Not make things difficult by asking things from him that he simply couldn't give. Not any more.

She wriggled out of her bra and undies—a little nervous. Because last time she'd pulled a stunt like this it hadn't exactly gone down well. But it was different now. She knew him. She knew what he liked and she knew he liked her touch.

He stirred. Mumbled something. She stroked his cheek. She didn't want him to wake yet, couldn't bear for him to reject her again. She just wanted to love him this one last time.

She moved slowly, smoothly, pressing a kiss to his roughened jaw.

'Stay asleep,' she whispered. 'It's just a dream.'

* * *

'Amanda.'

It wasn't a dream. Jared could feel her fingers, her hair as it trailed across his face. He could smell her—fresh and warm.

But he couldn't open his eyes. So tired, so comfortable—so wonderfully comfortable.

She was above him, he could feel her softness and it felt as if she was wrapped around him. Her hands touched the parts where he ached most—soothing, then stirring.

He really tried to concentrate. This shouldn't be happening. She was vulnerable. He'd stayed awake for hours last night, holding her, watching her sleep, wishing things were different. He'd drifted to sleep only as the first light of dawn was spreading in fingers through the three-quarters-drawn blinds and he was beyond tired now. Resistance was fading. Integrity slipping. Good intentions, oh, so quickly… gone.

His hands lifted and he clutched her to him. She was soft. So soft and she melted all around him, over him. Her hair, her warm body, her wide, moist mouth. Oh, she was sweet.

'Amanda?'

'Shh.' She kissed him. Kissed him as she'd never kissed him before and his mind refused to focus on anything else.

And then her mouth, her beautiful mouth was moving down his body—kissing…

'No,' he gasped.

She didn't understand he couldn't tolerate much. Too tired to maintain control. He'd come in another minute… another—

She moved. Thank God she moved. He breathed. But then she touched him again. With her wet, intimate heart this time.

He groaned, hoarse, aching. And as he instinctively tilted his hips, she slid down, enveloping him.

'Jared.' Her whisper, her plea, was his absolute undoing.

Never had anyone spoken to him like that, with such longing, with such—oh, God, was it love?

He cried out, voice mingling with hers as he both imploded and exploded.

Long moments later he could almost think—she felt so good, so utterly good but he was spent. The delightful darkness pulled him down; his eyes refused to open. He held her close. Never so content. Never so complete.

And then he slept.

He kept his eyes closed when he woke, but he couldn't stop the smile, enjoying the memory of that magic, hearing once more the way she'd said his name. *Jared.*

He sat up in a rush, powered by that memory, turning to talk to her, wanting to make it right, *now.*

He blinked at the empty stretch of bed beside him.

He reached out a hand, spread fingers wide on the sheet, the dented pillow—it was cool. He threw back the cover and went in search of her. Refusing to think. Refusing to—

It was there in the lounge. Unmissable, unavoidable.

For the second time in his life Jared stared at a piece of paper and knew his world had stopped. Over fifteen years ago his mother had left him one too but there wasn't even an envelope this time. Just a scrawl on a rough piece of paper that had been folded over. He didn't need to read it to know it would tell him the most terrible thing that anyone could. But still he lifted it, opened it. Read only the words that mattered, cutting through the waffle—ignoring the dishonest, trying-to-soften-the-blow crap.

I'm leaving. She'd already gone.

I'm sorry. Sure she was.

So far, so familiar. But then Amanda's note took an even worse turn that his mother's had.

Thank you.

For what? He scrunched it in his fist. The sex?

And then he felt it. The bitterness burning his throat and nose. He raced to the kitchen, gulped a glass of water to keep the nausea down.

Rage rose in its place. The glass shattered as he hurled it into the sink. Not enough, the smash wasn't loud enough, the destruction not big enough to slake his ravenous anger.

He gripped the edge of the cold steel bench, staring at the shards of glass, counting to keep control, waiting like rock for the need to lash out in savage violence to pass.

She'd left him.

She'd carved her name deep into his heart with the blunt edge of a dirty spoon and left the wound to fester. Poison flooded his veins and raced through every inch of his body. He turned, breathing hard, looked around his apartment— at the expensive furniture, the priceless art and the exquisite comfort. None of it mattered. He might as well be living under a bridge for all the happiness *things* brought. He had no peace. No satisfaction. No hope.

And whose fault was it?

His own. His rage turned inwards—on his thick-headed cowardice. He should have talked to her, should have told her what he'd been too scared to admit even to himself.

This unbearable pain was the flip side of love and he deserved the agony, didn't he? For she was the only woman he'd loved, the only woman he would ever love. And he'd been too terrified to tell her.

Now he'd lost her. And he knew she wasn't coming back.

He walked through the lounge, hating every inch of it— the rug they'd rolled on, the windows she'd strolled in front of. His eyes lifted, to the painting she'd so admired. His stomach cramped again. All pleasure was gone from it. No way was he looking at it for a minute longer—he'd sell it, give it away, anything, but it had to be gone.

He reached up with wide arms and lifted the thing from the wall. With the heavy load he turned; he'd put it face down on the table for now. But as he lowered it he exerted that touch too much pressure. It slid from him, falling fast, the canvas catching the corner of the coffee table. The rip was so quick he hardly heard it—but there it was, torn right through the middle.

He looked down at the thing of beauty he had just destroyed.

He was condemned.

CHAPTER SIXTEEN

AMANDA quickly walked to the entrance of the gallery, having checked everything she needed was in her bag. It was her fourth night out this week. But being busy didn't make it better.

She'd left the ad agency—Bronwyn had said she was sorry to lose her, but Amanda knew it was for the best. If they were doing yet more work for Jared, there was no way she could be involved and it freed up funds in the agency for them to employ someone more experienced.

She'd found another job on *Exclusively Auckland*—the monthly style and society magazine that was produced by the newspaper company. She'd gone for an advertising spot but somehow ended up as copywriter—covering arts and events. Those few communications papers she'd tossed in with her degree had come in handy, as had her photography hobby. But what had swung it all together were her social skills—while she wasn't a toff, she could fake it, converse politely with any of them. Funny how her time at Eastern Bay School for Girls had turned out to be one of her greatest assets.

And so in the last four weeks she'd attended every society event there was—exhibition openings, first performances, fundraisers, fashion launches, rugby matches and band debuts. And at each she'd talked to the VIPs, snapped the shots and written up the highlights. During the day she wrote fluffy advertorials on local fashion designers, artists and café owners.

She ran a hand down her little black dress, smoothing it. It was the second airing it had had this week. She'd had to become increasingly inventive with her accessories and combinations—but tonight she'd gone with pure simplicity.

Lifting her hand to check her hair, she caught the scent of the expensive perfume she'd sprayed on as she'd walked through a department store on the way. She patted the smooth French roll, satisfied it was neat—and practical as well.

The gallery owner smiled at her as she walked in. Already she was becoming known as 'Amanda from the magazine'. She moved into action; she had a mental list of the 'big guns' due to attend—the soap stars, the politicians, and the businessmen whose pictures would help sell the copy. They all wanted their fifteen minutes—all happy to pose for a head-and-shoulders shot that would make it into the 'been seen' section.

She'd circuited the vast interior once already before she stopped and actually looked at the walls of the gallery. There was some good stuff. Having checked off a few of her 'must snaps', she went to find the artists. Three were present. She talked with them, took photos of them beside their work.

The fourth artist was missing but she went to his wall— drawn to a wide landscape depicting the milky blue of the southern lakes and the mountains rising high behind. In the foreground a lone hawk gazed back at her. It was just the thing Jared would love too—he would see the predator; she saw its vulnerability. She forgot her job and simply stood in front of it for a long time.

'That one's already sold.'

She recognised the gallery owner's voice right behind her.

'The first to go tonight,' the woman continued. 'Let me introduce you to the buyer, he's—'

'We've met.'

Amanda's eyes closed for a heartbeat—the beat her heart had just missed at the sound of that voice. Her whole body flushed—hotter and then hotter still until it felt as if her skin were about to blister. It took another few beats before she was able to turn and look.

He was in a tux. She'd never seen him in a tux. And, being the lord of night, he was smouldering, dangerous and compelling.

'Right.' The gallery manager filled the century-long void. 'I'll leave you to chat, then.'

Amanda was fixed in place by those beautiful dark eyes. She gripped her pen harder, trying to regain some sense of reality—but all she could do was stare. There were a myriad emotions in his expression and she desperately wanted to understand each and every one. But it was hopeless.

'It's a beautiful painting.' She kind of got her larynx to work.

'I'm glad you think so.' He didn't look it. 'You want an interview with me, Amanda?'

'You don't do publicity.'

'It wouldn't be the first time I've made an exception for you.' His eyes raked over her. 'You've lost weight.'

'So have you.' His jaw was more defined than ever and her lips tingled—remembering the deliciously rough sensation of pressing against his skin.

'I've been busy.' She was staring so much her eyes were watering. That was why they were brimming, right? Because she hadn't blinked.

'So have I.'

He stepped closer and despite her heat she shivered. Fever—he was like some tropical disease that she hadn't a hope of beating, lost once more into the vortex of feeling she had for him: the burning black hole of love.

His head was on an angle, he was watching her so closely, reading every single subtle sign—the response that she just couldn't stop as he touched her, the lightest stroke of his finger across her nose, turning it so the back of his finger brushed down her cheek. She shivered more violently.

'Don't, Jared,' she whispered. *Don't make me want you even more. Not again.*

'Have you missed me?' His voice was so low and yet she heard it so clearly. Words that rubbed raw the deep hurt within.

His eyes penetrated, darkly going below her flimsy layer of protection—did he see everything?

With every breath she'd missed him. What would he do if she answered with that honesty? Yet she could not go back to how they were—couldn't not have all of him.

But he'd stepped closer and her body was begging for him to come closer still. Her heart hammered unevenly, madly, and her breathing was short and quick as she tried to get enough oxygen in—enough to be able to think, to protect. She had to protect herself. Her mind raced; she had to stop this.

'I don't want to be your mistress.' She blurted the words out. 'I understand if you don't want to keep paying for Colin's home and I'd appreciate it if you could let me know as soon as poss…as…poss…'

She stammered and stopped. Her eyes were so wide they burned as she watched his face go white, the angle of his jaw sharpening, and a pale ring appear around his lips.

He breathed in, lips parting only a fraction. As he spoke they barely moved more. 'Get out. Go.'

Fear flooded her. The look in his eye had been pure rage. Knowing he meant it, she ran, lightly stepping out of the side entrance to the gallery and cutting across the car park. She'd gone five paces when she heard his footsteps on the concrete behind her—fast and furious. With strides double the length of hers it was only a moment before he was right behind her.

'Do you really think I'd do that?' He grabbed her arm and pulled her round. 'What the hell kind of person do you think I am? How could you think I'd do that to you?'

Her heart thudded so fast she thought she might faint, or choke, or both. 'I don't know what to think of you, Jared.'

'Do you really think I'm such a sleazy bastard as to use your grandfather? God, Amanda. That's not what I want.'

'I don't know what you want. But I don't want to owe you. I'll pay you back—I've got a new job and I'm saving and I'll—'

'You owe me nothing!' he shouted. 'This was a debt I owed.'

Looking at him hurt so much but she couldn't stop.

His chest was heaving and his eyes were full of bitter accusation. 'You walked out on me.'

'And you just told me to go.'

'What the hell do you want from me?' The words were torn from him.

'Everything!' She couldn't hold hers back. 'I've always wanted everything from you. But you rejected me.'

'Is this about the night Colin moved up? The night I—'

'Said no to me.' When she'd needed him more than ever. He shifted, hands fisted as he loomed closer. 'It really does come down to sex with you, doesn't it, Amanda? All you want is sex.'

'Rubbish!' she shouted. 'I wanted you to *make love* to me because it was just a tiny part of what I *really* wanted.'

He frowned.

'I wanted you to love *me*,' she broke. 'It's all I've ever wanted. I know you don't. I know you want me like that but I'll never be the person you want by your side for ever. I don't know that you'll ever want someone by your side for ever.'

He closed his eyes, veiling an expression of pain so intense it cut across her heart.

'Jared—'

'Do you love me?' He sounded astounded.

'Of course.' She stared at him through the tears that were falling fast. 'What on earth did you think I felt for you?'

'I knew you wanted me.' He shook his head. 'You liked how I could make you feel.'

'That's just sex. And wonderful as it is it's nothing on how you make me feel the rest of the time.' She sniffed. 'I *hate* how you make me feel. So insecure. So miserable. So lonely. I didn't want to always be wondering when it was going to end.'

He stared at her, looking as if the sky had just fallen in on him, and as if he couldn't believe it.

'Damn it, Jared, I've loved you for years. I've always loved you.'

'Why?' He looked so stunned her heart broke all over again.

This, the boy who'd been abandoned by his mother and neglected by his father. Who knew women could want him, but never love him?

'How can you ask that? There's everything to love about you.'

He frowned again but she barrelled on. 'Yes, I love your

body. You know how much your body thrills me. You're sex on legs and you know it and, yes, you're the only man I've ever wanted like that and the extent to which I want that…you already know.' She'd wanted him so much she'd ravished him. Repeatedly.

'Your bank account I couldn't care less about. I mean, I love what you've done for Grandfather. Of course I do. It's just one example of how generous you are. How honourable. But I loved you for years before that. I loved the guy who came and worked on the farm and in Grandfather's office. The guy who was so serious and sullen and yet who could make my day just by looking at me.'

'Why didn't you tell me?'

'How could you not know?' she shrieked. 'I've been throwing myself at you for ever. And you always rejected me.'

'I thought you just wanted…I thought I was your bit of rough.'

'Oh, Jared.' She shook her head. 'I thought *I* was just sex for *you*. That was all you wanted, that was how you set it up.'

'I thought it was,' he said slowly. 'I really did. I thought the memory of you that night had somehow gotten under my skin—had become a fantasy that had to be played out.' He blew out a hard breath and stepped closer, cupping her face with hands that were trembling. 'Amanda, the truth is I love you.'

As the tears washed down her cheeks his voice broke— the words emerging frantic and fast. 'I've loved you for ever and I'll love you the rest of my days.'

He clutched her tightly to him and she tried to hold back the sobs and listen instead. 'You were the spoilt princess back then, and part of me hated you. I was jealous, you had everything. But I wanted you—so beautiful and wild. I couldn't have you—not when Colin had been so good to me. Meeting you again… I thought you were still the spoilt miss but once we started I found that all that was wrong. You were amazing—so generous, and I wanted more of what you could give. Finally I realised that just sleeping with you wasn't going to be enough. I wanted you to be mine. But I was terrified.'

'I didn't have everything, Jared,' she said painfully. 'Sure I might have had things and money. But I was lonely. So lonely and I saw you and I knew there was something in you that fit with me. And then when I got sent away? I hated you for that. I blamed you. I was so hurt.'

His arms were right around her now, cradling her close.

'Seeing you again it was like being in a time warp—all those feelings for you just came rushing back.' She'd been sixteen again and as out of control as ever. 'And they just grew. You were everything I'd thought you'd be and then so much more. The more time I spent with you, the more I wanted—all of you. Until you said you'd get an apartment for me.'

'That ended it for you.'

'It had to. I wanted so much more.'

'Was it fair of you?' he asked softly. 'To walk out? Without even talking to me?'

More tears tumbled as she absorbed how much he'd been hurt too. 'I couldn't bear for you to reject me again. I had to be the one to go. It had to be my decision.'

'I'm sorry. I wasn't rejecting you like that. You were in no condition to make love—as desperate as I was to. I didn't want to do that again until we'd sorted everything out.'

'You should have told me.'

'You were hysterical.' He tilted her chin and looked right into her soul with eyes that begged her to believe him. 'I never meant to hurt you.' He took a breath and said it again—the most important thing with the most intense conviction. 'I do love you, Amanda.'

She tightened her hold on him, suddenly terrified at what might not have been. 'If I hadn't run into you tonight we—'

'I knew you were going to be here,' Jared said. 'I was completely unprofessional and bullied Bronwyn into telling me where you were working. I couldn't stand another day without seeing you. But I wanted to surprise you, wanted to see your reaction. To see if—'

'I've never stopped wanting you.' She ached with the need of him, feeling it bite now, knowing he'd come for her, knowing he loved her.

'But it's more than that, isn't it?'

She nodded.

'Amanda, my feelings for you terrify me. The thought of losing you terrifies me. But I couldn't bear it if you didn't feel the same.'

'I love you.' She'd say it a million times a day if that was what he needed.

'You better mean it.' His arms held her tight and his head rested on hers. 'I'll never let you go. Not now. You've given me everything I never had, you know that, don't you?'

She did; she was just so incredibly relieved he wanted it. 'There's more to give.'

He looked at her.

'We could make a family together, Jared.' She spoke faster, seeing the shadows gathering in his eyes. 'We could be the parents we always wanted but didn't get. We'd shower them with love. Be there for them.'

'I don't think I know how to be a parent, Amanda.' He shook his head. 'I didn't have a very good example.'

'We'll learn together.' She smiled, leaning against him. 'We're good at learning—even if it is slow.'

'You're not a slow learner, sweetheart.' He blew out a shot of air. 'OK. We'll learn together.'

'You'll be great, Jared. You're great at everything you do. We can have everything together.' She hugged him close. 'Everything that matters.'

Hope. Faith. Love—a family.

'Don't you ever walk out on me again.'

Had he just cracked one of her ribs with the tightness of his embrace? She didn't care. All she wanted was to fill this gaping great ache inside him.

'I want to be with you for always. Believe me when I say it, Jared. I love you and I will never leave you.'

'Not until death do us part?'

'Not even then.'

'So you'll marry me?'

'Just try and stop me.'

'I wouldn't dare.' A smile. Finally, a huge delicious smile spread over his face. 'What Amanda wants, Amanda gets.'

'Yes.' Her eyes were overflowing again. 'I'm thinking soon. Really quiet and quick. Just us so we can get on to the good bit as soon as possible.'

'You don't want the big performance?'

'I just want us. All that matters is me and you.'

'What about your grandfather?'

'Oh,' she half sobbed. 'He doesn't have long, Jared. And I'd like him to be there.' She felt his uncomfortable twitch, the tiny withdrawal. She had her suspicions as to why. 'Want to know what I found?'

She stepped away from him and opened up her bag, carefully extracted the page from the zipped compartment usually reserved for things like keys or coins. She unfolded it. 'I found it in his file of important papers.'

It was that old alumni article, the one his mother had read before Jared put the ban on any personal publicity.

'He saw it. Cut it out and kept it, Jared.'

He took it from her and stared at the picture of himself.

'No man was ever going to be good enough for me. Not in his eyes,' Amanda said softly, suddenly feeling shy. 'But you're the only one he kept a clipping on.'

He looked at it a long time, she felt the rigidity in his muscles, but when he finally looked up at her the tenderness in his eyes made her bones melt. The relief in them turned her heart to mush completely.

'Why do you have it in your bag with you?'

She looked down and took the paper back from him. Looked at the image: Jared James in the dark jersey, looking like some Hollywood screen rebel—the dark eyes, the hint of that smile on his mouth.

'Why do you think?' She sounded as if she'd smoked thirty a day for the last fifteen years.

'You can do better than that.' He touched her hair lightly. 'You can have the real thing.'

His tenderness was laced with desire now. She watched as it grew and hers grew too—going from zero to two hundred in less than a second.

'I want it now.' She walked into the darkness, searching out his car.

'Amanda, we're in a car park. There are people around.' But he followed after her, fingers reaching forward to trail across her back.

There wasn't anyone else outside. They were too busy in the gallery hoovering up the food and drink.

'Then stay close, they won't see a thing.' She found his

car mercifully parked away from the streetlights, slipped her knickers down her legs, scrunched them in her hand and put them in his pocket.

'I always knew you had a wild streak.' He sounded hoarse, his hands hovering above his fly.

She leaned back against his car. 'Come on. I won't need long.'

His laugh was more of a choke. 'That's supposed to be my line.' He stood close to her, body and arms shielding the fact that she'd just pulled up the front of her dress. 'But the fact is I need for ever.'

'Give me a taste of it now.' She grabbed his hips and pulled him home.

'There's no denying you, is there, Demanda?' He groaned, body moving powerfully to claim hers.

'I'm so glad you finally see that, Jared,' she gasped.

His smile was smothered as they kissed and connected. She was right: neither needed long for that taste of for ever.

'*Jared.*'

He looked down, all the stars were in his eyes and she was soaring through them. She smiled and as his smile burst forth it was as if all the brilliant fireworks in the world exploded in her chest—filling her with colour and light and happiness.

She buried her face in his neck. 'Take me home.'

'Sweetheart…' he tightened his embrace '…we're already there.'

In each other's arms. For ever.

THE GOOD, THE BAD
AND THE WILD

BY
HEIDI RICE

Heidi Rice was born and bred and still lives in London. She has two boys who love to bicker, a wonderful husband who, luckily for everyone, has loads of patience, and a supportive and ever-growing British/French/Irish/American family. As much as Heidi adores 'the Big Smoke', she also loves America, and every two years or so she and her best friend leave hubby and kids behind and *Thelma and Louise* it across the States for a couple of weeks (although they always leave out the driving off a cliff bit). She's been a film buff since her early teens and a romance junkie for almost as long. She indulged her first love by being a film reviewer for the last ten years. Then a few years ago she decided to spice up her life by writing romance. Discovering the fantastic sisterhood of romance writers (both published and unpublished) in Britain and America made it a wild and wonderful journey to her first Mills & Boon® novel.

Heidi loves to hear from readers—you can e-mail her at heidi@heidi-rice.com or visit her website: www.heidi-rice.com.

To Abby Green, for seeing me to the end of this book,
and being a fabulous roomie in NYC 2011!

With special thanks to Michelle Styles,
who knows the Bay Area much better than I do.

CHAPTER ONE

'Don't look now, but he's here and he's right behind us.'

Eva Redmond's heart catapulted into her throat as the urgent whisper from her old college chum Tess sliced through the hum of polite conversation and the tinkle of champagne glasses in the upscale San Francisco art gallery. 'Are you sure?'

Tess looked past Eva's right shoulder. 'Tall? Check.' She nodded. 'Dark? Check. Handsome? Check. The only one not in a suit? Check.' She grinned at Eva. 'Yup, it's definitely your rebel scriptwriter.' Her gaze flicked past Eva again. 'And you're in luck. Not only is he alone. But he's even hotter than his photo.'

Eva stared blankly at the six foot square canvas in front of her—which was titled The Explosion of the Senses, but looked more like an explosion in a paint factory to her untrained eye—and swallowed down the knot of apprehension that had been tightening around her larynx ever since she'd boarded the plane at Heathrow that morning.

The knowledge that the man she'd travelled five thousand miles to meet was standing a few feet away made it feel as if she were trying to swallow a boulder.

'Goodie,' she muttered.

Tess laughed and nudged her. 'Don't sound so pleased.'

'Why would I be pleased?' Eva whispered back, fairly sure Nick Delisantro's extreme hotness was not going to work in her favour. If only he were a geeky academic. Sticking with what you knew might be dull. But dull had its advantages.

'Why wouldn't you be?' Tess countered. 'Giving a scorching hot guy the news that he's the heir to a fortune in Italian real estate is what I'd call a win-win situation.'

Eva nobly resisted the urge to sneak a peek over her shoulder. 'Yes, but I'm not you, am I?' she remarked wryly as she studied her friend dispassionately.

In her ice-blue, off the shoulder silk gown and six-inch designer heels, Tess looked elegant, slim, super-confident—and completely at home in the rarefied atmosphere of a gallery opening in San Francisco's Union Square neighbourhood. Which wasn't at all surprising. Tess had spent the last three years building a formidable reputation as an events planner in the US and even at university she'd been able to schmooze for England. Eva meanwhile had spent the years since she'd gained her first at Cambridge burying her nose in dusty antiquarian documents and computer research data. She couldn't schmooze to save her life—and she'd never felt more out of place than among all these beautiful people who had elevated socialising to an art form.

The admission touched some lonely place deep inside. She shook off the thought. She wasn't lonely; her life was exactly how she wanted it. Settled, secure, content. Until two days ago, when her boss Henry Crenshawe had demanded she travel halfway round the globe to be humiliated in public.

'And it's not as simple as telling him he could be the Duca D'Alegria's grandson. I'll also have to tell him the man he always thought was his biological father isn't.' Eva tensed at the thought of having such an intimate conversation with a stranger. A scorching hot stranger who had steadfastly ignored all her attempts to contact him in close to a month. 'I shouldn't have let you talk me into asking him for an appointment here. It's not appropriate.'

Tess gave an easy shrug. 'So don't ask him straight away. Flirt with him first. He'll be much more amenable. I guarantee it.'

Eva doubted that. She didn't know how to flirt and this man was a master at it. During her extensive research for the firm's high-profile new client, it was one of the few things she'd managed to discover about the elusive Niccolo Carmine Delisantro—the man who she had deduced was almost certainly the illegitimate grandson Don Vincenzo Palatino Vittorio Savargo De Rossi, the Duca D'Alegria, was offering a small fortune to locate.

The dry facts of Delisantro's life had told her very little about him as a person—North London runaway turned successful Hollywood scriptwriter and San Francisco resident who had scripted the biggest box-office hit of the decade five years ago—except that he was a wow with the ladies and he guarded his privacy like a hawk.

'You can take a look now, and see what you're up against.' Tess indicated with her champagne flute. 'Kate Elmsly's cornered him,' she finished, mentioning the perky and persistent gallery owner who had greeted them both earlier.

Trying to even her breathing, Eva turned. And her lungs seized to a halt. The back of her neck bristled as she took a hasty sip of her champagne cocktail. This was worse than she thought.

As she studied the man standing about ten feet away Eva realised she wasn't just out of her depth, she was in danger of drowning.

Tess was right. The grainy photo she'd managed to find on the Internet didn't do Nick Delisantro justice.

No mere human being had a right to that level of perfection. Thick wavy hair the colour of rich caramel curled to touch the collar of a worn black leather bomber jacket, which matched his thin black sweater and jeans. Sharp angular cheekbones with a hint of stubble, tanned olive skin to highlight his Italian heritage and a honed, muscular six foot plus physique combined to set him apart from the pampered crowd of local celebrities and dignitaries. His dark brooding masculine beauty drew female eyes, and hers were no exception—the relaxed, almost insolent way he leaned against the bare brick column as the gallery owner chatted effusively only made him seem more aloof. Surly, sexy, supremely magnetic, effortlessly successful as a hunter-gatherer but with a dangerous edge, Nick Delisantro was the perfect male prototype to ensure the survival of his species.

Eva sighed, a shiver running down her spine then sprinting straight back up again. While she was the female prototype to ensure it failed. An academic whose knowledge of men and sex included a few fumbled encounters as a post-grad and a secret passion for florid historical romance novels that had half-naked men with exceptional pecs on the covers.

She swung back to face 'The Explosion of the Senses,' her own senses imploding as her gaze skimmed down the designer gown Tess had lent her. 'This isn't going to work,' she murmured, more to herself than her friend. 'I look ridiculous.'

The crimson velvet creation with its split skirt and plunging neckline would look sensational on her friend, but Eva was two inches shorter and had several extra inches round the bust. The gown had made her feel exhilarated when she'd squeezed into it an hour ago, but now only made her feel like more of a fraud.

She wasn't one of those stunning damsels in distress with long flowing tresses and enough spirit to bring a marauding pirate captain to his knees. She was a risk-averse academic with a wardrobe full of beige who was still technically speaking a virgin at the ripe old age of twenty-four.

Tess placed a comforting hand on Eva's forearm. 'You do not look ridiculous. You look voluptuous.'

Eva crossed her arms over her chest. 'Flashing my boobs at him is not the way to go here,' she said, feeling more uncomfortable by the second. 'I should just go to his agent's office tomorrow morning and ask him for an appointment.' That would be the safe, smart thing to do, and had been Eva's plan all along until Tess had discovered through her many contacts that Nick Delisantro was attending tonight's gala opening and wheedled them both an invite.

'Cleavage is never a bad thing where men are concerned,' Tess asserted. 'And you said this commission is important,' she urged. 'If his agent blows you off, what are you going to tell your boss?'

Eva didn't have an answer for that. Mr Crenshawe had told her in no uncertain terms that Roots Registry valued the De Rossi commission, and if Eva delivered the missing heir before one of the rival companies the duca had hired located him too, she would finally be in line for a promotion.

It was a powerful incentive. Eva adored her job. Poring over diaries and journals and correlating the evidence left by birth, marriage and death certificates allowed her to imagine lives often lived centuries ago—their passions, their pain, their triumphs and tragedies. And the promotion she'd worked so hard for would finally give her the job security she craved.

Tess craned her neck to peer past Eva. 'It looks like he's shaken off Kate,' she continued. 'Go now.' She prodded Eva with her elbow. 'Brush past him on your way to the bar. The dress will do the rest.'

'And if it doesn't?' Eva asked tentatively, not sure the revealing dress was something she could actually control.

Tess shrugged. 'Then you haven't lost a thing. We'll go back to my place and you can try out plan B for Boring tomorrow.'

'Okay.' Eva took a shuddering breath, feeling as if she were about to walk the plank—in nothing but her underwear. 'I'll walk past him on my way to the toilet.' How hard could that be? 'But then we're leaving.'

She handed Tess her empty champagne flute and smoothed shaky palms down the luxurious velvet. The soft, seductive material brushed against her thighs as she concentrated on not falling flat on her face in the unfamiliar four-inch heels she'd also borrowed from Tess. She glanced towards him as she drew level, positive he wouldn't even have noticed her. And froze.

Heavy lidded chocolate eyes, as bold and insolent as the rest of him, caught hers and held. The image of Rafe, the pirate captain from her favourite, much-thumbed novel, shimmered like a mirage then cleared. A shaky breath gushed out as she stared back, transfixed by the way the overhead light caught the golden flecks in his irises. The colour was unusually striking and very familiar. She'd seen the exact same shade when the duca had arrived at their offices in London to hand over his dead son's journal.

His grandson's lips lifted a fraction on one side, as if he were enjoying a private joke, then his gaze dipped. Eva's heart punched her ribcage with the force of a heavyweight champ.

The lazy perusal raked over her sensitised skin like a physical caress, before his gaze met hers again. 'Do I know you?' he asked, the tone husky and amused, curt British vowels laced with the hint of a Californian drawl.

Eva shook her head, her tongue apparently stapled to the roof of her mouth.

'So why have you and your friend been spying on me?' he asked.

Good Lord, he has bionic hearing.

Eva's breathing choked to a stop. Then released in a rush as her common sense caught up with the kick of panic. He couldn't possibly have heard them—with all the hard surfaces the noise level in the gallery was loud and discordant. He must have spotted Tess watching him. Tess wasn't exactly subtle.

'We couldn't help it,' she said, trying to think of a viable excuse. 'You're a lot more intriguing than the art.'

'Is that right?' One brow lifted, making her breathing accelerate. 'I'm not sure that's a compliment. A daytime soap would be more intriguing than this stuff.' The disdainful comment was belied by the wry tone. 'What's so intriguing about me?'

Eva's breathing slowed and she began to get a little light-headed.

Was he flirting with her?

'You don't belong here,' she stammered, the fierce buzz of anticipation in her stomach coming from nowhere. 'But you don't care. That's unusual in a social situation. The normal response is to want to participate. To be part of the crowd. That makes you intriguing.'

The words trailed off as his lips quirked in a curious grin, softening his angular features.

Stop lecturing, you idiot. You sound like a professor.

He straightened away from the column, making her aware that he was at least half a foot taller than her, even in her borrowed heels.

Lifting his arm, he propped it against the column, angling his body so he shielded them both from the rest of the gallery. He stood close enough for her to smell the tantalising musk of soap and leather and pheromones. And see the crescent shaped scar drawing a white line through the shadow of stubble on his cheek. The pirate fantasy flickered at the edges of her consciousness. She forced it back, but not before the pulse of heat rippled over her skin and made her heart rate shoot back up to warp speed.

'You worked all that out after a few minutes?' he drawled.

Guilt tightened the muscles in her throat.

Not exactly.

'That's what I do. I'm an anthropologist.' *Of sorts.* 'I study people and their behaviour patterns. How they interact socially and culturally.' It wasn't exactly a lie, and she had a BSc to prove it.

'An anthropologist,' he said, savouring the word as if it were a rare single malt whisky. His gaze roamed over her, and her nipples squeezed into hard, aching points. 'I've never met an anthropologist before.'

And he wasn't meeting one now, she thought, her gaze flicking away from his. This was the perfect time to tell him the truth—that she was the woman whose phone calls and email messages he'd refused to return for three and a half weeks. But instead of seizing the opportunity to get down to the business of begging him for an appointment, the butterflies already fluttering in her stomach went AWOL, and she hesitated.

She'd never had the chance to flirt with a man like this before. Never been studied in that frank, assessing way, the pulse of awareness arching between them more potent than any drug.

'Anthropology can be fascinating,' she heard herself murmur, feeling inexplicably needy.

'I'll bet,' he said. 'Although you're wrong about me.' His gaze drifted over her hair, which Tess had spent an hour taming into a chignon. 'I belong here just fine.' Lowering his arm, he hooked one of the stray curls that had fallen out of the chignon. 'But you, on the other hand, don't belong at all.' The back of his finger brushed her cheek, the touch subtle but so unexpected, she jumped.

He chuckled. 'What are you afraid of?'

You.

Heat pulsed in that secret place between her thighs at the intimate question. She wasn't afraid of him, that would be ludicrous, it was just that she'd never been touched like that before, with a sense of entitlement.

'I'm not afraid,' she blurted out, the urge to run sudden and instinctive and oddly intoxicating. 'I have to go to the rest room.'

He tucked the lock of hair behind her ear with a care that made her heart throb in unison with her pulse points. 'Let's discuss anthropology when you get back.'

The suggestion was casual but proprietary and only disturbed her more. She might be a novice at this, but she didn't think this conversation had anything to do with anthropology any more.

Giving a non-committal nod, she rushed away, sure she could feel his golden gaze boring into the bare skin of her back—with the patient, predatory instincts of a lion hunting a gazelle.

The preposterous image made her breath catch. She had to get out of here—before she completely lost her grip on sanity. Plan B for Boring would have to do, because Plan A was way too terrifying—and exciting.

Colour me amazed.

Nick huffed out a rough chuckle as he watched the sexy anthropologist dash through the crowd and admired the swing of her hips in the stop-light red dress.

When was the last time he'd met someone so intriguing, especially at one of these tedious social functions?

He'd have to send Jay, his publicist, a thank you note for insisting that he venture away from his laptop tonight. Except that he hadn't really attended the gallery opening at Jay's insistence, but out of sheer boredom having spent the day staring at a screen full of rubbish.

Leaning back against the column, he closed his eyes, shutting out the hum of inane chatter and hoping to deter anyone from approaching him while he waited for the Woman in Red's return.

She'd captivated him, which was surprising in itself. He didn't appreciate being watched or whispered about, and he'd spotted her and her friend doing exactly that. But there was something about the way she had peered at him, with none of the usual calculation or confidence he had come to expect from the women that approached him. And then when he'd got a better look at her, his senses had kicked into overdrive like those of a hormonally charged teenager.

He kept his lids closed, picturing her, and tried to determine the trigger. Creamy, translucent skin? Wide blue eyes so dark they were almost violet? The flutter of her pulse visible in the graceful arch of her collarbone? Russet curls that had escaped the mass of hair artfully piled on her head? The swell of her breasts revealed by the plunging neckline of her gown? The fresh, simple scent of soap and spring flowers? The crisp, precise London accent that he hadn't heard in years?

Any one of those things could have turned him on. He was a guy after all. But still, she wasn't conventionally beautiful: not particularly tall; her eyes had been maybe too big, she had a slight overbite and her forthright observations about his character had unsettled him. Even though they could only have been a lucky guess.

Weird? There was no explaining the ferocity of attraction. Not really. Except maybe…?

He opened his eyes, found himself shifting round to look at the doors to the rest room.

And realised that by far the most captivating thing about her had been her unguarded response. Her breathing had quickened, her pupils dilating wildly as soon as she stopped in front of him. The truth was he'd always been jaded where women were concerned. Even as a boy. Once he'd grown up, he found himself craving sex as much as any man, but for him it had never been more than a physical release. And as a result in the last few years, ever since *The Deadly Touch* had made him one of the hottest properties in Hollywood, he'd developed a cynicism about the women he dated that meant while sex was satisfying, it had become less and less exciting.

He knew precisely which buttons to press to get the response from women he wanted. But when was the last time a woman had responded to him so instinctively—and with so little caution? She'd been so transparent, the instant physical connection between them so intense, he was sure it had to be an act. But act or not, he was still captivated. And intrigued. It was certainly a very long time since he'd felt this level of attraction. He glanced round, smiling at his own impatience, then pushed away from the column as he spotted her standing by the rest-room doors, talking into her cell phone. Not talking, pleading by the look of it. She snapped the phone closed, stuffed it into her purse, then rushed out of the back entrance of the gallery.

He was so astonished, it took him a moment to figure out that she'd left. Acting on impulse, he charged after her, snaking his way through the crowd.

Where the hell was she off to in such a hurry? He didn't even know her name. And he wasn't finished with her yet. Not by a long shot.

CHAPTER TWO

'HEY, wait up.'

Eva's head whipped round at the shout from behind her. She skidded to a halt, stumbling as she recognised the tall silhouette backlit by the light from the open doorway.

Strong fingers grasped her arm, steadying her. 'You okay?'

The firedoor crashed shut, throwing the alleyway into shadow.

'Yes,' she murmured, cursing the guilty blush burning her neck. 'Thank you. I'm not used to these heels.'

His fingers stroked down her arm, setting off a series of lightning bolts, before he let her go. 'I always wonder why women wear those ankle-breakers.'

'To make our legs look longer.'

He gave a gruff chuckle, the sound strangely intimate in the darkness. 'Is that so?' She saw his head dip as her eyes adapted to the low light. She took a staggered breath and his tantalising scent engulfed her, masking the aroma of wet pavements and disinfectant.

'You don't need any help on that score,' he remarked, his voice low and amused.

She wrapped her arms around herself, the chilled autumn air not the only thing causing her goosebumps. Was he flirting with her again? Why had he followed her? And why was his attention as intoxicating as it was terrifying?

'I suppose you're right,' she said. 'Given that broken ankles are even less attractive than short legs.'

He laughed again, the rough murmur chasing the blush into her cheeks.

Stop being so literal, you muppet.

'Where are you going?' he asked, mercifully ignoring her pathetic attempts at conversation.

'I…' She choked to a stop. She didn't have an answer. Her instinctive need to flee from him seeming even more ridiculous than her small talk. 'I wanted some fresh air. It's stuffy in there,' she lied.

Unfortunately, the lie didn't quite come off when she shivered.

'You're cold.' Shrugging off his jacket, he lifted her bag off her shoulder. 'Here.' Warm leather surrounded her. His scent clung to the garment, and she had to purse her lips to stop from sighing.

'Let's go for a ride.'

'I beg your pardon?' she stammered, the tone of his voice making all sorts of inappropriate, but far too appealing, thoughts pop into her mind.

'A ride.' He buried his hands in his back pockets, hunched against the cold in the crew-neck sweater and nodded down the alleyway. 'I've got my bike round the corner. And I was looking for an excuse to escape myself.'

'You mean a motorbike?'

Placing a warm palm on the small of her back, he directed her towards the end of the alleyway, subtly leading her in the direction he wanted to go. 'It's a great way to see the city. You're a Londoner, right? Like me.'

'Um, yes,' she said, dazed by the little sizzles of electrical energy where his palm rested on her lower back.

'So when did you arrive?'

'I…' She paused. She should tell him now. But her tongue

seemed to get stuck in neutral again. 'This afternoon. I'm visiting my friend Tess.'

'The other nosey one?'

She gave a nervous laugh. 'Yes, sorry.'

'Don't be,' he said as they drew level with a monstrous black motorbike, its swirling logo and silver trim gleaming dangerously in the street lamp light. 'I like getting talked about by beautiful women.'

'Oh,' she said, not sure how to take the compliment. Was he trying to be funny? She looked good tonight, but no one would mistake her for beautiful, not unless they were seriously myopic.

Unlocking the box at the back of the bike, he lifted out a helmet. 'Put this on.'

She took the helmet without thinking. Standing dumbfounded as he mounted the huge machine with easy grace.

He glanced back at her. 'Hop on.'

'But I'm wearing a dress,' she said, struggling to slow things down a little. She'd never been on a motorbike before, especially not with a man of his… Power. 'And heels,' she added. 'What if I fall off?'

Placing a proprietary hand on her hip, he nudged her round to face him, took the helmet from her, and plopped it on her head. 'You won't.' He tucked the tendrils of hair into the helmet with a focused concentration that had her pulse throbbing in her throat. 'Not as long as you hold on tight.'

Fastening the helmet's strap, he ran his thumb across her chin. The tiny touch made her shiver and her tongue slipped out of its own accord, licking lips that had gone dry as a desert.

His gaze dipped and she pressed her lips together, the buzz of anticipation almost unbearable. When his eyes lifted back to her face, she could see amusement. And a disturbing intensity.

'Where do you want to go?' he murmured.

Anywhere you want to take me.

She slammed down on the impulsive thought and the much more impulsive thrum of tension that had her whole body vibrating.

She shouldn't be doing this. It wasn't just impulsive, it was reckless—bordering on inappropriate. And she'd never done anything before that bordered on reckless, let alone inappropriate.

But maybe that was exactly the problem, she realised, as the thrum of tension refused to subside. In that split second of indecision, her whole well-ordered and completely appropriate life seemed to stretch out before her in a rolling canvas of total and extreme boredom and the impulsiveness took hold of her tongue.

'I don't know. You decide,' she said, the whispered words so liberating she heard a strange sound come out of her mouth, which sounded suspiciously like a giggle.

Niccolo Delisantro chuckled back. 'See, that wasn't so hard,' he said, with surprising intuition.

Eva stiffened. Did he know how big a deal this was for her? That adventures were something she'd only ever read about in books? That her life was about as dynamic as magnolia wallpaper?

'Climb aboard and let's get this show on the road,' he added, and she shook off the humiliating thought. How could he know? He didn't know the first thing about her.

She stifled the little pang of guilt at the thought of how much she knew about him. As soon as the ride was over, she'd tell him who she was. And face the consequences. But just this once, she wanted to give in to impulse.

She adjusted the helmet on her head, then hesitated, studying the enormous machine and the small segment of leather seat available to her.

Adventure was one thing, but how on earth did you climb onto a motorbike that large? In four-inch heels and a figure-hugging designer dress?

He stood up to stamp on one of the pedals and the monster roared to life. She jumped at the explosion of sound.

'Um…I'm not sure how to…' She shouted above the engine noise. 'How do I…?' He adjusted his wrist and the noise subsided to a dull rumble. 'Do you have any instructions?'

The colour charged back into her cheeks at the easy grin he sent her over his shoulder.

So much for Eva Redmond, wild child. What kind of a loser asks for instructions on how to mount a motorbike?

Swivelling round, he lowered his gaze to her legs. 'I'm guessing you'll have to hike the skirt up.' The mischievous glint in his golden eyes made colour race over her scalp and stand the fine hair on the back of her neck on end. He leaned over and flipped open a short rubber pedal that stuck out above the gleaming silver exhaust pipe. 'Step on that and then take my arm.' So saying he held out his hand.

Biting into her bottom lip, she gathered the skirt clumsily up her legs. 'Here goes,' she mumbled as she gripped his arm. Feeling the muscles of his forearm tense, she slipped while placing her instep onto the pedal.

'Easy,' he soothed. 'There's no hurry.'

She gave him a hopeful smile, praying that her blush was dimmed somewhat by the low lighting and that she wasn't about to knock the two of them into a heap on the pavement. Then took a deep breath and launched her leg over the bike.

He gave a sharp tug as she did so, and she landed on the leather bench with a huff. Her breath sucked into her lungs at the sudden, explosive mix of sensations. The bike's heavy vibrations shuddered up through her backside, her nipples hardening into peaks as they touched the unyielding slopes of his back. The skin of her inner thighs sizzled alarmingly as the dress hitched up and she came into intimate contact with the rough denim of his jeans.

The tight muscular contours of his backside flexed through his clothing and the blush intensified.

Oh, God. She'd never been this close to a man before. Ever. The sensations racing through her were both exquisite and yet petrifying on some elemental level. She leaned back, worried he'd feel her nipples poking him, but that only intensified the pressure of his denim-clad butt pressing into her spread thighs. She fanned her hand in front of her face, convinced she was having her first hot flush thirty years too soon.

What had possessed her to agree to do this? What if she passed out from sensory overload and fell off the bike? Then got flattened by a cable car and ended up horribly mangled in the middle of a San Francisco street?

'Put your arms round my waist.' The rough command sliced neatly through her panic attack and she obeyed him instinctively. Circling him, she pressed her cheek against the silky smooth cashmere sweater and linked her fingers, trying desperately to ignore the tensile strength of his abdomen beneath her palms.

She squeezed her eyes shut as the bike jerked forward off its stand. He revved the engine, signalling another sensory overload as the shudder of leashed power made her pulse jump.

'Relax.' One large palm covered the back of her hands, still locked round his waist. 'You're safe. I swear.' She felt the rumble of his chuckle through her cheek and tried to loosen her death grip.

'My name's Nick, by the way,' he said, his warm palm letting go of her hands to steer the bike off the pavement and into the road with a jolt. 'Nick Delisantro. What's yours?'

'Eva,' she said, the renewed stab of guilt going some way to calming her rioting nervous system. 'Eva Redmond,' she added, then tensed at the realisation that he might well recognise her name and call a halt to the whole fiasco.

She frowned. The fact that she would be desperately disappointed if he did, despite the mix of terror and anticipation making her stomach churn, had to be yet more evidence that she was probably having some sort of weird emotional meltdown.

'Nice to meet you,' he said, clearly oblivious to her deception.

She breathed a ragged sigh. But as her cheek brushed the velvet steel of his back she made herself a solemn promise. She would definitely tell him who she was once their wild ride was over. No more evasions.

Assuming she survived her wild ride.

Her heartbeat slammed into her throat as the bike leapt forward like a savage beast, and reared away from the kerb. Eva's legs squeezed his backside while her arms tightened around his waist, her fingers clasped so tight she was in danger of dislocating a knuckle.

'Welcome to San Fransisco, Eva the anthropologist,' he shouted back at her.

More like Eva the Fraud.

The quick burst of shame did nothing to dim the heady kick of adrenaline as the bike tilted into a turn and then accelerated up the steep hill into the night.

Eva clung on tight and for the first time in her life allowed herself to rejoice in the thrill of doing something reckless. And unwise. And inappropriate.

And completely and utterly intoxicating.

Terror gave way to fascination as the scent of roasted duck and Szechuan spices made Eva's stomach rumble. She swivelled her head back and forth trying to take in the kaleidoscope of people as the bike wound through the traffic choked

thoroughfare. The oriental faces and exotic hieroglyphics on
the signs and posters marked the area out as Chinatown. But
almost as soon as she had registered the fact, they took a sharp
turn and left the crowded street behind. A cable car trundled
past on the cross street in front of them, like something out of
a bygone era, but for the tourists in shorts and T-shirts with
cameras round their necks sandwiched onto the bench seats.
Shuddering over the cable-car tracks, the bike climbed and
dipped through hills of ornate Victorian town houses, stopping and starting on every corner. Eva's heart thumped against
her chest wall, the emotion swelling in her throat at the overwhelming beauty of the city gilded by the dying sun.

She threw her head back, let the evening air brush a few
escaped tendrils of hair against her cheeks.

Her eyes stung with tears. How could she have spent the
first twenty-four years of her life never having done anything
remotely spontaneous or daring?

Her parents had been in their fifties when they'd had her.
Both of them brilliant academics dedicated to their chosen
fields. When she'd been conceived by accident, they hadn't
had a clue how to factor a child into their busy lives. So she'd
adapted instead. Which had meant being cautious and responsible and respecting the boundaries they set, even when she
was a teenager and every other person she knew was busy
tearing them down.

No wonder she was such a coward.

But maybe adventure didn't always have to be bad. Or contained within the pages of the romance novels her parents had
always insisted were 'a foolish indulgence'.

She blinked furiously and clung tighter as they edged down
another steep incline. The man in front of her felt so solid,
his broad back sheltering her from the lengthening shadows.
Then the bike hit a major road. Suddenly they were leaving the picture-postcard houses, the steep slopes and stepped

pavements behind. Trees and parklands sped past and then Eva gasped, her eyes widening in wonder as the Golden Gate Bridge reared up before them, a huge geometric monolith of rusty red steel lit by the dying sun.

The bike thundered through the fingers of fog drifting over the road, the rush of air and noise both cold and thrilling as they zipped past the occasional car, and a monstrous shiny yellow eighteen-wheeler. Squeezing her eyes shut, Eva hugged the only still thing in her universe and felt them both take flight through the traffic, hurtling across the water. The ball of emotion broke lose. Firing up her torso, it burst out of her mouth and she let out a gleeful yell that whipped away on the wind.

She'd been walking through a fog her entire life but now the cloying veil of conformity was being ripped away—making every colour more vivid, every scent more acute, every sense more vibrant.

To think she had lived her whole life and never experienced anything as thrilling as a sunset ride across San Francisco Bay?

Adrenaline and affection blossomed as she clung to Nick Delisantro. How could she ever thank him enough, for giving her this?

CHAPTER THREE

As the bike wound through the nature reserve on the Marin headlands, taking the climb towards Hawk Hill, Nick glanced at the fingers knotted round his waist and smiled.

He'd hazard a guess that Eva the gorgeous anthropologist had never ridden pillion before, given the way she was attached to him like a limpet. Not that he was complaining. Once she'd got the hang of leaning into the turns, the feel of her clinging to him had been very nice indeed. Her shocked little gasp when they'd hit the Bridge on 101, and her spontaneous shout as they'd raced across it had only added to the heat. Seemed the prim and proper Miss Eva had a wild side. When you factored in the familiar adrenaline kick of being on the bike and the awe-inspiring view as they topped the rise and drifted to a stop at the overlook…

No, he definitely didn't have a single complaint about his split-second decision to invite her along. It had been far too long since he'd enjoyed the city like this—or the feel of a woman's soft, pliant body plastered against his.

He felt her expel another sharp breath as he cut off the bike's engine.

'Wow.' Her hushed murmur sent a delicious tingle through the short hairs at his nape. 'It's so beautiful.'

He tilted the bike onto its stand, flattened his feet onto the ground. 'Yeah. This is the best view of the bridge.'

They sat for a while in silence, admiring the majestic span

of the Golden Gate, blazing a trail across the bay in the sunset, the fog sitting like a carpet of mist over the water and the lights of the city laid out behind.

Reluctantly, he placed a hand over hers, glanced round at wind-stung cheeks and wide violet eyes. 'It's safe to let go now.'

Pulling her hands out from under his, she sprang back. 'I'm so sorry. Was I holding on too tight?'

Her cheeks flushed a becoming shade of pink, and, despite the camouflage of his leather jacket, he caught a tantalising glimpse of her cleavage.

With a figure like that she couldn't possibly be as innocent as she seemed. Guys would have been all over her since puberty. But it was still an intriguing act.

'You've my permission to hold on as tight as you like,' he murmured. 'But if you want to stretch your legs for a minute and enjoy the view…'

'Yes…Thank you, I would,' she said in that very proper London accent, but didn't budge.

He waited a beat. 'You'll have to dismount first,' he prompted, stifling a grin when the colour highlighting her cheekbones flared again in the fading light.

'Oh, yes, of course.' Shifting back on the seat, she gathered her dress and then bit into her bottom lip as she concentrated on her dismount. It took a moment for her to execute the manoeuvre, during which he got an eyeful of lush thighs and trim calves displayed in silky nylons. He held back a groan, the clumsiness of her dismount making the view even more enticing as her many curves jiggled. Clearly it had been far too long since he'd had that much lush, scented female flesh within touching distance.

Swinging his leg over the bike, he stood behind her as she lifted the helmet off. With her back to him as she gazed out across the city, the top of her head barely reached his chin.

Curls of reddish-brown hair, no longer contained by the arrangement at the top, fell in disarray around the graceful column of her neck. Would her hair look all soft and rumpled like that straight out of bed? He stepped close enough to hear the staggered rise and fall of her breathing and to catch a whiff of her through the scent of sea-salt and earth. Spring flowers and soap, the fresh, unsophisticated scent seemed somehow exotic. He wanted to caress the back of her neck so badly he could almost feel her skin against his fingertips.

Burying his hands into the back pockets of his jeans, he tried to recall for about the fiftieth time since he'd spotted her in the gallery why he'd sworn off romantic entanglements a few months ago. Something to do with a script that wasn't happening, a looming production deadline and the unpleasant scenes when Lisa, his last girlfriend, had finally figured out that he'd meant it when he'd told her he wasn't *that* interested in her. But as the once convincing reasons swirled through his mind again, they didn't stop the urge to reach out and touch.

'It's really an astonishing feat of structural engineering,' she said.

'Uh-huh,' he replied. Although it wasn't the bridge's astonishing feats of engineering that he was admiring at the moment.

He caught the words 'truss arches' and 'cantilevered suspension' as she continued to talk, the words rushing out as if she'd swallowed an architectural textbook, and he found the grin tugging at his mouth again. He'd crashed out of school at sixteen and never gone back, so why did he find that serious, studious tone so damn sexy? He let his gaze drift down to the round swell of her backside lovingly spotlit by the bike's headlamp in rich red velvet—and decided maybe it wasn't so much the tone, but the contrasting packaging that was so appealing.

As the four-syllable words continued to tumble out she

hugged the helmet to her midriff like a long-lost child. She was nervous. The thought added a nice little ego-boost to his attraction. It was kind of intoxicating to get the chance to do the chasing for a change.

As he waited patiently for her to wind down and look at him, something he suspected her lecture on the Golden Gate Bridge was being used to avoid, he pulled one hand out of his pocket.

Time to refocus her attention.

Angling his thumb under the line of dangling curls, he skimmed it across the whisper-soft skin of her neck just above the collar of his jacket.

The lecture cut off and she shot round, her eyes fixing on him at last, her skin pale in the light from the bike's head-lamps.

He smiled. She couldn't have looked more shocked if he had poked her with a cattle prod. He held out his hand, his thumb still tingling from the subtle contact. 'You want to give me the helmet? I'll stick it on the bike.'

She glanced at the helmet, as if she'd forgotten it. She relaxed her hold, and those amazing violet eyes met his again. 'Thank you,' she said, passing it to him.

He walked the few steps to the bike and fixed it to the handlebar.

'Sorry,' she said again when he turned back to her. 'I talk too much.' She looked away. 'I just…' Even white teeth worried her bottom lip and he imagined nipping at the plump flesh and then gliding his tongue across to lick it better. 'I read an article about the bridge's construction in the in-flight magazine. It was fascinating.'

'It's a cool bridge,' he agreed, letting his gaze linger on her lips. Her bottom lip trembled and then her tongue flicked out to moisten it. The answering jolt of heat hit his groin like an Exocet missile.

His eyes locked on hers as he let out a strained laugh. 'But right now, I'm finding you a lot more fascinating.'

'I…' Eva clamped her mouth shut, before she swallowed her tongue. Or, worse, started spewing loads more twaddle about the Golden Gate Bridge like an overzealous tour guide.

His eyes took another leisurely trip down to her toes and she clasped her arms harder around her midriff, the worn leather of his jacket offering very little protection from the zip and zing of awareness.

Ever since he'd brushed his finger across her nape, she felt as if she'd been wired up to a nuclear reactor. And everywhere his gaze wandered felt as if it were being zapped with several billion kilowatts of energy.

She'd always adored reading about the instant overpowering sexual chemistry between the bold heroines and the impossibly masculine heroes in her favourite romances. But she'd never believed it actually existed in real life. Had simply assumed it was as fictional as all the hyper-real emotions and lavish derring-do. After all, none of her kind and conscientious male colleagues, or Phil, the chess club president she'd dated briefly in college without getting past second base, had ever made her giddy. Her physical reaction to Nick Delisantro, however, was forcing her to reconsider, because it felt every bit as out of control and extraordinary as the most fantastical romantic fantasy.

All this man had to do was look at her, his heavy-lidded eyes dark with erotic promise and warmth flooded every single cell of her body. The skin of her nape was still tingling from the barely there brush of his fingertip, for goodness sake.

She let out a shuddering sigh as she curled her toes in the ankle-breaking heels, forcing herself to meet his gaze. 'You must be easily fascinated.'

He cocked his head, observing her with nerve-racking intensity. 'Not true.' His lips quirked. 'If you knew me better, you'd know I'm next to impossible to fascinate.'

She pushed out a little laugh, guilty knowledge tying her stomach in knots. She wondered how fascinated he would be if he knew the truth. That underneath the glamorous camouflage of Tess's designer dress lurked dull and dependable Eva Redmond?

'I do know who you are,' she said, quelling the dreadful stab of disappointment. 'Our meeting tonight wasn't an accident. I've been trying to contact you for over three weeks to make an appointment with you.' The twist of curiosity on his lips died. 'I went to that gallery opening tonight because it's imperative that I speak to you about—'

He touched his finger to her mouth, silencing her confession. 'Shh.' To her amazement his lips curved in a wry smile. 'I get it.' He shrugged. 'If all you want is an appointment, we can meet at my agent's office tomorrow afternoon.' His hand fell away and he shoved it back in his pocket.

She stared at him, astonished, not only that he was taking her deception so well, but that he seemed to have been expecting it. Then the greasy knots of tension dissolved and she grinned, giddy with relief. He knew who she was. He knew why she was here. He must have recognised her name after all from all the messages she'd left with his agent and his publicist.

'If, on the other hand, you want more,' he continued, and giddy relief turned to giddy shock, 'then I'm happy to explore how much more. Tonight.' His rough palm cupped her cheek, the husky tone of voice making the erotic intent unmistakeable. 'But whatever we do tonight has no bearing on what happens tomorrow. I don't do favours for sex.' The light tone made the implication that she might have been suggesting such a thing seem amusing rather than insulting. 'Even really good sex.'

'What if it's not really good sex?' she asked, the question popping out before she could stop it.

His brows flew up and he choked out a laugh. A hot flush fired into her cheeks.

Good grief, Eva, shut up. It's not like you're actually going to take him up on his offer.

But then he brushed the callused skin of his thumb across her bottom lip. And every single reason why she couldn't possibly allow herself to be seduced by a man as dangerous as Nick Delisantro flew right out of her head.

'Why don't you let me worry about that?' he murmured.

She sucked in a breath, the throb of heat between her thighs painful.

Kiss me.

The words echoed in her mind. But his gaze flared, as if he had heard her plea and he leaned close, surrounding her in his spicy scent, then pressed firm lips to hers. She let out a staggered breath, the contact as unexpected as having the silent yearning instantly fulfilled.

His tongue traced her bottom lip then explored in expert strokes, his hand capturing her head. She opened her mouth to let him in, her palms flattening against his chest, fingers clutching at the soft wool of his sweater as heat sizzled across her skin. Her tongue delved back, timid at first, then growing in confidence, coaxed into action by the warm, wet skill of his lips, his tongue.

The kiss seemed to go on for an eternity, and yet ended too soon.

He lifted his head, those golden eyes locked on hers. Her breathing rasped, her heartbeat hammered, the frantic pounding drowning out the distant hum of passing traffic, the keening cry of a bird of prey.

'You taste good,' he said, before nipping at her bottom lip.

'So do you,' she replied, mesmerised.

A drop of water splashed on her cheek and she jumped.

'Damn,' he cursed softly, brushing the rain off her cheek-bone with his thumb. He held his palm up to the sky. 'We better take this indoors. It's about to rain.' His eyes took on a feral gleam in the dark. 'You want to come back to mine?'

She knew what he was asking, knew what would happen if she took him up on the bold invitation. And knew at every other time in her life before now she would have refused. But the rebellious instinct that had made her climb on his bike and made her hoot for joy as they crossed the bridge geysered up inside her again, like a volcano of need forced to be dormant for far too long. And the refusal got stuck somewhere around her solar plexus.

Tomorrow she would meet him at his agent's office, give him the details of his inheritance and arrange his first contact with the Duca D'Alegria. Roots Registry would get their all-important commission, her promotion would be secure and she and Nick would never see each other again.

Nick Delisantro was *not* a tormented pirate captain about to forsake his wicked ways so he could declare his everlasting love. He was a flesh-and-blood man who was clearly exceptionally well adjusted to his wicked ways.

And she wasn't a gullible fool despite the guilty pleasure she took in reading larger-than-life romantic fantasies. She knew what Nick Delisantro was offering was strictly a one-night deal.

But why shouldn't she take that crazy leap into sexual fantasy and indulge in the heat of the moment, just for tonight?

She sucked in a calming breath. This was crazy thinking. Was she seriously considering racing headlong into bed with a man she barely knew?

Her breath gushed out and she heard herself say, ever so politely. 'I'd love to, thank you.'

That would be a yes, then.

The fierce arousal in his gaze was anything but polite as he nodded back. 'Great, let's go.'

He gripped her hand, hauling her towards the bike as she picked her way across the rocky ground in the heels.

The lights of the bridge blurred in the drizzle of autumn rain as the powerful machine lurched down the hill in the darkness. Eva's pulse lurched right along with it, the thunder of her heartbeat drowning out the engine's roar as she clung to her fantasy man and refused to contemplate the notion that she'd just made the most catastrophic mistake of her adult life.

CHAPTER FOUR

THE trip back sped past, despite the stop to pay a toll on the bridge, the bike travelling through a tunnel before emerging into parkland. The spitting rain hit Eva's cheeks, soaking her clothes as she huddled behind Nick's back and tried not to envision herself hurtling full pelt towards disaster.

It had taken her all her adult life to come into contact with someone as potent as Nick Delisantro. What if she had to wait another lifetime to meet someone this attractive again? This was a once-in-a-lifetime opportunity, which she refused to regret. At least until tomorrow.

Edging the park, they entered a neighbourhood decorated with psychedelic murals and scribbled graffiti. People in colourful slickers stood outside bars, defiantly smoking in the rain, while down-and-outs huddled in doorways and under awnings. Eva knew from her research that Nick lived in an area called Haight Ashbury, a place that had become famous during the Flower Power days of the late sixties. As they drifted past a cornucopia of hippie chic—from smoothie bars, to vegan cafés and a New Age market with a marijuana leaf logo and enough neon-coloured tie-dye clothing in the window to make your eyes bleed—Eva figured the Haight hadn't quite left the Summer of Love behind.

Turning off the main street, the bike rumbled to a stop on a wide tree-lined avenue in front of a five-storey Victorian terrace. Pale blue wooden siding, giant bay windows, elaborately carved trim and a stunning pergola at the top gave it a kitsch antique grandeur that wouldn't have looked out of place on Disneyland's Main Street.

Shifting round, Nick shouted, 'There's a gizmo in the jacket pocket. Give it a buzz.'

Finding the smooth plastic device, Eva pressed the button and a large door beneath the front steps lifted with an electric whine. Harsh neon lights flickered on as Nick drove the bike into a musty cellar garage. Shelves crowded with boxes lined one wall while a washing machine and drier stood in the opposite corner.

Eva clambered off the bike as the door whirred closed, but not before every one of the doubts that she'd been busy trying to pretend didn't exist sneaked in with her. She levered off the helmet. Her hair plopped onto her shoulders, the artfully arranged chignon now a mass of wet tangles. The velvet of Tess's beautiful dress clung to her thighs in sodden patches.

Inadequacy assailed her as she watched Nick dismount and shove the bike onto its stand. His tall physique only looked more spectacular in the soaking jeans and jumper. Spotlighted by the brittle white light, the denim moulded to long, lean thighs while damp cashmere clung to the sleek musculature of his chest and shoulders.

Maybe this hadn't been such an excellent idea after all. She looked about as sexy as a drowned collie while he looked like Adonis. Her stomach squeezed. Maybe she simply wasn't capable of being a bad girl, even for one night.

He disengaged the bike key and shoved it in his back pocket, then swiped his hair off his forehead. Drops of water dampened the concrete as she debated how best to decline his offer without seeming rude.

But then he whisked his wet jumper over his head—and she forgot to breathe, let alone look for an escape route.

'It's always freezing down here,' he said, crossing towards her. 'Even in the summer.'

She stared, her gaze riveted to his naked chest. Not just giddy any more but light-headed.

Goodness.

She'd never seen anything so beautiful. Bronzed, olive skin defined the bunch of muscle that looked so much leaner and tougher than the steroidal excess of the romance cover models she'd once fantasised about. She certainly wouldn't be fantasising about them any more.

A faded tattoo of a coiled snake writhed on his left bicep as he rubbed the garment over his hair, making it stick up in rough spikes. Her gaze locked on the springy curls of hair under his arms, which also grew much more sparsely around flat brown nipples. The dusting of hair angled down into a thin line that bisected the ridges of his six pack before disappearing beneath the low waistband of his jeans. Her heartbeat bumped against her neck as she noticed the thin white scar that stood out against the bronzed skin of his abdomen, slashing across his ribs to follow the line of his hipbone. She struggled to breathe, horrified and yet entranced by the other smaller scars she spotted marring smooth skin. She'd known he was dangerous, but she hadn't realised quite how dangerous.

Her eyes jerked to his face as he lobbed the wet sweater into a wicker laundry basket beside the washing machine. Stepping closer, he lifted the helmet out of her hands, a confident smile edging his lips. She could have sworn she could feel the heat of his skin. Or maybe that was just her body temperature going haywire, because she was about to pass out?

She drew in a lungful of air. And tasted the clean spicy scent of him.

'You cold?' he asked, dumping the helmet on a shelf. She shook her head, knowing speech was probably a bad idea.

'Come on, the apartment's a lot warmer.'

'Okay,' she mumbled, as if she needed any more heat.

Having retrieved her bag from the bike box, he hooked it over her shoulder, then guided her towards a wooden staircase that led out of the back of the garage into the rain. 'You'll need to lose the ankle-breakers,' he said, the weight of his palm on her back causing the now familiar sizzles of electricity. 'The stairs get slippery in the rain.'

She nodded, still mute, and slipped off the slingback shoes. Before she could bend to pick them up, he scooped them off the floor.

He clasped her hand and they dashed through the rain together, drops splashing on the wooden decks as they climbed to the top landing. Her breath sawed out as he led her through terrace doors into a long, narrow room with high ceilings and a marble fireplace thrown into shadow by the twilight. The starkly modern leather sofa and chairs and huge flat-screen TV contrasted with the old-world charm of the cornices on the ceiling. A light clicked on illuminating a spotlessly clean, granite and glass kitchen at the far end of the room.

'I'll get some towels,' he said, disappearing down a corridor to the right of the kitchen.

She shivered violently. The room was warm, cosy even, with the sound of the sleeting rain lashing the terrace doors, but the sight of his naked back retreating from view did nothing to stop the shaking.

Dropping her bag on the kitchen counter, she spotted her mobile in the side pocket, its message light flashing.

She read the text from Tess. *'Where r u???'*

She paused with her fingers over the key pad. What should she say? How did she explain where she was and what she was planning to do? She took in a shuddering breath.

Keep it brief. Keep it simple. And don't go into too much detail or you might chicken out.

She keyed in: *'I'm with Nick.'*

The mobile buzzed almost instantly with Tess's reply. *'OMG! U wild woman.'*

A smile quirked on Eva's lips, excitement dispelling the last of her terror. Finally, dull, swotty Eva Redmond was having a conversation like the ones she'd once overheard in the changing room before PE class or in the common room at university. The conversations she'd listened to with avid interest and secretly envied, but had never once been a part of. Because the girls she'd eavesdropped on—the pretty, confident girls who had boyfriends and a social life and didn't stress about their exams or their homework nearly as much as they did about their next date—those girls had never talked to Eva. In fact they had probably never even known she existed.

Eva tapped out: *'Don't w8 up,'* the last of her doubts lifting off her shoulders. Who knew it would feel so liberating not to be invisible any more?

Tess's reply flashed back. *'LOL. Go 4 it!'*

She shoved the phone back into the bag, next to the file folder that contained her notes on the D'Alegria case. A wayward grin spread across her face. There would be time enough for work tomorrow. Tonight, Eva Redmond was finally going to get the chance to play.

She peeled off her wet tights and buried the sodden mass in the pocket of the leather jacket. Maybe she didn't look her best, but she planned to look as presentable as possible. Clammy water dripped down under the collar as she heard the soft pad of footsteps in the hall.

Appearing out of the shadows, Nick walked towards her with predatory grace, a towel draped around his neck and his feet now as bare as his chest. The exhilaration caused by her girly text conversation peaked and Eva's teeth chattered.

Without a word, Nick took the tab of the jacket zip between his fingers. The rasp of the tiny metal teeth releasing cut through the soft patter of the slowing rain. He pushed the jacket off her shoulders, tugged it down her arms and dumped it on the sofa. Carefully locating the last of the pins in her hair, he pulled each of them out then ran his fingers through the wet curls, gently parting the tangles. The rain glistened in his damp hair as he drew the towel from around his neck, then gathered the ends of her hair and rubbed.

Eva stood trembling under his ministrations, her heartbeat rioting. A muscle in his jaw flexed while he concentrated on the task. The bodice of the dress felt like a corset closing off her air supply. Her heavy breasts swelled against the constriction as the ends of the towel fluttered over her cleavage.

Finally satisfied, he looped the towel round her neck. Holding the ends, he tugged her up onto her tiptoes. She opened her mouth on a little gasp and his tongue plundered as she placed her hands on his stomach to steady herself. The hot smooth skin tensed under her palms and her fingers touched the rough edges of the scar. As he lifted his head her breathing became so jagged she felt as if she were about to faint.

He let go of the towel, and she dropped back onto her heels. His palms cradled her elbows, his thumbs stroking the sensitive skin on the inside as his lips lifted on one side in a lopsided smile. 'I'll have to take the dress off, to dry you properly.'

The rough murmur seemed to prickle over her skin, scraping over each of the places that throbbed with need. She looked back at him, and felt the spark of impulse, the sizzle of desire and anticipation. All her life she must have had this wildness lurking inside but it had taken a man like Nick Delisantro to locate it and bring it galloping to the surface.

'I'd like that,' she heard herself murmur, her voice low and sultry and nothing like her own.

His lips quirked as he placed his hands firmly on her waist. 'You would, huh?'

She nodded.

He didn't reply, but anchored his hand on her hip and turned her to face the terrace doors. Lifting the hair draped over her shoulder, he trailed tiny kisses down her neck, sucking and nibbling and sending her senses into overdrive. The reflection of them, backlit by the kitchen light, was so erotic her knees trembled. He stood behind her, his head dark against the stark white skin of her collarbone. The zip at the back of the dress released, freeing her breasts from the too-small bodice as firm fingers eased the straps of the dress down. His eyes met hers in the rain-splattered glass as he undid the hook on her bra with a deafening click. He peeled the purple lace off leaving her naked to the waist.

His teeth fastened on the cord in her neck, feasting on the sensitive spot as his fingers traced the outline of her areolas. She raised limp arms, fastened them around his neck and arched into his hands, desperate to feel more, to have it all. She sobbed, her breath trapped in her lungs as hot callused palms cupped her breasts and caressed.

She shuddered, the pleasure so intense her knees buckled.

He swore, the harsh expletive making her eyes fly open. Grasping her waist, he spun her round to face him, then cradled her breast, and fastened his lips on the aching peak.

She held his head, the hair damp against her palms as he teased the swollen tip with his tongue, his teeth. Her thighs quivered and she moaned, scolding heat scorching down her torso to the bundle of nerves at her centre.

He raised his head, ending the devastating torment, and then shoved the dress past her hips. It settled around her ankles, leaving only the tiny swatch of lace covering her sex. She'd never felt more vulnerable, more exposed in her life, but as she saw the glazed desire in his eyes power surged.

'Put your hands round my neck,' he demanded. She obeyed, mesmerised by the hard glint of passion darkening the golden brown as he swept her up in his arms. Kicking the heavy velvet out of his way, he strode across the front room, then down the narrow corridor to the back of the apartment. Shoving open a door, he walked into a large room, its hexagonal shape marking it out as the pergola she'd admired from below.

Her breasts ached, and every inch of her skin tingled as he laid her on the large bateau bed that dominated the room. Moonlight streamed through the window, highlighting the harsh beauty of his torso. She panted, trying to calm her breathing, wipe the fog of arousal from her mind as he grabbed a foil packet out of the bedside table and flung it onto the coverlet. She clasped her arms across her swollen breasts, the heady feel of his teeth, his tongue still a visceral memory as he unsnapped his jeans, ripped open the button fly and kicked off the wet denim and cotton boxers beneath.

Her heart rammed into her throat as she got her first sight of the column of erect flesh that thrust out from the nest of hair at his groin. A shocked gasp escaped her lips as she gauged the impressive length and thickness.

Her mind engaged, and she felt a flutter of panic as the blaze of lust flooded between her thighs. She knew all about the mechanics of sex, had spent years day-dreaming about this moment. But she'd never seen a naked man in the flesh before. Let alone a naked man who was fully aroused. And she hadn't day-dreamed about anything quite that…She took a steadying breath, desire and panic twisting together in the pit of her stomach. Anything quite that enormous.

He grasped the foil packet off the bed, rolled on the latex sheath with ease and efficiency. She glanced up as he settled onto the bed beside her, dragged her easily into his arms, his erection now butting her thigh.

'Hey, what's this?' he said, sounding puzzled and amused

as he took her wrists, to lift her clasped arms away from her breasts. 'Don't get shy on me, now.'

She struggled to breathe, knowing she had to relax, or this would be a thousand times more uncomfortable. Should she tell him? That this was her first time? But then he dipped his head, captured one aching peak between his teeth, and she raised off the bed, pushing her body instinctively into the exquisite torture.

Don't think. Just feel. And don't tell him, or he may stop.

As her fingers fisted on the sheet, her body bowed by the renewed onslaught of sensation, she knew that, however painful the initial penetration, she didn't want him to stop.

He explored her body with his tongue, his teeth, his lips. Suckling hard then drawing back, transferring from one breast to the other. His hand flattened against her belly. She bucked, shocked by the intensity of sensation rocketing up from her core as he cupped her, then discovered the slick burning nub. He circled and retreated, teasing her with fleeting caresses that took her to the brink but were never enough. She clung to his shoulders, sobbed out incoherent pleas for him to do more.

He gave a rough laugh. Then he touched, right at the heart of her. She opened her thighs, bumping against the knowing brush of his thumb, the nerves exploding.

She cried out, the orgasm cascading through her in strong, sure, wonderful waves.

Quivering, shaking, she kissed his cheek, laughed with delight, the rush of achievement, of abandon sensational as she floated in afterglow.

'Thank you. Thank you,' she murmured, tears of emotion, of joy sliding down her cheeks.

The sense of validation was triumphal. Sex was more wonderful, more fulfilling than her wildest fantasises, all she'd had to do was wait—for the right man to unlock the secret passion inside her.

'You're welcome.' He chuckled, sounding surprised and amused. His brows drew together as he stared down at her in the moonlight. He touched his thumb to her cheek, lifted a drop. 'That was quite a show. Do you always cry when you come?'

The inquisitive, vaguely mocking tone brought her sharply back to reality, the hazy joy clearing to be replaced with embarrassment. Appalled at how exposed she felt—and at how much she'd let him see.

This means nothing to him.

'Not always,' she lied. She choked out what she hoped was a frivolous laugh. 'You're good at that.'

He grinned, the flash of pride almost boyish. 'Only good, huh?' he said, clasping her hips in large hands and positioning her beneath him. 'Let's see if I can do better.'

She had a moment to tense, prepare for the devastating entry and then he plunged hard.

She cried out, the pain raw and shocking, as his girth thrust through the barrier of flesh.

'What the hell?' He reared back, stopped dead, the penetration so deep she could feel every inch. 'Are you okay?'

She nodded, robbed of speech, the pain still raw, still brutal. 'Don't stop,' she said, through gritted teeth, determined to bear it.

He cradled her cheek, still lodged impossibly deep. 'Are you sure? You're so tight.'

'It'll be all right in a minute,' she said and prayed that it would be.

'Relax,' he murmured. 'You're tense.' He stroked his hand down, pressed his thumb to the punch of her pulse. He didn't move, didn't thrust. And slowly the pain receded. To be replaced by an impossible pressure. He smiled down at her, and she wondered if he somehow knew.

'Let's see if we can go for better than all right,' he said, then lifted her hips.

She sucked in a sharp, ragged breath as he settled deeper still. She gave a low groan, grateful when the pain didn't return, even though the pressure increased. His forearm strained beside her head, the muscles of his bicep bunching and releasing, as he held his weight off her. Then he drew his other hand down. Delving into the curls at her core with expert fingers, he exposed the swollen nub and flicked it with his thumb. She jerked, thrusting against him, the sudden rub of intense sensation both exquisite and shocking.

He continued to play, continued to circle and rub and flick until slowly, gradually, the swell of pleasure built again, unstoppable, unrelenting this time. The pressure then turned to a new exquisite pain as he began to move at last, rubbing some spot so deep inside, the pleasure intensified. She moaned, gripping his bicep to anchor herself and moved too, meeting the expert thrust of his hips with her own untutored movements.

She heard his harsh grunts against her ear. Felt him swell to even greater proportions, the fullness of his penis triggering a brutal, pulsing series of contractions that rolled over her. Then shattered, shooting her into oblivion.

Feeling, sensation, sanity returned in tiny incremental bits and pieces. The ragged pants of his breathing rasping in her ear, the musty scent of sex and sweat overlaying the clean fresh scent of rainwater and him, the muscled shelf of his shoulder resting on her collarbone, the large, but softening column of his erection still impaling tender flesh.

'Damn.' His low murmur cut through the silence. 'That was good.' He sounded as dazed, as disorientated as she.

He lifted off her, pulled out gently. She flinched, a groan

escaping as her swollen flesh released him, the soreness a cruel reminder of the initial pain. She rolled away from him, and shifted across the bed.

As incredible as that had been, she felt fragile and wary. She'd never imagined, never realised, sex would be anything like that. The heady romances she'd read certainly hadn't prepared her for something so brutal, so basic, the elemental nature of it nothing short of animalistic.

'Hang on a minute.' One muscled forearm banded around her waist, drawing her back into his chest. 'Where are you off to?' His lips nuzzled her neck.

'I need to…' *Get away from you,* she heard her mind shout, shocked by the renewed blast of arousal as his thumb played lazily with her nipple. She hurt, all over. She couldn't possibly want to do it again. But still the molten heat between her thighs gushed back.

She lay motionless, clamped down on the need to struggle out of his grip. She didn't want him to figure out the truth, that their coupling had been a life-altering experience for her.

She couldn't bear for him to know now that she'd been a virgin. It would make this far too intimate. And it was intimate enough already. She'd assumed this would be anonymous sex, only to discover that the intimacy of the act meant there was probably no such thing.

'I need to use the bathroom,' she said.

'All right.' His hand stroked her belly in an oddly possessive manner. 'There's an en suite over there.' His chin touched her shoulder as he nodded towards a door in the opposite wall. 'I'll keep the bed warm,' he murmured, his hand skimming down her buttocks before he released her.

The proprietary words reverberated in her head as she shot across the room naked.

She couldn't have been? Could she?

Nick frowned at the moonlight reflecting off the polished

wood of the bathroom door, the niggling suspicion slowly but surely clawing its way through the sweet, heady buzz of afterglow.

Rolling over, he snapped on the bedside light, and flipped the duvet back. Then blinked several times at the two dark red splotches on the pale blue linen bed sheet.

He jerked upright, then cursed softly.

No way. Not possible.

He stared blankly for several long minutes at the evidence before him. Then raked his hand through his hair, the contraction in his chest forcing him to finally process the truth.

Eva the sexy anthropologist was a virgin. Correction, had been a virgin. Right up until the moment he'd ploughed into her.

He swore again, a lot more forcefully this time. And pushed back the sickening wave of guilt at the memory of her face, white with shock.

How the hell was that even possible? How could a woman as alluring and spontaneous and mind-blowingly sexy as she was have waited into her twenties to have intercourse? And why had she?

A picture of her wide blue eyes, petal soft skin and the tempting sprinkle of freckles across her shoulder blades formed in his mind. He gulped down the constriction in his throat. Damn. Assuming she was in her twenties. Why hadn't he stopped long enough to ask her? To be sure?

He acknowledged the residual hum of heat in his groin, and had his answer.

Because he'd been spellbound. That was why. Even now, the memory of her lush body writhing in his arms, the weight of her full breasts in his palms and the sound of her stunned gasps as he ran his hands over the puckered pink flesh had the blood surging south. He'd been mesmerised by her ever since he'd spotted her in the gallery. And once he'd got her back here, got her naked, the last semblance of restraint had been swept away on a wave of lust so intense he'd been determined to have her.

Hearing the trickle of running water coming from behind the bathroom door, he slid out of bed and stripped off the stained bed sheet, feeling thoroughly disgusted with himself.

He'd lost control, let instinct and lust take over—something he'd worked really hard never to do again—and had sex with a woman he hadn't bothered to find out a damn thing about. He knew her name, that she had studied anthropology and that she had written a script she wanted him to look at, which had to be why she'd been so keen to meet him.

Lobbing the soiled linen into the laundry basket, he grabbed a fresh sheet out of the drawer and wrestled it on while riding out the dull flush on his cheeks.

He'd admired her honesty and her forthright manner when she'd told him their meeting hadn't been accidental. And been hopelessly turned on by her refreshingly artless approach to sex and then blinded by her quick and instinctive response to his caresses. So much so that he hadn't stopped to question her.

He let out a calming breath.

Stop beating yourself up. You're not exactly an expert on virgins.

Despite his varied and extensive experience, he'd never been any woman's first lover before. How could he have known her innocence wasn't faked? That the sheen of grateful tears in her eyes when he'd stroked her to orgasm was a sign of her inexperience and not, as he'd assumed like a conceited jerk, his superstar abilities in the sack?

He hadn't forced her. She'd been willing. More than willing. And while the possibility that she might be younger than he'd thought bothered him, surely she couldn't be a teenager. She'd been far too intellectually astute and not nearly self-absorbed enough for that.

All of which meant he was off the hook. He slung the duvet

back onto the bed, but as he settled under it to wait for her return the tight feeling in his chest refused to go away.

Maybe he didn't need to feel responsible. But unfortunately he did, because while he'd had one of the most mind-blowing orgasms of his life, he'd hurt her.

His eyes narrowed, trained on the bathroom door. Which brought them to another burning question. Why hadn't she said anything? Before letting him barrel into her like that? He'd seen the shocked look on her face when he'd been putting on the condom. He was a fairly big guy, and for all her lush curves she was a small woman, but even so if she'd said something, anything, he would at least have attempted to get a stranglehold on his desire and use some degree of finesse.

A sick feeling settled in his stomach. Had she wanted him to hurt her?

The horrible suspicion that she might have been intending to use her virginity to give her some leverage tomorrow, when she showed him her script, sprang into his head. And was thankfully almost as quickly quashed. If she were that devious, wouldn't she have mentioned her virginity straight afterwards? Made a bigger deal of it? And her seduction techniques were hardly practised. Just the opposite in fact. Plus, how could she have known he would find her refreshingly untutored reaction to him such a major turn-on? Hell. He wouldn't have suspected he'd find it a turn-on himself until tonight.

He forced himself to relax back against the headboard and folded his arms over his chest, the insistent beat of his heart punctuating the seconds ticking by as he waited for her to reappear.

One thing he did know: when Miss Eva the sexy anthropologist finally ventured out of his bathroom, she was going to have a whole lot of explaining to do.

CHAPTER FIVE

CONCENTRATING on the two deep grooves bisecting her brow in the bathroom mirror, Eva forced her fingers to release their death grip on the sink.

Hiding out in Nick Delisantro's bathroom for the rest of the night is not an option.

The metallic tinkle of rain hit the fire escape outside and she shifted her attention to the partially open window. Then sighed, stifling the urge to leap onto the vanity unit, wedge herself through the small gap and run off into the night.

'Don't be ridiculous,' she whispered to her pale reflection.

Apart from the fact that she was stark naked under Nick's oversized robe, her bag was still on the kitchen counter and it was the middle of the night, she was in a strange city in a strange country and it was pouring with rain. If she didn't die of hypothermia, she'd probably get arrested. So running away was not an option either. The frown on her forehead deepened.

Plus she had an important appointment with Nick tomorrow, which she couldn't duck out of. As difficult as it was going to be to assume any kind of professional etiquette after sleeping with him, he'd probably throw her out on her ear if she showed up after doing a vanishing act in the middle of the night.

Which left option number three: be mature and dignified, something that had eluded her so far this evening, face up to her responsibilities, and give the man some kind of explanation—*before* she ran out on him.

She straightened away from the sink and glanced at the door. Assuming, of course, she ever got up the guts to stop cowering in his bathroom.

Not that she intended to tell him the truth—that her secret fantasy life had taken one wild leap into reality during the space of one motorbike ride. Not only would that be way too much information for a one-night stand, but he'd probably think she was a lunatic.

She twisted on the tap, and splashed one last dose of cold water on her cheeks. The scarlet hue making her freckles look like bullet points faded to a dusky pink.

At least she'd had one lucky break. She hadn't bled very much, so he need never know what a pathetic cliché she actually was. A twenty-four-year-old virgin, whose experience of men and sex up until fifteen minutes ago had been gleaned from the pages of romance novels.

Unfortunately she now knew the truth. That the novels had lied. Or at least been guilty of omission. They really ought to have mentioned how mortifying it was to face a complete stranger who had given you two stunning orgasms after the haze of afterglow had cleared.

Time to stop prevaricating—and face the fire. She could save the self-flagellation for tomorrow, when she was safely on the plane back to the UK, with his signed agreement to a DNA test tucked in her bag.

She yanked the lapels of the robe up to her chin and retied the belt. The sooner she faced Nick, the sooner she could start putting her night of insanity behind her. The next ten minutes were going to be awkward in the extreme. No question. And it was a pity she hadn't considered that a bit sooner. But the good news was he'd probably be just as keen to get this whole episode over with now as she was.

Her courage rallied as she gripped the door handle in a determined fist. You never knew, he might even have fallen asleep, then she could simply leave a polite note.

Eva took two paces into the room, then stopped dead, her heartbeat and her pheromones both leaping into frantic action as her gaze landed on the bed.

With his back propped against the headboard, Nick Delisantro sat watching her.

'You're still awake.' She winced at the inane remark and the rush of blood to her nether regions. With his arms crossed over his chest, his pectoral muscles looked even more well defined than she remembered them.

Oh my. She took a steadying breath, riveted to the spot. How could she have forgotten how beautiful he was?

'Hello, Eva. Long time, no see,' he said dryly.

She felt the dusky pink rise back to scarlet. 'I'm sorry I took so long. I didn't mean to keep you awake.' She gestured down the corridor with her thumb. 'I should probably get—'

'Come here,' he said, releasing his arms and beckoned her with one finger.

She crossed to the bed as if drawn by an invisible string. It would probably be better to get this over with—her eyes dipped and then jerked back to his face—and not notice how low the duvet sat on his hips.

He patted the mattress beside him. 'Sit down.'

She perched on the edge of the bed. 'I really ought to be going,' she managed, her mouth so dry the words rasped against her throat like sandpaper. 'Tess will be wondering where I am.'

His eyes searched her face and then he lifted his hand, and brushed his thumb across her cheekbone. She stiffened, the contact unexpected. 'How old are you?' he asked gently.

'Twenty-four.'

He released a long breath. 'You look younger without make-up on,' he murmured.

'I should go,' she said more demonstratively this time, the insistent melting sensation between her legs getting more acute.

She tried to stand, but he grasped her wrist, and held on. 'I don't think so.'

'Why not?' she asked breathlessly, the feel of his thumb absently caressing the thin skin of her wrist not doing a thing for her sanity issues.

'Why didn't you tell me?'

'Tell you what?' she asked, the blood surging into her cheeks as her stomach dipped. Did he know? How could he know?

'That this was your first time?'

She swallowed convulsively, looked away from his seeking gaze, the blood coursing so hard now she was fairly sure her cheeks could double as fog lamps. 'I don't know what you're talking about...' Her voice trailed off as she faced him. She'd never been a good liar, and from his penetrating stare it was clear he wasn't fooled.

'I had to change the sheets,' he said matter-of-factly, and her cheeks burst into flame.

She stared down at her hands, clasped in her lap, and his long fingers still looped around her wrist. Could he feel her pulse hitting his thumb like a jack-hammer?

She croaked out a laugh. Forget about awkward, this was now officially the most humiliating experience of her entire life. And given her pitiful history with members of the opposite sex that was quite an achievement.

Hooking a finger under her chin, he raised her gaze to his. 'Why didn't you say something?'

Good question.

And one she had no intention of answering in any detail.

'I thought…' She paused, gave a stiff shrug. 'I thought you might stop if you knew.'

His thumb continued to circle her pulse point in lazy strokes. 'Why would I have stopped?'

'I don't know…' she murmured. 'I thought you might not want the responsibility…Or something.'

He sent her a puzzled smile. 'You're an educated woman who's past the age of consent. Why would your virginity be my responsibility?'

The blush flared back to life. 'It's not. Obviously it's not,' she said, backtracking furiously to cover the excruciating embarrassment. 'That's not what I meant.'

He tipped his head to one side, considering. 'So what did you mean?'

How had she dug herself into such a huge hole? And how was she going to climb out again with even a small measure of her dignity in tact? 'Just that, if you knew I didn't have a clue what I was doing, you might not want to…' She mumbled, the last of her confidence leaking away under his unwavering gaze. 'You know…Do it…With me.'

Her pride crumbled to dust when he choked out an incredulous laugh. 'You're not serious?'

The astonished amusement in his tone crucified her. He was laughing at her, and while she already knew how ridiculous she was, she couldn't see the funny side. 'I have to go,' she said, tugging on her hand.

Instead of letting go, his fingers tightened. 'Shh, calm down, sweetheart.'

The careless endearment touched that lonely place deep inside her she'd always tried so hard to ignore and her abject humiliation was complete. She'd always known she was a pathetic cliché, but she'd never known quite how pathetic.

She pulled back, wanting not just to run away now but to hide under a very large rock.

He gripped her other wrist and drew her back towards him. Still chuckling, he pressed his forehead to hers. Then to her astonishment placed a kiss on her temple.

'Eva, you're one of the sweetest, cutest, sexiest women I've ever met. How could you not know that?'

He gave his head a little shake, the stunned pleasure the compliment caused making her chest hurt.

'Really?' she asked, then flushed redder, realising how needy she sounded.

But he didn't seem to notice, the mocking twist of his lips disappearing as he smiled.

'Put it this way, I nearly lost it in the living room and I hadn't even got you naked.' His voice had roughened, scraping over her skin. 'Are you in any pain?' he asked softly.

She shook her head. 'It's a bit tender, that's all,' she said, her senses reeling as the swell of emotion thickened her throat. She swallowed, forced the boulder back down. He couldn't possibly know how much it meant to her to know the passion between them had been mutual.

Giving a gentle tug on the tie of her robe, his hand snuck under the towelling and settled on the curve of her waist. 'Come to bed.'

The husky invitation sent all sorts of fireworks off in her nerve-endings, but she caught his wrist, stopped his hand from wandering. 'I don't think I can do it again yet.'

He grinned. 'I meant, so we can get some sleep.' Taking his hand out of her robe, he rubbed his thumb under her eye. 'You look shattered. And for that I am responsible.'

She opened her mouth to try and deny it, but it stretched into an enormous yawn.

He laughed. 'I rest my case.' He lifted the duvet and scooted back to make a space for her. 'I won't ravish you again tonight. You have my word.'

Given the smouldering look in his eyes, she wasn't sure she

could trust him. But the sight of his muscular body, shadowed by the duvet, was so tempting, and the thought of spending a little more time in his arms, however meaningless, so seductive, she nodded.

He'd been patient and understanding and surprisingly gallant. And he'd told her she was the sexiest woman he'd ever met. Which was obviously a lie, but a really nice one.

She settled into the lee of his body, curled her back into his chest. He anchored one arm around her waist, bundling her into the towelling robe like a child, and kissed the back of her head. 'Sleep tight.'

The feel of his big body cocooned around hers felt so safe, so comforting she drew in a deep breath, let out a shaky sigh. Her wild night hadn't been a complete catastrophe after all.

While the whole experience had been a lot more affecting than she would have anticipated. Not to mention exhausting. She'd remember Nick Delisantro—and the rainy autumn night in San Francisco she lost her virginity—for the rest of her life.

She closed her eyes, the lids weighing several tons, and drifted into a sleep filled with wonderfully vivid and earthily erotic dreams.

Nick watched the rain run in rivulets down the bedroom's bay window, the droplets tinged orange in the dawn light, and diligently counted the streams. Eva shifted beside him, her flannel-clad bottom bumping his hip. He sucked in a breath, heat surging back to his groin, her scent flooding his senses—and he lost count of the rivulets. Again.

What had possessed him to suggest she stay the night? He wasn't a snuggler, and he wasn't responsible for Eva despite the dark smudges under her eyes or the astonished wonder on her face when he'd told her how sexy she was.

But even knowing that, he'd been lying here for hours now, kept awake by the double whammy of an erection that shot back to attention every time she brushed against him and the questions that refused to stop bouncing around in his head like hyperactive sheep.

How had a woman as passionate as Eva stayed a virgin for so long? And why had she? And why the hell had she picked him, of all people, to be her first? A guy who'd left innocent behind a lifetime ago.

Easing his arm out from under her shoulders, he rolled away from her onto his side.

The answers didn't concern him. They didn't matter. He shouldn't even be asking the questions. Just as he'd told her—and she'd agreed—those were her choices, not his. But somehow, he couldn't stop the questions from circling like buzzards, and pecking away at his certainty.

He stared at the early morning light shining on the ugly antique dresser he'd inherited when he bought the apartment two years ago. He should wake her up. Call her a cab. He had to be up in a couple of hours, had to get the first draft of the script he was working on finished this week if he was going to meet the production deadline. But somehow he hadn't been able to find the will to do it while her soft, scented body was curled so trustingly by his side.

For some strange, inexplicable reason, he'd wanted to keep her with him. For tonight.

He shut his eyes, felt the tired, gritty texture on the lids that signalled insomnia. Willing himself to ignore the murmur of her breathing and the aroma of spring flowers and talcum powder that teased his nostrils, his brain finally began to unwind, and the erection to soften.

As he fell into a fitful sleep he promised himself he would hustle her out first thing in the morning no matter how soft and tempting she looked in his bed. This was physical attraction. Pure and simple. All he had to do was control it, the way he'd been doing for years.

And he wasn't going to ask a single one of those damn questions either.

Those were her choices. Her business. And nothing whatsoever to do with him.

CHAPTER SIX

NICK rolled his shoulders to ease out the kinks, and tried to persuade himself the freezing shower had refreshed him. Grabbing a pair of old sweatpants and a UCLA T-shirt out of the dresser, he slipped them on, his eyes fixed on the woman still curled on his bed.

He felt the familiar tightening in his groin. The sunlight streaming through the window gave her pale skin a soft glow and cast a halo of light over the curls of hair mussed around her cheek. She looked cuter than a Botticelli angel. His gaze dipped to the sliver of cleavage visible above the lapels of the robe she'd slept in. An exceptionally sexy Botticelli angel.

He pushed the drawer shut, a little too heavily, and steeled himself against the tinge of guilt when her eyes fluttered open.

It was nearly eleven. He needed to get going. He had a lot to do today. Especially if he was going to meet her for that appointment he'd promised. Which, now he thought about it, he wished he hadn't. Seeing her again probably wasn't the smartest idea.

She scrambled upright, her dazed expression finally focusing on him. The robe fell off one shoulder and she clutched the lapels together, covering herself too late to stop the shot of arousal hitting his crotch. He shoved his hands into the pockets of the sweatpants.

She pushed the hair out of her face with an unsteady hand. 'I-I'm sorry, I overslept,' she stammered, her voice smoky with sleep. 'I should…' She glanced around, disorientated. 'I should get going.'

The apologetic tone kicked off his temper—which wasn't in the best of conditions anyway. He'd had a total of four hours' sleep and his body still seemed to have a mind of its own, despite the ice-cold shower he'd treated it to. 'Stop apologising.'

'I'm sorry?'

He propped his butt against the dresser, braced his hands against the surface as he studied her. 'You just did it again.'

'Did what?' she asked, chewing on her full bottom lip, and making him want to chew on it too.

'Said sorry.'

'Oh, yes, I see. I'm sor—' She stopped.

'See what I mean,' he said sharply, irritated by the flicker of vulnerability and confusion in her eyes. 'Why do you keep apologising?'

'I've outstayed my welcome,' she said at last, which was hardly an answer. She lifted the duvet and he got a good look at her slim calves as she put her bare feet on the floor, reminding him how naked she was under his robe. 'I'll get my clothes, then get out of your way.'

'They're over there.' He nodded towards the window seat in the bay.

He'd headed straight to the kitchen after waking up, to gulp down a gallon of water—but his throat had dried right up again when he'd spotted her clothing, draped across the living area. It had been hard as hell not to fantasise about taking the skimpy bit of lace and the heavy velvet gown off her as he'd gathered them off the floor and dumped them in the bedroom.

Hence the freezing shower.

'Thank you.' She crossed the room to the bay. 'Do you mind if I use your bathroom? I promise not to hog it this time.'

As she bent to pick up the clothes the robe gaped, and he spotted her nipple, before she covered it hastily.

'Sure,' he murmured, determined not to ask the question making his head hurt or give in to the desire to tug the robe off, and make the ripe peak harden against his tongue.

But then she walked past him and his hand shot out to grasp her forearm as the fresh sultry scent of her filled his nostrils. 'Why me?' he demanded.

She jerked to a halt, her violet eyes huge. 'Sorry?'

'Stop apolo—' He cut off the surly command, seeing her flinch. 'What made you pick me?'

Her long lashes hit her cheeks as her gaze dropped away, but she didn't answer.

'To be your first?' he prompted, although he was pretty sure from the nuclear blush fanning out across her chest and spreading up her throat she had understood the question.

'I don't…' She hesitated, her chin still tucked against her chest. 'When you looked at me that first time, it made me feel…' She addressed her toes, the words trailing into silence.

It made her feel *what?* But then he recalled how she had writhed in his arms when he'd undressed her, and figured he knew.

Her chin lifted. 'I think, possibly, on an entirely subconscious level, when I researched you, I must have decided you would be a good choice. Because you're so assured, sexually. And I'm not.'

When I researched you.

He released her. Okay, that was intrusive.

'Right.' He dug his fists back into his pockets, trying to muster the required anger at what she'd revealed. Because if he'd understood her right—and, given his sleep deprivation and the fact that all of his blood had drained out of his head, that was debatable—she'd just told him she'd dug into his private life so she could engineer a meeting with him. But she sounded so earnest and sincere, those Bambi eyes were doing funny things to his equilibrium.

'I need coffee.' He scrubbed his hands down his face. 'I'll call you a cab while you're in the shower,' he grunted, not as enthusiastic as he should have been at the thought of getting rid of her.

'A cab would be great, thank you,' she said, before she hurried away with her clothes.

He frowned as he headed for the kitchen. He rarely did sleepovers, because he preferred not to deal with the morning after. And the demands on his time that inevitably followed.

The fact that Eva Redmond hadn't made a single demand—hadn't even seemed surprised when he'd offered to call a cab—should have pleased him. It didn't.

He'd made a rash decision, and led with his lust instead of his common sense last night. So why was he so tempted to make another one this morning?

He emptied the coffee pot, started going through the ritual of brewing a fresh pot. Time to mainline caffeine, before he lost his mind completely and invited her to stay for breakfast... So he could bombard her with all the questions that had kept him awake most of the night. And then sweet-talk her back into bed.

Nick inhaled the first precious sip of scalding black coffee and tried to ignore the buzz of the mobile phone coming from Eva's bag. He glanced down the corridor to the bedroom door.

Where the hell was she? He wanted her gone before the last of his will power seeped into his pants. The ringing cut off, then started right back up again.

He slapped the mug down and grabbed the bag. After rummaging for a few seconds trying to locate the phone, he dumped the contents onto the countertop. An array of female paraphernalia poured out: pens, a make-up case, a roll of antacids, a notebook, a sheath of papers, tissues, a cotton sweater. Finally he spotted the buzzing mobile under a file folder.

Swiping it up, he clicked the answer button. 'What?' he barked into the receiver.

There was a slight pause, then a succinct female voice asked, 'Oh, hello. Is that Niccolo Delisantro?'

'The name's Nick,' he corrected, but softened his tone, the woman's precise English accent reminding him of Eva. 'I take it you're the busybody friend,' he added, vaguely recalling the long, skinny girl in the blue dress from the previous evening.

The woman laughed. 'Correct. And being a busybody, I'm busy trying to find out where Eva is.'

Leaning back against the countertop, he lifted his coffee mug to his lips, took another satisfying sip. 'She's in my shower,' he said, the odd feeling of satisfaction coming from nowhere.

'I see.' The woman didn't sound particularly surprised at the revelation. 'Is she spending the day with you, then?' she asked.

His heart bumped. 'No,' he said, too quickly. 'She's leaving once she's dressed.'

There was a longer pause, then the woman came back on the line. 'Could you ask her to give Tess a call?'

'Sure.'

'Excellent. Thanks. It's been nice talking to you,' she said crisply.

'Yeah.' He clicked the phone off, dumped it back on the countertop. And glared at it. What was with the heart bump? He didn't want to spend the day with Eva. Didn't want to know her secrets. The sooner she left, the better.

He contemplated the bedroom door again as he sipped the coffee, not even sure he could convince himself. What was it about her that made her different from all the other women he'd slept with? It had to be the whole virginity business.

Somehow he'd got hung up on it. Crossing to the coffee maker, he refilled his cup.

Snap out of it, Delisantro. You're not thinking straight.

This ended here. Now. No more questions. And no more answers. It would only make her more of a distraction.

He stared at the debris sprawled across the counter, briefly contemplated looking through her stuff. But then dismissed the thought. He ought to stick her things back in her bag. Snooping would imply a level of interest in her he didn't have.

Picking up the file folder, he started to shove it back in her bag, when he spotted the words typed neatly on the label stuck across the top: Delisantro/De Rossi.

He lowered the mug, his heart beating right into his throat. What the…? Why did she have a file on him? And who was De Rossi?

He flicked up the flap and peered inside, not caring any more about her privacy. Stapled to the top of a sheath of typed pages was an old press clipping. He recognised the grainy black and white photo at the centre of the layout instantly, even though he hadn't seen it in more than twenty years.

Coffee sloshed over the rim of his mug as his heart punched his larynx. He placed the mug on the countertop.

The innocuous headline: 'Family-Run Trattoria Brings Taste of Tuscany to Tufnell Park' blurred as he stared at the picture of his family below it—or, rather, the people he'd thought were his family—standing outside the tiny Italian restaurant in North London where he'd grown up.

There was his little sister Ruby, eight years old and already stunningly beautiful, showing off her best Sunday Mass dress while grinning precociously at the camera. He stood to her right, looking lanky and uncomfortable as he tugged at the starched collar and tie threatening to throttle him. And on Ruby's left stood Carmine Delisantro, with the ready smile spread across his robust features Nick would always remember. A band of emotion tightened around his heart as he blinked, noticing that Carmine's mane of hair was already thinning in his early thirties, and his head had been level with Nick's. How could they have been the same height? He'd only been twelve when the photo had been snapped by a local journalist doing an article on the family restaurant. Always in his memory Carmine had seemed like a lion of a man, his warm, vocal presence so much larger than life.

Dad.

The word echoed in his head as his thumb touched the faded newsprint. The band squeezed painfully, but just as the guilt and regret threatened to choke him his gaze settled on the woman standing on Carmine's other side in the far left of the picture, with her arm looped around her husband's waist and her head tucked on his shoulder. Nick studied her striking face, her statuesque figure, the lush lips, the glorious waves of hair, so like his own, and those dark sultry laughing eyes that had held so many cruel secrets.

Confusion and anguish washed over him, until the tide of grief turned into a wave of resentment.

Isabella Delisantro. His mother.

Eva paused at the entrance to the living room, not sure what to make of the scene before her. Nick stood with his back to her, his head bent. But why was her stuff strewn across the kitchen counter? Had he been going through her things? She tried to feel affronted, but all she could manage was dismay.

However much she might have researched about him in the last fortnight, and however intimate they had been last night. She didn't know him. And she knew even less about what to do in this situation.

Why had he been so surly when she'd woken up? Was he just not much of a morning person? Or had she done something wrong? Something she was unaware of? Was he entitled to look through her stuff, because they'd slept together? Did it give him certain rights she didn't know about? Because she'd never been in a relationship with anyone before, she didn't know if the normal rules of privacy still applied.

She was completely clueless about morning-after etiquette. She crossed her arms over her chest, desperately self-conscious about the plunging neckline of the velvet gown, and her total lack of relationship knowledge.

'Um…Hi,' she murmured, talking to Nick's rigid back. 'Did my bag explode?'

He spun round, the hard glint in his eyes making her take an involuntary step back.

'What's this?' The frigid tone of voice matched the glacial expression on his face. He held up the papers in his hand, and she recognised the contents from the De Rossi file.

'Those are my research notes,' she replied as the shiver of apprehension shimmered up her spine. If he'd seemed surly in the bedroom, he seemed coldly furious now.

'Your *research* notes?' His voice rose to a shout as he emphasised the angry words by slapping the papers down on the counter. She flinched, shocked by the barely suppressed violence in the gesture.

He braced his palms on the countertop. 'Who the hell are you? And who's De Rossi?'

She tensed. 'I'm Eva Redmond. I work for Roots Registry.' She cleared her throat, ashamed at the quiver in her voice. 'I…I thought you knew. Vincenzo De Rossi, the Duca D'Alegria is our client. I emailed your agent, countless times.' She'd only given minimal details, had intended to tell Nick the whole story face-to-face, but even so she'd assumed he knew who she was. Why she had wanted the appointment.

'I don't know any Duca D'Alegria.'

'He's an Italian duke, the last in the direct line of the house of De Rossi in the province of Alegria.' She tightened her arms, trying not to be put off by the sharp frown on his face. 'The duca's main residence is the Alegria Palazzo on the banks of Lake Garda,' she babbled on. She should have clarified the situation last night, before she'd got onto his bike. Why hadn't she? Heat pulsed in her cheeks, swiftly followed by guilt. She knew why. And it had had nothing to do with her job. 'The family owns sixty-thousand acres, a thriving olive pressing business, two vineyards and several properties in the Tuscan—'

'Stop right there!' He held up his hand to emphasise the point. 'What the hell has any of this got to do with me?'

'He's your…' She paused, her tongue going numb. He looked so angry. Resentment was rolling off him in waves. She couldn't tell him the rest. Not like this. Not after what they'd done together. Maybe it hadn't meant much to him, but it meant something to her. And however little she knew about him, she didn't want to hurt him.

He slapped his hand on the counter. 'He's my *what?*'

'We have reason to believe…' She swallowed, the sick feeling in her stomach surging up her throat. 'We have reason to believe his son, Conte Leonardo Vittorio Vincenzo De Rossi, may have been your biological father.' But the truth was there was no maybe about it. Having met the duca, and seen photos of his son, as soon as she'd got a good look at Nick Delisantro she hadn't had a single doubt about his ancestry. 'Which would make the duca your grandfather,' she continued. 'And you his only direct descendant.'

She let out a breath, her throat aching at the thought of what might be going through his mind. About the man he had believed to be his biological father. The man he'd spent the first sixteen years of his life with.

'I'm so sorry. I realise this news must come as a shock.'

But he didn't look shocked, she realised as his gaze bored into hers. In fact, he was displaying none of the reactions she had prepared herself for—shock, disbelief, confusion or, worse, hurt. Temper flashed once more in his eyes, and then his gaze raked over her. And all she saw was disgust.

'So that's his name. Leonardo De Rossi. Thanks,' he said, contempt dripping from every syllable. 'I've always wondered who my mother screwed.'

Eva drew in a shaky breath. Not sure she'd heard him right. But how could she mistake the bitterness in his tone, or the look of derision now levelled at her?

'And you're on some kind of commission,' he asked, but it didn't sound like a question, 'to locate me, right?'

She shook her head. 'I receive a salary, but the company does get a commission from our client, once he's satisfied that you're the baby mentioned in his son's journal. Leonardo wrote a…'

He flipped up a palm and she stopped in mid-sentence, the explanation dying on her lips. 'Spare me the details. I'm not interested in the duca, or his son.' He folded his arms over his chest, propped his butt against the countertop. 'But I am interested in you.' He flicked his gaze back over her figure. 'You're quite the little operator, aren't you? I've got to admit, the virginity was a nice touch. It threw me off for a while.' He huffed out a contemptuous laugh. 'What were you doing? Saving it up for the perfect mark?'

The lump of emotion swelled in her throat as the heat soared into her cheeks. He couldn't mean what she thought he meant? That wasn't possible. This wasn't the man who had held her last night, whose arms she had slept in. Who had treated her with a care and consideration she knew now she probably hadn't deserved. She opened her mouth, to explain. Then closed it again. He was looking at her as if she were scum. Worse than scum.

'I don't…' She pushed the words out, nerves and guilt and

horror writhing in her stomach like venomous snakes. 'I don't know what you're trying to imply.'

'Really?' He laughed again, the harsh sound echoing against the room's hard surfaces. He strolled easily round the counter. She stepped back as he approached, rubbed her hands over her upper arms, the heat of his temper searing her skin.

'You can stop the innocent act now. I'm wise to it.'

'I don't understand.'

He cupped her cheek, his rough palm cool against her burning skin. 'Damn, but you're good.'

'I'm not…' The denial caught in her throat. 'Whatever you're thinking, it isn't true.'

He wrapped his arm round her waist, jerked her against him. 'You know what's ironic?' he murmured as his scent filled her senses, the outline of his arousal shocking her almost as much as the melting response at her core.

She pressed her palms against his chest, tried to push away from him, but he only tugged her closer, buried his head against her neck.

'You played your ace for nothing,' he whispered against her ear, his lips brushing the pulse point hammering her throat.

She braced her arms, horrified by the sizzle of response shimmering down to her core, the moisture flooding from her thighs. The man thought she was some kind of con artist. How could she still be so susceptible to him?

He nipped at her ear lobe. 'What a shame you didn't do a better job with your research. If you had you'd know I'm not the noble type.' His hand cupped her breast. And she gasped, the nipple puckering through the velvet as he rubbed his thumb across the tip. He chuckled, the sound hollow and smug. 'You were saving it up for nothing, sweetheart. But let's not let it go to waste. Right?'

'Please don't do this.' The tears stinging her eyes only

added to her humiliation. She bit into her lip, desperate to get out, to get away, before he saw her cry.

He lifted his head at the blare of a car horn from outside. 'Well, what do you know? Saved by your cab bell.'

He let her go, and she scrambled back.

'Go on, get lost,' he said, the mocking twist of his lips brutal in its contempt. He swept a hand towards her stuff. 'And take your *research* with you.'

She lifted her bag from the counter, shoved the contents back into it, her hands shaking but her back ramrod straight. The tears scoured her throat as she gulped them back.

You have to hold it together, long enough to get out of here.

She slung the bag over her shoulder, made herself face him. 'I'm sorry. I thought you knew who I was. I didn't mean for any of this to happen,' she said, politeness the only shield she had.

'Then I guess we're both sorry. Aren't we?' he said, his voice as flat and expressionless as his eyes.

Somehow even his anger was better than his contempt. She rushed through the terrace doors. Her bare feet slapped against the wooden decking as she fled, not just from him, but from her own stupidity and inadequacy.

She clenched her teeth, pressed the heel of her palm against her breastbone as the cab whisked away from the kerb. The pain and confusion felt fresh and raw and jagged as the romance of her one wild night shattered inside her like the fragile illusion it was.

How could she ever have believed, even for one night, that she could be anything other than what she was? A cowardly academic who'd spent her whole life day-dreaming about being reckless and adventurous and then doing exactly what she was told.

CHAPTER SEVEN

'WHAT is going on, Eva? Bob informs me he finally got a reply from Delisantro's agent and the guy told him Delisantro not only wants nothing to do with this company, but he specifically doesn't want anything to do with you.'

'I'm so sorry, Mr Crenshawe.' Eva gripped the polyester weave of the seat cushion and hunched into the seat, the pain as fresh and raw as it had been a week ago. Sweat pooled under the armpits of her tailored suit. 'I had hoped Mr Delisantro would be more willing to cooperate with Bob,' she mumbled, the jagged little shards of agony piercing her chest at this renewed evidence of Nick's contempt.

Hadn't she suffered enough for her foolishly reckless and fanciful behaviour a week ago?

She'd confessed to her boss, Henry Crenshawe, that her trip had been a failure as soon as she'd got back from San Francisco. Mr Crenshawe had subjected her to a ten-minute lecture on her appalling lack of people skills, and then taken her off the account, which she'd been pathetically grateful for. She didn't want to have to contact Nick again.

But she'd been far too humiliated by her gross lack of judgement and professionalism—not to mention the presence of those jagged little shards that came back every time she thought of Nick—to admit the whole truth to her boss or anyone else. That she'd got carried away by some ridiculous flight of fancy and the nuclear blip to her usually tame libido as soon as she'd set eyes on Nick Delisantro—and lost sight of everything that was important in her life in the space of one night. Her responsibilities to Roots Registry and to her job hadn't even entered her head. And for that she felt not just guilty and embarrassed but so angry with herself she wanted to scream. She'd put a job she adored in jeopardy. But what upset her more was the knowledge that Nick's contempt still hurt so much, a week after he'd kicked her out of his apartment.

How foolish was she to have believed that he might have reconsidered? And decided that she wasn't such a terrible person after all? And why should it even matter? She was never going to see him again.

'Yeah, well he isn't cooperating.' The irritation on Henry Crenshawe's face made it quite clear she wasn't going to be given any slack. 'What exactly is it that Delisantro has against you? Because if we knew that, we might be able to fix it. Get back in his good graces. The company needs this commission—it's prestigious as hell. The publicity is priceless. Alegria has three other heir-hunting companies that I know of looking for his heir. And we've got the jump on them. Because we've already located the guy.' Crenshawe yanked at his collar, his pudgy face going a mottled red. Eva's heart, the jagged little shards still prickling, sank to her toes.

She would have to tell her boss the truth. 'It's a private issue, between myself and Mr Delisantro,' she mumbled, desperate to stave off the inevitable.

'Private how?' Crenshawe demanded. 'You were only in San Francisco for one night. I know your people skills are non-existent,' he said, his voice rising. 'But even you couldn't have annoyed him that much in one night.'

She could hear the incredulity in Crenshawe's voice, and knew what he was thinking. How could his quiet, timid and inconspicuous researcher even have been noticed by a man as dynamic as Nick Delisantro, let alone have made enough of an impression on him to annoy him to this extent?

The realisation triggered something inside her—and the jagged little shards of misery were obliterated by a surge of anger.

Eva straightened in her chair, and her gaze lifted to the man who had always regarded her with benign contempt. Mr Crenshawe wouldn't expect Nick Delisantro to notice her, because like most of the people she knew, he had never really noticed her either. Henry Crenshawe had always taken her work completely for granted, had never given her the credit she was due.

Roots Registry hadn't located the Duca D'Alegria's missing heir, *she* had—after weeks of painstaking research on the historical data, most of which had had to be translated from Italian. It had been a mammoth task, checking marriage records, tracing the movements of every young bride within a fifty-mile radius of the Alegria estate in the year in question and then correlating the birth certificates of the babies born to them.

And it wasn't the first time her concentrated and creative investigation of the known facts and her diligent attention to detail had pulled in a major account. Even so, she'd been the only one of Crenshawe's researchers not to be considered for a promotion when the company had expanded a year ago. She was paid less than all her male colleagues and she'd only had one modest bonus in three years. While she adored the job she did at Roots Registry, she'd always shied away from any contact with her boss, because she knew he was a sexist blowhard who didn't understand or appreciate the work she did…Except when it came to the bottom line.

What made her temper spike, though, was the fact that Crenshawe's scorn towards her and her efforts had been partly her own fault, because she'd never once stood up for herself.

Until now.

Yes, she'd made a mistake sleeping with Nick Delisantro. But his negative reaction to the news of his grandfather's existence had not been caused by their night together. He'd clearly already been aware of his illegitimacy before she'd said anything. And the deep-seated resentment there had nothing whatsoever to do with her.

But more than that, Crenshawe was wrong about her. She wasn't the mouse he clearly thought she was. Not any more.

Nick Delisantro *had* noticed her. She hadn't been invisible to Nick. And while it might have been better for her employment prospects if she hadn't had sex with him, she was through feeling guilty or ashamed about what she'd done. She didn't deserve Henry Crenshawe's contempt, any more than she deserved Nick Delisantro's.

'I slept with Nick Delisantro that night,' she announced, pleased with the firm tone and her refusal to relinquish eye contact when Crenshawe's eyebrows shot up to his receding hairline. 'And he misconstrued my motives the following morning.'

'You did *what?*' Crenshawe yelped, the sheen of sweat on his forehead glistening. 'You…You…' His double chin wobbled with fury, the mottled colour in his cheeks turning scarlet. 'You stupid little tart.'

He was going to fire her. She could see it in the vindictive light that came into his beady eyes as he stomped around the office, gesticulating wildly and throwing out a series of increasingly personal insults about her and her work.

Her fingers released on the seat cushion and she kept her chin thrust out, more than ready to take the blow, an odd sense of calm and detachment settling over her.

Well, what d'you know? Mr Crenshawe has noticed me at last.

* * *

Nick tapped the parting line of dialogue into the template on his computer. Then paused to reread the scene he'd spent all morning sweating blood over. And groaned.

His detective hero sounded like someone with a borderline personality disorder. He ran his fingers through his hair, then stabbed the mouse to close the script window on the laptop.

Getting up from the desk, he crossed to the window, glared down at the street below which was all but deserted in the middle of the afternoon on a workday. Maybe if he got out of the apartment for a few hours, took a ride on his bike and blew the cobwebs out of his head. But as soon as the thought registered he dismissed it.

The bike was out. He'd gone for a ride yesterday, and somehow ended up on the Marin Headland, the memory of Eva Redmond's lush body plastered against his back and the high-pitched whoop of her laughter as they'd crossed the bridge reverberating through his subconscious every inch of the way.

Why couldn't he get her out of his head? It had been a full week since that night. The woman was an operator, had investigated him and his origins and then had the gall to sleep with him without telling him the truth about who she was. That should have been more than enough to end his fascination.

He swore softly, slung a hand into the pocket of the sweatpants he wore when writing. How had she got her hooks into him so deep?

He squinted against the afternoon sun shining through the study window and pictured her face the last time he'd seen it. The pallor of her skin, her lips trembling and those wide translucent blue eyes, the pupils dilated with shock.

Instead of the resentment, the cleansing anger that had sustained him for the last seven days, he finally acknowledged the trickle of guilt.

'Hell!' The expletive cut the quiet like a knife.

Eva Redmond might not have been one hundred per cent forthcoming about who she was, but there was no getting around the fact that he had seduced her. Not the other way around.

As soon as he'd spotted her in the Union Square gallery, her glorious curves displayed to perfection in red velvet, her shy but direct gaze locked with his, he'd wanted her. And while he'd become a lot more cautious in the last decade or so, a lot more discerning about who he pursued, one thing hadn't changed. When he saw a woman he wanted, he went after her.

The only difference with Eva was that he had been more relentless, more eager and more determined in his pursuit. There had been numerous signs of how innocent, how out-of-her-depth she was, long before he'd taken her virginity, and he'd chosen to ignore every one of them to have her. So whose fault was it really that he'd ended up getting burned? Plus when he replayed all the conversations they'd had during their evening together—something he'd done with alarming regularity in the last seven days—he could see she'd tried to tell him who she was. And he'd stopped her elaborating, because he hadn't wanted to hear anything that might stop him getting her into bed.

He braced his hand on the window sill, forced himself to confront the truth. He'd done a lot of crummy things in his life. None of which he was proud of. But some of them had been necessary to survive. When you ran away from home at sixteen with just the clothes on your back and a belly full of anger, you ended up doing a lot of things that you would later regret. And he'd done more than his fair share.

He was enough of a pragmatist, though, to realise that he couldn't go back and undo those things now. And in many ways, he wouldn't want to. He wasn't a hypocrite and he knew that what he'd managed to make of his life had been largely due to that feral survival instinct—and the burning anger that had kept him strong and resilient in the face of often impossible odds. You couldn't go back, you had to go forward. But that didn't mean he could keep repeating those mistakes over and over again.

The only way he was going to be able to put this episode behind him was to see Eva Redmond again—and wipe that vision of her eyes bright with unshed tears out of his head.

Unfortunately, seeing Eva had the potential to open up a whole other can of worms.

He huffed out a harsh laugh, felt the hum of heat pulse through his system as he recalled the sight of Eva reflected in the glass, her nipples large and distended, and her soft sighs of pleasure spurring him on. He'd woken in a hot sweat every night since that night. His sex hard and erect, and throbbing with the urge to bury himself deep inside the tight clasp of her body. He'd got so damn wound up by the erotic memories he hadn't been sleeping properly, had barely been able to write—and everything he had written was terrible.

So the urge to see Eva again wasn't entirely altruistic. Given the shoddy way he'd treated her the morning after, he doubted she was going to be all that amenable to jumping back into bed with him—but that didn't seem to bother his libido.

The bright trill of his phone had him jerking upright. He turned to stare at it flashing on his desk. Probably his agent Jim wanting to know how the script was going. Not a conversation he really wanted to be having, seeing as the damn thing was going nowhere fast. But even so, he picked up the handset. Better to be lying to Jim than wrestling pointlessly with the apparently insolvable problem of Eva Redmond.

'Hi,' he said, struggling to inject some enthusiasm into the greeting.

'Hello, may I speak to Niccolo Delisantro?' replied a male voice with crisp and efficient British diction.

'Speaking, although the name's Nick,' he corrected, curious even though he didn't want to be. The only people who had called him Niccolo in recent memory were Eva and her friend Tess.

'I'm terribly sorry, Mr Delisantro. Nick,' came the effusive and fawning reply.

'Who is this?' Nick said, feeling less curious and more annoyed by the second.

'My name is Henry Crenshawe, I'm the managing director of Roots Registry. We're based in the UK. We do genealogical research for high-profile clients who wish to discover the—'

'Cut to the chase, Henry,' Nick interrupted the flow of unnecessary information as the short hairs on the back of his neck tingled. Roots Registry? Wasn't that the name of Eva's employer?

He heard a slight pause on the other end of the line, then Crenshawe's voice came back, the tone oily and obsequious. 'This is a very delicate situation, Mr Delisantro. I'm calling to offer my sincere apologies for the reprehensible conduct of our former employee Miss Eva Redmond. I can't stress enough our absolute—'

'What do you mean your *former* employee?' Nick asked as his heartbeat kicked up a notch.

'We fired her, of course,' the man replied, in an officious voice, and the trickle of guilt turned into a torrent.

'As soon as we discovered her grossly inappropriate behaviour during her visit to San Francisco,' Crenshawe continued in the same pompous tone. But Nick couldn't really hear what the guy was pontificating about.

Eva had lost her job over their night together.

'And I'd like to assure you she will never get another job in the genealogical research industry again after this incident—'

'Wait a minute,' Nick cut in, his temper finally putting in an appearance. 'How did you find out we slept together?' Was he being watched by these people?

He thought he heard a slight choking sound, then a super-cilious little laugh. 'Um, well, Miss Redmond admitted to the indiscretion, Mr Delisantro, this afternoon.'

He raked his fingers through his hair.

Damn it, why had she told them? But even as he asked him-self the question he could see the guilty flush on her cheeks when she'd admitted to being a virgin—as if she'd tricked him or something—and he knew the answer. Because she was an honest and forthright and hopelessly trusting person. Unlike him.

And to think he'd accused her of being an operator. What a joke. Eva Redmond was about as devious as Snow White.

'Here at Roots Registry we couldn't possibly condone that kind of behaviour,' Crenshawe continued with the same self-righteous indignation. 'We're a reputable company in every respect and we value our reputation above all else.'

'But not your employees,' Nick remarked coldly, his anger at the man rising.

'I beg your pardon, Mr Delisantro?'

'You heard me—how long did Eva work for you?'

'Approximately three years,' Crenshawe replied with af-fronted dignity. Nick could almost see him puffing up his chest.

'And during that time, did she ever do anything like this before?'

'Well, no, of course not. She was a quiet and, we thought, demure employee—we never had any reason to suspect she would—'

'But even so you didn't think she was worthy of a second chance?' Nick interrupted again. The creep had sacked Eva without a moment's notice and by the sounds of it was intend-ing to blacklist her too—and all because she'd succumbed to the explosive physical chemistry between them that even Nick, with all his sexual experience and cynicism, hadn't been able to resist.

'Some things simply aren't excusable,' the man said, but he'd lost a lot of his bluster and sounded more confused than self-righteous.

'Yeah, right,' Nick sneered, but even as his scorn for the bureaucratic jerk curdled his stomach he knew he had to take a large share of the blame for Eva's predicament.

'So I take it you won't be making a complaint?' the man said tentatively.

'Of course not,' Nick barked, thoroughly sick of the whole situation now.

He hadn't felt this guilty about anything since he'd refused to return to the UK seven years ago and see Carmine Delisantro one last time, despite his sister Ruby's tearful pleas.

He'd done the same thing then that he'd done a week ago. Put himself and his feelings, his wants and desires first, above everyone else's. He hadn't wanted to see Carmine again, because he'd been so bitterly ashamed of how he'd behaved as a teenager towards the man who had raised him. He'd thought at the time it had been the right thing to do, not to risk digging up all that anger and unhappiness and resentment about the miserable circumstances of his birth all over again. But as the years had passed, and he'd never been able to forget Ruby's phone calls, and the funeral invitation that he'd thrown into the trash as soon as he'd received it, he'd finally had to admit the truth. That he'd taken the easy way out. He hadn't done the right thing—he'd just done the right thing for him.

'Well, that being the case, Mr Delisantro,' Crenshawe's voice buzzed in his ear, distracting him from the unpleasant memories, 'I'm eager to talk to you on another matter entirely,'

'What other matter?'

'As I believe Miss Redmond informed you, she was working on the Alegria account.'

Here it comes, Nick thought bitterly. *The real reason for Crenshawe's call.* 'Yeah, what about it?'

'We have reason to believe that Vincenzo Palatino Vittorio Savargo De Rossi, the fifteenth Duca D'Alegria, is your paternal grandfather.' The eagerness in Crenshawe's voice sickened Nick, but he listened.

Maybe he could work this to his advantage. Crenshawe wanted something from him, and he wanted something for Eva.

'I already told Eva, I couldn't give a flying—' He paused, bit back the swear word that wanted to come out. 'I couldn't care less about this duc or his relationship to me.'

'I understand, Mr Delisantro. But I thought you should know that your connection to De Rossi, if it's confirmed, could possibly make you the sole heir to a substantial fortune in Italian real estate and assets. Not to mention the Alegria Palazzo on the banks of Lake Garda.'

'So what? I don't need it,' Nick said, and meant it.

Money had been the driving force of his existence at the lowest point of his life. How to get it had become an obsession that had consumed him every second of every day, so that he could eat, stay clean, stay healthy, find shelter. When you'd been at the very bottom, when the pursuit of a few pennies meant the difference between eating or going hungry, between curling up over a tube grate or having a hostel bed for the night, you discovered just how important money was. And you'd do anything you had to do to get hold of it.

But after he'd clawed his way out of the gutter he'd flung himself into at sixteen, and begun the long, slow and difficult process of remaking himself into the man he had eventually become, he'd made a conscious effort not to let money control his life any more. Sure, he'd pursued it with almost feral intensity long after he'd needed to, but he'd eventually learnt the painful lesson that to get over his past, he had to get over the insecurity of his years on the street, and the 'anything for a buck' mentality that had turned him into a less-than-stellar human being.

He knew that was still a work in progress. His decision not to go and see Carmine Delisantro on his deathbed, and his reckless pursuit of Eva were proof of that. But he had more than enough money now, not just to survive, but to prosper, and he certainly had no need of De Rossi's fortune. Maybe by some trick of genetics he was related to this guy, but he wasn't related to him in any genuine sense.

'But surely, Mr Delisantro, you must at least be curious about the De Rossi family? They are, after all, your blood relations.'

'Look, Henry,' he countered with deliberate insolence. 'Why don't you stop trying to butter me up and tell me what it is you want from me?'

'All right,' the man said warily. 'It's fairly simple really. We've spoken to our client about the results of our research on his behalf.'

'You mean Eva's research,' Nick clarified sharply.

Crenshawe cleared his throat. 'Yes, that's correct, Miss Redmond's research.' The guy at least sounded a little circumspect. 'And the duca would like to meet you. He has requested that you visit his estate in Italy, as a guest, and if things go well he would then involve his lawyers. Of course a DNA test will be required at some point, but he's insisting that he meets you first. On his home turf, so to speak.'

The cagey old bastard, Nick thought wryly. The duca might be looking for a biological heir, but he wasn't going to accept any Tom, Dick or Harry to inherit his precious real-estate fortune, whether they carried his son's DNA or not.

The idea of being inspected and deemed worthy or unworthy by some pompous Italian aristocrat whose own son had been a callow playboy, from the little Nick knew of the man who had seduced his mother, made Nick's temper burn. Who did this duca think he was?

'We'll be sending a representative from Roots Registry to accompany you,' Crenshawe continued. 'To make the introductions and then set out for the duca and his legal team the research we've carried out that supports your claim.'

And to make sure they got their commission out of the old guy, Nick suspected, as he hardly needed an introduction, and any research documents could easily be emailed. But he didn't contradict Crenshawe, an idea forming in his mind.

'When does he want me to visit?' Nick asked.

'As soon as your schedule will allow,' Crenshawe replied, his voice perking up. 'The duca is an elderly man and he wants this matter settled as soon as feasibly possible.'

'And how long does he want me to stay?'

'He's asked for anything up to a month. If things go well, he would like to become properly acquainted with you—and teach you about the holdings you will be inheriting.'

'A month?' Nick almost choked. 'No way. I'm not hanging round in some castle in Italy for a month.' The truth was he didn't think the old guy would want him to stay too long once Nick had given him a few graphic details about his past. This wasn't going to be a heartfelt family reunion, so the quicker they got it over with, the better.

But he was going to go, because he wanted to see Eva again. And if he could get her her job back into the bargain, all the better.

'The final deadline for my latest script is the end of this week,' he continued. And now he had an added incentive to make sure he met it. 'After that there will be rewrites, but that's only after the producers, the director and the lead actors and their agents and assistants and pretty much every other nobody involved with the production company have read it,' Nick added, thinking on his feet, and steadfastly ignoring the little voice in his head that was shouting at him to stop and think this through. 'And it always takes a couple of weeks at least for that to happen.'

'I understand entirely, Mr Delisantro. Of course, we wouldn't presume to impinge on your valuable—'

'Shut up, Henry.'

What kind of pompous jerk used the word 'impinge'?

'I'll book a flight to Heathrow a week tomorrow. Eva can meet me there and you can arrange the connecting flights to Italy. But you'll have to tell your duca I can only spare a fortnight tops. And I want Eva with me at all times.'

He decided not to worry about the fact that the mere thought of having Eva near him again was making heat spread through his system. She might well hate his guts after the way he'd treated her, which would force him to get over her. And if she didn't, well…Two weeks in some luxury palazzo in Italy would be a good way to figure out what had got him so obsessed with her in the first place.

'But, Mr Delisantro, Miss Redmond is no longer in our employ,' Crenshawe said hesitantly.

'That's your problem, Henry. Not mine. But let me give you some advice. If she's not waiting for me at Heathrow a week from tomorrow, you can kiss your commission goodbye.'

CHAPTER EIGHT

EVA reread the monitor in Heathrow's Terminal Five for the fiftieth time and tried to even her breathing. She was starting to hyperventilate.

'In the arrivals hall.' She whispered the words above the hum of conversation and the indecipherable drone of the terminal announcer's voice.

Pulling the two tickets to Milan out of her handbag, she studied the flight numbers for the twentieth time. Then shoved them back in and fastened the bag.

Think pretty thoughts.

But instead of puppies gambolling on a bed of wild flowers springing to mind, the less-than-pretty picture of Nick, his eyes glittering with contempt, leapt into her head. Her breath clogged her lungs, taking on the consistency of treacle.

Breathe.

She pushed out a breath. Gulped in another.

She'd never had a panic attack before, but seeing Nick Delisantro again was exactly the sort of extreme-stress situation that could trigger one. She sucked in several more painfully shallow breaths, exhaled slowly.

Focus. Because quite apart from the humiliation factor, you don't have time to pass out.

Nick's plane from San Francisco was already half an hour late. Their flight to Italy was due to take off in two hours. She had to get them to Terminal One, and ensure they checked in at least an hour prior to take-off. And then…

She swallowed down the lump of treacle cutting off her air supply as heat seeped into her cheeks.

And then she would be spending the next two weeks at Nick Delisantro's beck and call.

She still wasn't quite sure how she'd got into this fix. Everything had happened so fast and so unexpectedly. She'd been scouring the job ads last Tuesday morning, trying to figure out a way to make her meagre savings last while she reinvented her shattered career, her confrontation with Mr Crenshawe not making her feel quite as courageous as she would have hoped, when she'd received a frantic call from her ex-boss—begging her to return to work and claiming that her sacking had all been a terrible misunderstanding. When she'd hesitated momentarily, from shock rather than reluctance, he'd immediately doubled her salary as an incentive.

It was only when she'd arrived at work that afternoon, trying to ignore the inquisitive stares from her co-workers, that she'd discovered the enormous catch in her sudden change of fortunes.

First there had been the astonishing news that she was back on the Alegria account, promptly followed by the heart-stopping information that Nick Delisantro had not only consented to travel to the Duca D'Alegria's estate in Lake Garda, but that he was insisting she accompany him as Roots Registry's representative.

She'd left her boss's office in a daze, her fingers whitening on the printouts of the Alegria client presentation Bob had already started work on, as the whole terrifying scenario had slotted into place.

Nick Delisantro was the only reason she'd got her job back. Mr Crenshawe hadn't had a sudden change of heart, and if she refused to make the trip he would kick her right back out of the door again.

So she'd agreed to go to Italy.

And then endured seven whole days of extreme agitation while she tried to figure out Nick Delisantro's motives. Why had he insisted she go with him? When he couldn't stand the sight of her?

The only possible scenario that had made any sense was that he had devised this trip as some new way of punishing her. As if shouting at her, humiliating her and kicking her out of his apartment weren't enough.

At first she'd panicked. Horrified at the thought of not only having to deal with his anger all over again, but having to spend two whole weeks with him using her as his whipping boy. But after a long phone conversation with Tess, during which she'd given her friend a pared-down version of her one-night stand, Tess had made her realise that she had every right to be mad at Nick and not the other way around.

Unfortunately, despite her show of bravado in finally standing up to Mr Crenshawe, Eva wasn't sure she had enough courage to stand up to someone as dominating as Nick.

The truth was she had even less experience of confrontational situations than she did of sexual ones. As a child she'd always been a champion conciliator, had hardly ever even uttered a cross word at the dinner table—because she'd always been far too aware of the weight of her parents' disapproval if she did. Not that her parents had been bad parents—they hadn't. They'd never been aggressive or unkind towards her, and they hadn't even been particularly strict, except about her schoolwork. But they had never been very affectionate either. They simply hadn't been demonstrative people—and unfortunately she was. She'd longed for the spontaneous hugs and kisses, the casual praise and all those other unconscious signs that demonstrated you were loved and cherished, which she saw her school friends receiving from their mums and dads, but her own parents had never been capable of. And as a consequence of that childhood yearning, she'd become pathetically eager to please. Nick had accused her of always apologising. And he'd been right.

But as Tess had pointed out rather forcefully on the phone yesterday afternoon from San Francisco, he hadn't been right to turn on her the way he had after they'd slept together. He'd accused her of things she hadn't done. Things that, once she'd had a chance to think about it, didn't even make sense. Why on earth would she have needed to sleep with him to tell him he was in line to inherit millions? Surely most people would have been overjoyed to receive that news? The fact that he hadn't been must have something to do with his past.

When had he discovered he was illegitimate? she wondered. Had it been a particularly traumatic experience for him?

Eva frowned at the dwindling line of passengers coming out of the arrival gates, and swallowed down the wave of sympathy.

Don't even go there.

She needed to nurture her indignation and work on her confrontation skills—or Nick Delisantro was going to walk all over her a second time, and the little shards that he'd somehow inserted in her heart would never go away. She definitely did *not* need to feel sorry for him. So making assumptions about what might have happened to him as a child was out.

She peered towards the gate and smoothed damp palms down the lower half of the power suit she'd chosen that morning, after trying on six other outfits. With its knee-length steel-grey pencil skirt, matching tailored jacket and demure white cotton blouse, it made her look one-hundred-per-cent professional.

She was calm now, she noted. Or calm enough. She gripped the handle of her wheel-around suitcase. Her hands had stopped quivering and she was breathing, if not evenly, at least fairly regularly. Once she'd got over this first meeting, established how she was going to play things—calm, detached, not given to emotional outbursts of any kind—everything would be fine.

Then she spotted the tall, well-muscled man strolling out of the gate in a worn T-shirt and low-slung jeans. His caramel brown hair was shorter than she remembered it, hugging his head and curling only slightly around his ears. But there was no mistaking that devastatingly handsome face, the olive skin, or the dark gaze that scanned the crowd, then locked onto her face with a focus and intensity that reminded her of their first meeting.

Her grip flexed and tightened on the handle to stop the trembling in her fingers and the quick, shallow gasp of breath. But it didn't do a thing for the swell of heat beneath her pencil skirt that dampened the gusset of her panties.

She bit down on her bottom lip as he strolled towards her, his strides measured but exact, and the expression on his face completely unreadable.

Ignore the heat. Stay calm, stay professional and, whatever you do, do not say sorry. You're not the one who should be apologising.

She stood rooted to the spot. Determined not to give in to the sudden instinct to lift the hem of the confining pencil skirt and leg it straight out of the terminal building.

She'd flown once before, and he'd caught up with her. What she had to do now was fight.

Fight for composure. Fight to regain her dignity and fight to maintain control of this situation for the next two weeks. Not to mention fight an attraction that for some inexplicable reason had not gone away, despite the appalling way this man had treated her already and the unpleasant way she was sure he intended to treat her again.

Unfortunately, her hormones paid absolutely no attention whatsoever to her mission statement. Because as Nick Delisantro got closer, they began jumping and jigging about as if they'd just won the lottery.

She squeezed the fingers of her free hand into a fist, released them and then thrust out her palm as he stopped in front of her. 'Good afternoon, Mr Delisantro. I hope you had a pleasant flight,' she said, her voice satisfyingly polite and professional despite her jackpot-hitting hormones. 'But I'm afraid we need to hurry or we'll miss our plane to Milan.'

His fingers closed over hers, making electricity zing into her palm and then shoot up her arm.

'*Mr* Delisantro?' One dark brow arched as a mocking smile curved his lips. 'Isn't that a bit formal, given that I've seen you naked, Eva?'

The confidence in his tone, and the spark of humour in his eyes, made it clear he wasn't asking a question. And her temper finally got the better of her hormones.

'Formal works for me, given that you're not going to see me naked again, *Mr* Delisantro,' she fired back, tugging her hand out of his grasp.

Nick chuckled at the steely hint of aggravation in her tone.

Damn, how could he have forgotten how direct she was? And how much he enjoyed that about her?

He let his gaze drift over her, and enjoyed the view too. While the buttoned-up two-piece suit should have made her look a lot less appealing, somehow it didn't. She'd tied her riotous hair back in a ruthless bun, but those big baby blue eyes, full kissable lips and petal-soft skin were as exquisite as he remembered them, belying her attempts to disguise her beauty.

Had she disguised herself especially for his benefit? The

thought gave him a nice little ego-boost and confirmed the decision he'd come to on the plane.

He was through feeling guilty about the way he'd lost his temper with Eva the morning after their night together. He'd got Eva her job back—and was submitting to being judged like a prize stallion by a man he'd never met before, plus he was travelling all the way to Italy for the privilege. So as far as he was concerned, his conscience was now clear on that score.

Which had rather neatly paved the way for the second decision he'd come to a split second ago, as his libido had rioted right back into overdrive at the sight of her. He hadn't been able to forget her in two whole weeks now. And he was through trying. They were going to be stuck together in Italy for a fortnight. And he for one couldn't see the harm any more in making the most of it. Especially given that flush of arousal turning her pale cheeks a rosy pink.

'Now that sounds like a challenge,' he teased.

Her eyebrows lifted all the way to her neatly brushed fringe. 'It's not,' she said swiftly, but the firm words were contradicted by the tiny tremble of her bottom lip.

'If you say so, Eva,' he replied, his eyes drawn to her full breasts, which quivered deliciously under the prim shirt she wore.

Heat punched his groin. He wanted to feel the weight of her breasts again. Wanted her straining against him and begging for his touch the way she had a fortnight ago.

That could take a while, he acknowledged, as his thought processes finally kicked in, certainly longer than the first time, given that she didn't seem entirely pleased to see him.

Good thing they had more than one night.

'We have to get to Terminal One,' she said, glancing at her wristwatch and avoiding his eyes. 'The flight to Milan leaves in less than two hours.'

'I'm all yours,' he said, his voice husky with innuendo.

The colour in her cheeks hit critical mass, but she only sent him a wary glance, before shooting off towards the terminal entrance. He followed at a more leisurely pace, easily keeping up with her short strides. And wondered if she realised the tailored skirt did nothing to disguise the seductive sway of her hips.

He was playing some sort of game with her. That had to be it, Eva thought as she stared out of the aeroplane's small window and the puzzled frown on her face reflected in the perspex.

But she didn't have a clue what game. Why did he keep sending her those long, smouldering looks? And what was with the husky tone of voice? The sexy teasing? Had she imagined it, simply because she was so relieved that he was being cooperative instead of cruel?

She cast a look over her shoulder, to find him lifting his bag into the overhead locker. His T-shirt rose up his waist, to reveal a narrow strip of lean, tanned belly, dusted with dark hair. Her eyes traced the jagged white scar that defined the hollow of his hipbone. And the moisture dried in her mouth, and gushed elsewhere. His arms dropped and the tantalising glimpse disappeared. She squeezed her knees together and jerked her gaze back to the window.

But then her hearing became impossibly acute. She listened to the muffed thump as he sat down, then the creak of the seatback as he adjusted his long legs in the business class seat and finally heard the deafening metallic click of his seat belt fastening.

She stared out at the dull, concrete terminal building, rolled her lip under her teeth.

What was going on? Why was he being so reasonable? He hadn't raised a single objection as she'd rushed them over to

Terminal One, dealt with the check-in and then directed him straight to the queue to get through Security.

He'd stood in line behind her for what felt like several millennia but had only actually been about twenty minutes. She'd made some pointless attempts at small talk, until nerves at the penetrating looks he kept sending her had forced her to shut up.

But despite his silence, he hadn't been disdainful, or even annoyed. He'd been relaxed, amused even.

While she felt as if she were on a knife-edge. Why was she so unbearably aware of his physical presence? Maybe it was simply his height, that imposing physique. She hadn't really noticed how much taller than her he was, until now. That had to be why he seemed to tower over her, why it felt as if he were standing too close. When he really wasn't.

But that hardly accounted for the sudden attack of paranoia. Every time she looked away, she could have sworn she could feel him watching her. The fine hairs on the back of her neck were prickling alarmingly, even now, as if she were being shocked with static electricity. Her brow creased some more in the perspex. She was being ridiculous. A look could not possibly have a physical manifestation. She had to be imagining it.

Soft hairs brushed against her forearm on the arm rest and she jumped. She laid her arm across her lap, and sent him a tight smile to disguise her skittish reaction. 'It's only a two-hour flight. I hope your jet lag's not too bad.'

He sent her a steady look. 'I'll survive.'

'The duca is sending a car to pick us up at the airport. His social secretary said in her email that the drive to his home is about two hours, apparently.'

'Fine,' he said, sounding indifferent.

'What made you change your mind about meeting with the duca?' she asked, on impulse.

His eyebrows lowered slightly, but he didn't reply.

'You didn't seem inclined to pursue your inheritance, before,' she said, trying not to wince at the memory of exactly how disinclined to pursue it he'd been.

'My *possible* inheritance,' he said carefully. 'There's no conclusive evidence that we're related. And I'm not taking a DNA test.'

The reply was deliberately evasive, and only made his decision more confusing. If he had no intention of pursuing this, why was he even going to Italy? 'I doubt the duca will insist on a DNA test,' she remarked.

'Of course he will,' he said, dismissively. 'He'll want proof.'

'He won't need proof once he sees you.'

'Why not?' he said, the hint of irritation surprising her. It was almost as if he didn't want to be related to the duca…

'Your resemblance to his son is uncanny.'

His eyebrows rose fractionally but then his mouth flattened into a thin line. 'I see.' He hissed the words under his breath, just as the steward announced the details of the in-flight services.

'I have a photo of your father, if you'd like to see it?'

Nick looked at Eva blankly. 'My father?' he asked, momentarily confused. Was she planning to whip out the newspaper clipping of Carmine Delisantro? Then he realised who she was talking about, and he had to stifle the renewed stab of annoyance. 'You mean Leonardo De Rossi?'

She blinked. 'Yes, I'm sorry, I meant your biological father. I should have clarified that. I realise this must be hard to—'

'He's not my father,' he interrupted her sharply, not liking the way her features softened.

I don't have a father, he almost added, but didn't. Instead he grabbed the in-flight magazine out of the seat pocket, flipped a few pages to find something to read. But when she took the hint and didn't say anything more on the subject, he began to feel churlish, like a sulky child. Plus biting her head off for no good reason probably wasn't the best way to persuade her he wasn't such a bad guy after all.

He stuffed the magazine back in the pocket. Turned to find her switching off her mobile.

'As far as I'm concerned De Rossi's a sperm donor,' he clarified, careful to hide the bitterness in his voice. 'He means nothing to me. And neither does this inheritance.' He wasn't about to admit that the main reason he'd agreed to come was to see her again, so he added, 'I'm just a bit curious to find out what kind of man could make my mother forget her marriage vows.'

She said nothing for a long time, but he had the strangest sensation she could see right past his show of indifference. The truth was he was more than a little curious about the duca and his son, and why his mother had betrayed his father, or the man he had always thought of as his father, all those years ago.

He felt the unfamiliar flush of colour rise up his neck under her unwavering gaze, then her fingers touched his arm.

'You seem to have a lot of unresolved anger towards your mother.'

'What?' he croaked. *Where had that come from?*

'Your mother,' she said softly. 'You seem to have a lot of unresolved anger towards her.'

That was what he thought she'd said. He gave a half-laugh. 'Is this a joke?'

Her eyes widened as if she was surprised even at the suggestion. 'No, not at all.'

He chuckled, but the sound was hollow. He'd admit to curiosity, but anything else was ludicrous. He propped his elbow on the arm rest to study her. 'My mother died of breast cancer when I was still a kid. Believe me any anger I had towards

her for what she did—unresolved or otherwise—is long gone.'
He leaned closer, skimmed his thumb across her cheek and
watched her eyes darken delightfully. 'Let's talk about something else.'

Her eyes flickered away for a moment, then flicked back
to his, the determination in them more than a little unsettling.
'Leonardo wrote a journal, the duca discovered it a year after
his death and read it. That's how he found out his son had fa-
thered a child. You should read it,' she said, the earnest tone
as disturbing as the sympathy in her eyes.

'No, thanks.'

'It's written in Italian, but I have an English translation if
you need—'

'My Italian's fine. I don't want to read it,' he said stiffly.

'But don't you want to know what actually happened?' she
murmured, the pads of her fingertips touching his arm again.
'If you read the journal you'll see that your mother wasn't to
blame for…'

'I don't care what happened between them.' He tugged his
arm off the seat divider. Taking a calming breath, he kept his
voice low and even. 'And I never have.'

It wasn't strictly speaking true. He'd cared a lot when he
was a teenager, tortured by the thought that his father was not
the man he loved, the man he had always tried to emulate,
and live up to, but actually some slick Italian playboy who his
mother had screwed and then lied about for years.

But he didn't care about it any more. And he certainly didn't
want to read about their illicit affair in the playboy's journal. That would just open up all the old bitterness and anger
that had followed him around like a bad smell throughout his
teens and early twenties, making him do stupid things, take
pointless risks—and hurt the only people who had ever really
cared about him. He'd finally managed to outrun the anger,
finally calmed down enough to make a success out of his life

and put all the mistakes behind him—but he'd never be able to apologise to Carmine Delisantro.

The last thing he wanted was to drag any of that guilt up again. Fine, he could admit to mild curiosity about the duca and the man who had impregnated his mother. But he had no intention of playing happy families.

And if that meant he had some unresolved anger, well then maybe he did. But he could live with it just fine. 'Listen, Eva I'm all grown up now, and I couldn't care less about what happened a generation ago between De Rossi and my mother.'

'Okay,' she said, nodding carefully. 'I just thought you might be interested in—'

'I'm much more interested in talking about you,' he cut in, the sudden desire to change the subject almost as acute as the need to wrestle back control of the conversation—and her.

He didn't want to talk about the duca, or his son, or his own past. He was much more fascinated by the woman sitting beside him. And the unprecedented effect she still had on him. Which seemed to have become more acute since their first night. Instead of less.

Even while she'd been asking those intrusive questions, he'd felt the residual hum of arousal at the provocative tilt of her chin, and the softening in her gaze. The small patch of skin where her fingers had touched his arm still sizzled. He'd never been this aware of a woman before.

'What do you want to know?' she asked warily.

Reaching towards her, he drew his thumb across the little indent under her bottom lip, heard her sharp intake of breath. 'Let's start with how you got that tiny scar on your belly?'

As expected the intimate enquiry had hot colour firing across her cheekbones, but her gaze didn't falter. 'It's an appendix scar,' she said, both direct and delightfully flustered.

He leaned close, whispered: 'Want me to kiss it better?'

She didn't reply, but stunned arousal darkened her irises to a rich cobalt as her eyes flew wide.

He closed the gap, caught that full bottom lip between his teeth and gave a soft nip before sliding his tongue across it.

She jerked back, thudding against the aeroplane wall. 'No, I don't,' she said, more breathless than outraged.

'That's a shame.' He chuckled, noting the frantic rise and fall of her breathing, the pink flush on her neck. She fascinated him all right. And what fascinated him most of all was the way she responded to him. And how much her instant, untutored response turned him on.

Even when she was trying really hard not to.

He kissed me. Why did he kiss me?

Eva rubbed her hand over her mouth, unable to relinquish her fixed stare out of the window.

And why did I let him?

She pressed her lips together where the tiny bite still tingled. The jet taxied down the runway, forcing her body into the seat as it tilted into its ascent.

It hadn't been much more than a playful little nip, followed by a quick brush of his mouth against hers. It wasn't a case of letting him or not letting him. It wasn't that big a deal. She mustn't overreact. This was all part of the game he was playing.

But why wouldn't her lips stop buzzing?

This was worse than she thought, she realised as she heard the ping of the seat-belt sign switching off and her fingers white-knuckled on the arm rest.

Not only did she not have a clue *what* game Nick Delisantro was playing, but she had an awful feeling that whatever game it was, he planned to win.

CHAPTER NINE

THE chauffeur-driven car wound through the carefully manicured hedgerows of the Alegria estate, the red geraniums splashing vibrant colour into the intense green. The duca must have a small army of gardeners, Eva calculated, to keep the flowers blooming in this heat. She slipped open another button on her blouse, careful to keep her body turned to the window and away from her fellow passenger, who'd folded his long body into the seat next to her over two hours ago and promptly fallen asleep.

She'd lost her jacket as soon as she'd been positive Nick wasn't faking sleep to lull her into a false sense of security. Despite the air-conditioning, the sun glaring off the tinted windows, and the overwhelming presence of the man sleeping next to her, had made the interior of the limo stifling. She glanced down at her cleavage, glad to see only the smallest glimpse of flesh and the slight glow of perspiration. She wanted to look as professional as possible when they arrived, and she also didn't want to give Nick any ideas. He'd taken more than enough liberties already on that score. Although quite why he had, she still hadn't figured out.

She risked a look over her shoulder. With his chin tucked into his chest, his arms folded and his long legs crossed at the ankle and stretched out in front of him in the limo's spacious seat well, he'd hardly budged during the journey.

But how could he have fallen asleep so easily?

How could he be so apparently uninterested about meeting his grandfather for the first time? He hadn't asked a single question on the plane about the duca, or her research—or even the estate. In fact, apart from that moment of teasing and the kiss—she pressed her lips together—which she refused to think about again, he'd hardly spoken at all. Instead, he'd opened an expensive laptop not long after take-off and typed at a steady pace, pausing only to order a tomato juice.

When she thought of how absorbing she found tracing the ancestry of people who had been long dead and who she had no connection with whatsoever, she was even more astonished by his attitude. How could he be so calm and composed about meeting a man he was actually related to?

But even as the question echoed in her head she recalled his flat refusal to read Leonardo's journal. To even discuss the man. And the brittle anger in his voice. Maybe he wasn't indifferent about his past and his heritage at all. Maybe he was simply defensive about it. Because discussing the affair between his mother and Leonardo De Rossi brought back painful memories?

She watched him, the vulnerability of sleep making his harsh dominant features look almost boyish, and felt the little blip in her heartbeat at the thought of what he might have suffered when he discovered that Carmine Delisantro was not his father.

The crunch of the car wheels on gravel had Eva blinking back the sentimental thought.

Stop it—you promised yourself you wouldn't do this.

Romanticising Nick's reactions, and reading an emotional response into this visit that almost certainly wasn't even there, would only get her into trouble. She should never have probed about his relationship with his mother, but curiosity, and a stupid desire to soothe the anger she'd seen flash in his eyes, had got the better of her. Nick wasn't a little boy, as he had already pointed out, he was all grown up now. And the secrets of his past were none of her business.

The car swept out of the hedged driveway and rolled to a stop in front of the Alegria Palazzo. Eva sucked in an awed breath, craning her neck to get a better view. She'd seen photographs of the duca's estate, but nothing could have prepared her for the size and grandeur of the structure up close. Wide terraces separated the front of the building from the waterfront. The lake lapped against a wooden dock, where a couple of small sailboats were dwarfed by a muscular scarlet power cruiser.

Multicoloured formal gardens surrounded the mansion itself and stretched towards the forests that rimmed the property. In the distance the Dolomite Mountains created a dramatic natural backdrop to all the man-made splendour, towering over the northern tip of the Lake. She'd done her research on the Ducal Palazzo. Had discovered that it was originally a summer house built on the shores of the lake in the eighteenth-century to take advantage of Garda's pleasant micro-climate and provide the De Rossi family with an escape from the gruelling summer heat of their Tuscan olive plantations. But she hadn't expected anything quite this grand. Obviously a summer house to a duca was a little different in size and magnificence from an ordinary summer house.

Two women in stylish dark-purple uniforms and a man in a matching dark purple suit came out of the palazzo and hurried down the limestone steps that led to the driveway.

Nick hadn't stirred, and she debated whether to wake him, when the chauffeur whisked open her door and bowed. *'Noi siamo arrivati, signora.'*

'Grazie, Paolo,' she said in her rudimentary Italian.

She turned to wake Nick only to find him watching her out of hooded eyes.

'We've arrived at the palazzo,' she said, a bit inanely.

He stretched and then flicked a brief glance out of the window. 'Yeah,' he murmured. If he was as blown away by the duca's estate as she was, there was no trace of it as he climbed out of the car.

The staff had lined up to greet them, the butler standing so stiff and erect, Eva was half expecting him to salute as she and Nick approached. The man cleared his throat and rattled off a stream of Italian, only some of which Eva understood. Nick replied in the perfectly accented Italian she'd heard him use at the airport, then shook the man's hand and nodded at the two female staff, apparently unperturbed by the way all three of them were gaping at him as if they'd seen a ghost. She would hazard a guess the staff must all have worked for the duca when Leonardo was still alive.

She muddled her way through the introductions with Nick interpreting in short, staccato sentences. For a moment she thought he might be nervous. But he didn't look nervous as he strolled into the house beside her and they were directed to a drawing room just off the entrance hall. The room smelled of lemon polish and old wood, the elegant furnishings as ornate and luxurious as the palazzo's terracotta façade. Floor-to-ceiling shelves loaded with musty leather-bound volumes marked the room out as some kind of library, the partially closed shutters on the casement windows cast long shadows on the tiled flooring. The air felt cool and pleasantly dry after the muggy heat of the outdoors.

A slim middle-aged man in a perfectly tailored suit stood as soon as they entered and walked towards them. He was a few inches shorter than Nick, his clean-shaven jaw and sleek designer clothing in sharp contrast to Nick's worn jeans and day-old stubble. The man spoke in rapid Italian.

Instead of replying in Italian as he had done outside, Nick held up his palm to halt the flow of information. 'You'll have to speak English,' he said firmly. 'Or get a translator. My Italian's not that good.'

Eva blinked, taken aback by the statement. Hadn't he told her he was fluent on the plane? He certainly hadn't had any difficulty conversing with anyone else.

'I understand, Signor Delisantro,' the man switched neatly into lightly accented English, pronouncing the words with the crisp, clear diction of a natural linguist. 'My name is Luca DiNapoli, I am the head of Duca D'Alegria's legal team. Firstly I must inform you that you are very welcome in Don Vincenzo's home as his guest. But that your invitation here in no way obligates—'

'Silenzio, Luca.'

The gruff words came from behind them. And it was only then that Eva noticed the elderly man sitting at a desk in the far corner of the room. He walked into a stream of sunlight, his patrician bearing as regal and dignified as one would expect from a high-ranking member of the Italian aristocracy.

The familiar golden gaze that Nick had inherited flickered over her face. 'We meet again, Signorina Redmond. A pleasure,' he said, the musical lilt of his accent adding an old-fashioned charm to the greeting. He took her hand, lifted it and then bowed slightly to buzz a gallant kiss onto the knuckles.

But during the whole exchange, his eyes remained fixed on Nick. The mechanical ticks of a carriage clock on the mantelpiece chanted the passing seconds with the deafening crack of rifle fire as the Duca D'Alegria took his time studying his grandson. Slowly, the intelligent, astute, assessing gaze softened, until the rich gold shone with tears.

'Leo.' The old man whispered the name like a prayer, his body trembling.

Eva stepped forward and touched his elbow. 'Are you all right, Your Excellency?' He looked every one of his eighty-eight years all of a sudden, and nothing like the forceful, indomitable and naturally poised man she had met two months ago at Roots Registry's offices.

The duca gave his head a slight shake, then sent Eva a brief, unbearably sad smile. 'Yes, I am well. Thanks to you, Signorina Redmond.'

Before she had a chance to process his meaning, he collected himself, the moment of fragility vanishing as he addressed his solicitor. 'You may go, Luca.'

The man tried to protest in Italian.

The duca raised his hand. 'We speak in English, Luca, for the benefit of our guests. And don't be foolish. You have only to look at Niccolo to know there is no need for any of that now.' His gaze settled on Nick as he continued to address the other man. 'Leave us, I am tired of your talk. I will contact you tomorrow.'

The solicitor said his farewells. If he was annoyed by the abrupt dismissal, he was well trained in hiding his displeasure.

The same couldn't be said of Nick though.

'Would you leave us too, Signorina Redmond?' the duca asked. 'I would talk to Niccolo in private.'

'She stays,' Nick interrupted before she could answer.

The older man waited a moment, as if assessing his reply, then nodded. 'If you wish.'

'And the name's Nick, not Niccolo,' Nick replied, the cold tone bordering on rude.

The duca stiffened, but instead of ordering Nick to leave, as Eva had half expected, he only inclined his head towards an antique leather sofa and two wide wingbacked chairs, arranged in front of a huge stone fireplace. 'Let us sit. The staff are bringing refreshments.'

'That would be love—' Eva began.

'I don't think so,' Nick cut off her acceptance. 'I've been

travelling for close to twenty-four hours. I need to crash for a while.'

As if on cue, the two female members of the duca's staff entered carrying silver trays laden with a coffee service and plates full of dainty sugared pastries and slices of fresh fruit. Continuing to watch Nick, the duca clicked his fingers and redirected the staff in Italian. The maids left and the butler rushed in, concern etched on his face.

'Eduardo will take you to your rooms,' the duca announced, but the hollow melancholy had left his voice. He sounded stern and his eyes were sharp and completely lucid now as they assessed Nick. 'I dine at nine. Eduardo will show you where.' It wasn't an invitation, but a command from a man who spoke as if he were chastising an errant child, and was willing to be patient, but only up to a point.

Despite the dictatorial tone, Nick shrugged. 'Maybe, if I don't sleep through.'

The reply was insolent, clearly stating that Nick had no intention of obeying the command. Eva had the strangest impression of two stags, one a young buck, the other the leader of the herd, their antlers poised as they prepared to fight for control.

But instead of locking horns, the duca simply inclined his head. 'Eduardo will wake you in good time if you fall asleep, Niccolo,'

Nick sent the old man a hard stare, but didn't reply to the obvious challenge before they were led out of the room by a worried looking Eduardo.

They'd gone a few feet into the lobby area, when a young footman appeared bearing Eva's case. 'Signorina Redmond, we have the room for you in the garden house,' he said in faltering English.

But as she went to follow him Nick took her wrist and she

jerked to a stop. 'We're together. I want her in the room next to mine.'

What?

Heat raged up her neck and burned her scalp. She twisted her hand free.

'I don't think that's entirely necessary,' she said to Eduardo, who was already redirecting the footman up the stairs with her case, the mortification on his face plain. 'Anywhere you want to put me is absolutely—'

But before she could say any more, Nick began talking over her to Eduardo in his supposedly rusty Italian. From the look of concern on Eduardo's face and the way he was practically genuflecting to Nick it was clear her protests would be futile.

The Prodigal Grandson had spoken and that was that.

Within minutes, she was being ushered up the wide, sweeping central staircase of the mansion right behind her suitcase, her wishes having been ignored as Nick continued to converse in Italian with the butler.

Not fluent, my butt.

She fumed every step of the way up the stairs to the first floor and then down a long corridor, shock and embarrassment warring with indignation. The footman opened a large door leading onto an enormous room, dominated by a four-poster bed on a dais. Laying her rather worn-looking suitcase on a dressing table, he whipped back the drapes and opened terrace doors onto a wrought-iron balcony that looked out over the lake. Sunlight flooded the room, but the awe-inspiring view did little to calm her rising temper.

Nick had made her sound like his lover.

The footman paused as he crossed back to the door, gave a quick bow. 'Your bathroom is shared with Signor Delisantro,' he said and she was sure she could detect a little Italian smirk of approval. 'This was the room of the contessa.'

Which one? Eva wondered as the footman left, assuming

he was referring to one of Conte Leonardo De Rossi's four wives, the last of whom he'd divorced two months before his death. From the grandiose furnishings and the deluxe silken bedspread, she would have guessed the last contessa. A French supermodel who had been under half of Leonardo De Rossi's sixty-five years of age when they had married during a spur-of-the-moment ceremony in San Moritz.

But she wasn't Signor Delisantro's wife. Or his mistress. In fact she wasn't even his girlfriend. Despite what he'd implied. And she didn't want an adjoining room. Her role here had become completely redundant as soon as the duca had set eyes on Nick. She doubted he would even want to see the PowerPoint lecture she'd worked a week on to explain her research and how she had come to identify Nick's mother as the heartbroken girl Leonardo's journal referred to only as *'il frutto proibito'*—the forbidden fruit.

Roots Registry would get their commission without her having to prove the validity of her research. And as if her situation weren't already untenable enough, Nick had now made her look like a convenient bit of totty rather than a certified genealogical research fellow. Which was probably all part of the nasty little game he was playing with her.

She unzipped her case and swore under her breath. A word she hadn't used since her teens. Her eyes landed on the bathroom door as she heard the muffled voices of Nick and Eduardo from the hallway. Dumping her treasured collection of lace lingerie into the polished maplewood dresser, she slammed the drawer closed.

The time for playing games was over. She stalked to the bathroom door and sailed through it. Barely sparing a glance for the magnificent marble bath, and the gilded fixtures and fittings, as she headed for the connecting door to Nick's suite. Her hand tightened on the handle.

Forget professionalism. Forget demure, efficient and composed. Forget being a damn conciliator and worrying about stepping out of her comfort zone. She didn't need to put up with Nick's arrogant behaviour a moment longer. She was going to throttle the man.

CHAPTER TEN

Eva gave a quick rap on the door, then marched into Nick's room without waiting for a reply.

She was a rational, level-headed woman who would do pretty much anything to avoid an argument. But she'd never had to deal with anyone as hard-headed, self-absorbed and insensitive as Nick Delisantro before. And there was a fine line between being diplomatic and being a doormat.

And whatever he might believe her role here to be, it wasn't as his doormat…Or as his personal punching bag.

'I want a word with you,' she announced as she stepped onto the thick silk carpeting, and took in the palatial splendour of the master bedroom, which was even bigger than her own suite next door. He stood by the large casement window, with his back to her and his hands dug into the rear pockets of his jeans.

He twisted round, but didn't say anything.

She wrapped her arms round her waist, her temper stuttering slightly under that intimidating gaze. The piercing look in his eyes had little tingles of electricity sizzling across her skin. 'You totally undermined my credibility, my professional integrity and my position here as a representative of Roots Registry by insisting we be roomed together.'

He turned fully towards her. 'Did I?' It was the amused twist of his lips that did it. She felt something inside her crack, and her temper boiled like molten lava flooding through a volcanic fissure.

She strode across the room. 'You know perfectly well you did.' She stabbed her index finger into the centre of the motorbike logo on his T-shirt. 'You made me sound like your mistress. In front of Eduardo and the footman. It was humiliating.'

He pulled his hands out of his pockets and glanced at her finger. She whipped it back, too aware of the unyielding chest muscles beneath.

'And you did it deliberately,' she added, struggling to focus on the lava. 'You…You…' She sputtered, trying to think of a suitable name to call him. Unfortunately, she didn't have a particularly wide vocabulary to hand. She never called people names. 'You…' She racked her brains. 'You berk.'

He gave a rough chuckle and the molten lava burned. 'Berk? Seriously? You need to work on your insults, sweetheart.'

Heat pounded into her cheeks. 'Don't call me that.'

It was the same generic endearment he'd called her two weeks ago. Before he'd kicked her out of his apartment. And she was sure it meant nothing to him. He probably used it with every woman he slept with. But for her it had been special, had made her feel special. And hearing it again now, when all he wanted to do was humiliate her only made her feel more foolish.

'Why not?' he said, apparently oblivious to her runaway temper. 'You *are* sweet.'

He cruised a finger down the side of her face, and she jerked back, the tiny touch like an electrical zap of energy to every one of her pulse points.

'Stop it,' she said, panic making her shout.

He stepped forward, invading her personal space. 'Stop what?'

'Stop playing games with me.' She stood her ground, despite the shock waves of awareness making her whole body tremble and yearn to step towards him—like a vertigo sufferer about to leap off a high ledge. 'It isn't fair and you know it.'

'What games?'

'This game.' She spread her hands, took another step back, the force field of raw machismo pumping off him making the heat pound hotter between her thighs.

How did he do that to her? When she didn't want him to?

'The flirting and the innuendo and the…The kiss,' she babbled. 'The kiss you gave me on the plane. And that look,' she finished in a rush, knowing she sounded like a nutcase, but desperate now to make him stop his little charade. So her body would come to its senses.

'What look?' he asked, but she knew he understood, because he was giving it to her again. Her nipples tightened painfully under the lace of her bra, and throbbed in unison with the tender spot between her thighs.

'*That* look.' She pointed at him. 'That look right there. That says you want me. When we both know you don't.'

The air crackled with tension, and then he had her cheeks in his palms and his mouth on hers.

His lips were firm, warm, seeking and tasted of coffee and need. Without warning, hunger flared, and the craving for him that she'd been pretending didn't exist charged through her system with turbo-powered intensity. He opened his mouth to take more, and her tongue thrust back, drinking him in like a long cold glass of icy water on a hot summer day.

His fingers thrust into her hair as he angled her head to take the kiss deeper—she placed her palms on his waist, her fingers gripping soft cotton and hard muscle and rose on tiptoe, to let him. Searing heat fired through her body as they devoured each other. She wanted him, wanted this, with a power that overwhelmed her.

He stopped first, the breath expelling from his lungs in a couple of ragged pants. She heard her own staggered breathing. Dazed with the sudden rush of sexual hunger and the realisation that she'd forgotten to breathe.

He reached out, pressed his thumb to her raw, swollen bottom lip.

'I'm not playing games.' His thumb trailed down, to where her pulse hammered against her neck, and all she could do was stare blankly back, scared to move in case she swayed towards him like a cat in need of stroking.

His hand dropped away. 'And from the way you kissed me back, I'd say neither are you.'

'We can't do this,' she said. 'It's not appropriate.' The denial sounding absurd after the kiss they'd just shared. But her mind was engaging again, and the stupidity of what she'd just done was staring her in the face. The wild woman had returned.

'Who cares if it's appropriate?' he demanded, his face fierce, his tone tight with impatience. 'We both want to. And we've got two damn weeks here…' She saw it then, the flash of something she would never have expected. Something she'd failed to spot before because she'd been too busy trying to control the uncontrollable.

'Unless I can get His Highness to kick me out sooner.' He turned away, buried his hands back in the pockets of his jeans. But now that her mind had engaged, it wouldn't stop engaging.

'This isn't about me,' she murmured, suddenly understanding the game he had been playing all along. This wasn't a game of humiliation—it was a game of avoidance.

But instead of feeling used, or insulted, all she felt was a choking sense of sympathy. 'I'm just a convenient distraction.'

He glanced over his shoulder. 'You've lost me?'

'It was all an act, wasn't it? That sullen "I don't care about any of this" act you put on downstairs. You're not indifferent, or bored. You're scared.'

Scared? Was she nuts?

Nick pushed a laugh out past the ball of tension that had lodged in his solar plexus. 'You may be a distraction, but you sure as hell aren't convenient,' he said.

And she'd just become even less convenient.

Why had he kissed her? He hadn't meant to. The plan had been to take things slow and easy, to tease her and tempt her and wait for her to give into her passionate nature again and come to him.

But then she'd stood there in front of him, insisting that he couldn't possibly want her, and all the frustration that he'd been keeping a lid on smashed through the barrier of his will power, and he'd been the one to crack. Not her.

And now he had an erection the size of the Eiffel Tower pressing against the button fly of his jeans to go with his foul mood.

'Stop changing the subject,' she said.

'The only subject I'm interested in is you and me getting naked.' If he'd expected the surly tone to send her packing, he'd been sadly mistaken.

She tilted her head, regarded him with those clear blue eyes that saw much more than he wanted them to. 'Why can't you admit that meeting your grandfather is a big deal?'

He heaved a sigh. Why couldn't she give this a rest? 'Because it's not,' he said, deciding not to correct her once again about the spurious nature of his relationship to the man. Vincenzo De Rossi wasn't his grandfather, any more than Leonardo De Rossi had been his father.

Sure that look of recognition, of stunned affection and hope on the old guy's face in the library had unnerved him.

But only because he hadn't been expecting it. And because it had brought with it an unpleasant revelation about his relationship with his mother.

Until Eva had mentioned it, it had never even occurred to him that he might bear a physical resemblance to the De Rossis. The thought had made him uncomfortable. But what had been worse was the jolt of memory, when the look in De Rossi's eyes had reminded him of what he'd often seen in his mother's eyes. It had been the same damn look of recognition, but with one crucial difference—instead of the hope, the excitement, the stunned pleasure he'd seen in De Rossi's eyes, what he'd always glimpsed in his mother's eyes had been despair and regret. He'd refused to acknowledge it as a boy, had always just strived harder to please her, in the hope that one day she would look at him the same way she looked at his sister Ruby.

His mother had never been cruel to him, never been deliberately unkind, if anything she'd let him get away with a great deal more than his sister, but there had always been this distance between them. Her affection for him had always felt guarded, dutiful, and so unlike the full, rich, boundless love she'd lavished on her husband and her daughter. And he'd never understood why. Until now.

Today, in the Alegria Palazzo's library, while Vincenzo De Rossi had stared at him with tears in his eyes, he'd finally understood why his mother had always found it so hard to love him. Because as he'd grown older, and begun to resemble Leonardo more and more, she would have become painfully aware that he was Leonardo's son. When she'd looked at him, all she had ever seen was the evidence of her sin.

His mother had died years ago, an excruciatingly painful death. She'd told Carmine the truth about his parentage on her deathbed. Two years later he'd run away from home. Unfortunately he hadn't been able to run far enough and the destructive anger—much of it aimed at his mother—had followed him around for years. But he'd eventually come to terms with it and moved on. He'd forgiven his mother—so none of this was a big deal, not any more.

Unfortunately, from the sympathy he could see shining in Eva's eyes, she was obviously on a mission to share and discuss. Not something he had any intention of doing.

Seeing her mussed hair, and the rash on her chin where his stubble had burned, it occurred to him that there was a much more effective way of changing the subject.

Gripping the hem of his T-shirt, he lifted it over his head and flung it on the bed.

Heat soared in her cheeks, making the tiny sprinkle of freckles across her nose stand out. A spontaneous smile edged his lips. Her eyes had glazed over with stunned arousal, exactly as they had when he'd taken his sweater off in the garage of his apartment two weeks ago.

She might have lived her life like a nun up to now, but the bad girl was well and truly out of the bag, if that look and the kiss they had just shared were anything to go by. All he had to do now was get a stranglehold on his emotions and not crack first again—if he wanted to keep the upper hand in this seduction. And he damn well did.

'What are you doing?' she said. 'We're having a conversation.'

'You may be. I'm not.' He rubbed his palm over his chest. She followed the movement with rapt attention, her tongue peeping out to moisten her bottom lip. The jolt of arousal felt good this time. He was in charge again, in control.

He eased open the first button of his jeans, watched her eyes dart down. 'I'm shattered and I'm taking a shower.' He popped another button.

'You can't,' she said, a little too breathlessly.

His erection swelled back to life under her attentive gaze. 'And after my shower, I'm going to bed.'

'But we haven't finished talking about…' Her voice dried up as the third button went.

'If you want to join me—you're more than welcome.' He ran his hand across his belly, eased his fingers down, under the waistband of his boxers.

Her gaze shot to his face, the colour in her cheeks now radioactive, and the flare of arousal unmistakeable.

'But I should warn you, there's not going to be a lot of talking,' he added.

'I…' She swallowed convulsively. 'I'll see you at dinner,' she murmured and shot off towards the connecting door as if the hounds of hell were snapping at her heels.

The first genuine laugh he'd had all day echoed after her.

Eva Redmond might not be a convenient distraction, but she was a really entertaining one.

CHAPTER ELEVEN

Eva's body was still humming four hours later as she headed through the palazzo's labyrinthine corridors to the terrazzo, where Lorenzo the footman had informed her the duca would be hosting pre-dinner aperitifs for her and Nick.

She wanted to believe it was indignation that had made her throat go dry and other more sensitive parts of her anatomy feel moist and swollen as she'd lain awake on the satin covers of her four-poster, listening to the muffled splash of running water from the bathroom—and imagined Nick Delisantro's naked chest gilded with soap suds—but she wasn't sure indignation quite covered it.

Maybe sexual obsession would be more appropriate. Or complete insanity.

But one thing was certain. She'd always been more comfortable studying the lives and loves of people she didn't know—people in parchment documents, in ledgers of births and marriages and deaths, people who were either long dead or lived lives completely removed from her own. Her life had been exceptionally dull, but also sensible and secure, because she'd never had the guts, or the inclination to take what she wanted and damn the consequences.

Nick Delisantro, on the other hand, didn't have the same reservations. He'd lived his life on the edge and forged a successful career out of taking risks. Which made him extremely dangerous.

Huge French doors lined the airy corridor and opened out onto the estate's vast ornamental gardens. The scent of jasmine and lavender perfumed the air while the dying sun added a redolent glow to the riot of colours.

Eva stared at the lavish gardens and felt the flicker of panic and confusion that had been dogging her all afternoon. Unfortunately, Nick Delisantro's wild, uncivilised behaviour and his reckless approach to life had somehow rubbed off on her.

All he had to do was look at her in that surly, sexy, I'm-going-to-eat-you-alive way he had, and her hormones shot into hyperdrive. She touched her fingers to her chin, felt the slight sting of the mark he had left on sensitive skin.

The low heels of her sandals clicked on the polished stone flooring as she continued down the corridor, frowning into the mirrors that lined the walls. She'd made the stupid mistake of losing her virginity to a man she found it impossible to resist. Even though their one night hadn't exactly been the most comfortable experience, her body seemed to have forgotten the pain.

The sheen of sweat dampened her breasts in the simple summer dress she'd been forced to change into for the evening—because the tailored suit had felt unbearably restrictive. She walked briskly to the open door at the end of the corridor.

She was in serious trouble. Her one wild night with Nick Delisantro had not been a roaring success. The man was taciturn, moody, demanding and unpredictable. And had a temper that she didn't want to be on the receiving end of again. Plus, she'd almost lost her job.

But even knowing all that, everything she knew about herself as a person—her caution, her common sense, her obedience—was on the verge of collapsing around her ears, and she seemed powerless to stop it happening. In fact if the kiss she'd given Nick was anything to go by, all he had to do was take off his shirt and she'd happily fling herself into the inferno again without a second thought.

The only possible solution was to stay away from him… But how could she do that when she was now sleeping right next door to him? For two whole weeks. And he seemed more than happy to exploit her lack of control. She needed a plan, and she had to come up with one fast. Because her will power was non-existent and the rational, sensible behaviour she'd always relied on in the past seemed to go up in flames whenever he was within ten feet of her.

She let out a small sigh of relief when she stepped onto the wide, flagstone terrace situated at the end of the house, and found the duca sitting alone at a wrought-iron table laid with drinks and canapés. She needed to gauge her situation with Don Vincenzo and see if he would be happy for her to fly back to London once she had given him her PowerPoint presentation. She'd considered all the possible permutations, and it seemed like the only option. There was no reason for her to stay longer than a day or two. Don Vincenzo was her company's client, not Nick, so how could he insist she stayed if her job was done?

'Signorina Redmond, you look beautiful,' the duca said in his flawless English as he greeted her with a glass of Prosecco. 'And well rested I hope.'

'Very much so, Your Excellency,' she said, accepting the flute of sparkling wine and the compliment, although she doubted its veracity. She'd had the quickest shower in human history, worried that Nick might walk into the bathroom and press his advantage, and she hadn't managed to get a wink of sleep during her so-called nap. Because she'd been far too busy having inappropriate thoughts about the man in the room next door. 'But, please, call me Eva.'

'Then you must call me, Vincenzo,' he replied, directing her to a bench rimmed with climbing vines that bloomed with purple wisteria. 'My title is little more than an old man's vanity, after all, as we have been a republic in Italy for many years now and rightly so.'

'You're not a monarchist?' Eva said, surprised by the statement. The laws of Italian nobility were notoriously complex and confusing, and fake titles had abounded since the dissolution of the monarchy after the Second World War, but she knew that the Duca d'Alegria's family was one of the few who could claim a direct lineage to the throne—and as such she had expected him to be a strong supporter of pomp and circumstance.

'I am a pragmatist,' he said, the lines of his face more pronounced in the dusky early-evening light. 'My noble title has given me a very comfortable life, several beautiful homes and a pretty crest to put on the bottles of olive oil we produce at the Savargo Estate. And for that I am grateful.' He took the seat opposite her. 'But it did not make me a noble father, nor help me to raise a son I could be proud of.'

'You mean Conte Leonardo?' she murmured, taken aback by the intimate nature of the confidence—as well as the weight of disillusionment in his voice.

'Let us call him Leo,' he said. 'My son always insisted on being addressed by his full title when he was alive. However, he did not deserve it, nor did he honour it, so I refuse to address him by it in death.'

The duca didn't sound bitter or angry, just weary, his voice heavy with regret.

'I didn't realise you had such a low opinion of your son,' she said, feeling desperately sorry for the old man.

'You have read Leo's journal,' he stated. 'So you know my low opinion was well earned.'

She nodded, not sure what to say. How could she argue with the truth? Leonardo's journal had revealed a man who had been given everything he could ever want but who had always wanted more. Reading the translations, she had tried to remain impartial, not to judge, to maintain a scholarly distance while analysing every word and phrase for clues that would help her to identify the young farmer's daughter Leonardo had been introduced to on her wedding day, and then ruthlessly pursued until he got her pregnant. But it had been next to impossible not to despise the author for his arrogance, his reckless pursuit of his own pleasure and his selfish disregard for everyone's feelings but his own. She could understand why a man of principle would find it hard to be proud of such a son.

'Can you tell me,' Don Vincenzo asked, contemplating his glass, 'has Niccolo read his father's journal?'

She shook her head. 'No, he hasn't.' She didn't elaborate, deciding Vincenzo didn't need to know the whole truth—that Nick had refused to read it.

The old man bowed his head. 'So that does not explain his dislike of me.'

'Nick doesn't dislike you,' she countered, her sympathy for the duca increasing. She was beginning to realise that this reunion meant a great deal to the old man, and not just for reasons of heredity. Did he hope to forge a relationship with his grandson to replace the unhealthy relationship he seemed to have had with his son? From what she knew about Nick, she suspected the duca was doomed to failure but she didn't want to add to his pain. 'Nick doesn't even know you,' she continued. 'I just think he's a little overwhelmed by the whole…' She paused, trying to think of a suitable explanation for Nick's animosity. 'By the prospect of the title.' She finished lamely, knowing perfectly well Nick was as disdainful of the duca's title as everything else.

'But Niccolo cannot inherit the title.' The duca lifted his head, concern making his voice crack. 'The rules of primogeniture are clear on the matter. I can only pass the title to a legitimate male heir.'

She had known, and now wished she hadn't said anything. She laid her hand on Vincenzo's gnarled fingers. 'Don't worry about that, I'm sure Nick doesn't expect—'

'Does Niccolo know he cannot inherit the title?' the duca asked carefully.

'Nick doesn't want the title.'

Eva's head whipped round at the abrupt interruption. Nick stood on the edge of the terazzo, his legs crossed at the ankle and his hip propped against the low stone wall.

How long had he been standing there? From the stark look on his face she suspected quite a while and her heart fluttered uncomfortably. Had he heard her presuming to know what his thoughts and feelings were on the subject of his inheritance? And worse, had he heard Don Vincenzo talking about his son? She was suddenly grateful he hadn't taken her up on her offer to read the journal. While it might help him to forgive his mother, did anyone really need to know they had been conceived in such a reckless, loveless way?

'Niccolo, you have joined us.' The old man stood, his face carefully wiped clean of emotion. 'We are indeed honoured.' The pleasure in Vincenzo's voice was tinged with irony.

Seeing Nick's brow furrow, Eva felt a slight smile tremble on her lips at the evidence of his frustration.

Nick might want to despise his grandfather—and believe he had nothing in common with the man—but she had a feeling he wasn't going to find it as easy as he had probably assumed to deny his heritage. The Duca D'Alegria was a man of honour and integrity, a man for whom family and tradition meant a great deal, but more than that, the man had a sharp intelligence and a dry wit. Surely even a loner like Nick would find that hard to resist?

As the two men continued to spar over Prosecco and canapés it occurred to Eva that she would miss watching the two of them lock horns as they got to know each other over the next two weeks.

But the wistful thought cleared abruptly as the three of them were led into dinner by Eduardo and Nick's hand settled on her lower back under the pretext of directing her into the dining salon. Heat from the brief touch shimmered through her entire body before she could step out of reach. As Lorenzo the footman held out her chair she looked up to catch Nick's eyes watching her, his heavy-lidded gaze dark with knowledge.

As Eva choked down the first course of asparagus tips wrapped in Parma ham, she let the men's stilted conversation wash over her and studiously avoided meeting Nick's gaze again. She was way out of her depth here.

Nick wasn't vulnerable, or insecure—he was reckless and unpredictable and a dangerous man to get involved with, on any level.

She had to leave the palazzo before she did something monumentally stupid. Again.

'Don Vincenzo, I was wondering if it would be okay for me to return to the UK tomorrow after I've done the client presentation?' Eva heard the clatter of Nick's cutlery but kept her gaze fixed on their host.

She'd waited through their starter, a pasta course of crab linguini, an entrée of rabbit cacciatore and summer vegetables and a dessert of strawberry tiramisu, listening to Nick's monosyllabic answers to all his grandfather's questions, while apprehension tightened her stomach and she struggled to swallow a single bite.

Vincenzo lifted the bottle of wine they had been sharing out of its wine bucket and topped up her glass. His gaze drifted past her to Nick, whom she suspected was glaring at her, but she had to be grateful he hadn't said anything. At last Vincenzo addressed her. 'I never speak of business while I am dining, Eva. It is an Italian's prerogative to do everything in their power not to spoil their digestion.'

'I'm sorry.' The tension stretched taut, but she soldiered on. 'I understand completely, but maybe we could discuss it tomorrow then,' she added hopefully, not wanting to be put off. This was her way out, because she was very much afraid that her resolve wasn't going to stand up to more than one night in the room next door to Nick.

'I have arranged for you to travel to Milan tomorrow to see Luca, while I take Niccolo on a tour of my properties in Riva del Garda,' Vincenzo said easily. 'But once you have shown your research to my solicitors, I see no reason why you should not return to London.'

Eva sent him a tremulous smile. It was a lifeline, if not much of one. Surely she could keep her hormones in check for a couple of days. 'Thanks, that would be—'

'Eva comes with us to Riva del Garda.'

Eva whisked her head round, to find Nick sipping his wine, his gaze willing her to challenge him. 'She can see the lawyers another day.'

'Excuse me, but it's not your decision to make,' Eva said through gritted teeth. How dared he presume to intervene? This was her job. 'It's up to Don Vincenzo when I—'

'Now, now, children.' Vincenzo gave a gruff laugh, holding up his hands to silence her tirade. 'While my grandson's manners could do with improvement,' he said, casting a quelling glance at Nick, 'he is right. There is no rush for Luca to see the presentation. You are more than welcome to accompany us to Riva del Garda, Eva.' Vincenzo rang a small bell, signalling the staff to clear their plates. 'In fact, I insist you come. It is a magnificent little town, full of history. You will enjoy it.'

'It sounds lovely,' Eva said politely, her jaw tense as she

realised Nick had managed to manipulate the situation again without even trying. 'And I appreciate the invitation, but I—'

'It is settled, then,' Vincenzo announced, steamrolling over her objection. 'I will inform Luca to expect you another day.'

Eva was forced to nod her assent as her lifeline vanished. 'I'll look forward to it,' she murmured, her jaw so rigid now it was a wonder she hadn't cracked a tooth. It seemed Nick and his grandfather had more in common than just their looks, she thought as Lorenzo whisked away her dessert plate.

'Do you mind if I excuse myself, Don Vincenzo?' she said laying her napkin on the table. She needed to get out of here, before she gave into the overpowering urge to give Nick a good solid whack on the shins under the table. 'I'm exhausted.'

'No of course not.' The old man rose too, shooting Nick another stern look when he remained seated. To Eva's silent astonishment, Nick took the hint and, throwing his napkin onto his plate, pushed his chair back and got to his feet.

As she dashed back to her room through the palazzo's corridors she conceded two things: even if Don Vincenzo managed to teach Nick some much needed manners, he would never be remotely civilised—and she needed a new plan. Fast.

When she reached the bedroom, she flipped the lock, then eyed the connecting door that led to their shared bathroom—which she already knew didn't have a lock.

Dragging an inlaid-gold armchair that stood next to an antique writing desk across the thick silk carpeting, she propped it under the gilt handle, tried the door, then stood back to admire her work. Okay, it was a little desperate and extremely lowering to realise she didn't trust herself to resist that hungry look in Nick's eye should he pay her a surprise visit.

But at least she had a new and brilliantly simple strategy to keep him—and herself—under control. For tonight at any rate.

CHAPTER TWELVE

Rafe's mane of midnight black hair caught the wind, the tempest of emotion on his face as wild and unyielding as the thunderous roar of the sea pounding the ship's deck. 'Ye shall not deny me another night, Shanna,' he yelled. 'I own ye now.'

'Take me then,' Shanna hurled the words through the lashing rain. 'But you shall never own me,' she cried, the fire in her belly igniting as his manhood plunged deep.

EVA groaned and closed her favourite book. It was no good. However hard she tried, instead of seeing Rafe the Pirate Captain and Shanna the fiery beauty who had brought him to his knees, she kept seeing Nick and herself. But Nick wasn't the one being brought to his knees.

Her head shot up at the muffled thump on the balcony. An all-too-familiar silhouette appeared in the open terrace doors. She shrieked and jerked upright in bed—and *The Pirate's Captive* flew out of her hands and landed on the carpet with a thud.

'Nick!' The figure strolled into the room. 'What are you doing?' she squeaked.

'Paying you a visit,' he said, his breathtakingly handsome face illuminated by the dim light from the bedside lamp. 'What does it look like?'

She leapt out of bed, determined not to be caught lying down, and cursed her own stupidity. Her brilliantly simple plan had a major flaw. The palazzo had no air conditioning, so she'd left the balcony doors open to let the lavender scented breeze from the gardens cool the still air. She'd noticed the neighboring balconies on the bathroom and Nick's room, but hadn't given them a second thought, because they were a good three feet apart. How on earth had he got across? Without breaking his neck?

'You can't come in here.' She headed towards him, deciding to lead with her temper and ignore the pump of adrenaline making her limbs tremble. 'You have to leave.' She thrust her forefinger towards the balcony doors to point him in the right direction. 'Now.'

Instead of following her perfectly succinct order, he walked right past her. 'That's gratitude for you,' he said lazily. 'When I've just risked life and limb to safeguard your reputation.'

She slapped her palms on her hips. *'My reputation?'* she snapped. 'You're in my room in the middle of the night!' she whispered furiously.

Just because her breasts were tingling beneath the skimpy silk of her nightgown, and she'd been imagining him ravishing her on the deck of a pirate ship she definitely did not want him here. 'How is that going to safeguard *my* reputation?'

'No need to get your knickers in a twist,' he countered, the statement making her uncomfortably aware that she had no knickers on to get in a twist. 'No one knows I'm here.'

Before she could tell him that was hardly the point, he gestured to the chair propped against the bathroom door and swore softly. 'I knew it,' he muttered, exasperated. 'You barred the door.' His eyes drifted down her frame. 'Now how childish is that?' he drawled, a slow smile appearing.

Her nipples puckered into hard points, so she crossed her arms over her chest.

'It's not childish,' she muttered, the swelling in her breasts and the pounding between her thighs making it impossible to maintain an adequate level of scorn in her voice. 'Certainly not as childish as climbing about on balconies in the middle of the night,' she added.

He shrugged, picking up the summer dress she'd left flung over a chair. 'I wanted to see you.' He raised the dress to his face and took a deep breath.

She forced down the blip in her heartbeat at the possessive tone, the sensual gesture. 'Well I don't want to see you,' she countered, and tried to make herself believe it.

'What have we here?' he murmured, spotting something on the floor as he flung her dress on the bed. Bending down, he rose holding her discarded paperback. 'Well, well, I never would have guessed it.' He gave a gruff laugh, examining the battered cover—which bore a colourful illustration of a bare-chested Rafe and an all but bare-breasted Shanna in an extravagant clinch. 'You read porn.'

She gasped. 'It's not porn.' She tried to grab the book, but he held it easily out of reach. 'It's romantic fiction.'

He chuckled. 'Girly porn, then.'

'It's not porn of any kind.'

'Let's read it and see.' He held the book down, began to rifle through the pages.

She snatched the paperback out of his hands. 'It's *not* porn,' she said, whipping the book behind her back. 'You'll have to take my word for it.'

No way was she letting him read the book, especially the passages she'd dog-eared. It would only inflame the situation—and her. And her body was already on fire. His big body brushing hers as he backed her into a corner.

Her back hit the wall with a soft thud.

'Eva.' His voice reverberated over her skin as he braced his hand above her, caging her in, the scent of musk and man filling her senses. 'Why read about it, when you can do it for real?'

'Because I don't want to,' she blurted out, seeing the hungry promise in his eyes as the breeze brushed her bare legs, and a delicious tremble of reaction shimmered down to her toes.

He touched his lips to her ear lobe, and whispered: 'You're lying.'

She opened her mouth, but the denial got stuck in her throat. She could feel the slickness of her sex, the tenderness of her breasts, hear the rasp of her own breathing.

One rough palm settled on her leg, cutting off her air supply completely. Her thigh muscles quivered and bunched, her breath expelling from her lungs in a rush as his hand trailed upwards.

'You want to know how I can tell you're lying?' he murmured.

She shook her head, but revelled in the zing of sensation as his callused palm rose up her leg.

His thumb brushed across her hip and traced the top of her thigh. She shuddered, her fingers releasing the paperback, the gentle thump as it hit the floor barely registering as his thumb dipped into the curls covering her sex. 'You're wet and ready for me right now, aren't you, Eva?'

'Please…' she begged as longing blazed through her. She *was* wet, and ready. Ready to forget everything. Her job, her sensible well-ordered life, her sanity, if only he would touch her more. Touch her there.

He bit into her ear lobe, the sharp nip a delicious counterpoint to the painful shock of pleasure as his thumb found the perfect spot at last and rubbed.

She sobbed, clutching the muscle of his bicep, and clung on, riding his stroking thumb to increase the torment. Her swollen breasts arched into his chest as the orgasm swept through her in one tumultuous, all-consuming wave.

She forced herself to let go of his arm as she drifted back to her senses. She pressed back into the wall, knees still weak from the intensity of her climax. But instead of the smug expression she had expected, all she saw in his face was fierce lust burning the golden brown of his irises to a molten chocolate.

'I rest my case,' he rasped, lifting his thumb to his lips and licking.

'You're right,' she said, her voice as shaky as her legs. 'I do want you, but you scare me too.'

Was what she felt for him more powerful, more overwhelming than simple lust? She swallowed heavily, looked away from his penetrating gaze, ashamed of her own cowardice, and worse, terrified that he would see the yearning in her eyes. And realise how needy she was.

He lifted her chin, and her eyes met his, the tenderness and concern in them making the frantic beat of her heart increase. 'Don't be scared, Eva,' he said gently. 'I won't take you until you're ready. Not this time.'

'What do you mean?' she said, confused by the note of self-loathing she detected.

He stepped back, huffed out a breath. 'I did that once before and look what happened. You lost your job.'

'That wasn't your fault,' she corrected, more confused than ever. What was he saying? That he felt responsible for her losing her job?

'Whatever.' He shrugged. 'The point is, it doesn't matter now because you've got it back.' The words were delivered in an offhand manner, as if the information was irrelevant, but as soon as he said them something she had never understood suddenly became blindingly obvious.

'Oh, my goodness!' She pressed her palm to her mouth, her

shock as real as the disturbing rush of emotion at the thought of what he'd done. 'That's why you agreed to come here. That's why you changed your mind about meeting your grandfather. To make Mr Crenshawe give me my job back.'

She'd thought he'd done it out of some vindictive desire to punish her, when what he'd really been doing was helping her.

He gave a strained laugh. 'Yeah, like I'm really that noble,' he said, but she wasn't fooled.

'But you are,' she said, all the more convinced because of his attempt to deny it. 'You didn't have to insist I accompany you. But you knew Crenshawe would have to re-employ me if you did.'

'Stop being so naïve,' he said, frustration sharpening his voice. 'I engineered this whole thing so I could have you again. You getting your job back was just a nice fringe benefit.'

'I don't believe you.' She thought of his defensiveness when she'd spoken about his mother. His prickly response to his grandfather. And the emotions swirling in his eyes when she'd confronted him that afternoon. Why would he go through all that just to sleep with her, when he could have any woman?

'Yeah, well, you should.'

'You did something good. Something kind and sweet,' she shot back. 'Why is that so hard for you to admit?'

He swore, flattening her body against the wall. 'Because, damn it, I'm not kind and sweet.' Large hands grasped her waist, lifting her, until the long, hard ridge in his jeans pressed against her. 'Feel that—that's what I want from you. That's the only reason I'm here.'

Firecrackers of need exploded in her sex at the memory of his thick girth lodged deep inside her, stretching pain turning to blinding pleasure.

She writhed and he gave a harsh laugh. 'I'm not one of the good guys, Eva. Remember that,' he snarled, his erection grinding into the juncture of her thighs. 'But I'm going to wait for you to come to me this time. So you know exactly what you're getting into.'

He let her go.

'But I already know,' she said, the words shuddering out on a shocked sob.

'No, you don't.' He ran his thumb down her cheek. 'Because you're way too sweet and naïve for your own good.' Tucking his forefinger beneath her chin, he raised her gaze to his. 'Sex is all I'm looking for. There aren't going to be any hearts and flowers like in your book. Not with me. And I want you to understand that before we go any further.' He placed a firm, possessive kiss on her lips. 'Now go get me Leonardo's journal.'

'I…Why?' she stammered.

'I need something to help me sleep. And your girly porn isn't going to cut it.'

She nodded, skirting around him, and then crossed to the antique dresser, her thoughts whirring at what he'd revealed. Why was he so convinced he was one of the bad guys?

She pulled the leather-bound book from her suitcase, handed it to him.

Her heart plummeted at the sight of his long fingers closing over his father's diary. Reading the truth of that cruel, long-ago seduction would only make this trip harder for him.

'I'm afraid I only have the original,' she said and bit back the urge to snatch the journal from him, knowing he would only scoff at her concern.

He flipped the book up, caught it one-handed. 'That's okay.' He touched the spine to her cheek, trailed it down her throat, and traced the neckline of her gown, her bosom rising and falling in jerky spasms. 'Get a good night's sleep, Eva Redmond.' A suggestive grin flashed across his handsome features. 'Because it may be your last.'

She gave a nervous little laugh as he walked through the

terrace doors, clamping down on the urge to call him back. To tell him to finish what he'd started, that she wanted him now, that she was ready.

The wrought-iron railing creaked as he jumped onto the balcony and disappeared into the night. She returned to her empty bed, climbed beneath the sheets, and turned off the bedside lamp.

Nick Delisantro wasn't right about himself. He was a better man than he believed himself to be. And he wasn't right about her either. She wasn't naïve, she was only inexperienced. And just because she got a vicarious pleasure from reading about virile pirate captains and their beautiful captives, she did know the difference between fiction and reality—thank you very much.

But he was right about one thing. She needed time and space to analyse her feelings, to consider the situation rationally and sensibly before she did something wild and reckless again—and then discovered she couldn't control the consequences.

CHAPTER THIRTEEN

> The smell of her arousal makes me hard. She's begging
> for it. Her husband is a fool, and as inexperienced as she
> is, he can't satisfy her, so I will. And afterward she'll
> always wish it was me between her thighs and not him.

NICK slammed the book closed and growled out a guttural
expletive, his fingers digging into the worn leather.

What a creep.

He slung the journal onto the coffee table. If he'd learned
one thing over the last two sleepless nights waiting for Eva to
come to him, apart from the fact that he was his own worst
enemy, it was that Conte Leonardo Vittorio Vincenzo De
Rossi had been a lecherous, egotistical, misogynist jerk who
had about as much restraint as a horny schoolboy and a lot
less literary talent.

Nick levered himself out of the armchair and stalked across
the bedroom to the balcony. The night air was still and silent
but for the quiet chirping of some unknown insect. He took
a deep breath into his lungs. The perfumed scent of the garden's flowers mingled with the fresh scent of lake water and
went some way to clearing away the stench that clung to him
after reading Leonardo's grubby little secrets.

The light spilling from Eva's open terrace doors had the
last of the grim thoughts clearing away to be replaced by a
healthier frustration.

Shoving his fists into the pockets of his sweat pants, he leaned back against the balcony rail, and contemplated his own stupidity. And the miserable thought of spending another torturous night without Eva's lush little body under his.

Why had he said he'd wait for her to come to him?

Then the image of her trusting blue eyes, wide with confusion, and her body trembling with arousal yesterday evening came back to him. And he knew he hadn't had much of a choice.

She'd responded so beautifully, come apart so easily in his arms. After the smallest of touches she'd been wet for him, pleading for release. When she'd climaxed, he'd been so close to burying himself up to the hilt and satisfying both their hungers that it was making him hard just thinking about it.

But then she'd whispered that line about wanting him, but being scared of him too—and his conscience had as good as kicked him in the nuts.

She'd sounded so young and so impossibly vulnerable. And things had only got worse when she'd got some insane idea into her head about him coming to Italy to get her her job back, when his motives hadn't been anywhere near that pure. And then started spouting loads more nonsense about him being a nice guy. Nonsense he could see she actually believed.

He braced his hands on the balcony, stared out into the night, his frustration making the muscles in his shoulders throb.

Him? A nice guy? Hardly.

The woman had led a seriously sheltered life if she believed that. She'd certainly read way too many of those racy books that peddled all that happy-ever-after stuff and made women think that hot sex equalled love.

He gave a harsh laugh. As if real life were anything like that.

He propped his butt against the balcony rail, alert to even

the slightest sound from her room. But all he heard was the cricket going berserk and the water lapping on the dock below. His nose wrinkled, the citrusy aroma of lemons floating up from the tree under his balcony reminding him of the sharp, fresh scent of Eva.

He dropped his head back and gazed at the stars sprinkling the night sky, the tension in his shoulders almost as pronounced as the tension in his groin.

But wasn't that just the problem with Eva? She hadn't had a real life, not yet anyway. How could she have and still have been a virgin at twenty-four?

He let his chin drop and cursed. Which was why he had to treat her with a little more care than any of the other women he'd slept with. Not only did she not know the score, she probably didn't even know there was a score.

He knew how much she wanted him. That sure as hell wasn't in any doubt. If it hadn't already been obvious after her live-wire response to his caresses last night, it had been even more so today during their scheduled trip to Riva del Garda.

He'd heard her strangled little gasp when his thumb had lingered on the inside of her elbow as he'd helped her into the duca's motor launch. Had smelt the glow of sweat forming on her nape when he'd stood just a little bit too close as they were escorted round the duca's riverside offices. Had felt her body quiver when he'd stroked his palm down her spine, and left it resting above the curve of her buttocks to direct her to her seat in the waterfront restaurant Don Vincenzo had booked for lunch. Had seen the way her eyes darkened when he'd brushed a lock of silky hair behind her ear during their pre-dinner drinks at the palazzo.

Truth was, he'd been so damned attuned to every one of her responses—every single sight, scent, sound and touch—he'd actually been grateful to have the duca there chaperoning them, or he wouldn't have been able to stop himself dragging her off and forgetting about his stupid promise altogether.

The woman was driving him mad. He'd never been particularly good at deferred gratification. And he was getting less so every second he spent in her company. Even now he could taste the sultry scent of her arousal, hear her shocked gasp as he circled the stiff nub of her clitoris.

The blood pumped into his groin. His teeth clenched and his back muscles knotted as he spent several fraught moments contemplating the quick journey from his balcony into her bedroom—and the feel of soft, slick skin, dewy with need.

Damn it, Delisantro, get a grip. You're worse than Leonardo.

The repulsive thought doused the fire like a bucket of icy water. He sucked in a breath, pushed out another, thrust shaking fingers through his hair, and shoved away from the balcony to head back into the bedroom. Sick loathing made his stomach muscles clench when he spotted Leonardo's journal on the coffee table.

Stop torturing yourself.

Stretching out on the bed, he punched the pillows into submission and switched off the bedside lamp. He had no connection to Leonardo. So what if he looked like the guy? He had more than enough sins of his own to deal with, without shouldering the blame for someone else's.

Folding his hands behind his head, he watched the moonlight cast eerie shadows in the velvet canopy above his head and waited for the nausea to go the hell away. The light citrus-scented breeze gradually cooled the sweat on his brow and replaced the acrid taste in his mouth, bringing with it comforting memories of Eva. And her nutty insistence that he was a nice guy.

Welcome heat curled in his abdomen.

No, he wasn't a nice guy. Or a particularly patient one. But he'd proved that he could be decent, or decent enough, by giving her some time to realise he wasn't one of her storybook heroes.

That said, he wasn't a masochist—which meant he'd be doing his very best tomorrow to ensure he didn't have to spend any more nights alone with only Leonardo's creepy journal for company.

CHAPTER FOURTEEN

'YOUR mind is elsewhere today, Niccolo?'

Nick glanced up from his lunch, to find Don Vincenzo's astute gaze steady on his. He sighed inwardly. He'd stopped bothering to correct the old guy about his name yesterday, when he'd figured out the man was as stubborn as he was. And yeah, he was a little preoccupied all right.

He hadn't expected Eva to be gone this morning before he'd woken up. He also hadn't expected her to sneak off to the lawyers' offices in Milan without bothering to mention it to him. But worse had been the panic that had skittered up his spine when he'd found her room empty at ten o'clock and figured she'd run off back to London. He'd felt pretty stupid about that when Eduardo had told him the truth. But that hadn't stopped him sulking for a while, and then watching the clock all morning waiting for her to return.

Make that a lot preoccupied.

But he wasn't about to talk to an octogenarian he barely knew about the dismal state of his sex life.

'I guess I'm still jet-lagged,' he muttered.

Don Vincenzo nodded, as if digesting the information, then said: 'Eva tells me you have read my son's journal.'

Nick put down his fork. 'Yeah. Some of it.' Where was this headed? Because talking about Leonardo's journal was even less appealing than talking about Eva's disappearing act.

'So now you know—' Don Vincenzo's hand shook as

he laid his napkin on the table '—that I raised a vain, self-absorbed man, who preyed on women simply because he could.'

Nick hitched a shoulder. 'I guess,' he said, wishing he couldn't see the pain in the old man's eyes.

'I owe you an apology, Niccolo, on behalf of the Alegria family.'

Nick stiffened. 'It's not your job to apologise for what he did.'

'I was his father, I should have—'

'And anyway, I don't need an apology.' Nick interrupted, hoping like hell to put an end to the conversation. 'I did okay.'

He hadn't wanted to like Don Vincenzo. Hadn't wanted to feel anything for the old man at all. But it was proving next to impossible not to.

He knew what the old guy wanted. Had figured it out yesterday as Don Vincenzo had squired Eva and him round his properties in the picturesque town of Riva del Garda and spoken with pride and hope thickening his voice about the estates and businesses he owned in Tuscany.

Don Vincenzo was looking for someone who would care about the Alegria legacy and the various properties and businesses he had nurtured and watched grow for the last forty years. But more than that, the old man wanted a grandson who would love and respect him, to replace the son who never had.

And Nick simply wasn't that guy. His life was in San Francisco, where he wrote about the dark underbelly of urban life, because he'd once been a part of it himself. He didn't know the first thing about managing a business, or the day-to-day running of an ancestral estate. And he didn't do love and respect either. He didn't want to be a part of Don Vincenzo's family, because he hadn't shared that connection with anyone. Not since he'd been a kid. And look what a staggering success he'd made of that.

'How can you say that?' Vincenzo asked dispassionately. 'When you ran away from home?'

Nick flinched. 'How do you know about that?' he asked, but he could already guess. Don Vincenzo was a shrewd businessman, of course he would have had him investigated.

Don Vincenzo bowed his head. 'When Henry Crenshawe informed me of your name, I endeavoured to find out all I could about you.' Anger flashed in Vincenzo's eyes. 'Why did you run? Did Delisantro reject you after he found out you were not of his blood?'

'You've got it all wrong.' A shame Nick thought he'd buried years ago lurched back to life. 'Carmine Delisantro was a good man and a great dad, but when I found out about…' He paused. Why couldn't he say Leonardo's name? 'I rejected Carmine, not the other way around. So if anyone needs to apologise it's me.'

'You were a boy.' Vincenzo sighed. 'No child should have to find out what you did. If the man who raised you was as good a man as you say, I'm sure he forgave you.'

'He did.' To his horror, Nick felt his voice crack. He stared at his plate, recognising the grinding pain in his stomach for what it was. Guilt.

Carmine Delisantro had forgiven him all right, and he'd carried on loving Nick right up until his dying day. But Nick had been too much of a coward to admit he felt the same. So what did that say about him?

Don Vincenzo's hand covered the fist Nick had on the table. 'I will be travelling to Milan tomorrow to change my will. As you know, to my great regret I cannot pass the title to you, because you are not a legitimate heir.'

'There's nothing to regret. I don't want the title.' Nick's fingers released and the grinding pain began to dim. Thank goodness, the old guy had finally realised Nick wasn't cut out to be anyone's grandson.

'Very well, then.' Vincenzo patted the back of his hand and sent him an easy smile. 'I have a second cousin in Palermo who shall become the sixteenth Duca D'Alegria.' The man's lips quirked in a benevolent smile. He gave the ornate dining room a quick survey before his gaze fixed back on Nick. 'But to you, Niccolo Carmine Delisantro, I shall take great pleasure in leaving the rest of my estate and the Alegria Palazzo.'

'What?' Nick's shoulder muscles spasmed as he leapt out of his chair. 'Why would you do that? You don't even know me. I told you I don't want—'

'Sit down, Niccolo, and stop panicking.' To Nick's astonishment the old man simply laughed, the sound gruff and genuinely amused. 'My doctors tell me I have a few years yet before you need worry about receiving this gift.'

'But damn it, I don't want your gift.' He slapped his palms on the table, rattling the plates. 'And I sure as hell don't deserve it.' The thought terrified him. Not just the responsibility he would have to maintain the land, to manage the staff and the property and the businesses, but also the connection, the debt he would owe to the man.

Instead of looking appalled, or even annoyed by Nick's outburst, Vincenzo cocked his head to one side, his oddly penetrating gaze disturbing Nick even more. 'Why would you think you don't deserve it?'

'Forget it,' Nick replied, the panic starting to choke him. He didn't have to explain himself to Don Vincenzo or anyone else. He'd made his own life, free of family, free of emotional ties and that was the way he intended to keep it. 'I don't want this inheritance. And you can't make me take it,' he said, slinging his napkin on the table and turning to leave.

'We shall talk of this later, when you have calmed down…'

The buzzing in Nick's head drowned out the rest of Don Vincenzo's words as he strode across the room, desperate to escape from the misguided hope and affection in the old man's eyes.

He knew he sounded like an ungrateful kid, the same ungrateful kid who had once thrown everything away that mattered because of pride and temper and stupidity. But so what? The past was gone. He couldn't go back and change it. Any more than he could change who he had become.

He raised his eyes from the floor and stopped dead at the sight of Eva standing in the doorway, her hands covering her mouth, her blue eyes round with sympathy.

The silk-papered walls of the elegant parlour rushed towards him.

How much had she heard?

His vision dimmed, the sudden claustrophobia forcing him to move.

'Nick, are you all right?' she whispered, reaching out.

'I'm fine.' He shrugged off her fingertips as he strode past her, through the palazzo's marble lobby and straight out of the entrance doors. The burning heat of the afternoon sun did nothing to dispel the shocking chill creeping into his bones.

He was running away all over again.

But he had to get out of here, get away from his grandfather's misguided trust—and the sparkle of distress on Eva's lashes.

CHAPTER FIFTEEN

'NICK, come back.' Eva rushed down the steps of the palazzo after Nick's retreating back. Kicking off her heeled sandals, she left them on the hot stones and ran barefoot, desperate to catch him as he headed towards the dock at the end of the waterfront.

She hadn't meant to eavesdrop. Hadn't meant to listen in to what was clearly a private conversation. But when she'd entered the pleasantly cool lobby after her exhausting trip to Milan, she'd been flushed with pleasure at the sound of the muted voices coming from the dining salon. How wonderful to hear Nick finally conversing with his grandfather in full sentences. But then she'd stood in the doorway, heard the raw emotion in Nick's voice, had actually registered the words—and been stunned into silence.

Why was he so angry and upset at the thought of inheriting the Alegria estate? And why would he think he didn't deserve it?

The crippling sense of responsibility had hit her first. Nick had come to Italy to help her get her job back. But that had been swiftly followed by the desire to soothe the hurt and panic she had seen in his face.

He'd looked stunned and had clearly been horrified she had witnessed his outburst. But how could she ignore his pain and confusion now she had?

Seeing him step onto the cherry-red power cruiser moored

at the end of the dock, she picked up the hem of her skirt and ran down the worn wooden boards.

She could help, but only if she caught up with him.

'Nick, hang on.' She skidded to a halt on the dock, panting as the duca's dock keeper released the thin nylon line mooring the cruiser to the quay. 'Where are you going?'

'For a ride.' He caught the line the dock keeper threw across. 'Alone.'

After sending a perfunctory salute to the man beside her, and tying off the line, he crossed the boat's deck and leapt up the steps to the pilot's cabin.

The powerful boat kicked to life, water churning as it glided away from the dock. Without taking time to think about it, Eva took two steps back, and then ran at full pelt, squeezed her eyes shut and launched herself off the dock and into mid-air.

The soles of her feet slapping on the deck were accompanied by the alarmed shout of the dock keeper. She pitched onto her knees then grabbed onto the handrail, her knuckles whitening as the boat lurched forward.

Okay, that wasn't the most graceful thing she'd ever done, but at least she hadn't drowned.

Fighting the sway of the boat as it rode the swell, she clambered up the steps to the cabin.

Nick glanced at her, a dark scowl on his face as he swung the boat's steering wheel into a turn to direct the boat onto the open lake. 'You little fool, you could have hurt yourself.'

'You could have waited for me,' she said, unperturbed by his reprimand, and perched on the leather bench seat behind him.

With his legs akimbo, his T-shirt moulded to his muscular chest and his caramel brown hair whipping about his head he looked savage and uncivilised. Like a pirate captain at the bow of his ship, ready to maraud and pillage anything that took his fancy.

Eva shook off the fanciful thought. This wasn't a romantic fantasy. It was real life. And she wasn't scared of Nick. Not any more.

'I wanted to be alone.' He glared at her, a muscle in his jaw twitching as his gaze narrowed. 'What part of that didn't you understand?'

She clutched the leather cushion as the boat skimmed over the wake of a couple of wind-surfers and rounded the point, leaving the cove that sheltered the palazzo behind. 'You don't always get what you want.'

Nick let out a harsh laugh. 'You don't say,' he murmured, his voice thick with innuendo as his gaze flicked to her cleavage.

Eva's cheeks hit boiling point, awareness shimmering, but she refused to rise to the bait. He was trying to provoke her. And divert her attention.

She touched the soft hair of his forearm. 'What are you so upset about?'

The sinews in his arm tensed, and the muscle in his jaw bunched. But that was his only reaction to the question.

He grasped a lever on the dashboard, which looked like a throttle. 'You wanted to ride,' he said, yanking the lever down. 'So let's see what this baby can do.'

The engine roared, lifting them up and throwing Eva back against the seat. Then the boat powered across the water as if catapulted out of a sling, skimming over the choppy surface as they shot towards the sun. Eva's bottom bounced on the bench, the wind and spray refreshing as she screwed up her eyes and held on tight, the punch of adrenaline making her heart pound.

Nick stood, his hands gripped on the steering wheel as he negotiated the leisure traffic with practised ease.

He looked fierce, indomitable. And yet she'd seen the moment of vulnerability when his gaze had met hers in the dining salon. Meeting Don Vincenzo, learning about his biological father had been hard for him. Probably much harder than he had imagined or would ever admit. And her heart went out to him, even if he didn't want it to.

Minutes passed as they drove to the far end of the lake, leaving the crowds of smaller craft and the heavily developed shoreline behind. Heading back into the shallows, the boat rounded a rocky outcropping and entered a quiet cove. The engine slowed as they approached a ramshackle dock that listed to one side. A stone shrine topped with a crucifix nestled among the plants and bushes edging the water.

She had no idea where they were as Nick eased the throttle down and the boat kicked and settled in the water. But wherever they were, they were alone. The gentle lap of the water on the powerboat's hull the only sound above the rasp of her own breathing. She could feel the prickle of heat and anticipation shimmering over her skin, the mist from their ride dampening her cotton blouse but doing nothing to cool the heat pulsing through her veins. His hooded gaze locked on her face, the fine spray of water on his hair sending it into unruly furrows as he whisked it back from his forehead.

He looked wild and untamed, the anger when she'd jumped on board replaced by fierce arousal. But the harsh desire on his face didn't frighten her, because she'd had time to think about what she was letting herself in for.

Nick wasn't looking for love or commitment. But then neither was she. He was a complex man, who guarded his feelings and his vulnerabilities and, she suspected, found it next to impossible to trust anyone because of the circumstances of his birth. She'd really have to be a romantic fool to think that she, with her limited knowledge of relationships, could have any hope of changing that.

But that didn't mean they couldn't share something worthwhile together for the short time they had. He'd warned her that this could only ever be a purely sexual adventure. But she already knew it was more than that. Because whatever Nick wanted to believe, she already cared about him, and he cared about her.

Propping his butt on the control panel, he crossed his legs at the ankle and beckoned her with his forefinger. 'Come here,' he said, his voice husky with hunger.

She stood still, the desire burning.

Leaning forward, he hooked his forefinger in the waistband of her skirt and yanked. 'I said, come here.'

She stumbled towards him, flattened her palms on his chest. Rough, urgent hands lifted her skirt, caressed her thighs and moulded her buttocks, his lips fastening on her throat, his teeth nipping at the place where her pulse hammered.

She dropped her head back to give him better access, ground her backside into his palms, whispering: 'I thought you wanted to be alone?'

'Not any more,' he growled, the demand urgent in his voice. Rough hands snuck under the waistband of her panties, then ruthless fingers found the zip on her skirt and dragged it down.

She looped her arms round his neck, hoping he couldn't feel the quiver of trepidation as he sat on the bench seat and yanked her down to straddle his lap.

She grasped his shoulders as he captured her mouth. Moist heat flooded between her thighs, his erection confined by soft denim rubbing against the damp cotton of her panties as she let the hunger that had built in the last two days consume her.

She rode his length, revelled in his staggered breathing and threaded her fingers into the hair at his nape. Then urgent seduction turned to violent need. He ripped at her blouse, buttons popping. She dragged his T-shirt over his head, exploring the ridged steel of his abdomen, the velvet steel of his chest.

The brown of his irises darkened before his mouth covered her breast through the delicate lace of her bra. She cried out, the keening sound of pleasure echoing away on the breeze as he tasted and teased with his teeth, then suckled strongly. Eva bowed back, arching into his mouth to feel more, to take more. Clever fingers released the bra's hook, peeled away the wet lace. She shivered, the nipple tightening, swelling. His lips feasted on naked flesh: hot, hard, perfect.

She lost focus, delirious with longing and exhilaration. He needed this, needed her as much as she needed him.

He swore softly, banded his arms round her waist. 'Hold on,' he croaked, lifting them off the bench together. 'We're taking this below deck.'

She wrapped her legs round his waist, clung on, as her dazed brain registered the rumbling hum of a passing speed-boat. He staggered down the steps into the boat's cabin, then strode through the galley to the bedroom.

She landed on the wide double bed that took up most of the compact space. Rising on her elbows, she watched him kicking off his deck shoes, struggling out of his jeans and boxer shorts, then grabbing a small foil packet from the back pocket.

Her breath expelled in a rush. He looked magnificent. But she wasn't worried any more. Rising on her knees, she touched the powerful erection. Marvelling at the hardness, she cupped the generous weight of him in her palm.

Gazing up, she met eyes ablaze with arousal. 'Can I kiss you there?' she asked.

'No,' he groaned.

He threaded her fingers through his, pulling them away from his flesh before he rolled on the condom.

He climbed on the bed, forcing her back. Cradling her cheek, his fingers trailed down her neck to stroke the curve of her collarbone. 'Later,' he murmured. 'Or this is going to be over way too soon.'

His hand shaped her breasts, caressed her hip, cradled her buttocks, then long, talented fingers delved into the wet curls at her core.

She bucked, clamped her knees together, the shocking touch almost more than she could bear.

'Open for me,' he urged.

Her knees weakened, loosened for him of their own accord. He rubbed, stroked, circled the burning nub. She heard her own broken sobs as his fingertip skimmed over the heart of her. She cried out as the slick heat built to an impossible crescendo. She couldn't breathe, couldn't think, but as she clung to that desperate edge, her senses screaming, she knew this wasn't how she wanted it. Not this time.

She closed her legs, shivered against him. 'Please…I want you inside me.' She choked out the bold request.

He rolled onto his back, pulling her with him, forcing her to spread her legs and bracket his hips. 'Then I want you on top,' he demanded.

Large hands cupped her buttocks, directing her to his shaft and then he drew her down. She shuddered, the shock of penetration too much as she took him in to the hilt. But then he began to move, bumping a place deep inside. The pleasure intensified as she moved with him, taking him deeper still in a wild, unstoppable ride to oblivion.

The orgasm hit hard, in a wave that went on and on until it crested with the speed and force of a tsunami. Slamming into her, robbing her of breath, it powered through from the tips of her toes to the top of her head. She heard his shout of completion, the sound a million miles away as her body shattered into glittery shards of ecstasy.

She collapsed on top of him, his sweat-slicked body slippery against her own.

His hands stroked her buttocks, roamed up her back. 'I

never thought I'd say this, but that was actually worth the wait.'

An exhausted grin formed on her lips as she settled beside him, and he tucked her under his arm. She rested her hand on his chest, stroked down the elegant line of hair, and her fingertips touched the raised edge of the scar that slashed across his abdomen. The grin died as tenderness engulfed her, and her heart careered into her ribcage.

Foolish tears prickled the backs of her eyelids. She blinked furiously, struggling to find something witty and clever to say to push the emotion back where it belonged.

Their love-making had been wild and uncontrolled. It had felt like more than just sex. But how much more? And why did the thought suddenly terrify her?

He tipped her face up to his. 'You okay? I was a little rough.'

'No, you weren't, I enjoyed it,' she said, her cheeks flushing at the smile that curved his lips.

Well, it wasn't exactly witty or clever, but at least it was accurate.

His thumb trailed down her cheek as he studied her face, his golden gaze still dazed with afterglow. 'So did I.' The soft words had her heart jumping into her throat again.

She traced the line of the scar and felt him tense. 'How did you get this scar?'

Sadness overwhelmed her when she watched the haze of arousal clear from his eyes and the familiar caution return.

Taking his arm from around her, he sat up with his back to her. She noticed the stiff set of his shoulders as he dragged his T-shirt over his head, covering the scar.

'We should head back,' he said, as if she hadn't said anything, then grabbed his boxers up and stood to put them on. 'Before they come looking for us.'

She reached for a bed sheet to cover herself, acutely aware

of her own nakedness, and swallowed down the stupid lump of hurt at the way he had ignored her question. What they had wasn't permanent and her curiosity was just that. Curiosity. If he didn't feel comfortable talking about his past, he certainly didn't have to.

'Do you think the duca will guess what we've been doing?' she asked, concerned about what the old man might make of their behaviour. She doubted he'd be all that impressed.

'Maybe.' He shrugged, glancing over his shoulder while fastening the button-fly of his jeans. 'But who cares? I expect Eduardo will inform him we're sharing a bedroom before too long.'

She shot upright, clutching the bed sheet to her bosom. 'We can't share a bedroom.'

'Yeah, we can,' he said easily. 'And we will.'

'But…Then everyone will know,' she said, worrying her bottom lip. 'Maybe we could just—'

'Eva, sweetheart,' he interrupted her panicked reasoning, sitting down on the edge of the bed. 'As much as I enjoy playing pirate captain to your damsel in distress—' he tucked a strand of hair behind her ear '—no way in hell am I risking my neck on that balcony every night to have you.'

She let out a jerky breath, the tenderness of his touch making the foolish emotion rush back. 'But you don't have to. We have the connecting bathroom. You could easily—'

'No, I couldn't.' He silenced her with a quick kiss. 'I'm not sneaking around like some horny teenager. I want you in my bed at night.' He gave his eyebrows a saucy lift. 'And in the morning—and any other time in between that takes our fancy. We've got another week and a half here and I plan to have you as much as is humanly possible. If you don't want me, all you have to do is say so.'

'I *do* want you,' she said. 'You know I do.'

But did she want him too much?

They only had a week and a half, and she had to keep sight of that. She mustn't let her romantic nature and her affection for him—not to mention their thrilling sexual chemistry—get in the way of her common sense.

But she could take that risk, she decided. She was ready—and she was through being a coward about her own needs and desires.

'Well, good.' His smile turned to a triumphant grin. He grasped her waist and tumbled her back onto the bed. 'But you'd better get dressed pronto,' he added. She shrieked, giddy with excitement, as he wrestled the sheet off to nuzzle her exposed nipple.

'Or I'm going to make you prove it.'

And then he did.

CHAPTER SIXTEEN

'THERE you are. What are you hiding in here for?'

Eva looked up from the exquisite parchment that had the Alegria family tree hand-drawn on it by fourteenth-century monks, to see Nick striding into the palazzo's library with a frown on his face and a picnic basket under his arm.

'Studying your ancestors,' she replied, acknowledging the flutter of excitement that always gripped her when she saw him again.

'Don't start. I've already had a lecture about my so-called ancestors from Don Vincenzo today,' he said, but to her joy he sounded exasperated rather than upset.

It had been over a week since she'd eavesdropped on his lunch with Don Vincenzo—and since then she'd enjoyed watching his relationship with his grandfather soften and grow. She knew Nick was still opposed to inheriting the palazzo, but Don Vincenzo had proved to be patient and kind and surprisingly astute—and he'd worn down Nick's resistance to him on every other front. The two men had a lot in common, despite Nick's attempts to dwell on their differences, and it had been sweet to see him struggling to cope with his growing affection for the old man. She wondered if he knew he was making an attachment here he would find it hard to break.

'I thought you had a whole day of meetings with Don

Vincenzo's lawyers in Milan?' she said, inordinately pleased to see him back so soon.

'Not any more.' Grabbing her wrist, he hauled her out of the chair. 'I gave them the slip,' he said, dragging her out of the room and down the corridor. 'We're playing hooky for the rest of the day.'

'We are?' she asked, excitement making her voice rise.

He squeezed her hand and grinned. 'Yeah, we are.' He lifted the wicket basket. 'And I've bought supplies so we don't have to come back till we start to starve.'

She giggled, like a child escaping from the classroom, as he led her out of the palazzo's back door, then climbed the steeply terraced ornamental gardens towards an overgrown orchard of lemon trees. As they trekked down the country lane through the trees Eva struggled to keep pace with his long strides and control the ecstatic flutter of her heartbeat at the promise of a new adventure.

She'd become addicted to the adrenaline rush of being Nick Delisantro's lover. Their time together had rushed past in a haze of hot passion-filled nights and long lazy days as they explored Lake Garda and its surrounding towns and villages—and every inch of each other's bodies. He never ceased to surprise her, to arouse her, to provoke and excite her—and she'd found herself conquering every challenge and rejoicing in every risk.

In fact, she was a little bit afraid she might have become as wild as he was. But she couldn't seem to find the will to worry about it too much. And if there were moments when she held him a little too tightly, when she had to bite back the urge to ask him to confide more about himself and the demons that she knew still haunted him, or wondered about how she was going to cope back in her old life when their time was up, she refused to dwell on them. This was a once-in-a-lifetime adventure that had already changed her for ever. She'd become so much bolder, so much more independent and she was loving the new, improved, devil-may-care Eva Redmond far too much to force her back into her shell even when her dangerous lover was no longer by her side to tempt her into trouble.

And she didn't need to know about Nick's past, because she'd already come to terms with the fact that they had no future together. There were only two days left until he returned to San Francisco and she went back to London. And while neither of them had mentioned it, they both knew it was coming.

Eventually they reached a sloping meadow, a good mile above the palazzo, edged by ancient trees, and carpeted with wild flowers. She toed off her sandals and let her bare toes sink into the course grass and fragrant blooms. A light breeze tempered the scorching heat of the summer sun.

Dumping the basket on the ground, Nick flopped down on his back beside it. 'We're stopping here,' he said, hooking his hands behind his head. 'That thing weighs a bloody ton.'

Eva laughed. 'Fine by me, Romeo,' she teased.

'Hey, don't get cocky. I wheedled lunch out of Maria, didn't I?' he grumbled, mentioning the palazzo's chef, just one of the many members of staff who Eva knew adored him—so she doubted much wheedling had been involved. 'And hefted it all the way up here,' he finished.

'Fair enough.' She grinned, kneeling next to him to open the basket. 'I'll carry it back.'

'Big deal,' he said, lifting up on an elbow to pluck out a chilled bottle of Pinot Grigio, while Eva laid out the checkered cloth Maria had packed. 'It'll be empty by then.'

She snorted out an unladylike laugh at the disgruntled expression on his face as she laid out the array of mouthwatering anti-pasti dishes.

Finding a corkscrew, he twisted it into the bottle in a few efficient strokes and yanked the cork with a satisfying pop.

'Laugh all you want, sweetheart, but I intend to exact a high price for all my hard work.'

He handed her a chilled glass of the pale amber wine.

'Oh, goodie!' she said cheekily, enjoying the way his eyes darkened dangerously as she took a fortifying sip.

Nick watched Eva eat as he devoured his meal—and thought about devouring her. The agonising sexual tension tightened deliciously every time she flicked him a flirtatious glance over the rim of her wine glass, or when she tore open a ripe fig and bit into the succulent fruit or licked the sweet juice off her lips.

God, she was so gorgeous. So lush and sexy and playful and provocative. She turned him on to the point of madness, simply by breathing. And yet she'd proved to be a surprisingly calming influence when it came to dealing with all the tangled emotions that the time he spent with his grandfather seemed to bring to the surface.

Even on that day over a week ago, when he'd overreacted so spectacularly to Don Vincenzo's decision to leave his estate to him, having her on the boat beside him, being able to lose himself in her had been enough to take the turmoil and the anger away.

He still didn't want the damn inheritance, not that Don Vincenzo would listen to any of his objections, but he didn't feel nearly so trapped now, so scared of accepting the old man's affection. And the main reason for that had been Eva's presence. He didn't know how or why. But he did know he was going to miss her when he had to go back to San Francisco alone—her bright sense of humour, her easy affection, even her foolish concern for his feelings about this reunion or her misplaced faith in his integrity, not to mention her sexy, responsive little body. She made him feel lighter and more carefree than he had since he was a boy.

He hurled the hunk of ciabatta he'd been eating into the

underbrush. No need to worry about their parting yet, he still had another couple of days to enjoy her. Brushing his hands on his hiking shorts, he crooked a finger at her. 'Picnic's over, sweetheart. It's payback time.'

Putting down her paper plate slowly, she darted a glance to her right. 'Only if you catch me first,' she said, then, to his amazement, leapt onto her feet in one fluid movement and shot off like a gazelle.

He swore and levered himself up to chase after her. She was a lot faster than he would have given her credit for, plus he had a belly full of food to contend with. So they were both breathless and laughing hard when he finally tagged her round the waist and slung her to the ground, rolling over to take the brunt of the fall and then settling on top of her.

Holding her wrists in one hand, he levered them above her head and looked down into her laughing eyes as she wriggled furiously trying to buck him off. 'So finally I know how you stayed a virgin so long,' he joked. 'You run faster than an Olympic sprinter.'

Her body stilled and she looked away, the flags of colour on her cheeks flying high.

'Hey, I'm kidding,' he said. He'd embarrassed her and he hadn't meant to.

She looked back. 'That's okay.'

'No, it's not. Tell me what's wrong.'

'It's nothing,' she said, but the vivid colour on her cheeks said otherwise.

He let go of her wrists, but kept her pinned to the ground. 'It's not nothing. What did I say?'

He saw her swallow, knew that shuttered look that meant she was building up the courage to ask something. 'Does it still bother you? That I was a virgin?'

He wanted to laugh off the question. Say of course it didn't bother him. But the problem was it did. Now more than ever.

Because however hard he'd tried he couldn't explain away the feeling of responsibility towards her that kept growing every time they made love. Every time she clung to him and begged him for release. Every time she sobbed out his name while reaching orgasm. Every time he taught her a new way to please him, or showed her a new way he could please her. The truth was he loved knowing he was the first man who had ever made her feel that way—and apart from making him feel like a Neanderthal jerk, it scared the hell out of him, because it made no sense at all. He didn't have any claim on her, any more than she did on him, and he didn't want to have, so why did he feel so possessive?

'Fine.' He forced a self-deprecating smile to his lips. 'It does bother me a bit.' His hands settled on her waist, the thin satin of her dress brushing his palms. 'I want to know why it took you so long.'

'If I tell you,' she began, her hands covering his, her eyes thoughtful, 'would you tell me something about yourself in return?'

Damn, he should have seen that one coming. But instead of evading her, as he had always done before, he nodded. 'It's a deal.' Holding her hands, he leant forward and kissed the warm sun-kissed skin on the tip of her nose. 'So what's your answer?'

'You have to promise not to laugh,' she added, colouring again, and looking so vulnerable his heart lurched in his chest.

'I won't laugh,' he said, and he knew he wouldn't. Whatever reasons she had for denying the passion inside her for so long, he had a feeling he wasn't going to like them.

'Can I sit up?'

He wanted to say no, but could see she needed the distance. 'All right.' He lifted off her.

Hugging her knees to her chest, she looked out into the meadow at the afternoon sun dipping towards the trees.

'Actually it's remarkably boring,' she said carefully. 'I didn't do much socialising when I was a teenager.'

'Why not?'

She jerked her shoulder looking surprised at the question. Although he didn't know why she would be. She was such a lively, engaging person.

'I was horribly nerdy. My parents were academics and they wanted me to concentrate on my studies. And I wanted to please them.'

She made it sound simple. But he wasn't convinced. Why had she been so dead set on pleasing them?

'By the time I got to university I was two years ahead of my peers. And I didn't know the first thing about boys.' She gave a hopeless little laugh. 'Plus I think my love of pirate fantasies may have given me some unrealistic expectations. And by the time I got over that, and realised that swashbuckling sex gods are quite thin on the ground in real life, I was stuck in such a huge rut it took someone spectacular to kick me out of it.'

The shy smile she sent him had his heart tripping over. He skimmed his thumb down her cheek. 'Please tell me you don't mean me.'

No one had ever thought he was spectacular before. And he knew he wasn't. So why did it feel so good to hear her say it?

She wiggled her eyebrows suggestively. 'Only in a sexual sense, you understand.'

'You little tease,' he said softly, framing her face. Then he kissed her.

Her lips softened, and he fed on the sweet, heady taste of figs and innocence. The soft sigh that issued against his cheek made it hard to focus. But he forced himself to draw back. Not to take her in the quick greedy gulps he wanted to.

'It's kind of ironic, don't you think?' he said, trying to

lighten the mood and dispel the feeling of hopelessness that threatened to engulf him. 'That you were a good girl and did what your parents wanted, while I was a rebel and did the opposite. And yet we both ended up regretting it.'

Her eyes flickered with something that looked like sadness. 'Why *did* you run away from home?'

The sixty-four-thousand-dollar question, he thought grimly.

'Was that your question?' he asked, stalling.

She nodded. He debated giving her a sanitised version. Or making something up that would deflect her from the truth about who he really was. It wouldn't be the first time he'd lied to a woman after all.

But as he met her trusting gaze he knew he couldn't lie to her. Better to take the stars out of her eyes, once and for all.

'When my dad came home from the hospital the night Mum died, I was fourteen,' he began, the horror of that long ago summer night making his gut churn. 'I thought my whole world had collapsed. But it hadn't. Not yet.'

Eva could hear the tension in his voice, see the rigid control in his face and wanted desperately to take the pain away he was trying so hard to hide.

She touched his arm. 'It's okay, Nick. You don't have to tell me.'

'Yeah, I do,' he said, the tone gruff. 'My dad was wild with grief. She'd told him the truth. That I wasn't his biological son. And he lost it for a while.'

Tears pricked her eyes. She hated to think what that meant—and how deeply he had been hurt by an incident that even now he couldn't bring himself to describe.

'He apologised a few days later at her funeral,' Nick continued, plucking a tuft of grass, flinging it away. 'He said it didn't matter. That he still loved me, still considered me to be his son. But I wouldn't believe him.'

Eva sniffed, scrubbed away the tears.

Nick's head shot up and he scowled. 'Don't you dare cry, Eva. Not for me.'

'Why not? It must have been dreadful for you.'

'It wasn't that bad,' he said, as if the trauma he had suffered that night had been nothing at all. When she knew how bad it must have been, if he was unable to acknowledge the pain, even now.

'I made him pay for that lapse for the rest of his life,' he said grimly. 'Him and my sister Ruby. I made their lives hell for two years.' He thrust his fingers through his hair, the gesture defensive and full of frustration. 'I got into fights, bunked off school, argued with him constantly. And then I ran off and got up to much worse on the streets. And I didn't go back. Ever. Even when Ruby begged me to. Even when he was dying.'

The loathing in his voice was so intense, so bitter, she didn't know how to get past it. 'You mustn't blame yourself,' she said, the tears flowing freely now. 'You were a frightened, confused child.'

'You think?' he said, the cynicism brutal and unyielding— and nothing like the warm, wonderful man she had discovered in the last two weeks. 'I know what I'm capable of,' he added, his lips twisting in a bitter smile. 'I've known it ever since I was a kid. And now I've read Leonardo's journal, I know why.'

Standing up, he walked back to the picnic basket.

She ran after him, pulled him round to face her. 'You're wrong. You're nothing like Leonardo,' she blurted out, knowing it was true, wanting to make him believe it, but not knowing how.

He shook his head, his expression closed off and unreadable, deliberately shutting her out. 'How would you know?' was all he said—and her newfound courage deserted her.

Kicking the lid of the basket closed, he shoved it under his arm and glanced at the grey clouds that had covered the sun. 'We better get back to the palazzo—it's going to rain.'

She looped her arm through his as they walked back, but she could already feel him slipping away. And felt powerless to do anything about it—the fresh citrus scent of the lemon orchard a cruel reminder of the short-lived new Eva.

He made love to her that night, bringing her to orgasm countless times, and taking his own pleasure with ruthless efficiency, the seduction brutal and relentless as if to prove that sex was all he had ever wanted—until she fell into an exhausted sleep.

She woke groggy and sore the next morning to find him gone—and opened the note sitting on the dresser with trembling fingers.

Stay sweet, Eva. And go find one of the good guys.

And then she sobbed as if her foolish romantic heart were shattering.

Because it was.

CHAPTER SEVENTEEN

'HEY, what's the matter, man? Something wrong with the beer?'

Nick tuned out the comment from his publicist Jay, his gaze locked on the tall, willowy blonde standing on the other side of the art gallery. He'd recognised her as soon as she'd walked in a minute ago.

Eva's friend, Tess…Something. He'd been to three different openings at this godforsaken gallery in the last six weeks, ever since he'd returned to San Francisco, and he had never admitted to himself the reason why he kept coming back here.

But the miserable truth was suddenly staring him in the face with startling clarity. Because as soon as Eva's friend had appeared, his heartbeat had rocketed into his throat—just as it did every night when he struggled to fall asleep in his empty bed, or when he switched on his computer only to spend the rest of the day staring at a blank screen.

He hadn't got over Eva. Hadn't been able to forget her. Because even the most tenuous link to her made him feel like crap.

'Hey, Earth to Nick,' Jay said, swinging his palm in front of Nick's eyes.

Nick passed the lukewarm beer to his publicist. 'Hold this,' he said, ignoring Jay's puzzled frown as he headed through the crowd.

Sweat popped out on his forehead and made his hands feel clammy. He ignored it.

This wasn't a big deal. He wasn't going to make it a big deal. Maybe all he really needed was closure? Something he'd denied himself by not saying goodbye to Eva properly. And here was the perfect opportunity. He could have a quick chat with Eva's friend, just to see how Eva was doing. And then he'd finally be able to stop thinking about her. Every damn second, of every damn day. And every damn night.

He'd waited patiently for her to contact him. To ask him to come back. But it had been six weeks, and she hadn't. So he had to let it go now.

As he approached the woman he formulated the best way to introduce himself casually in case she didn't remember him. But then she lifted her head, laughing at something her friend had said, and spotted him.

The laugh died on her lips and her eyes narrowed sharply as he stopped in front of her.

'Well, if it isn't the playboy screenwriter,' she said.

He frowned at the outright hostility in her tone. Seemed she remembered him all right. 'The name's Nick.'

'I know your name.' She flicked a derisive glance over him that had his temper prickling. 'Although I can think of several other names which would suit you better.'

'Have you got a problem with me?' To hell with polite introductions. He'd hardly slept in close to two months, his writing had been shot to hell, and now he was getting the third degree from someone he barely knew. What was up with that?

She glared back. 'You treated the kindest, sweetest, most genuine woman I know as your personal plaything. Then dumped her like she was nothing. So yes, we do have a problem.'

'What are you talking about?' His voice cracked, the shock

at her attack nothing compared to the emotion banding around his chest.

That wasn't the way it had happened at all. He'd done the decent thing. He'd had no claim on Eva and very little to offer her. So he'd walked away. And left it up to her. Even though it had nearly killed him. Was still killing him. He deserved a damn medal.

'Don't you get it?' She fired the words at him. 'You destroyed her, you creep. She cried over you for weeks. And she never cries.' The girl's diatribe washed over him as temper gave way to regret and confusion. If she'd felt that much for him, why hadn't she contacted him?

He'd given her a choice. Why hadn't she taken it?

'But the good news is,' the girl continued, her eyes boring into him, 'she's over you now. She's met a great guy. And he treats her right.'

The hell she had. The temper he'd been trying to muster came surging back to life.

'What guy? What's his name?' He'd strangle the bastard.

She couldn't have got over him so easily—not when he wasn't over her.

'It's…' The girl hesitated. 'It's Bill and he's a…' Another slight pause. 'A computer programmer.'

A computer programmer called Bill! What the…?

No way. Eva wouldn't be happy with someone like that. She needed adventure. She needed passion and excitement in her life. She was like a beautiful flower burst into bloom. And she'd damn well bloomed with him. Which meant she didn't get to bloom with anyone else.

'The hell with that,' he snarled under his breath. Then turned and walked out of the art gallery, the emotion burning his throat bursting into flames.

So she thought she could just take up with someone else? *I don't think so.*

It wasn't over. Not till he said so. He'd done the decent thing and given her a damn choice. And she'd thrown it back in his face. He still wanted her. And he needed her. And she needed him. Not some computer nerd called Bill. End of story.

Hailing a cab, Nick shouted at the driver as he launched himself into the back seat. 'Take me to the airport. I've got a plane to catch.'

He'd been through six long weeks of torture and now she thought she could just blow him off. Well, she could forget it. He was through hanging around. And he was through pretending to be a nice guy.

'Eva, it's me, Tess. We need to talk.'

'Tess?' Eva glanced at the clock on her computer—just past two o'clock in the afternoon London time on a Saturday afternoon. 'Is everything all right?' Why was Tess calling so early in the morning? She never got up before noon on a weekend.

'Everything's wonderful,' Tess's voice came down the phone line, but she didn't sound too sure.

'Okay,' Eva said carefully. Tess could be a bit of a drama queen, but she sounded genuinely worried. 'So what do we need to talk about?'

'I did something a tiny bit rash last night. And I thought I should let you know.' There was a long pause. 'In case there are consequences.'

'Consequences?' That didn't sound good. 'What did you do?'

'I bumped into Nick Delisantro at the Union Square gallery.'

'Oh.' Eva felt the sharp tug of grief at the mention of his name, and hated herself for it. 'I see' she said dully, forcing the words out.

She was over him. She had to be. It had been over a month and a half since she'd woken up in the master suite in the palazzo to find him gone. And she'd changed beyond all recognition from that devastated woman who had cried herself hoarse for two solid weeks, until she was hollowed out and exhausted and simply had no tears left in her.

Admittedly, it had taken her even longer to call a halt to her pity party and put her wild fling with Nick Delisantro into its proper perspective.

Yes she'd fallen for him. Hard and fast and far too easily. And once she'd finally got past the howling grief of losing him, it had been pathetically obvious to figure out why.

In his own way, Nick Delisantro had been everything she'd always fantasised about in her dream man. Tough and untamed, unconventional and wildly exciting on the outside but surprisingly tender and thoughtful and troubled on the inside. He'd made her feel beautiful and exciting and vivid. He'd lifted her life out of the ordinary and made it extraordinary. And most of all he'd made her feel important. The way her parents never had.

But it wasn't until she'd received an email from Don Vincenzo a little over a month ago that she'd realised the bold, exciting person she had believed herself to be with Nick was as much of a fraud as the timid, mouse-like person she had been before she met him.

The duca had been as devastated as she was to find Nick gone that morning without a word. But unlike her, he hadn't been willing to simply accept Nick's departure. According to the email the duca had sent her a fortnight later, Nick had refused to acknowledge his many attempts to contact him and Eva could tell that had devastated the elderly man. But the duca had finished by thanking her for her part in his reunion with his grandson and stating that he hadn't given up hope—assuring her that however stubborn Nick was, the Duca D'Alegria was more so.

Eva hadn't doubted the old man for a moment, and as she'd

read the email at her cluttered desk in Roots Registry she'd felt the first stirrings of something other than misery.

A fragile glimmer of hope had peeped through the fog of despair and then she'd had a devastating moment of enlightenment. Nick wasn't responsible for her courage, or her lack of it. She was. He couldn't give her the guts to be herself. To be the bright, bold, confident woman she'd always wanted to be. Only she could do that. And even though she couldn't make Nick Delisantro love her or make him accept the love she had for him in return, she could still be that woman.

And so she'd walked into Henry Crenshawe's office that afternoon and handed in her notice.

The next month had flown past as she'd pushed her broken heart to the back of her mind and concentrated all her efforts on remaking herself into the real Eva Redmond. She'd chucked out her wardrobe full of biege. She'd got a business loan, moved out of her dull suburban semi, moved into a chic little studio flat in Stoke Newington, and launched her own web-based heir-hunting and ancestral research business. Her client list was still small, but, with her overheads minimal and the two big contracts she'd secured from her contacts at Roots Registry, she had made an excellent start.

The only big blot on her horizon had been her complete inability to start dating. Which she had a terrible feeling derived from some subconscious belief that she'd never be able to find anyone to replace Nick.

She clutched the phone tighter, forcing back the urge to slam it down.

'How is he?' she heard herself ask Tess.

She could do this. She could have a conversation about him without bursting into tears. She had to. If she was ever going to be free of him for good.

'Really angry actually,' came Tess's reply.

'Angry with whom?' Eva said, curiosity going some way to dim the pain.

'With you.'

Eva's eyes popped wide. 'Why would he be angry with me?'

'It has to do with Bill, the computer programmer.'

'Bill? Bill who? I don't know anyone called Bill,' Eva said, not just curious now but completely confused.

'Bill's…Well, Bill's a long story.' Tess's voice rose, getting more dramatic by the second. 'And he's sort of beside the point,' she added evasively. 'The thing is, I saw Nick. And he was looking all sexy and intense and gorgeous. And then he came up to me. I think to ask about you. And I got so angry with him I totally lost it and stupidly told him how devastated you were when he dumped you.'

'Oh, Tess, you didn't.' The thought of Nick knowing about the extent of her meltdown had humiliation stabbing under her breastbone right alongside the pain. In those dark days after his departure, the one thing she'd had was her pride. She could always feel relieved that she'd never blurted out the truth to him and told him how hard she'd fallen for him.

And now she didn't have that any more.

'But listen,' her friend began. 'There is a good side to this. Because, Eva, from his reaction, I'm totally convinced he's not over you. Honestly, he went pale. And then he got all fired up when I told him about Bill. He stormed out of the gallery.' Tess huffed out a deep breath, the frantic tumble of information stuttering to a halt. 'I think he might be coming to London. To see you.'

Eva squeezed her eyes shut, let the wave of misery wash through her.

Nick wasn't coming to see her. Why would he? If he'd wanted to be with her, he never would have left her the way he had. Or at the very least he would have contacted her long before now. Tess with her overactive imagination and gung-ho personality had simply misinterpreted his reaction and read into it the most ridiculous scenario possible.

'Look, Tess. Thanks for letting me know.' She drew in a steadying breath. 'But don't worry, I'm sure nothing will come of it.'

She ended the call as quickly as possible and settled the phone back in its cradle. Then took a deep breath.

Stop that right now.

She wasn't going to let herself get sucked under again. She was a stronger person now. A more confident, more independent, much less fragile person. Who was not going to get all choked up about a guy who had always been wrong for her.

Pushing away from the desk, she made her way to the hall closet and pulled on her raincoat. That said, she might as well admit that after Tess's call she was unlikely to get any more work done today. She'd go for a walk to Clissold Park. The new café there was always buzzing with people and the chilly autumn air would do her good and stop her moping around the flat, thinking about things—and people—it would be better for her not to think about.

The brisk wind ruffled her hair as she stepped out onto the pavement and locked the door behind her. She noticed the taxi stopped at the kerb in front of the house, just as a tall, painfully familiar figure got out.

'Eva?'

Shock came first, before the tumult of emotions she'd thought she'd conquered surged back up her torso.

'What are you doing here?' Her voice echoed from a million miles away.

'I want you back.'

She stared at him. That sharply handsome face that had haunted her dreams. And knew she couldn't do this. She wasn't ready.

She had a good life. It wasn't safe and secure any more. Thank goodness. Now she had challenges. Now she was her own person. Now she was the real Eva Redmond who had guts and courage galore. But he could take all that away from her…If she let him.

'Don't…' She shook her head fiercely. 'I can't.'

Ignoring the look of confusion on his face, she turned and ran.

'Eva, wait! Damn it. Come back here!' Nick shouted, his voice raw.

He'd been riveted to the spot by the unexpected sight of her walking out of the building. She'd lost weight, and her eyes, those luminous blue eyes, had lost the trusting look he remembered. But then he registered the sound of her feet pounding on the pavement and he sprinted after her.

He caught her in a few strides, grabbed her round the waist and hauled her back against him.

'Let go of me.' She stiffened, struggled, tried to prise his arms from around her waist. 'I can't do this. Go away.'

He inhaled, smelt the glorious scent of spring flowers in her hair, and held her tight, the slope of her breasts warm against his forearm. 'We have to talk.'

She bristled, her fingers digging into his forearms. 'You have to let me go,' she said. 'I don't want to talk to you.'

He lowered her feet back to the floor, released his arms, and she spun round to face him.

'I don't want you back,' she said, but her voice trembled and he saw the flicker of uncertainty in her eyes. She was lying. He knew she was. She still wanted him. His heart stopped kicking his ribcage and swelled into his throat.

Grasping her hand, he squeezed hard, the euphoria of having her close again overwhelming him. 'Yes, you do,' he murmured, already anticipating the reunion he'd been obsessing about during the long, sleepless night flight from San Francisco. 'Dump Bill.'

She yanked her hand out of his. 'There isn't any Bill. Tess made him up.'

'Huh?'

'You heard me. I don't have a boyfriend. But I don't need one to know I'm not going to fall for you again.' Her eyes sparkled with temper, making the dark blue turn to a vivid violet. She looked indomitable and wilful and more beautiful than even he could remember, and he remembered a lot. But he had no clue what she was talking about.

'Fall for me?'

'Oh, come on, Nick. Let's not be coy.' She thrust her chin out in a gesture he did remember, but this time there wasn't an ounce of hesitation about it. 'You know perfectly well I fell hopelessly in love with you. That's why you turned tail and ran.'

He'd heard the declaration before, from other women, delivered in clinging, dulcet tones, or in simpering desperation. Tons of times. And it had never meant anything to him. He'd never once heard it delivered like a slap, with the spark and sizzle of anger and indignation and the underlying tone of misery. And this time it meant everything.

But instead of taking her declaration and trying to make himself believe it, he said, 'You don't love me—you can't,' in automatic defence. However happy he was to see Eva again. However much he'd missed her. However much he might want her back. He would never ask for that. Would never expect it. Especially not from her. Not when he would only hurt her. The way he'd hurt everyone else who mattered.

'Don't tell me how I feel.' She hurled the words at him. The moment of fragility he'd witnessed disappearing as quickly as it had come. 'You arrogant…' she sputtered. 'You egotistical…'

'Berk?' he offered.

Her eyes narrowed, but not before he saw the unshed tears. 'Yes, berk,' she said, the anger subsiding to be replaced by something much more disturbing. 'You broke my heart, Nick, when you dumped me, but I've spent the last six weeks healing.' She hitched a shaky breath into her lungs, and the bottom dropped out of his stomach. 'And maybe I haven't healed all the way, yet. But I will.' She shoved her hair back behind her ear, her fingers trembling slightly. 'Goodbye.'

She turned her back on him, started to walk away.

'I didn't dump you,' he said, his voice hoarse, but the words surprisingly clear despite the swish of passing traffic on the rain-slick streets. 'That's not how it was. I left to protect you.'

Eva stopped dead at the low words, turned round. 'To protect me from *what* exactly?' she asked. Did he really think she was going to believe that?

'From me,' he replied, frustration edging the words. 'What the hell do you think?'

Her eyebrows shot up her forehead. 'You're not serious!' She could see it in his eyes, the shuttered, defensive look making her heartbeat stumble. But as much as she wanted to give in to the tenderness, to hold him close and tell him he was mad to think so little of himself, more than that she felt anger. At what he'd put her through. At what he'd put them both through. With his stupid inability to accept the truth about who he really was.

She marched back to him and socked him hard in the chest. 'You stupid berk!' she shouted, having no difficulty whatsoever remembering the name this time.

He stumbled back, his eyes widening. 'What was that for?'

'I cried for weeks after you left me that stupid note. And now you're telling me you did it for my own good.' The more she thought about it, the more she wanted to hit him again.

'Like I was a silly immature little girl who couldn't make up my own mind about who to love…'

'You were a virgin, damn it,' he shouted back, rubbing his chest where she'd punched him and looking aggrieved. 'How could you know you loved me? When you'd never been with anyone *but* me.'

She waved her hand, her temper growing and intensifying like a living thing. 'Oh, for pity's sake, will you please just get over that now? I'm not a virgin any more.' And then she remembered the wording of his note. The note that she'd mooned over and soaked with her own tears for weeks, and her temper ignited. 'That's what it meant.' She fired the words like bullets, glad when he flinched. 'That crass line about me finding one of the good guys. You wanted me to sleep around. Because until I do I can't possibly have the emotional maturity to know how I feel—is that it?'

'What?' He looked horrified, his face going bloodless beneath his tan. 'I *did not* tell you to sleep around.'

'Didn't you?' She slapped her hands on her hips, warming to her theme. 'Tell me something, Nick. Exactly how many guys do I have to sleep with before I can be trusted to decide for myself who I love?' She poked a finger into the middle of his chest. Hard. 'You should probably give me a number, so I can be absolutely sure.'

He grabbed her finger, pulled her close. 'Forget it. You're not sleeping with anyone but me,' he yelled back, his own temper rising to match hers. 'I gave you the choice and you fell for me anyway. You said so.' He wrapped his arm round her waist, pulled her flush against him. 'So now you're stuck with me.'

Her heart soared at the angry words, and heat pulsed low in her abdomen. This was what she'd dreamed of after he'd left her. That he'd come back. That he'd stake a claim, make a declaration, and finally get past that warped sense of honour that had made him believe he wasn't good enough for her.

But even as euphoria rushed through her, she refused to give in to the heady thrill. She struggled out of his arms, stepped back. What he offered wasn't enough. And the new powerful, risk-taking Eva Redmond wasn't willing to settle for second best any more. She didn't just want the dream. She wanted the reality—but that meant risking everything.

'You walked away from me, Nick,' she said, her voice low. 'You didn't give me a choice. You didn't tell me how you felt. You didn't give me the chance to tell you how I felt. You simply made the choice for me.' She blinked back the threatening tears. She had to do it. For his sake as well as her own.

'That's not true, I—'

She pressed a finger to his lips, to cut off the denial. 'What if Tess hadn't told you I had a new boyfriend, Nick? Would you have come here? Or would you have let me keep on waiting?'

She didn't need to hear his answer, she could see it in his face. See it in the way he stiffened and thrust his fists into the pockets of his jeans. 'I wanted to leave it up to you,' he muttered.

She shook her head. 'You ran away, Nick. Just like you've been doing all your life. When things get hard, when things get scary or complicated. When you can't control the way you feel. That's what you do, you run away.' She sniffed, scrubbed away a solitary tear.

'I *do* love you.' She cupped his cheek, felt the rasp of his stubble and the muscle in his jaw tighten and knew that however much she'd tried to deny it, that would always be true.

'I love the dangerous, wild and exciting man you are in bed and out. And the kind, tender and stupidly noble man you don't even know is there. And I feel nothing but sorrow for the boy you were. Who discovered something devastating about himself at the most difficult moment imaginable, and couldn't cope.' She let her hand slip away from his face. 'But I don't want another fling. I want to make a life with you. And I can't do that unless you love me back enough to finally let that boy go and stop running.'

Her panicked heartbeat flicked in her chest and she swallowed hard, the boulder of emotion in her throat threatening to choke her. She straightened, scared of what he was going to say. Had she pushed him too far? Did he even want to make a life with her? She didn't know. But one thing she did know: if he ran now, if he rejected her, if she'd asked too much of him, it was better to know. Because she would rather survive the heartache, than live with a lie…

'You've changed,' Nick said, his heart so swollen, he was pretty sure it was about to burst. He couldn't believe she'd offered him everything. Knew he would never deserve it.

She gave a stiff nod, the wry tilt of her lips crucifying him. 'I know. I'm not a doormat any more.'

He choked out a laugh. Then grasped her wrists, hugged her to him. 'You were never a doormat. You were just so…' he searched for the word '…sweet.'

She cringed. 'I'm not sweet. And I don't want to be.'

She was. And she always would be. But he knew that wasn't what she needed to hear.

'The point is, I'm strong.' She looked up at him. 'You don't have to run away, you can just tell me to my face you don't love me. And I'll survive.'

He clasped his arms round her back, and sank his head into her hair to inhale her wonderful scent. 'Yeah, you'll survive.' He hugged her trembling body to his. 'But I sure as hell won't,' he said, wanting to absorb her into him so he would never be without her again. 'I don't just love you, Eva. I'm pretty sure I can't live without you.'

He drew away, held her at arm's length, then saw the smile on her face and took courage from it. 'The last six weeks have been agony. I wanted to contact you countless times, but it was easier to pretend I was being noble, that I was giving you the choice, than admit the truth. That I was scared out of my wits you'd already come to your senses and realised I didn't deserve you.'

'But that's mad, you do deserve—'

He framed her face in his palms, placed a tender kiss on her lips to silence her.

When he pulled back, the stunned pleasure on her face sent his heart soaring into the stratosphere. 'It doesn't matter any more. Because I'm through running. And I'm going to spend the rest of my life proving that I *do* deserve you.'

She flung her arms round his neck, leaned into his body. 'You really don't have to do that,' she said, sending him a saucy look under her eyelashes that had lust swelling right alongside the joy. 'But if you insist, I know a very good place you can start.'

He threw back his head and laughed—the sheer elation making him light-headed.

Sobering, he let his hands travel down to caress her buttocks through the bulky raincoat, then pulled her against his hardening erection, eager to begin the rest of his life with this sweet, smart and incredibly strong woman by his side.

'That's funny, because so do I,' he murmured.

EPILOGUE

'MAYBE this wasn't such a great idea after all.' Nick stared at the imposing Hampstead mansion block out of the windscreen of the hire car he and Eva had picked up at Heathrow airport an hour ago.

Traffic had been lighter than he'd expected for the day after Boxing Day. Way too light in fact. Was he really ready for this?

Eva's hand settled on his thigh and rubbed gently. 'If you don't want to do this, Nick, you don't have to,' she murmured as if she'd read his mind. 'We can go book into the hotel.' She gave a quiet little laugh. 'From the pictures on their website, the honeymoon suite is amazing.'

Covering her hand, he let go of the breath he'd been holding.

'You booked the honeymoon suite?' He gazed at his wife, and huffed out a laugh, pathetically grateful for her attempt to lighten the mood. 'When we've been married for over six months?'

She wiggled her eyebrows. 'It has the best bed,' she countered, her blue eyes sparking with humour. 'And anyway, they won't know how long we've been married, will they?'

'Really?' He placed his palm on the firm mound of her belly, felt the familiar ripple of love and pride at the thought of the life they'd made together growing inside her. 'This is a bit of a giveaway, don't you think?'

'Not necessarily,' she said laughing. 'We could have been living in sin.' Her brows rose mischievously. 'In fact, we would have been if you hadn't turned out to be such a square,' she finished, a mock pout on her lips.

He chuckled, remembering her initial attempts to persuade him that they didn't *have* to get married just because they'd had a slip-up with their birth control and were becoming parents a lot sooner than planned.

'Sweetheart, give it up…' He curved his hand round her neck to draw her close, touched his nose to hers. 'Your wild days are over.' He nuzzled her lips, letting his hand linger as it caressed the soft hair at her nape. 'I wasn't about to miss the chance to get my ring on your finger. The baby just helped seal the deal.'

Had it really only been two years since she'd agreed to move to San Francisco? She'd changed him so much. Made him a braver, better man than he'd ever thought he could be— making him realise that your life wasn't defined by the mistakes you made, but how you dealt with them.

He'd faced so many of his demons and learned to conquer them with Eva by his side. Best of all, he'd made his peace with Don Vincenzo and the truth about his biological inheritance. With Eva's help, he'd come to accept that he wasn't so much Leonardo's son as Vincenzo's grandson. And getting to know the old man, over the summer months they now spent at the palazzo, and become a part of his family, had given him back the important foundation that he'd lost at sixteen. His lips curved at the memory of Vincenzo's elation when his grandfather had greeted him and Eva as they arrived for Christmas in Lake Garda and spotted her pregnancy.

Nick sighed, and faced the austere mansion block again, where his PA had discovered his sister Ruby now lived with her husband of six years, Callum Westmore. His lips firmed.

The question now was, did he have the guts to finally deal with the biggest mistake of his life?

'Seriously, Nick. You don't have to do this,' Eva said, her voice full of the sweetness and support that had become such an important part of his life.

He looked into her eyes, the smile returning. 'Yeah, I do. It's past time. I want our child to know Ruby.' He rested his palm on Eva's leg. 'I just hope to hell married life has calmed her down a bit, because the kid I remember could create quite a scene when she set her mind to it.'

He climbed out of the car, skirted the bonnet and opened the passenger door for Eva, then slung his arm round her waist. The solid feel of her against his side giving him the courage he needed.

Because the truth was, he'd take a scene any day to what he really feared. That Ruby would cut him dead, the way he deserved.

Eva squeezed Nick's hand as he pressed the buzzer on the mansion's intercom. She could feel the tension vibrating through him, knew how much this meeting meant to him. And while a part of her hoped that Ruby Westmore was a woman with a big heart and a forgiving soul, if she wasn't, Eva already had a contingency plan. No one got to hurt Nick, not even his sister. So the woman would have to go through Eva to do it.

'Who's there?' The high-pitched enquiry crackled out of the panel.

Nick frowned at Eva, clearly as puzzled as she was by the abrupt question. 'Um…We're here to see Ruby Westmore.'

The door buzzed and Nick shoved it open.

They climbed the brightly lit stairwell to the first floor, the building's wrought-iron balustrade and marble flooring matching the gothic frontage. Just as they reached the landing a door opposite the stairwell opened and a little girl standing on a chair peered out. 'My mummy's Ruby Westmore and she's making turkey for dinner. Again,' she announced, her nose wrinkling comically. 'And Daddy's giving Arturo a bath.'

'Oh, I see,' Eva said, when Nick simply stared at the little girl, clearly struggling to process the fact that this stunningly beautiful child with her cap of honey-brown curls and her bright emerald eyes had to be his niece.

'What's your name?' Eva asked.

'My name's Alessia and I'm four and a half. My big brother Max is five and three quarters and he's on a sleepover with his best friend Becca,' she continued without any prompting. 'Daddy says Alessia means trouble in Italian.'

Eva bit into her lip to hold back a grin at the non sequitur. She could just imagine how much trouble.

'It's nice to meet you, Alessia,' she said. 'I'm Eva and this is my husband Nick and we'd really like to talk to one of your parents.'

'Hello,' the girl replied, her gaze dipping to Eva's stomach. 'Do you have a baby in your tummy?' she asked bluntly, happily ignoring the request for parental intervention. 'Mummy had Art in her tummy for ages.' She rolled her eyes and gave a long-suffering sigh worthy of an eighty-year-old. 'But he's out now and Daddy says he's even more trouble than me and Max.'

'Ally, get down off that chair this instant,' a male voice boomed from inside the apartment.

Far from looking worried or even chastened, the little girl shot Eva and Nick an impish grin and whispered loudly from behind her hand, 'That's my daddy.'

The door swung wider and a tall, strikingly handsome man with jet-black hair and the same intense emerald eyes as his daughter stood before them with a cherubic baby haphazardly wrapped in a towel held securely in the crook of his arm.

'Hi, I'm Callum Westmore,' he said tightly, looking harassed with his hair furrowed into rows and a large damp patch on his T-shirt. 'Sorry, I didn't hear the doorbell.'

Before either Eva or Nick could introduce themselves, he turned to his daughter, who had wrapped her arms round his waist from on top of her chair.

'Ally, you little terror,' he said, sounding more exasperated than annoyed. 'How many times have I told you not to answer the door?' he said, his voice softening as he folded his free arm round his daughter's shoulders. 'You're supposed to tell me or Mummy if you hear it ring. Remember?'

The little girl nodded sheepishly, then turned beseeching eyes on her father. 'I forgot, Daddy.'

'I'll just bet you did,' he muttered, but, from the way he was stroking the little girl's shoulders, it was fairly clear he was putty in her hands.

Eva smiled at the tableau Callum Westmore and his children made as he turned his attention back to them. 'Sorry about that. My daughter is like her mother and doesn't follow instructions very well,' he said dryly. 'How can I help you?'

Eva opened her mouth to reply, when Nick answered, his tone stiff. 'I'm Nick Delisantro. We're here to see Ruby. I'm her—'

'I know who you are,' Westmore interrupted sharply, his voice harsh, his brows lowering over eyes that had gone as hard as flint. 'I also know how you treated my wife.' His gaze swept over Nick. 'What makes you think she wants to see you?'

Nick straightened. 'That's between my sister and I.'

Barely restrained violence crackled in the air as the two men squared off across the threshold to the apartment.

Eva placed a restraining hand on Nick's arm, determined

to calm the situation down, when little Alessia pointed at her and said happily, apparently oblivious to the tension, 'Look, Daddy, Eva has a baby in her tummy, just like Mummy did.'

Callum Westmore's gaze shifted to Eva and he stared blankly for several seconds before his gaze lowered to her belly. She realised the exact moment he registered, not just her presence, but her condition as a dull flush appeared on his cheeks. 'I…'

Eva thrust out her hand to rescue him. 'Hello, Mr Westmore, I'm Eva Delisantro, Nick's wife,' she said gently. She might have wanted to dislike the man for his aggressive dislike of Nick, but she couldn't, when it was obvious his anger stemmed from an unflinching loyalty to his wife.

It was also hard not to feel sympathy for his current predicament as she saw him process the fact that he was going to have to back down, with his children looking on and a pregnant lady on his doorstep.

He shook her hand. 'Hello, I didn't mean to—'

'Cal, what's all the commotion? Who's at the door?' a smoky female voice asked before a statuesque beauty appeared beside him.

Eva took in the caramel-coloured curls piled high on the woman's head in a casual knot, the lush, outrageously curvaceous figure that looked stunning even in the simple cotton dress and the captivating chocolate-coloured eyes that went wide with shock as the woman whispered the single word, 'Nick?'

No wonder these two had produced such beautiful children together, Eva thought.

'Hi, Rube,' Nick said, his voice breaking on the nickname. 'I'm here to apologise. For what I did to you and to Dad. Can you forgive me?'

She gave her head a little shake, her lashes dampening with tears. 'Nick,' she murmured again, covering her mouth with her hand. But Eva didn't see anger or derision on her face, all she saw was surprise and an emotion so fierce it was overwhelming.

'Why are you crying, Mummy?' Alessia asked, blunt as ever.

'Ruby, you don't have to do this,' her husband said gently as the baby chortled in his arms. 'I can make him leave if you want me to.'

She glanced at her husband, sending him a spontaneous smile that literally beamed with the love the two of them clearly shared. 'Don't be ridiculous, Cal. He's my brother.'

Then she turned and flung her arms round Nick's neck. 'You idiot,' she said, the joy plain in her voice. 'What the heck took you so long?'

Emotion swelled in Eva's throat and her own eyes filled with tears as she watched Nick wrap his arms round his sister in return.

'Because I was an idiot, obviously,' he replied, wry amusement in his voice as he slanted Eva a smile filled with pleasure and gratitude. 'But I've come to my senses at last.'

'Your sister is a goddess. Her children are adorable and her husband is amazing. You do realize that?' Eva announced as she perched her elbows on her husband's naked chest and peered down at his closed eyes, excitement about what the next day promised making sleep impossible. 'I can't wait to meet Max tomorrow,' she said. 'Although I can't imagine he can be any cuter than Ally,' she continued. 'She certainly took a shine to you,' Eva added, recalling the way the little girl had insisted on sitting on Nick's lap all through supper.

Nick grunted, running a lazy palm down her back. 'Who knew a four-year-old could talk that much?' he said, his lids remaining firmly closed, but she could hear the pleasure in his voice.

The reunion had been an unqualified success, the two couples beginning to form the bonds of a friendship this evening that Eva already knew would last a lifetime.

'Junior's going to get quite a shock,' Eva said, resting a palm on her belly. 'When he meets his cousins.'

She stretched, rubbing seductively against Nick in the honeymoon suite bed, which—despite the gruelling journey from Italy that day and the emotionally exhausting evening they'd spent with Ruby and her family—they'd managed to give quite a workout.

'Don't you think?' she prompted, tapping her palm on his cheek to get his attention.

His lids lifted to half mast. 'Go to sleep, woman,' he grumbled, his voice thick with exhaustion as he gave her buttocks a firm pat. 'Or I'm going to give you another orgasm to shut you up.'

'Promises promises,' she teased, snuggling against him.

As his breathing deepened into sleep she touched her fingertips to his forehead, pushed the waves of thick caramel hair back from his brow and smiled.

'Guess what, Niccolo Delisantro,' she whispered. 'I found one of the good guys after all.'

* * * * *

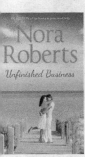 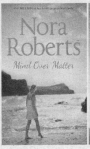 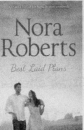 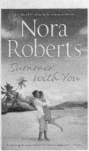
415_ST_11

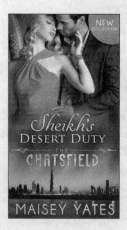

Join our *EXCLUSIVE* eBook club

FROM JUST £1.99 A MONTH!

Never miss a book again with our hassle-free eBook subscription.

★ Pick how many titles you want from each series with our flexible subscription

★ Your titles are delivered to your device on the first of every month

★ Zero risk, zero obligation!

There really is nothing standing in the way of you and your favourite books!

Start your eBook subscription today at www.millsandboon.co.uk/subscribe